THE RISING

THE IMMUNE
BOOK 3

DAVID KAZZIE

GRUB CLUB
PUBLISHING

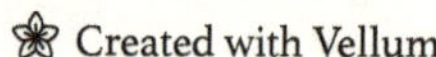 Created with Vellum

DEDICATION

*To my friend, my brother, my partner in crime, Matt, who
teaches me about bravery every day*

EPIGRAPH

If destruction be our lot, we must ourselves be its author and its finisher.

-Abraham Lincoln

THE STORY SO FAR...

In 2028, terrorists led by Dr. Miles Chadwick release the Medusa virus in New York City, which kills 99 percent of the human population. Adam Fisher, a physician immune to the virus, discovers his daughter Rachel may share his immunity, and he sets out across America to find her.

At the terrorists' Nebraska compound (the Citadel), Chadwick learns their vaccine, which they created to protect themselves, has made the women in his group infertile. Meanwhile, Adam travels west with survivor Sarah Wells, an Army captain with a terminal genetic condition. Adam and Sarah discover that the babies of surviving women may not be immune to the virus, leading to concerns about humanity's future.

Adam eventually learns Rachel is being held captive at the Citadel. With help from Sarah and other survivors, Adam locates and infiltrates the Citadel, which has captured dozens of naturally immune women they plan to use as surrogates. Adam and Sarah rescue Rachel and other captives, but Sarah sacrifices herself to prevent Chadwick from releasing more viruses.

Thirteen years later, Rachel lives with her mysteriously healthy 11-year-old son Will - the only known post-pandemic child to survive infancy. After Adam is killed in an attack, Rachel and Will flee, eventually ending up at a boarding school in Colorado. The headmaster betrays them to a woman named Priya, who's interested in Will's survival.

Now taken captive by Priya, Rachel discovers a facility called Olympus, run by Leon Gruber—the mastermind behind Medusa. Gruber reveals he and Rachel's grandfather created Medusa together. Rachel learns she was immunized before the outbreak at her grandfather's request, using a different vaccine variant than the one that caused infertility at the Citadel.

When Rachel refuses to join Olympus, Gruber tries to kill her. During an attack by Priya's group, which destroys Olympus, Rachel manages to rescue multiple children and secure a supply of the vaccine. She kills both Gruber and Priya, escaping with the survivors and the means to potentially ensure humanity's future.

PROLOGUE

THREE WEEKS BEFORE THE OUTBREAK

His name was Adrian West, and he was going to save the world.

Adrian had laid all the evidence on the large table before him. It was everything he needed to take down Miles Chadwick and his insane band of doomsday lunatics, all the evidence he had carefully curated over the last two months. Documents, secret recordings, photographs, flash drives. Everything. Eight weeks of work to ensure that he'd be taken seriously. Eight weeks of holding his breath, looking over his shoulder, wondering if he'd been made.

They would not hesitate to kill him—of this, he had no doubt.

There were three of them working together to bring it all down. It was risky. As the saying went, *three people could keep a secret, if two of them were dead.*

But they had been clever. Careful. They had taken no one else into their confidence. Everything was done in person: no emails, no text messages, no phone calls. They met weekly to discuss their progress.

But time was running short.

He did not know where or when the attack would take place, as that information had been kept secret at the highest levels of Penumbra. But it would be soon. Activity had accelerated, and pieces were being moved into place. The operatives were scheduled to arrive at the Citadel the following day. There, each would collect a designated canister and fan out to the attack sites.

Absently, he brushed his hand against his shoulder, the site of the PB-815 vaccine injection he'd received after signing onto the project. If everything went according to plan, he would never need its protection. The vaccine's nanoparticles would circulate through his veins for time eternal, looking for an invader that would never come.

He carefully placed each item of evidence into his briefcase, closing and locking it when he was done. He spun the dial of the briefcase's combination lock to three random digits and set it on the ground. A quick check of his watch. It was just past two-thirty in the afternoon. His meeting with Special Agent Dan Hughes was less than an hour from now, at a diner in Omaha, roughly twenty minutes away.

He had to ensure that Chadwick never deployed the canisters. If Chadwick got the first hint that he'd been made, he'd release the virus early. That was the demented beauty of his plan. Once the virus was ready, that was it. All they had to do was open one at an interstate rest stop. That would probably be sufficient. The world sat precariously on a knife's edge, and it had no idea. Humanity's only hope was that Chadwick would adhere to the carefully orchestrated schedule he'd constructed years earlier. That was why Adrian had been so careful, so meticulous, in building his case. He would get one chance. Civilization would get one chance.

Adrian stood up and stretched, the ligaments and

muscles in his back popping deliciously. He was a tall man, pushing forty, and his life was dedicated to his work. The ravages of age were rearing their ugly heads: a trick knee that was sore more days than not and a hip that screamed if he sat at his desk too long. He had never married, had kids, or had a proper relationship. His destiny had lain on a different path, bringing him here.

He wandered over to the window, looking east toward downtown Omaha. The other buildings in the office park glinted in the hot July sunshine. He had rented this tiny office space for his work, paying in cash for three months. It was an irregular arrangement, but occupancy in the park had been well below expectations, so the property manager had agreed to Adrian's unusual proposal. The office was sparsely furnished — a high-speed copier, a desktop computer, a landline phone, and a file cabinet. These few items had been his trusted allies in his secret war against Miles Chadwick.

The day Chadwick told him played on a constant loop in his head. He was an epidemiologist with Penumbra, hired to analyze genomic data, conduct modeling, and analyze machine learning data to help the team monitor interactions between host and pathogen. He had left a successful career with another pharmaceutical company, drawn in by the prospect of cutting-edge work. The selection process had been rigorous: physical examinations, psychological evaluations, and a series of inoculations.

And the first few weeks had been cutting edge, out in the wilds of Nebraska. The facilities were top-notch, and the team was stocked with the most brilliant minds he had ever encountered. Then, one Friday afternoon, he was summoned to a meeting. Miles Chadwick was waiting for him.

It was a meeting unlike any other he had ever attended.

"Do you know why you're here, Dr. West?"

That was the first question Miles Chadwick had asked him.

When Adrian did not answer, Miles continued nonplussed, as though it had been a rhetorical question.

"It's because we are on the brink of a paradigm shift. And we need people of your considerable talents."

This was an innocuous comment, one he expected. Every lab believed it was on the brink of a paradigm shift. It revealed nothing about the nightmarish few minutes that would follow. When Chadwick had finished laying out his dark, twisted vision, Adrian could barely breathe. But he kept up appearances because he suspected very strongly that failing to do so would be like signing his death warrant.

It was time to go. Adrian gathered his briefcase and small suitcase and rolled out to the parking lot. It was hot, the sun beating down on the asphalt, cooking the weeds that somehow found purchase in even the tiniest crack in the pavement. A quick scan of his surroundings. Nothing out of the ordinary.

He guided the car out of the lot and onto Route 73, heading north toward Omaha. The traffic was thick, but he kept a wary eye on his mirrors for any potential trail. At Route 221, he turned east onto a lonely two-lane highway that would feed into the western Omaha suburbs. The land was flat, and the road cut through the plains like a bullet.

Ten minutes from Omaha, he noticed the black SUV in his rearview mirror, closing in fast. His heart leaped into his throat while he simultaneously dismissed his concern as his paranoia working overtime. His hands grew damp on the steering wheel as the truck grew more prominent in the mirror. They had entered a heavily foliaged section of the highway. The trees were heavy with the summer leaves, their branches reaching across the road to form an arboreal tunnel.

"Go around, go around," he whispered.

He eased off the accelerator, hoping to encourage the driver to go around him. The westbound lane was empty as far as the eye could see; it would be a simple pass if the driver's motivations were not malicious. As he slowed, he heard the truck's big V8 engine roar in the summer stillness. A second later, the vehicle was on top of him. A man leaned out from the passenger-side window, bearing an automatic weapon. But he did not fire. The truck slammed into his rear bumper, causing Adrian's sedan to shimmy badly. He whined in fear as he mashed the gas pedal to the floor. But it was useless; the bigger, faster truck stayed on his tail. It backed off momentarily and came in hard at Adrian's left rear bumper, forcing him off the road and onto the shoulder.

The car screamed over the side of the road, sending Adrian's heart into his throat. It had happened so suddenly that he hadn't had time to be afraid. The car bottomed out on the shallow embankment as he struggled to regain control. But abject terror quickly flooded through him as the car went airborne, giving him a clear view of the large tree blocking his car's flight path.

The car struck the trunk of the tree and spun wildly before crashing hard to the ground and rolling over onto its roof. Adrian, who had blacked out from the impact, slowly came to, hanging upside down, still restrained by the seatbelt. The airbag had deployed and was pushing against his face.

Alive!

He was still alive. Every single muscle and bone hurt and

maybe there were internal injuries, but he was still in the game for now. He released the seatbelt and dropped to the ground. The briefcase was wedged into the passenger-side footwell. As he reached for it, his lungs and chest burned with pain. But he had to get to it. As his fingers wrapped around the bag's strap, he heard movement outside the car. He saw a pair of boots loping casually toward the vehicle.

"Can you please call 911?" he called out weakly.

There was no reply as the boots stopped outside the crumpled window frame. Perhaps the good Samaritan had not heard him. He started to call out a second time when the person dropped to their knees and peered in through the window frame. He was a big fellow, his face hard and jawline sharp. His black hair was slicked back. Most alarmingly, a gun the size of a cannon was pointed at Adrian.

"Wait," Adrian said meekly.

They always said that at the end, your life would flash before your eyes, but it wasn't like that for Adrian West. As the woods echoed with the report of the large-caliber round, a single, solitary thought flashed through his mind before everything went dark.

He would have a lot of company soon.

∼

1

———

SIXTEEN YEARS LATER

The group reached the outskirts of Dixon's downtown area two hours before sunset. Their shadows stretched out ahead of them, elongating with each passing minute and painting the sides of the buildings as a partially veiled sun dipped toward the western horizon. The skies had cleared temporarily, bringing the travelers their first taste of sunshine in several days.

But another front was approaching from the west. Rain would fall again soon, but that was something to which they had become accustomed. Rain had fallen virtually every day for the past week. Cold rain. The kind of weather that was most excellent for curling up under a blanket with a good book and a cup of hot tea. A bourbon, if that floated your boat. Not so good for traipsing across a continent mostly emptied of its people.

The clouds backfilled the sky more quickly than Rachel Fisher anticipated. A single drop of rain struck the nape of her neck. She reached back and wiped it away. For all the good it did. One plink on her rain jacket quickly turned into many.

Rain.

Rachel was sick of rain.

It was mid-autumn, late October by Rachel's estimation. Still a bit early in the season for snow, but it would be a different story in a few weeks. The approaching winter had injected their road trip with a sense of urgency. They needed a place to call home, and they needed it soon. The group was running on fumes physically and emotionally. Their supplies were dwindling. The toll on her own body was building: nagging injuries that never fully healed, brutally chapped lips, and clothes disintegrating.

They were eighteen miles southwest of St. Louis. The Missouri River, the smaller cousin of the mighty Mississippi, lay half a mile to the east, bisecting the small city of Dixon. Before Medusa, this had been a popular bedroom community, a leafy, tree-lined exurb of the St. Louis metro area. The road was mostly clear of the dead traffic jams that had marked humanity's final gasp. Abandoned cars and trucks and SUVs lined the shoulders. At least half the vehicles still housed the skeletal remains of Medusa victims, those who had been unable to escape mankind's final traffic jam before the disease claimed them.

Rachel paused at the crest of a hill, the two-lane road descending toward the bridge crossing this section of the Missouri River. Like virtually all bridges they'd found coming across the country, this one had long been commandeered as an income-producing asset. A series of barricades had been erected at the bridge approach; a pair of sentinels kept watch. Rachel did not begrudge folks this kind of entrepreneurship; you got by any way you could. Better than committing highway robbery, she supposed. And most bridge tolls were reasonable. Anything of value was usually enough to get you across.

Intact bridges had become prime real estate in the last decade. Absent regular maintenance, many of the nation's water crossings had succumbed to the elements since Medusa had finished its nasty work. The Mississippi River, in particular, saw heavy traffic across its longitudinal spine. As a result, enterprising folks had turned these crossings into the ultimate side hustle. The tolls generated by a critical crossing could support an entire community indefinitely. Rachel did not know how long this bridge had been under its current management, and she didn't much care. All she cared about was getting them safely across.

The bulk of Dixon's downtown sat on the west side of the river. An overgrown park converted into farmland bordered the riverbank. At the top of the embankment stood a handful of office buildings and condo towers. The buildings were green with mildew; ivy and kudzu grew wild along the foundations and walls. Low-slung storefronts that had once been home to trendy restaurants, boutique shops, and independent bookstores broke up the skyline. The land on the far side of the bridge was less developed. Across the river was a brewery with a large open patio that looked back toward downtown proper. The town that had sprung up around this new economic engine was heavily fortified.

At the barricade, the guards checked in a pair of travelers ahead of Rachel's group. An older man in his early sixties and a woman maybe twenty years his junior. They did not look dangerous, but Rachel had kept her troupe well back of the couple. She eschewed contact with strangers at all costs. As she watched through binoculars, the guard directed each individual to sign a logbook. Almost certainly aliases. Rarely did anyone give their real names. That said, just knowing how many people were coming through was useful intel. The pair continued onto the bridge, headed for points east.

As Rachel's group had neared the Mississippi, they saw more of these small fortress towns. Before the plague, much of the U.S. population had been concentrated east of the Mississippi, so it made sense there would be more survivors in this section of the continent. There weren't *that* many people, to be sure. After all, Medusa had spared only about one percent of the U.S. population. Moreover, the pandemic had softened things up for the other horsemen of the apocalypse, and the population shrank even further in the intervening years. War, famine, disease, and lawlessness constantly chipped away at the population.

They crested one more gently sloping hill; from there, the road descended another hundred yards to the barricade. Rachel pushed a bramble of branches out of her face, a tree growing out of the buckled asphalt. The others brought up the rear, one at a time. Four children and three adults, including herself. Seven little dots on a map.

There had been twice that many when they'd fled the ruins of Olympus more than two years earlier, but fundamental disagreements had led to the group's fracture. Initially, they had gone west toward the coast, the mild weather a big draw and Rachel wanting to see San Diego again. But wildfires were common, pushing them back before she had made it to her childhood home. It was a slow trek; the search for a permanent residence was challenging for many reasons. You couldn't well walk into a strange town with half a dozen kids born after the pandemic. People might have questions. Eventually, the group had split; Andy, Eloise and three of the children disappeared one night. To this day, Rachel did not know what became of them.

Rachel flexed and unflexed her fingers, hoping to get blood flowing into her chilled extremities. It was drizzling, the air heavy and damp. The group had gathered behind an abandoned panel truck. The kids sat on the curb, worn out by the long day of walking. While the others rested, Rachel eased ahead to the front of the truck to get a better view. Will was by her side, as he often was. It was different now, though. Once upon a time, he stayed near her because he depended on her for so much. But now, a different dynamic had taken hold. Someone who wanted to learn. As much her apprentice as he was her son.

A stiff breeze blew across Rachel's body, chilling her even more. Her boots pushed into the mud running along the curb. They were new, thick and sturdy, and she enjoyed the sensation of dry feet. Simple pleasures were often the only pleasures any of them had these days.

The Missouri had been in Rachel's sights for weeks. Beyond that, it was a short journey to the Mississippi River, where Rachel hoped to find a proper home for the winter. It was time to put down roots, even though that meant revealing the children's existence. After all that, she had landed in the same place as Andy and Eloise. The last two winters had been extremely rough, just the small group making their way, living off handouts and what they could scavenge.

Dozens of small communities dotted the riverbank from its northern headwaters to its mouth into the Gulf of Mexico. It was as if humanity were going back to the beginning, starting near the river, a place where things grew in the ground, a place to fish and hunt, a place to access clean water. It was the culmination of a long trek across America, one that Rachel had carefully mapped, finding the right balance of safety and access to resources until they could navigate a soft landing.

Stopping at this checkpoint filled her with anxiety; they were so close to their destination. Exposure to populated areas was kept to a minimum. It was impossible to avoid them entirely, so they were judicious in choosing their way stations. There had to be a reason. The potential benefit had to outweigh the risk.

And today's fit that bill.

A crumbling elementary school stood about three blocks shy of the barricade ahead. A two-story building, brick and a lot of glass. The natural light flooding the interior had once stimulated learning and mood and growing brains. Even after a dozen years of inattention and exposure to the elements, the brick green with mildew, it was still beautiful.

The rectangular marquee in front of the building still bore its final message.

First Day of School – August 26!

A reminder, a warning from the past.

Nothing was ever guaranteed. Not even the first day of school.

Because by August 26 of the Year of the Plague, Medusa had all but finished its brutal and terrible work. There would be no school to return to, not that year and not in the many years since.

Carla Greyford, a member of their group, approached Rachel from behind. She was thin and severe, her skin pasty white and stretched tightly across her frame. If a scream waiting to be screamed were a person, it would be Carla. Rachel got on with her well enough, but they were anything but close. Two mercenary cowgirls hired to wrangle a herd of cattle. The mission to keep these children safe joined them together—their common goal.

These extraordinary children.

"What do you think?" Carla asked.

"This is the safest way through," Rachel said.

The main highways were safest. Drifting too far off the beaten path could land you in territories controlled by militias and warlords. That was a quick recipe for disaster.

"Kids," she called back over her shoulder. "Hoods up."

The children complied immediately. It was part of their backstory, a fictional construct that had served them well. As the kids tightened their drawstrings, largely obscuring their faces, Rachel brushed her fingers against the backpack secured over her shoulders. She did it dozens of times a day.

Because in the pack was the future.

It was a small valise lined with dark red felt; fifty factory-sealed vials lay tucked into the small cutouts. The vials contained twenty doses each, the last known supply of the Medusa vaccine. The one true vaccine. The serum with which Rachel herself had been vaccinated more than fifteen years ago. It had protected Rachel from certain death. It was how Will had been possible, how any of these children had been possible. Because for all the devastation Medusa had wrought, she had saved her cruelest joke for the survivors. Every person immune to Medusa invariably carried the virus inside them; although it posed no threat to women, the infection was catastrophic for the babies they carried. It was always fatal to newborns. And it posed a massive threat to the continued viability of humanity.

There were small pockets of survivors who had never been exposed to Medusa, but they were few and far between. Rachel and Will had come across such a community several years earlier. Assuming unexposed survivors could procreate in sufficient numbers to save humanity was a risky bet, one she was not willing to take. For all she knew, they were still vulnerable to a slap from their old friend Medusa. No, she had to ensure she vaccinated as many women as there were vaccines.

Rachel could vaccinate nearly a thousand women with these vials—a seed community. Hopefully, those women would bring twice that many lives into the world, and so on, with each passing generation growing exponentially until humanity's future was secure. She had already shared the vaccine with a few women here and there, unable to resist the urge to help, to provide a beacon of light when the darkness seemed eternal.

It would never be like it was, of course. Too much had been lost. Maybe in a hundred years or two hundred years, they could get back to where they had been. To a golden age of technology. An era of waking up in New York, jumping on a plane, and having dinner in Los Angeles that very night. But would they want to? After all, was it not technology that had made it possible for Leon Gruber to unleash his terrible weapon on the world?

Even before Medusa, technology had irrevocably divided the country and the world. The internet had spawned a dream of uniting the world. But they'd ended up with anonymous trolls threatening to shove Jewish journalists into ovens. Bomb throwers sharing fake videos about anything and everything under the sun. From war crimes to police beatings to looting to simple acts of resistance. Sometimes, and it was a terrible thing to think, a thought she shared with no one, Rachel Fisher believed humanity had gotten what it deserved.

When the kids were appropriately cloaked, she directed them to wait in the cover of the abandoned truck.

"Wait for my signal," she told Carla.

Carla nodded.

Rachel patted Will on his shoulder.

"You remember the script?" she asked.

"Yeah, Mom, I got it."

She chuckled softly. The kid was asserting his independence more often these days, a welcome development, although it broke her heart a little. She reminded herself that this was how it had to be in their world. He was fourteen years old, having celebrated his birthday just weeks earlier. He had been a fall baby, and with the season turning toward winter, his birthday had come and gone.

She didn't know exactly which day it had been because they had lost the calendar some years before, never to find it again. That saddened her immensely. She would never tell Will that she no longer knew exactly when his birthday was; instead, she had picked a nice day after the leaves had turned. He was a sharp kid; he probably knew that she had just plucked the day from the ether; that day was his birthday because she had said so. A box of generic cream-filled sponge cakes she had found outside of Kansas City accompanied her birthday wishes; still factory sealed, the treats edible even after fifteen years. Well, the cake had been a little dry. That icing, though, was forever.

There was no guarantee she would live long enough to see Will become a man. That was why she had to build him into a man as quickly as she could. Was it fair? No, but fairness had left the station the day Leon Gruber had unleashed the Medusa virus on the world.

"You ready?" she asked.

"Let's go."

2

Rachel was checking her gear when she sensed a presence by her side.

"Miss Rachel?"

Elijah was tugging at her jacket.

He was the youngest member of the group, maybe five years old. He was incredibly attached to Carla. His parents had died in the final battle at Olympus, leaving him orphaned. He was a sweet little boy. A little stuffed tiger was clenched in his chubby little fingers.

"What?" she said, a bit more harshly than intended.

He stepped back from her, taken aback. He squeezed his stuffed tiger tightly against his chest. Guilt coursed through her. She hated losing her cool around the kids, even for a second. Things were hard enough for them.

"Sorry, honey," she said, kneeling to his level. "What do you need?"

"I'm hungry."

"Yeah?"

He nodded. Tears filled his eyes.

"Okay," she said gently. "Let's see what Miss Rachel can do."

A bare hint of a smile ran across his face.

As he scurried back to the other kids, she suddenly felt lightheaded. Her vision narrowed to pinprick cylinders. She steadied herself, waiting for the moment to pass. It had been a while since the last episode like this one. There were moments, even now, when she thought she was enmeshed in history's longest, most vivid, most realistic, and most terrible dream. The moments were brief, just flashes, like the silver streak of a meteorite scratching across the blank sky. There and then gone again. Indeed, this could not be happening; this was not how her life had turned out. Leading a band of refugees across a post-apocalyptic wasteland. Sometimes, the sensation stopped her in her tracks, and she would wait for it to pass, sure that she was about to wake up but strangely, equally sure that she was awake.

"You okay?" asked Will, taking her gently by the elbow.

She took a shaky, deep breath and let it out slowly as the sensation passed.

"Yeah," she replied. "Fine. Come on. Burning daylight here."

Rachel and Will approached the first barricade, their hands out, as was the norm.

Carla and the kids dropped out of view, taking cover behind the elementary school. They would be safe there while Rachel and Will took stock of the situation. Negotiating the price to cross. Keeping the children safe was her prime directive, her reason for being. Her biggest fear was losing the kids. Any decently sized group could overwhelm them. It was yet another reason why they needed to find a permanent home. A place where she could distribute the vaccine. Once the vaccine was in play, once the flow of babies began, these kids would be safe because they would no longer be rare.

Beyond the barricade, an eight-foot-high wall guarded the western edge of downtown Dixon. It had been cobbled with repurposed sheet metal, pressure-treated lumber, and some brick. It was hard to tell how long it had stood. Parts of it appeared new, while other sections looked to have withstood the test of time. The two-lane road continued east toward the bridge.

Will looked at her suspiciously as they approached the crossing.

"Let me do the talking," Rachel said, pushing his concerns aside.

He nodded and whipped his head to the side, flipping his hair out of his eyes the way boys his age did. It must have been ingrained in the DNA of teenage boys. It wasn't as if he'd seen the cool kids in homeroom do it. It reminded Rachel of her school days when the boys had done the same. The handsome boys who had their pick of the girls, down in the luxurious basements of their wealthy parents' homes. Boys who were handsome like Will. He grew more attractive by the day, now favoring his late father, Eddie, more than she cared to admit.

"Mom?" he said, slowing to a stop.

"Yeah?"

"Someone's been following us," Will said with a heft in his voice. A maturity that you only saw in fourteen-year-olds who'd come of age after the end of the world.

His revelation took her by surprise. She was usually adept at picking up a trail, but if Will was correct, this one had eluded her.

"Are you sure?"

"Very," he said. "I didn't want to say anything until I was certain. He's a few hours behind us. Maybe less."

"How did you figure it out?"

Will had developed an important skill, one that she needed to learn herself.

"His campfire. He throws sage into it. I've also heard him whistling. The same tune every night."

She chuckled. Both markers had escaped her. Young ears held a significant advantage over those just a few years older. And Will probably had better hearing than the average pre-Medusa adolescent; his ears hadn't been subjected to music blasting through earbuds, slowly damaging his hearing. As for her olfactory senses, she was disappointed in herself. She should have noticed it.

"Any idea who it is?" she asked.

"No," he replied.

"We'll discuss again later," she said, pressing an index finger to her lips as they drew within earshot of the barricade.

"Hold there, friends," said the guard.

A balaclava cloaked the man's face and head. He wore jeans and a denim jacket, a hedge against the chilly breeze swirling across the river. It was hard to tell how old he was, but he moved well, belying a man in his thirties or forties. A machine gun hung from his left shoulder, and a belt of ammunition was draped across his chest. The second guard watched quietly; his rifle was up, but the barrel was angled downward.

The guard eyed them briefly, and then he waved them to approach. Rachel and Will exchanged a glance before moving toward the barrier. A small table and a pair of camping chairs were positioned at the barricade; an insulated travel mug and a small package wrapped in foil sat atop the table. Next to it was a deck of cards set out in a game of gin rummy.

"Help you folks?" he asked.

"Looking for a way across the river."

He poked a thumb over his shoulder at the bridge.

"This here is it," he said. "Unless you fancy hoofing it twenty miles north."

"Not particularly."

"Just the two of you?" the man asked.

"How much to cross?" Rachel replied, answering his query with one of her own.

"Is it just the two of you?" he asked again.

"Nine of us," she said.

The man's brow furrowed. He peeked around them theatrically.

"Nine? Got any invisible friends back there?"

He laughed heartily at his terrible joke.

Rachel smiled her most disarming smile.

"All adults?"

"Four adults, five kids."

"Kids?"

"Teenagers."

"Don't see many that young anymore."

That was because most of Medusa's youngest survivors, the infants and toddlers lucky enough to be immune to the virus and who would have been teenagers now, had suffered a fate worse than the virus. Abandoned in their cribs, their parents dead in their beds. Wandering alone. Dead of thirst or starvation or accident, lost to the depraved minds of those who would do harm to children and would never face justice for it. Other than these kids from Olympus, there were virtually no survivors born after the pandemic. But most adults weren't good at correctly judging children's ages, so the older cohort they passed off as fourteen and fifteen.

The two youngest, Elijah and Avery, were explained away as victims of a severe genetic condition affecting their growth. Found in a children's hospital in the aftermath of the plague. No, they probably would not grow much more, if at all. Passing the kids off as young teenagers was incredibly risky, but so far, the gambit had held. As they got older and bigger, the story became more believable.

This was the construct that Rachel and Carla had built over the months. As their travels had brought them further east, it had become increasingly difficult to conceal the existence of the children. Most survivors had never seen a child born after Medusa. In fact, Will's very existence had drawn an invasion force to their home in Nebraska three years earlier. They simply could not risk anyone finding out that these kids had been born *after* the pandemic.

For that reason, they needed this cover story.

They had tried a different story once upon a time. A tale that the kids had been born to parents who had never been exposed to Medusa in the first place. People who had hunkered down during the acute phase of the outbreak while the virus chewed away at humanity until only the immune remained. Immune survivors did not transmit the virus (except in utero, evidently, and wasn't that the world's worst cosmic practical joke). At least, that's what they all hoped.

But that approach had created its own problems.

The myth and legend of children born after the pandemic held an almost talismanic sway over people. It didn't matter if they'd been born to Medusa-naïve parents. What mattered was that they'd been born at all. The group was still intact, coming across the southwestern corner of

Nebraska. It was a warm summer evening, pleasant, the kind of day you hoped for. They crested a hill, spotting a large tent city spread across the plains near McCook, Nebraska. A farming community before the plague, it had become a collector city in its aftermath thanks to its proximity to the fertile lands of the Republican River Valley.

In hindsight, it might have worked if there had been only one kid. But trying to pass off a handful of kids as children of parents never exposed to Medusa was a bridge too far. For that reason, they abandoned that act. It had nearly caused a riot, and they had been lucky to escape with their lives.

It was a moment she regretted to this day.

"What's your name?" she asked. "I'm Rachel. This is Will."

"Ezekiel."

"A pleasure," replied Rachel. "Can I bring them up here?"

He nodded, chewing his lower lip in anticipation. He peered around Rachel and Will as though the kids might form out of thin air. She nodded at Will, who whistled loudly, the shriek piercing the late afternoon stillness. The rest of their group emerged hesitantly from the back of the elementary school a hundred yards away. Slowly, Carla and Jessica led the children toward the cage. Both women were on the shorter side, which helped advance the illusion that the kids were older than they were.

"Awfully small, ain't they?" asked the second guard.

He was older than Ezekiel, probably in his early fifties. A tall fellow, easily over six feet. He was thick through the chest, and his arms were like tree trunks. The kind of bulk that came from field work rather than from time in the gym. A tattoo of a snake coiled around his left forearm.

Rachel noticed his grip on his weapon had tightened. A skeptic. She'd need to tread carefully here. Her heart was pounding as the women approached with the three children. As they'd practiced many times, the older kid, Marshall, took the point, staying in front of Elijah and Avery. Jess and Carla flanked the younger ones.

"The two little ones were babies when we found them," she said, her voice steady and firm. "An orphanage. Kids with special needs and whatnot. Couldn't well leave them there."

"They don't look like teenagers to me," said the other guard. "They look like they're eight years old. What the hell's going on here?"

"I know they don't look it, but they're both around thirteen. They have dwarfism."

The second guard continued to eye her suspiciously, but the muzzle of his weapon dipped toward the ground. He took a step back, deferring to Ezekiel.

Ezekiel threw the man a glance before returning his attention to Rachel.

"So how much to cross?" Rachel asked.

"Well, that depends," the man said.

"On what?"

"On what you're willing to pay."

3

———

R achel considered her reply carefully. The stewards of the various water crossings, especially up and down the Mississippi and Missouri, were known to drive hard bargains. Not too hard, though, because that just drove travelers to a different crossing. Healthy competition was good for everyone. But you still had to be careful.

"What's it gonna cost us?" asked Rachel.

"What do you have to offer?" he asked. "We have a lot of needs, and those change from day to day. Got any weapons?"

"None that we can spare."

Truth be told, they did not have much to offer in payment. Guns and ammunition were like gold in their world. They were just too valuable. Often, a party's arsenal was the difference between life and death on the roads. Rachel knew down to the last bullet what the group was currently packing. Will and Carla each carried a Glock. Rachel carried Sarah's M-4 rifle, and Jess was entrusted with the AR-15. Their arsenal also included four flash-bang grenades and three boxes of ammo for each of the firearms.

"You folks ever have any live music around here?" she asked.

He looked at her quizzically.

"No, I can't say we have."

"We're a singing group," Rachel said. "We can entertain the town."

This was, hard as it was to believe, a fact. Old eighties tunes. Their catalog was deep, and damn if they couldn't sing. Carla had taught the kids music back at Olympus, and the little ones weren't bad either. Over time, it became a thing they did in the evenings after making camp. For obvious reasons, they only sang on the nights they bunked indoors. Carousing around a campfire was a good way to draw unwanted attention.

It was an escape from the dark of the world locking down the day. For those few minutes when they sang their songs, it felt like they had cracked open the world's darkness and let a bit of light in. A bit of light from the world Rachel and the other adults had known. A world that the kids had never known.

He laughed derisively.

"Before you laugh us out of here," Rachel began, "I want to ask you something."

"Shoot," he said.

"Have you seen anything beautiful today?" Rachel said.

The man smiled at first. Then he chuckled.

"You putting me on?"

"I assure you, I am not."

He opened his mouth and then closed it again. Then he spoke.

"It's funny you ask," he said wistfully. "I was up early this morning, thought I might catch the sunrise. But it was cloudy. And I missed it."

Rachel did not reply.

The question continued to turn over in his head.

"I've seen a lot of sunrises," he said. "They get old after a while, to be honest."

"Ezekiel, do you like music?"

Rachel recalled a folk song that her old friend Erin Thompson had written years ago. The lyrics were largely lost to her, but one stanza remained rooted in her mind.

In the still of the night, the shadows they howl...
Whispers of the past, memories that scowl...
But with hope in my heart, dreams that won't bow
Slide away darkness, slide away now...

"Yeah, sure," Ezekiel said.

He clicked his tongue against his teeth as a memory unspooled for him.

"They used to have this concert on Friday nights during the summer," he said. "You know, before. My wife made us go every week. It wasn't anything big. All we could afford back then."

Before Medusa. Back when the world was big and loud. When there were concerts every summer Friday night in every town in America. When you stood on a large tract of land and stared up at the stage, a twelve-dollar beer sloshing in your hand as you swayed to the music of an up-and-coming artist or a Queen cover band.

He tucked his lower lip under his upper teeth and his eyes glistened, but he did not cry. Rachel didn't need to ask what had become of the man's wife. There wasn't a family on Earth that Medusa hadn't cast asunder.

"Remember how that felt?" she asked.

He nodded.

"Let us do this," she said. "Isn't that worth a decent meal?"

He shook his head hard like he was clearing it of silly thoughts. Shallow, vapid thinking.

"Nine mouths to feed," he said, more to himself than to Rachel.

Rachel wasn't picky. If they needed help in the fields, they would help in the fields. Anything, within reason, was worth a good night's sleep and a hearty meal.

He glanced up at the sky.

The second guard took a step forward and whispered into Ezekiel's ear. Rachel did her best to pick up scraps of his message, but his words remained just out of earshot. Ezekiel cut him a glance and nodded.

"It's kind of an unusual offer," he said. "I'll have to check with someone higher up on the food chain."

He returned to his post, opened the ledger to a blank page, and then turned the book toward Rachel.

"Sign in here," he said, handing her a pencil.

Rachel scrawled their aliases on a blank page, one name per line. She watched Ezekiel from the corner of her eye. Taking the kids public was scary, especially with their admittedly shaky cover story, but there was little choice. Keeping them hidden forever was unrealistic, so it was best to do so under her terms. There was always the chance someone would take them, the way a woman named Priya had tried to take Will. But the children were also living proof of the vaccine's effectiveness; when the time came to distribute it, its promise would be certain.

The second guard opened the gate for Rachel and the group.

"Follow me," Ezekiel said.

RACHEL FELT eyes on them the moment they set foot inside the barricade. As they filed into town, she rechecked the kids, noticing the cloaks and thin facemasks she hoped would conceal their actual age. As they cleared the threshold, the second guard threw the gate home. It clanged shut with a disquieting finality.

As Ezekiel led the group deeper into the town, she glanced again at the kids. Every visit to an unfamiliar settlement made Rachel uneasy, but what choice did she have? They were hungry. And if Will was right, someone was on their trail. This was the least bad option.

In the fading light of the day, Rachel could just make out the fence protecting the town's northern border. The main gate opened on a town square, a grassy expanse dotted with trees and perfectly square gardens, mostly barren at the end of the growing season.

To the east lay a quilt of condos, empty restaurants, abandoned retail spots, urban parks, and office space. The long fencing bordering the town enclosed a space of a few hundred acres. Unsurprisingly, every speck of open real estate had been converted into farmland, dedicated to growing their lifeblood.

It was a common sight these days and growing moreso as the environment recovered from the nuclear-fueled insanity of the last days of Medusa. Honestly, it was a wonder humanity hadn't vaporized its surviving remnants in the plague's chaotic final spasms. The summer just behind them was the warmest Rachel could remember since the pandemic. There was hope that the starvation that had become endemic would soon be a thing of the past.

The field on the left had been a park, but now it bore the hallmarks of regular agriculture. As they went by, the workers in the nearby field stopped to take a gander at their guests.

"Last harvest of the season," Ezekiel said. "Pulling up broccoli, kale, cabbage this week. They don't mind a little cold. Lotta greens actually are like that."

"Looks like you've got a good operation here," said Rachel.

"We work hard at it."

"How many folks you got living here?"

"Ohh, we do okay," Ezekiel replied cryptically.

Rachel did not push further. Something in the tone of his voice made her uneasy. Not enough to change her current approach, at least for the moment. For now. A data point. Safety was never guaranteed. Nothing was. You made the best choice you could with the intel available to you. And you were constantly assessing situations, collecting data, and, if necessary, adjusting on the fly. You always had to be ready to walk away.

They turned at a small courtyard fronting a six-story office building, following the winding path through a garden that was still vibrant with the hardy vegetables of the late growing season. A pair of goats worked at the park's edge, chowing down on weeds. Somewhere unseen, a cluster of chickens clucked away.

"This here is our nerve center," Ezekiel said. "Step inside with me, and we'll see what's what."

Ezekiel held the door open and ushered the group inside. Carla took the lead while Rachel waited at the rear, keeping an eye out behind her. Will fell in behind the kids, and Rachel followed him inside. They were in the building's lobby, which was bustling with people. It took Rachel aback to see this many folks in one place. Granted, *bustling* was a relative term these days. It wasn't like Times Square on New Year's Eve.

A reception desk sat in the center of the lobby. A suite of offices ran along either side of the floor. An older man sat at the desk, his head down in paperwork. His head popped up as he sensed their approach. He glanced back down before doing a double take at the unusual group approaching.

"Wait here," Ezekiel said, pointing at a small sitting area. Three old sofas were perched around a coffee table.

Carla, Jessica, and the kids collapsed onto the couches. Rachel and Will stayed on their feet, pacing back and forth. Ezekiel and the older man were locked deep in conversation. Her eyes drifted to the back of the room, where she spotted a younger girl, maybe fifteen years old. Kids like her were essential to the safety of Rachel's group. It took the edge off seeing a group with younger kids.

"What are they talking about, you think?" Carla asked quietly.

"I don't know," replied Rachel, shaking her head slowly.

She pressed an index finger to her lips as Ezekiel made his way back toward them. Rachel moved toward him, hitching her pack higher on her shoulders. Another ripple of unease. Another data point. She filed it next to the initial one. A dull ache formed in her jaw, a byproduct of her terrible habit of grinding her teeth. It intensified during periods of increased stress, which was just about all the time.

"Got some good news for you," Ezekiel said.

Rachel's eyebrows popped up.

"They're gonna let you work tomorrow for your supper tonight. You cross after lunchtime."

"Can we cross after dinner?"

"No," he replied quickly. Perhaps too quickly. "We close the bridge at sunset. Safety reasons."

There were murmurs of excitement behind her.

"Just need you to wait down the way here," he said. "They'll bring you your dinner shortly. There's just one condition."

"What's that?"

"You'll need to surrender your weapons during your stay," he said. "We'll return them on your departure."

Her face tightened, and Ezekiel must have noticed it.

"Please understand, you will get them back," he said. "But this is non-negotiable."

This was common in many settlements. After all, their hosts needed to be sure they weren't about to be attacked by bandits.

"Fine."

She nodded to Will. They relinquished their arsenal to Ezekiel, who carefully recorded each weapon and round of ammunition in a notebook at the reception desk. Rachel verified his entries in the log and signed the book. He countersigned the logbook and locked the weapons in a safe under the desk. She watched him type the code and filed it away in her memory.

Sloppy, Ezekiel. Very sloppy.

When he was done, he stood up and clapped his hands twice.

"Follow me, everyone."

Rachel's stomach rumbled. She could not deny that she needed to eat something. There had been scraps here and there for the last few days, but eventually, the deficit caught up with you. It always did. Your legs got weak. Your decision-making got hinky. And the allure of a hot meal in your belly could push thoughts of anything else out of the way.

As Ezekiel took a step down the corridor, Rachel paused. Something her dad had taught her resurfaced in her mind.

Once is an accident. Twice is coincidence. Three times is enemy fire.

She was sitting on two.

Two data points.

She glanced back at her group. Tired, hungry faces looked back at her.

"Come on, everyone," she said, gesturing toward the corridor.

~

4

———

Ezekiel guided the group to a small conference room at the end of the corridor. Three of its walls were painted a soothing blue. One glass wall looked over a small courtyard sandwiched between this building and a shorter one to the north. Lanterns sat perched on a pair of sconces on either side of the room, filling the room with warm but dim light. An oval laminate table sat in the center of the room. Six chairs were strewn askew through the room.

"Just have a seat here," Ezekiel said. "We'll be back with your dinner in a few. Hope you're hungry."

As he left, he started drawing the door closed behind him. Rachel reached out and grabbed the edge of the door before he latched it shut. The sudden stop of the door mid-flight caused Ezekiel to stumble a bit.

"If you don't mind," she said sweetly. "I'd prefer to keep it open."

A look of disappointment flashed briefly across his face, but he recovered quickly.

But not quickly enough.

Data point number three.

"Of course."

She hovered in the doorway as Ezekiel retreated down the hall. He was moving with a bit more urgency than one would expect, all but confirming Rachel's suspicions. When he was out of earshot, she turned back to the group.

"Everybody up," she said. "We need to get out of here."

Jess and Carla's eyes widened. A scattering of murmurs among the children.

"Why?" whispered Jess.

"We're being set up," she said. "Someone's been following us."

Looks of dismay spread across their faces.

"Why?"

"I don't know," she said. "But we need to get out of here."

The others exchanged nervous glances as they processed Rachel's news. Even the little ones seemed to sense trouble.

"Quick," Rachel snapped, her voice a harsh whisper. "On your feet. Now."

The group complied with her request, albeit reluctantly. Undoubtedly, their minds focused on their empty bellies and the food that would no longer fill them. Rachel didn't like going hungry any more than the others. But tonight, it was a necessary sacrifice. She tightened her backpack straps. The vaccine had to be kept safe at all costs.

And they had to go now.

"Follow me," she said. "Will, stay behind me. Then the kids. Carla and Jess bring up the rear."

Rachel's heart pounded as she shifted into a wartime footing and led her party out of the conference room. Ezekiel had made a mistake by not locking the door, but insisting on it would have been risky. Lantern light flickered in the corridor, which was chilly and dank. Rachel pushed close to the wall. Will gestured to the younger kids to keep pace.

Rachel stopped near the end of the corridor, holding up a fist to signal the others. The group was silent but for the ragged breathing of the little ones. The kids were easy to frighten; not much could be done about their anxiety. At least they were being quiet.

Rachel peered around the corner, back to the main reception area. Ezekiel was deep in conversation with a woman she did not recognize. The exit door was just beyond them. Outside, darkness had started to fall. Rachel did not relish another night on the road, but there was little choice.

Ezekiel's companion turned and left the building, leaving him alone in the reception area. His next move would determine Rachel's course of action. He stood there in thought, tapping his chin. Then he committed. He turned back toward the corridor leading to their erstwhile conference room-slash-cell.

Keeping an eye on the man, Rachel gestured behind her back, directing the others to move deeper into the corridor. Her decision was made; she ducked out of sight and pushed against the wall. As Ezekiel turned the corner, she clenched her hands together and swung her fist into his midsection. He grunted hard, doubling over from the force of the blow to the sternum. He gasped for air, grunting in surprise. Rachel delivered her second blow, clubbing him under the chin with her forearms. Her wrists vibrated with pain, but it was worth it. He staggered against the wall before sliding to the ground. He was still conscious, barely so. She grabbed his hair and slammed it once against the wall, knocking him out. She found a gun tucked into his waistband, which she secured for herself. They hustled toward the reception area, which was largely deserted.

"Now," she said, looking at the others. "Right for the door. Don't stop, don't look at anyone. Jess, Carla, y'all need to get across the bridge while there's still time."

"What if there are guards on the other side?"

"They'll assume you're clear to cross."

"What if they have walkie-talkies or some way to communicate?"

"Jess. That's what this is for."

Rachel handed Ezekiel's gun to the woman. She drew in a sharp breath, and Rachel placed a hand on Jess' shoulder.

"You can do this," Rachel said. "For the kids."

Jess nodded firmly.

Although no one had discovered Ezekiel yet, time was already running out. He'd be back in play soon, albeit with one hell of a headache. They needed to be out of the building post haste.

Sending Jess, Carla, and the kids ahead was a risk worth taking. Night had fallen, and the group would blend into the darkness on their way to the bridge.

"But they're guarding the bridge."

"It'll be clear. But not for long. You'll need to be close to the bridge."

"How will we know when to cross?"

"You'll know. We'll meet you on the other side. Thirty minutes."

"I don't want to split up."

Rachel was shaking her head before Jessica finished her sentence.

"It's too dangerous," she snapped. "I mean it. Someone is looking for us. Here. Now. Get across the bridge as fast as you can. Run."

She tapped the side of her backpack. Jessica's eyes widened with fear. Then she glanced toward the door, perhaps wondering what lay beyond it. Rachel squeezed Jessica on the shoulder as the woman examined the firearm in her hand. Jess and Carla herded the children to the door and quickly exited the building.

Once they cleared the door, Rachel and Will cut behind the desk toward the unattended safe. She knelt and spun the dial to the appropriate notches. The door swung open, and Rachel gathered the three firearms and boxes of ammunition. She kept one of the Glocks and M4. Will took the second Glock and the AR-15. They split the boxes of ammo and the flash-bang grenades. She cursed herself for checking their weapons with security. It had been a gamble, one that had not paid off.

A commotion erupted from the corridor, followed by a string of expletives.

"Now, Mom," Will said hurriedly. "We have to go now."

As they started toward the door, a man appeared on the other side, an apparition in the dark. He was dressed in black jeans and wore a heavy leather jacket. His head was turned to the side as he came in; it didn't appear he'd noticed them yet. Rachel and Will ducked low behind the desk. She froze, considering their options. Her best bet would be to push deeper into the building; the office likely had a rear entrance or loading dock.

Ezekiel came around the corner and connected with the man.

"Where are they?" asked the tracker.

"They must have run off," Ezekiel replied. His words sounded thick and dumb.

Rachel checked their rear. Another hallway stretched out behind them. Will glanced over at her, a quizzical look on his face. She tapped his chest twice and then repeated the gesture against her own. It was their universal sign for him to mirror his mother's next move.

"Bitch got the jump on me," added Ezekiel.

Charming.

She pressed up against the corridor wall, Will close behind her. The flickering candles nestled inside the sconces lit the way as the pair edged their way down the hallway.

A diversion. A diversion. A diversion.

Something big and loud.

They came to the building's rear exit. An old trashcan was near the back door, which opened onto a smaller court-yard. Will depressed the door's release bar and slowly swung it open into a narrow alley. Rachel quickly followed him outside, dragging the trashcan behind her.

"Follow me," she whispered after he had gently closed the door behind them. "And carry this."

Will tucked the trashcan under his arm and stayed on his mother's hip. They circled the perimeter of the building, coming around the eastern edge closest to the bridge. In the dim moonlight, she could see the pair of guards holding watch over the bridge approach. She needed to get close enough to draw their attention; it had to be a big enough cacophony to pull them off their posts. In the distance, she could make out the outlines of a small group of people.

She edged her way closer to the front of the building, bringing her and Will within twenty yards of the bridge approach. Near the corner, she stopped and set the trash can down. She lit the grenade's fuse and placed the device in the bottom of the can. Satisfied that the can was secure, she gently took Will by the elbow and led him toward a small grove of trees above an embankment descending toward the river. Around her, there was mostly silence. A few people were out and about for a late-night stroll. She spotted a two-man patrol circling the perimeter but paying little attention to their surroundings.

A few seconds later, the fuse reached its terminus. Then it happened: a sudden whoosh, followed by a bloom of fire. It made a hell of a noise, the trashcan's echo amplifying it tenfold. The two bridge guards left their posts and came running toward the source of the explosion. The fire quickly grew inside the trash can, which had tipped over, and spread into the grasses. Shouts filled the night as the cacophony drew instant attention.

"Come on, come on," she whispered, trying to will Jessica, Carla, and the kids out of their hiding spot. The time was now.

Then—movement.

The group burst forth from the shadows of a small grove of trees and raced toward the bridge, their footsteps clapping against the metal grate leading to the ramp. Carla took the point, the kids trailing behind and Jess bringing up the rear. Jess glanced over her shoulder, perhaps hoping Rachel was close behind. She continued rapidly up the ramp and disappeared into the gloom. It would take them about fifteen minutes to traverse the bridge on foot. The good news was that it didn't look like anyone had spotted them.

"OK," she said to Will. "Let's go. We'll catch up with them on the bridge."

Rachel took a single step clear of their hiding spot when she spotted him. The man tracking them loped toward the bridge, his movements quick and lithe. Briefly, she thought he would pursue Jess, Carla, and the kids, but instead, he took up a watch at the bridge.

The tracker was indeed after her. Well, at least the

others would be safe. Rachel eyed the man from her vantage point. Crossing the bridge was no longer an option; they were cut off from their group. She could only hope the women could keep the kids safe. Maybe they were better off without her and Will. Their presence was hazardous to a person's health. She needed a t-shirt with one of those black-box warnings they used to put on cigarette packs.

Two men approached the tracker at the bridge; they exchanged words but were too far away for Rachel to make out what they were saying. As they spoke, she considered their options. Beyond the northern perimeter fence stood a grove of trees thickened. A narrow riverbank ran parallel to the water.

The reality of their dilemma was coming into focus. The next bridge crossing was at least twenty miles upriver. On foot, it would take at least three days to catch up with the others, assuming she and Will could even pick up their trail. Unfortunately, there didn't seem to be any other option.

Activity at the bridge continued apace. More reinforcements arrived, carrying lanterns and weapons. Two continued onto the bridge, about ten minutes behind Carla and Jess. The wind shifted as the tracker barked new orders to the remaining group, sharpening the clarity of his words. His voice was strangely familiar. Rachel tried to identify its source, but she had no luck.

Moments later, the people near the bridge fanned out in pairs. It was time for them to go. She rued the loss of the bridge access, but what was done was done. Escaping with their lives would have to stand in as tonight's consolation prize.

She tapped Will on the shoulder and gestured for him to follow. They cut across the street parallel to the river and bounded down the embankment and around the edge of the fence. This narrow gap between the edge of the fence and the embankment was the town's one security failure. Here, the riverbank flattened out, creating a narrow path to negotiate. The pace was quick but manageable. Their long time on the road had taught them to move in virtual silence. The sounds of the river rushing downstream helped conceal the sounds of their passage.

Will kept a strong pace, never seeming to tire. He was still a kid, but the first hints of puberty were setting in. A sharp jawline and strong cheekbones were slowly replacing the once-round, cherubic face. He was still shorter than she was, by just a hair, but not for much longer. His shoulders now sat higher than hers, a strong indication that there was quite a bit of growing in his future.

It was yet another reason to find a permanent home. Will's body and mind were nearing a period of great change; a stable home would help ensure his physical and emotional transition from adolescence to young adulthood was as smooth as possible.

It took all her energy to stay on Will's hip.

They fled north.

5

Dr. Samir Malik wished people would stop doing this to themselves. After all, everyone knew how it would end—the same way every pregnancy here had ended since the end of the pandemic. And yet, they persisted, even all these years later. The indomitable human spirit, the stupid human spirit, the belief that life would find a way, hope—useless, thieving, lying hope—the notion that things would work out this time.

Even though they wouldn't.

The second knock was firmer than the first. An insistent *rap-rap-rap-rap* to deliver the message that this was incredibly important, never mind the time. Samir was awake, of course; he usually was, but that was not the point. He *could* have been asleep. Most people were. He was in his small living room, awash in lantern light. On the end table stood a large bottle of moonshine.

He'd opened it yesterday. It was about half empty now, and no one needed to tell him that was a bit more hooch than was acceptable in proper society. He knew that; of course, he knew that. He was a *doctor,* for God's sake.

Yeah, maybe I drink a little too much.

Still, it was nobody's business but his. It wasn't like he was going to perform heart surgery. Samir had been an emergency physician before Medusa, the pride of the Malik family.

His parents had immigrated to the United States from Syria just after the September 11 attacks (and hadn't that been a fun time to be olive-skinned in America!) and settled in Lawrence, Kansas, where they opened a Middle Eastern bakery. His mother had been nine months pregnant with him; his brothers followed in short order.

Initially, the locals weren't sure about the Arab newcomers, but Hussam, Samir's father, was as charming as they came. Traffic to the store grew quickly. The people of Lawrence might not have understood Islam, but they loved hummus, tabouli, and the seasoned meat pies known as *lahambajeen* they baked daily in their wood-fired oven.

Samir's parents had set their hopes and dreams on their son attending an Ivy League school, but none had admitted him, and they couldn't have afforded it anyway. Samir was reluctant to borrow six figures to finance his education. That said, he'd been a top-ten student, drawing a full ride from Kansas State. There, he excelled, finishing third in his class of six thousand and graduating with degrees in biology and English literature. He attended medical school at the University of Kansas before moving to a residency at a Dallas hospital. His chosen specialty, emergency medicine, had thrilled him; what he had not anticipated was the toll on his mental state.

The drinking had started slowly. A glass of wine after a shift turned into two. Two glasses became the whole bottle because it was an endless train of gunshots, overdoses, drunks with the shakes, and folks down on their luck using the ER for their primary care needs, generating massive medical bills most of them could never afford to pay. Maybe he had been naïve. Or just deliberately obtuse. His friends in private practice encouraged him to join them.

Samir, you're like a short-order cook. It's no way to live.

He didn't want to listen to them. He wanted to believe he could help.

His small apartment became a wasteland of takeout containers and empty wine bottles. The subtle hint of fermented grape hung in the air, a sweet sourness that lingered beyond the previous night's imbibement. The refrigerator was frequently empty; he was either at the hospital or he was on his couch watching old movies and drinking. More often than not, he woke up in the middle of the night on the sofa, his dehydrated lips stuck together, his head pounding, his heart racing.

It was an endless loop. Seventy-two hours on, twenty-four off. His life devolved into a blurry menagerie of counseling sessions, prescriptions, sexual trysts with anyone who would return the favor. Other doctors, nurses, even a patient once or twice, a profound violation of the regulations of the Texas Board of Medicine. He drank in the car on the way home.

He knew he was out of control. It was like there was a second Samir Malik, the spirit version of himself, floating in the air, but more than just an empty silhouette. A shadow that knew things. That knew the way things were. Screaming at and pleading with the damn fool below. What scared him, what truly terrified him, was the notion that the shadow was the Samir he wanted to be, the Samir he once had been. Maybe the alcoholic pill-popping menace below was the real Samir now. Perhaps that version of Samir was the boss.

He took a swig from the bottle and wiped his mouth. It flushed out the sourness of the previous evening's consumption. The knocking resumed, this time more frantically. He was still dressed, wearing a sweatshirt and a pair of jeans.

"Coming, I'm coming, Jesus," he muttered, perhaps loudly enough for his visitor to hear, perhaps not.

He didn't care. He could hear the baby hacking on the other side of the door.

He grabbed the lantern, got off the couch, padded to the entrance foyer, and opened the door. Ellen Trejo stood there with a desperate look on her face, a swaddled baby held close to her chest. The baby, whose name was Niko, was two days old. He'd begun showing signs of Medusa less than two hours after his birth. Samir couldn't remember a case of Medusa presenting so quickly. Maybe it was mutating. Maybe it would come for the rest of them next. Samir did not expect the boy to live much longer.

"Dr. Samir," she said breathlessly. "He's so sick."

His stomach fluttered with sadness. It still got to him, this sad, inevitable conclusion.

Every time.

"Let's head over to the clinic," he said.

Riverview made its home on the now-defunct campus of Ashby College, a small liberal arts school. Samir lived in a small suite in one of the university's dormitories, which housed virtually all of Riverview's five hundred residents.

Ellen nodded desperately, her eyes wide and bright, and followed him as he led the way toward Ashby's student commons. It housed their makeshift government office, the medical clinic, and the dining hall. Over the years, Samir had upgraded it with diagnostic equipment, surgical instruments, medications he scavenged from hospitals, pharmacies, abandoned homes and businesses, first-aid supplies, emergency life-saving tools, anything he could get his hands on. It was powered by their generator, which guzzled their precious fuel reserves, so he was extremely conservative with its use.

His head throbbed, and he wished to take another drink to help tamp it down. The science behind the hair of the dog had always eluded him, but there was no doubt that the next drink helped him bridge the pain and misery that had bloomed since the last drink.

Aware that his wits were not entirely about him, he kept a hand on the wall as they descended the stairs to the base-ment. He switched on the light, bathing the small clinic in harsh white. Their community's power supply was limited, mostly drawn from generators and a handful of small solar panels they had jerry-rigged over the years. It wasn't much, enough to support a few critical services. Ironically, Samir didn't think this qualified as *critical*; Medusa would do what she wanted to do whether he intervened or not.

In those hot, hellish days of that August long gone, virtu-ally every human being alive had been exposed to Medusa in extremely short order. Samir had come to believe that it only took a few seconds for an infected person to transmit the virus to its next victim. There was no avoiding it; there was only hoping you were in the one percent immune to the disease.

The R-naught factor for the virus was estimated at forty; a single person would infect around forty others, making Medusa the most contagious pathogen humanity had ever seen. Just two generations of transmission would result in fifteen hundred infections. A third generation pushed it over two million. That was how it had brought humanity to its knees so quickly. Once the acute phase of the pandemic had ended, it hadn't taken long to figure out that Medusa was the gift that kept on giving. Samir still remembered the first baby born to an immune mother that he'd seen die. It was extremely sad, of course, but by then, he was immune to seeing death.

He'd been in the emergency room of the University of Texas-Southwestern Medical Center the day Medusa had debuted in his life. It was late, well after midnight. An ambulance had brought in three roommates, all fresh out of college and living independently for the first time. He'd remembered them vividly. Two women and a man. Janine. Lydia. Anthony. He still remembered their names all these years later. All were burning with fever, all hemorrhaging, all delirious. Their neighbor had called 911 after finding Lydia barely conscious in the open doorway to their apartment. An hour later, the neighbor showed up in the ER complaining of fever and a bloody nose, and that was when Samir began to think something was very wrong.

The three roommates were dead before dawn. As the sun rose, the first bulletin came in from the Texas Health Department to be on the lookout for a possible outbreak of contagious disease. From there, things had deteriorated rapidly. So rapidly that Samir could scarcely believe what was happening. By the next day, everyone in the emergency department when the three index patients had arrived was symptomatic. Everyone other than Samir. Desperate to cut the outbreak off at the knees, the local health district quarantined the hospital, but it was too late. Hundreds of people had cycled through the emergency room that day, picking up a little viral souvenir and carrying it out to the world beyond.

It was after the second baby of an immune mother had died of Medusa that he began to fear something was, yet again, very wrong.

He guided Ellen and baby Niko to the examination table.

"Go ahead and set him down."

He hoped his voice didn't sound as defeated as he felt. Although his hope was gone, there was no need to let his despair wash over her. She'd be joining Samir soon enough. Things were hard enough on her as it was. The baby's father, a man named Zack, had checked out of Riverview upon learning Ellen was pregnant. He had not been seen since, leaving her alone to face their child's dark future.

Gently, Samir unwrapped the blanket cloaking the little guy. The boy radiated with fever; it was like holding a hand against a heating vent. He was coughing steadily, tiny, heartbreaking hacks. Blood stained his chin.

He glanced at Ellen, watching him with hopeful, needful, desperate eyes.

Stop looking at me, dammit! I can't save your son any more than I can walk on the damn moon! Actually, I've got a better chance of walking on the moon!

Samir rubbed the boy's tiny chest to break up the congestion, which sometimes provided relief for patients. The boy wasn't crying, which Samir found immensely depressing. The boy was too worn out to even cry. His chest rose and fell rapidly as he struggled to draw in air.

Samir became aware that Ellen was speaking.

"I said I think he's getting better," Ellen said. "He's not crying anymore."

He replied with a *hmmm*, not wanting to argue, not wanting to steal away her last bit of hope. They did not speak again. They stood there, hovering over the little boy for another hour. A massive seizure, the hallmark of end-stage Medusa, wracked his body, but mercifully, it ended as quickly as it began. Ellen sensed the end was near, so she picked up her son and held him close to her chest as he seized.

Parents of Medusa-infected newborns reacted in different ways. Some were resigned to their child's fate from the moment of birth, regretting their decision to challenge this inevitable force of nature by bringing doomed new life into the world. Others were delusional, certain that their baby would be the one to fend off Medusa's viral onslaught. And still others swung wildly between hope and despair, hoping beyond hope that the baby would live and then feeling that hope flicker out once the first symptom appeared.

Ellen Trejo fell into that third group.

He stepped away from the table and leaned against the wall, propping his foot behind him, his arms crossed against his chest. She set Niko back on the table, leaned in, and kissed his forehead. He was no longer breathing. Ellen caressed the thin layer of fuzz topping his head.

"Take as long as you need," he said.

She nodded. He heard an odd sound—her silent tears plopping on the table. There was no mournful sobbing, just the outline of her shoulders heaving up and down.

As he stood there with the mother of his patient, his mind drifted off toward the bottle sitting on top of his nightstand. Despite knowing exactly how this story would play out, he felt like another piece had been carved out of his soul. Somehow, he was numb to the horror while feeling like a raw nerve was exposed. It seemed particularly cruel that all Medusa had left to feed upon were children.

"Dr. Samir?"

He opened his eyes to find Ellen waiting before him.

"Can we bury him tomorrow?"

"Of course."

She left. The sounds of her footsteps on the stairs bore a muted, haunted quality. Samir wandered back to his suite, sat on the sofa, and poured another drink. It burned like a comet going down, but it was a small price to pay. It was the relief he sought, the sanding off the sharp edge of his hatred of Medusa.

The booze helped keep that feeling of hatred at bay. It reminded him that Medusa didn't do this out of malice. Medusa was not a rational, thinking entity. It was a piece of rogue code programmed to replicate itself. The way it did that was unfortunate for its hosts, but Medusa didn't know that. All it wanted to do was replicate.

But it hurt all the same.

Another child lost.

6

Rachel and Will were three days out from Dixon. After clearing the town's perimeter fence, they found the going difficult, slowed by a thick pine forest running north along the riverbank. The woods were deep and wide, the tree growth dense. On the plus side, the scent reminded Rachel of the Christmas tree lots of her youth. So, she had that going for her. No matter how many years were in the rearview mirror, pine trees would always equal Christmas.

The sun was at its peak for the day, casting its weak warmth down from an overcast sky. Will was tending to a small blaze, roasting a rabbit they had snared earlier that morning. It wasn't much, just a bit of protein to get them through the day. As he cooked, she snacked on pure snow— all the hydration they could ever want, right there for the picking. Even better was that neither she nor Will detected any sign of their tracker. The man showed his cards and made his play, and it had cost him.

It was cold, the sharpest chill of the season so far settling in. Typically, movement kept the chill at bay. But as the morning wore on, the chilliness persisted, and the cold seeped in even as they labored through the trees. The clouds were low and thick, casting an ominous gloom over them.

She sat close to the fire, rubbing her hands together. The blaze was smokeless, thanks to her and Will's carefully honed skill at building fires. Will tore a strip of meat from the roasted carcass and handed it to his mother. She took it gladly but insisted on him eating the bulk of the meat. He needed it more than she did.

One thing Rachel Fisher had learned in the sixteen years since Medusa had burned through the human race was that patience was a virtue. Rarely did things proceed according to anyone's schedule. It just didn't work like that. Their broken world dictated the schedule. The ones who thrived were those who could accept that—the ones who could exploit that fact. The ones who fought the reality of the world often suffered.

This thought bopped around Rachel's brain as they plowed quickly through their meal.

"How much farther to the next crossing?" he asked.

"A day. Day and a half."

They ate in silence. Rachel found herself daydreaming again.

"Mom?" he called out, breaking her out of her trance.

"Yeah?"

"You there?

"Sorry."

"Is the vaccine okay?"

Rachel shimmied the bag free from her shoulders and gently set it on the ground. After unzipping its large compartment, she carefully withdrew the valise and unsnapped the latches. Then, she lifted open the lid and carefully examined each vial. All were safe and intact, but for the one she had opened and from which she had distributed a handful of inoculations.

"They're fine."

"We have to do something."

Rachel did not reply immediately. He was right, of course.

"Because if we don't, something could happen to them."

Something *could* happen to them. And it would be her fault. It weighed on her every day, the responsibility she carried every day.

"I know."

Even her teenager knew the score. Eventually, their luck would run out; all her work these past few years would have been for nothing. And it was bigger than her. This wasn't just some sack of rations she was trying to keep safe. This was everything. It was for everyone.

It wasn't that she didn't want to distribute the vaccine. But she wanted to be sure. There weren't that many to spare. One thousand doses of vaccine needed to find the right one thousand arms. But thinking about how to distribute it was fraught with a single, almost impossible consideration.

Who should get the vaccine?

Merely considering the issue triggered waves of confusion in her mind. Pregnant women had to take priority—no one's need was more acute than an expectant mother. But that created its own dilemma. The supply of pregnant women almost certainly exceeded the supply of the vaccine she carried. Perhaps a few thousand. That group alone would exhaust her vaccine supply. But people weren't always easy to find these days. One might travel for days and not see another living soul. The survivors of the pandemic had scattered widely across the continent. Another option involved reserving a portion of the vaccine for women who weren't pregnant. But that created another problem—what if she wasted a dose on a woman who either did not or could not become pregnant? There were no doses to spare.

And how did you decide?

Who was she to play God? To tell one woman yes, you are worthy of motherhood, but to callously say no to another, as though you were passing them over for some entry-level job. It wasn't as if she hadn't distributed any doses at all. In their travels, she'd inoculated a handful of pregnant women. Women so close to birth, so close to the inevitability of Medusa's terrible fate, that Rachel could not bear to let them suffer. A few women out there right now, around ten, had given birth to Medusa-immune babies thanks to Rachel's gift.

This probably explained the tracker hunting them. Word of those immune babies had spread to the markets and communities, and someone might have figured out that there was a common thread tying them together. That was also a reason to find a new home for the winter: a larger population, plenty of women, and perhaps some guidance on establishing a vaccine distribution protocol.

But even if she found such a community, would they even believe her?

Would they believe that this stranger at their door carried with her the future of humanity? You didn't make it this far in their world without a healthy dose of skepticism. There was always someone out there trying to get something for nothing. For all anyone knew to the contrary, Rachel might just be injecting them with saline. Or worse.

"I know," replied Rachel. "But it has to be perfect. I can't afford to make any mistakes."

"Holding onto them too long could be the biggest mistake of all."

They finished their meal in silence.

"It's snowing," Will said absently.

Rachel glanced around; a light snow had started to fall. The campsite was silent but for the sound of flakes hissing against the flames of the fire. She looked at the sky. There were about five hours of daylight left. They would need shelter before then. By the looks of it, this was more than just a passing flurry.

"Let's get moving," she said. "We need a roof over our heads tonight."

Will nodded his understanding. She didn't sugarcoat things for him anymore. It was never a good idea in their world. Something as simple as a snowfall reminded her nothing was guaranteed. The epoch since the pandemic ended was just borrowed time for all of them. Honesty and candor helped keep them both alive.

Will extinguished the fire while Rachel covered any evidence of their presence. After clearing the site, she and Will were on the move once more. The snow fell more heavily as the afternoon wore on. The weather had not been terribly cold the previous week, so the snow was slow to accumulate; by mid-afternoon, however, a white blanket was stretched across the landscape.

An hour later, they reached a two-lane highway running west away from the river, snaking lazily toward the Gulf of Mexico this morning. Rachel looked longingly at the far bank of the Missouri, desperate for a way across. She'd kept her eye open for any stray craft that could ferry them across the river, but none was found. And the incoming storm would slow their progress even more.

As they turned onto the road, the tangy hint of

woodsmoke caught her nose. Ahead, a curl of white smoke rose into the sky through another grove of trees on the other side of the highway. There was little development out here. Any homesteads out here would be well isolated.

Will stopped beside her, his head tilted as though he was listening for something. She also paused and kept silent, relying on his young ears to divine vital intel from the air. He pressed an index finger to his lips as he scanned the trees. He gestured toward the trees on the far side. She nodded her understanding.

They crossed the roadway, blanketed with freshly fallen leaves swirling in the autumn breeze. They passed under a decaying billboard; once upon a time, it had advertised a local diner named Matty's Kitchen. Will's pace accelerated as they neared the tree line. She asked no questions, understanding that his alarm bells were sounding wildly. He pinballed through the woods, taking cover behind a large maple. Rachel followed him around the base of the ancient tree, keeping low.

"Someone's on us," he whispered.

Rachel clenched her jaw in frustration. Never a break. She drew her weapon, curling back around the side of the trunk for a peek back south. Behind her, the smell of smoke had intensified. The cabin was only a few hundred yards to their backs. The increased activity close to the homeowner's property undoubtedly drew their attention. Anyone who had made it this far into the post-Medusa world was nothing if not fully aware of their surroundings.

Movement in the trees across the highway caught the corner of her eye. A ripple of leaves and branches. Her gaze locked in on the spot, hoping it was an animal, bird, or just a breeze, but preparing herself for the worst. Then she spotted a flash of fabric, the familiar green, brown, and black of military camouflage. Then, another shimmer of movement. At least two pursuers now.

She glanced at Will and flashed two fingers at him.

There are two of them.

He shook his head and showed her three fingers.

Damn.

She'd missed one.

She nodded her understanding.

Whoever was after them was hellbent on finding them, that was for sure.

A plan bloomed in her mind. The cabin's residents would view all of them as threats. So, whether they knew it or not, she and Will were allies. A glance over her shoulder. It was about a hundred yards to the cabin, which sat in an open clearing circled by a ring of trees.

This was going to be tricky.

It would require her to draw the pursuers in as closely as possible while keeping an eye on their rear. An itchy trigger finger could end it for them right now. A trio of bandits emerged in a skirmish line from the tree line on the far side of the highway, wisely keeping ten yards between them. The remaining pair could quickly draw a bead on her even if she took one out.

As the group cleared the highway, she glanced at Will and motioned toward the cabin behind them. Together, they retreated, moving from tree to tree, hopefully drawing the men into a trap she still needed to set. That she still needed to think up. While collecting themselves behind a tree, she pointed her gun in the air and pulled the trigger. A single shot echoed through the woods. If their presence hadn't been detected yet, it was now.

But no return volley materialized.

She waited.

Then, a staccato burst of machine gunfire ripped through the air, tearing up a sapling not twenty feet away from them. The guns fell silent again. These attackers needed to be careful. If they shot her, the vaccine might be destroyed in the crossfire. And if she had hidden it some-where, its location would die with them. *Shoot first, ask questions never* was a popular mantra in the apocalypse, but today, her assailants might have other plans.

She bolted from the cover of the trees, Will right on her tail. The final ring of trees circling the cabin lay just ahead. The small structure was weather-beaten, gray but not decrepit. An old SUV was parked in the small circular drive-way. The truck was in good shape, its tires intact and inflated.

She tapped Will's chest and then tapped her own. He nodded. She bolted for the car, taking cover behind the hood, Will sliding in behind her. Another shot rang out, cracking the silence of the falling snow.

There was movement in the trees, both to her right and left. There was no need to conceal their movements any longer. They would try to pinch her and Will in now, one on each flank, while the third came in on a frontal maneuver. Rachel peered around the bumper toward the last line of trees.

The snow had picked up, adding a curtain of white, making it harder to see and providing an added layer of protection. Rachel glanced back at the cabin. The windows were dark and opaque. The shimmer of a curtain confirmed the presence of someone inside. Rachel could feel eyes on them right now—life inside the house, possible death out here.

This was a carefully kept home, a fortress of sorts. There was a rain barrel at the corner of the house. Just beyond were the remains of a vegetable garden, tended to but quiet in this dead season. A large stack of firewood sat against the house, covered under a tarp. The home's occupant was not a drifter. This was a permanent home.

Time to commit to a plan.

The snow was dusting her hair and eyelashes now. It showed no signs of slowing down—just a low gray sky in every direction. The bandits could bide their time. If the homeowner wouldn't come to the fight, Rachel would bring the fight to him. Ten yards of ground separated them from the front door. Rachel grabbed Will by the arm, tugging him toward the entrance to the cabin. She lowered her shoulder and barreled into the door. Her body struck the wooden door with a terrific thud, but it held fast. The cabin may have been old and weathered, but its primary access point was secure. She should have known better.

Pain lit up her left shoulder, and she slid to the ground in agony.

They were sitting ducks.

As she cradled her wounded arm close to her body, she fired two shots into the woods.

A whistle from the woods. A signal to move in for the kill.

Another volley of fire came in hot. She dove to the ground and pushed Will underneath her, kicking her left foot hard against the door over and over again.

She returned fire, spraying a few of her precious remaining rounds into the ether.

"Open the damn door!" she called out. "We're dead out here!"

A holly bush was next to the door; she grabbed Will and tugged him behind the meager cover it provided. They pressed up against the house's northern side.

"You okay?" she asked when the volley of gunfire ceased.

He leaned his head back and let out a shaky breath. His hand was pressed against his abdomen.

"I think so."

Then Rachel saw the blood spilling between his fingers.

7

"No, no, no," Rachel muttered desperately, placing her hand over Will's to stanch the flow of blood. She glanced up at him; his face had taken on an ashy tone. He shifted his seat but froze when a wave of pain washed across his body. Seeing her boy suffer made her heart cave in.

"Please!" she howled. "He's hit, he's hit!"

She didn't care if their assailants heard her desperate pleas for help. If this door didn't open in the next few seconds, they were dead anyway. Rachel tended to Will, waiting to live, waiting to die. Every second was an eternity.

There was additional movement in the trees.

The wind picked up, blowing snow in a violent swirl. She considered firing a shot at the door handle, but that would likely draw fire from inside, sealing their fate. All she could do now was hope a good Samaritan lived behind that door.

Will's eyelids fluttered and then closed. He was breathing, but it was shallow and rapid.

"Open your eyes, sweetie, open your eyes," she pleaded. "Don't you go to sleep on me."

He opened them wide and looked right at her.

"I'm okay," he said. Then he smiled dreamily before his eyes closed again.

Her hand was warm with his blood; she did not know how much he could afford to lose before it was *too* much. Panic rippled through her body. Fear of something terrible happening to Will had dwelled inside Rachel since he was born. It started with the assumed inevitability of his death by Medusa, back before she understood the truth about her family's connection to the pandemic. But even after he'd survived those frightening early days, the terror was never far from her mind. Their world was brutal and dangerous, and people died all the time for no good reason at all. Her late father's experience as a physician had made things easier, of course, but the fear was always there.

A rustle of activity behind the door drew her attention. A small port in the door slid open.

"I'm gonna open the door for five seconds," a woman's voice said. "I'll lay down cover fire for you. Get your asses in here."

"Got it," Rachel replied.

The door swung open, revealing a stocky woman on the threshold carrying an automatic weapon. As she fired a long burst from the gun, Rachel swung Will's right arm around her neck and grasped his wrist. With a mighty grunt, she pulled them to their feet and staggered toward the door, staying as low as possible. The woman stepped to the side while Rachel half-carried her wounded son inside the cabin.

The woman fired off an additional burst before slamming the door closed. She threw several deadbolts before doing a quick lap around the great room, throwing closed a series of heavy curtains.

"Kevlar curtains were a good idea, Mer," she said, mostly to herself, as a heavy burst of gunfire struck the side of the house.

Rachel was barely listening; she hurried Will to a sofa at the back of the large room and lay him down. She grabbed a throw pillow and pressed it against the wound in his abdomen, soaking up the blood still flowing from the wound.

"I need some towels," she called out.

"One second," the woman replied.

"Now, dammit, he's bleeding out here!"

"Shut your trap, or we'll all be dead!"

Rachel ignored her and pulled the pillow back to better look at Will's wound. The bullet had pierced his lower right flank; she gently rolled him onto his side in search of an exit wound. No such injury was immediately apparent. He grunted in pain, so she eased him onto his back once more. Rachel looked back at the woman, who had her eye pressed to the port in the door. A small object was in her hands, about the size of a computer mouse.

"Come on, you little bastards," she said. "A little closer. Just a little closer."

A few seconds later, she pressed a button on the object; a tremendous explosion followed. Layered in the folds of the sonic boom came desperate screams of pain and agony, which disappeared as quickly as they erupted.

She chuckled to herself.

"Well, that's three less bad guys in the world."

Again, her words were not directed toward Rachel; she seemed to be speaking to herself. She opened the door and confidently stepped onto the stoop. Whatever threat had been appeared to be neutralized. The acrid smell of fire wafted in from outside. Rachel tilted her head to look through the door. Dark grey smoke curled around a heavily damaged tree line on the far side of the clearing.

She closed the door and secured the deadbolts before joining Rachel at the sofa.

"What's happening with this sweet baby?" she asked.

"He took one in the abdomen," Rachel said through gritted teeth. "I don't know how bad it is."

"Sit tight," the woman said. "Name's Meredith. Keep pressure on that wound."

The woman, Meredith, disappeared into the house, making quite a commotion and talking to herself the entire time. A few minutes later, she returned to the room with a black doctor's bag, the kind used for house calls you saw on television, and a stack of towels.

"Let me see it," Meredith said, kneeling beside Rachel.

Rachel hesitated, fearful of trusting anyone with her son's life even as it hung in the balance.

"Sweetie, if I meant you any harm, you'd already be dead."

She chuckled to herself again.

Rachel had to concede the point.

"It's okay," she said. "I was a paramedic. Before."

Rachel let out a shaky breath. The woman had medical training. She moved to the side, giving Meredith a clear look at Will, who was drifting in and out of consciousness.

"Did the bullet come out the other side?" Meredith asked.

"I don't think so."

"Bad luck. We're gonna need to get that out."

"How?"

"We'll get to that. For now, we need to stop the bleeding. Press a towel against the wound while I get things ready."

Rachel folded the towel into quarters and held it against the wound, which was still leaking blood, although the flow had slowed a bit. She caressed Will's cheek; he was still awake, barely. Meredith opened a transparent bottle of rubbing alcohol.

"This is gonna hurt like hell," she said. "But I need to disinfect the wound."

Tears welled up in Rachel's eyes. The idea of Will being subjected to even more pain shattered her, even while she understood its necessity.

"Hold his hand and try to keep him still."

Rachel slid her arm under his neck, held him close against her shoulder, and kissed his clammy, sweaty forehead.

"Honey, I need you to stay as still as you can."

An almost imperceptible nod.

Rachel looked at Meredith and nodded.

"OK, move the towel."

Rachel complied. It was heavy with blood, which terrified her.

The woman wasted no time; she splashed a tablespoon's worth of clear disinfectant on the dark crevice left by the entry wound. As it made contact with his wound, his body locked up, and a terrible groan rumbled in his throat.

"One more. Almost there."

Another splash. This one drew a howling scream, one Rachel felt deep in her soul, carving away little pieces of her. Will bucked like a wild horse, nearly pitching over the side of the sofa and onto the floor.

"Okay, great job, kid."

She turned back to her kit, removing a large bandage and a roll of gauze.

"What's his name?" she asked as she readied the dressing.

"It's Will. His name is Will."

"You still with me, Will?" she asked.

His eyes fluttered, but he did not reply.

Nonplussed, Meredith continued with her work. With the smoothness of a seasoned pro, she slapped the dressing on the wound and secured it with several long strips of gauze. In just a few seconds, the wound was dressed.

"Won't it keep bleeding through?"

Meredith shook her head.

"The bandage is infused with a clotting agent," she said. "I don't have many, but this should buy us enough time. Help me get his feet up."

Rachel nodded, lifting her son's legs and bottom off the couch. As she did so, Meredith slid in a series of pillows, keeping his torso and legs above his heart as best as she could. This would help slow any continued loss of blood. Rachel kept her eye on the wound, fully expecting to see blood soak through the bandage and overflow onto his stomach.

"Enough time for what?"

The woman put her hand on Rachel's shoulder.

"He needs surgery," she said. "Soon."

Rachel's chest tightened with panic.

"There's a town a few miles north," she said. "Good doctor there. He might do it."

"Might?"

Meredith sighed.

"They're not as generous as I am. If you've got something to offer, it might grease the skids."

Rachel brushed her hand against the strap of her backpack. In the fog of violence, she had almost forgotten about it.

"I might."

"OK, let's get him to the car," she said. "It'll be dark soon, and they won't open the gate after sunset."

RACHEL SAT with Will in the cargo area of the old Jeep Cherokee as Meredith guided the vehicle north along the two-lane highway. She held his hand and stared blankly at the road behind them as they chewed up the distance between the cabin and their destination. Fallen leaves covering the road swirled around as they screamed through the falling twilight. Light snow showers dusted the ground.

Will was holding his own for now. His pulse was weak, but it was steady. He was breathing, maybe a little on the shallow side, but he was breathing, and that was what mattered. But an army of worst-case scenarios surrounded her sanity, ready to launch a full invasion. Paralysis. Brain damage. Death. Jesus, the day had devolved into an utter nightmare in the blink of an eye. Just an hour ago, they were eating roasted rabbit. The morning had dawned like so many others, and now, as the sun set, Will was fighting for his life.

Lose him. She could lose him. He could die tonight in this car. It was not an impossibility. A world without Will. Once he had entered it, she could not imagine it absent his presence. Her love for him had been instant, permanent, and all-encompassing. She remembered the night he'd been born, a rainy October evening, all alone but for her father overseeing the delivery. The other residents of Evergreen had resigned themselves to the inevitability of the baby's death.

That was when she knew it would always be her and Will alone. Sure, the others had come around when he survived, but it was too late. They had shown who they were. Not willing to stand with her, for better or worse.

And if he died, she would be alone. Everything she had done, all that she had sacrificed, would have been for nothing. She would be alone. There would be nothing to live for. Never again. This whole thing had been about building a world worth leaving behind for Will. If he was gone, she had little interest in what became of this broken place.

The Jeep decelerated; Rachel stole a glance through the windshield as the vehicle slowed to a stop at a checkpoint. A pair of armed guards stood watch before a wrought-iron fence flanked by two brick pillars. A stone engraved with the words Ashby College was set into the brick on the left. Established 1913. A college campus. The fence ran at least an eighth of a mile to the east before turning north. Nestled into the woodsy landscape was a series of Victorian brick buildings. As she craned her neck for a better view, one of the guards approached the driver's side. The man's movements were casual and unconcerned.

"Evening, Meredith," said the guard, a woman in her late twenties.

She leaned in the window, tilting her head toward the back and making eye contact with Rachel.

"Need to see Dr. Malik," replied Meredith, dispensing with the pleasantries. "Boy in the back's been shot. Needs surgery."

"Wait here a second."

Rachel was ready to explode. Every minute, every second brought Will closer to death. She bit her lower lip and closed her eyes; losing her cool would not help Will. She needed to let the situation play out.

The woman stepped back from the vehicle and spoke into a walkie-talkie for a few moments before returning. Her face was dour, and Rachel knew what was coming.

"Sorry, Mer, we're running low on things," she said. "The mayor said no."

"Wait, wait, wait!" Rachel called desperately from the back. She swung the door open and hopped out.

"Listen to me!" she said. "He's dying back there. Get your boss back on the horn."

The guard exchanged a glance with Meredith, who nodded. She thumbed the button on her walkie-talkie and waited for a reply.

"She wants to talk," the guard said. "Over."

"Go ahead. Over."

The guard handed the device to Rachel.

"My son, he's been shot."

"And I'm very sorry to hear that," a man said. "But that is more than we can handle right now."

"I can pay for the surgery."

Static filled the air while she waited for a reply.

"With what?"

"With a vaccine."

"What kind of vaccine?"

"The only one that matters."

8

Samir sat in the director's office with their fearless leader, June Richards, a cold, unforgiving woman, and her assistant, Alice Tirico. It was a strange little room that left him feeling uneasy. Richards had decorated it to match her quirky tastes. An autographed football encased in Lucite sat on the corner of the desk. It was signed by a former defensive end named Freddie Briggs. June's diploma from Louisiana State University hung from one wall. It was as if she wanted to forget the pandemic had ever happened.

Samir's head hurt. His mouth was dry, and exhaustion set deep in his bones. Maybe he was getting sick. Maybe Medusa had finally found him. Maybe somewhere out there, it had mutated into something to which they weren't immune and hunted them down. Some days, he had wished for precisely that. In so many ways, they were going through the motions and playing out the string like a baseball team eliminated from playoff contention.

But not today. Not right now.

Not since Alice had come to the clinic with news of this

woman's arrival. Her claim that she carried a Medusa vaccine, one that would protect babies in utero from their heretofore terrifying fate, had rocked him to his core.

If she were telling the truth, it would change everything. *Everything.*

Samir had been resigned to their fate for more than a decade now. Humanity was dying off, a little bit at a time, and there was no way to restock its pantry. He'd heard the stories, telling of female survivors who had never been exposed to Medusa, and thus, in theory, could give birth to a healthy baby. But he'd never seen one himself. And even if there were a few out there, it was doubtful there were enough to stave off humanity's extinction. There just weren't enough of them.

Moreover, there was no evidence that any immune survivor had given birth to a baby that had lived beyond infancy. It was maddening. If one to two percent of the population was naturally immune to Medusa, then a similar proportion of their offspring should also be. Samir, however, was not aware of any such infant survivor. He suspected a phenomenon known as maternal antibody interference. Although the antibodies protecting the mother from Medusa were transferred to the fetus, these microscopic guardians interrupted the development of a newborn's fledgling immune system. As such, babies could not mount a sufficient response to Medusa, and their little bodies were overwhelmed. A trip to the library had confirmed his suspicion, one dark evening spent reading medical textbooks by candlelight. This bizarre outcome had been documented in other diseases.

Fifty years from now, maybe sixty years, it would all be over. Lock the doors, turn out the lights, and give the planet back to Mother Nature. Knowing that he was part of humanity's last generation was weird. For two hundred thousand years, *Homo sapiens* had been at the top of the food chain, but in a few decades, their run at the top would end. A few decades after that, a few centuries at most, nature would fully reclaim everything it hadn't already taken back, and there would be no evidence that any of them had ever lived.

It really screwed with your mind.

Maybe in some distant future, beings from another world would stumble across this planet. Water, breathable air, organic life. And if those visitors dug a little deeper, they might find evidence of intelligent life. Networks of crumbling highways. Architectural ruins. Perhaps relics of beautiful things humans had made. And they would wonder where these bright and inventive creatures had gone.

Samir was thankful the pair had arrived at their gates before he'd begun his evening cocktail hour. He glanced at Alice Tirico, who likely wished she wasn't pregnant, but there wasn't much to do about that. She was eight months along now; the baby could come anytime. And then the baby would die.

The wounded boy and his mother were in the clinic, awaiting Riverview's final decision on providing the surgery the kid desperately needed. Time was running short; June needed to choose quickly or the boy's hemorrhaging wound would decide for them. Meredith had done a good job stitching up the boy, but her work had been a stopgap measure at best. He was bleeding internally while they held this ridiculous meeting. The surgery needed to happen soon. Samir could not believe they were even having this discussion. As though there was any debate to be had. Letting the boy bleed to death was not an option.

"I want to do this," Samir said. "I can save the boy."

"It's gonna cost us a lot," she said.

"The vaccine is worth more than everything Riverview has combined."

"You know the clinic is low on supplies," June said. "What do you need for the procedure?"

"Gloves, scalpels, sutures, among other supplies. Basic surgical tools."

"What if she's lying?" June asked.

"Then she's lying. And we save a young boy's life."

"We cannot save everyone," June said.

"But we can try," Samir snapped.

"Why would she have a Medusa vaccine? Where did it come from?"

"I don't know," replied Samir. "But it's a weird thing to lie about."

"So, because it's weird, we should believe her?"

"That's what I'm saying. It's so weird, so out there, that it almost warrants belief."

June tented her fingers at her lips.

"Pretty good position for her to be in," June said. "We have no proof the vaccine would work."

"The boy," Samir retorted. "The boy is awfully young. I've examined him. I highly doubt he's older than thirteen. Fourteen at the oldest. He's barely begun puberty. I think it's a virtual certainty that he was born after the pandemic. I think he's been vaccinated. It's possible they both have been."

"But you're not sure?"

"No," Samir conceded. "She could be lying."

A cold silence fell across the room.

"I'll take the vaccine," Alice said suddenly, shattering the quiet.

Samir's head swung toward the demure young woman

seated to his left. Her left hand caressed the swell in her belly, and her mind undoubtedly fixed on the dark fate awaiting her—a fate that had seemed inevitable until this afternoon.

"Absolutely not," June said. "We cannot risk your life on this lark."

"Dr. Malik?" asked Alice.

"Yes?"

"Do you think this woman is telling the truth?"

"I believe she is," he said. "But I can't be sure."

"Without a vaccine, will my baby die?"

His mouth watered, and he thought about his next drink. He did not want to tell Alice the truth because the truth hurt so badly, but she deserved nothing less. In their world, they deserved nothing less.

"Yes," he said. "Your baby will die."

"Then I don't care what happens to me."

Alice's bravery filled Samir with sadness. This young woman, who had already been through so much, would go even further to save the life of her unborn child. It seemed brutally unfair because it *was* brutally unfair. None of them should have to make these decisions.

"Alice," June was saying, "those vials could be filled with saline for all we know."

"I don't care. If there's a one percent chance it would save my baby, then it's worth the risk."

June thumped the table with a tightly clenched fist.

"I won't let this woman blackmail us," she said. "On nothing more than a promise."

Alice whimpered.

Samir placed a gentle hand on Alice's shoulder. She was a sweet woman and deserved better than this. June's casual dismissal of this opportunity sparked a fire in his belly.

"You do that," Samir said, a coldness in his voice he wasn't aware that he was capable of, "and everyone in this little community of ours will know."

"And what happens if word of this gets out?" June replied.

"If what gets out?"

"That we have a vaccine."

Samir considered this for a moment.

"We would have a lot of power."

She laughed.

"You see, you don't think about the consequences of this," she said coldly. "That's why you're not in charge. Every two-bit militia and warlord would be on our ass by sunset. What am I supposed to defend the town with? Your charming personality?"

He stood up.

"Well, then, that's your problem," he snapped. "I'm gonna go take care of that boy."

THE WOMAN WAS WAITING for him in the town's clinic, standing over her son like a hawk. He went first to the sink and washed his hands as thoroughly as he could, using the homemade soap, rinsing with the water drawn from the well serving the community. As he shook his hands dry, he glanced at the boy's mother. She was striking. She was only about five-foot-six, but her presence loomed large over the room. Her face was burnished brown from years in the elements. Small wrinkles creased the corners of her eyes, but she was about his age. The world aged them all quickly. He was forty, maybe forty-one, and his occasional glance at the mirror made him think he was looking at his grandfather. The woman's hair was tied back in a ponytail, framing her face in the room's dim light. Intensity radiated from her face as she kept vigil over her son.

Samir's chief nurse, Megan Franklin, was busy setting the surgical instruments on the tray beside the operating table. She was organized and careful; Samir trusted her implicitly. The air was sharp with the bite of rubbing alcohol. Will was anesthetized, the wound cleaned and disinfected, and he was ready for surgery. The room was quiet but for the hum of the generator powering the clinic.

"I'm Dr. Malik," he said as he approached the operating table. "Miss..."

"Fisher. Rachel Fisher."

She gestured to the unconscious boy on the table.

"This is Will."

He nodded, examining the boy.

"Sorry we're meeting under these circumstances," Samir said. "This will go much smoother if we can stay calm."

She nodded.

"I don't suppose you'll take my advice to wait outside?"

"No."

She was unequivocal.

"Didn't think so."

Megan handed him the scalpel, and he began cutting into Will's abdomen two inches below his rib cage. Blood pooled at the incision site; Megan worked to keep the operating theater clear of the obstruction. Surgery in a post-Medusa world was no joke. They worked without telemetry machines and relied on substandard anesthesia and home-grown antibiotics. It was a dangerous walk on a fraying tightrope. It was always the last resort—only when life hung in the balance.

As it did now.

Samir worked steadily, pausing only for Megan to mop his brow. For ninety minutes, things proceeded without incident. He located the bullet; the boy was lucky, as it had not hit any major arteries or organs. He clamped and slowly withdrew it, careful not to drag the jagged metal edges against the sensitive tissue surrounding it. Megan held out a small plastic tray; the bullet dropped into it with a satisfying clatter.

"Got the bullet, Mom," he said to Rachel without looking up.

Time to sew the kid back up.

Trouble struck around two hours into the procedure.

"Dr. Malik?"

Megan was frantically pulsing the balloon of the sphygmomanometer, their ancient blood pressure reader. A wash of panic crashed over him. He checked the surgical incision and noted an unusual amount of blood leaking inside Will's abdominal cavity.

"His BP is dropping," she said, removing the cuff from the boy's arm.

"He's losing blood," he said, looking for the site of the leakage.

"Eighty over forty," she said. "Still dropping."

He carefully but quickly examined each section of tissue, recalling his training to locate the nick in the artery.

Come on, come on, come on.

Lifting a flap here, a thread of tissue there.

"Still dropping, Doctor."

"Dammit, do something!" howled the mother.

She stepped around the table and sidled up beside Samir.

"Do you even know what you're doing?" she snapped.

He ignored her. This wasn't about him. This was a frightened mother looking out for her child. There was a wild look in her eyes, and for a moment, he thought she might take a swing at him.

"You need to trust me," Samir said calmly.

It was the calmest he'd felt in a long time. Knowing there was something he could do for this boy after years of watching one baby after another succumb to Medusa.

There!

He spotted the little geyser of blood erupting and bathing the surrounding tissue. It was incredible that something so small could cause such mayhem. The human body was a wonderful symphony, but for all its magic, the tiniest hiccup could trigger utter chaos.

"Megan, the quick clot."

She handed it to him. He dabbed the virtually invisible tear, stopping the bleeding quickly. He looked up at Megan, hoping.

"Ninety," she said, nodding. "One hundred. One fifteen and stabilizing."

He took a deep breath and let it out slowly. The crisis had passed. He resumed work on the boy's stitches.

"Is he okay?" asked Rachel.

"Yeah," Samir said, sighing. "Yeah, he's gonna be fine."

9

Samir went to check on the boy at midnight.

He knocked and entered the clinic's lone private room, where Will was recovering. Rachel was sitting by her son's side, stroking his arm with her left hand, propping up her chin with her right. Her face was heavy with fatigue. Dark circles under her eyes belied a woman desperately needing a good night's sleep. Despite the nap he had taken, Samir was still worn out and craving a long rest himself. It hadn't been the most challenging procedure, but even the simplest of surgeries took a lot out of you.

"Evening," he said to Rachel, pausing in the doorway.

"Hey there," she said, leaning back in her chair. She rubbed her eyes and stretched her back. It popped satisfyingly.

"Mind if I check on him?"

"Be my guest."

He moved toward the bed and began his examination. The boy's vitals were stable. His breathing was steady, about sixteen respirations per minute. The stitches in his abdomen were holding nicely, and for now, at least, there was no sign of infection.

She clicked her tongue.

"I'm sorry I got short with you in there."

Samir chuckled as he placed the stethoscope disc against his patient's chest. The soothing sound of a steadily galloping pulse made him smile.

"His heart sounds good."

"I mean, I shouldn't have spoken to you that way."

He hung the stethoscope around his neck. Doing the stethoscope thing always gave him a secret little thrill, one he would never admit to anyone.

"Oh, don't sweat it.

"Well, I'm sorry."

"Apology accepted."

"And thank you."

"You're very welcome."

He took the chair opposite Rachel.

"What's his name again?"

"Will," she said.

"And he was born after the pandemic, wasn't he?"

Rachel shifted uncomfortably in her seat. The question had taken her by surprise. It was an effective method for teasing out the truth.

"No point in lying about it," he said. "He's barely started puberty. The pandemic ended fifteen years ago."

Samir looked down at the boy's sweet, unlined face. It reminded him of an easier, happier time: his childhood in Texas.

She blew out a noisy sigh.

"Yes, he was born after the pandemic. Two years after it ended."

"Remarkable."

"Hmm," she said.

It was remarkable. This boy. This woman. This vaccine.

"So, it's true?"

"Is what true?"

"About your vaccine."

"You don't believe me? Why'd you do the surgery?"

"You think I would've let him die?"

She raised her eyebrows and tilted her head toward him accusingly. And it hit him. She really thought he would have let her son bleed to death.

"It's a tough world out there," she said. "Or perhaps you hadn't noticed."

"Indeed it is. But the day I turn away any patient, much less a pediatric patient, is the day I deserve a bullet in the head."

He was serious about that. Far too many people had been willing to sacrifice their humanity for survival. He'd seen it with his own eyes. The worst of human behavior had bubbled to the top these last fifteen years. The cream had not risen to the top. It was as if the human psyche had been looking for a reason to succumb to its darkest impulses. As if the civilization itself had been a façade.

It reminded him of the moment that had haunted him more than any other. Four years ago, five maybe now. He and Nicholas were scavenging in a town about thirty miles west of Kansas City. A supply run. Routine, ordinary, part of their everyday life. On their way back home, the weather had turned. A sharply cold wind began to blow ahead of a cold front. A funnel cloud appeared in the distance and began twirling toward them. Naked in its malice. The roar of a runaway freight train bearing down on them.

They took shelter in an old farmhouse east of town as the skies opened up. Black clouds surfed toward them on a wave of blue sky. He and Nicholas had just made it inside when the first fat raindrops began spattering the dusty patch of dirt surrounding the house.

Inside the dusty foyer, a sense of unease washed over Samir. He didn't know why, but the hairs on his neck stood up, and he felt cold. Something atavistic warned him that evil had been here. The air was thick with a strange, sickly sweet aroma. A certainty that something terrible had happened in this house swamped him. As tangibly as someone brushing past him in a crowd.

He readied his weapon, but his hands trembled with fear. Fear of whatever lay beyond the sweep of his vision. As thunder pealed loudly overhead, he took the point, edging deeper into the house with Nicholas trailing behind him. There was a great room on the west side, empaneled with mahogany wood, the kind you might find in a hunting lodge. Dim yellow light streamed through the broken windows.

A large deer head was mounted above a dark, cold fireplace on the south wall. But that wasn't what caught Samir's eye. A dozen human heads had been mounted on either side of the deer head and the remaining three walls. They were well preserved, meaning someone had taken the time to prepare them for permanent display. The faces—empty and dead—but somehow still full of life staring back at him. At least three of the faces had belonged to children. It had shaken him so badly that he'd wet himself a little.

A dozen human beings mercilessly slaughtered and converted into trophies.

It had been savagery for the sake of savagery.

They backpedaled away from the room, Samir gasping for breath as though the oxygen had been sucked right out of the house. In the foyer, the men collided and went down in a heap, and they crawled over each other in desperation to escape. They fled through the front door and hiked ten more miles through the storm, the skies laced with deadly lightning and roaring with thunder. The danger meant little to him. A bolt could have struck him down that afternoon and that would have been okay. Anything would have been better than waiting out the tempest inside the house.

Nicholas had taken his own life some months later. Samir could never be sure, but he believed what they had seen in that old farmhouse had driven the poor man to his breaking point. And Samir had considered it himself. The reason he hadn't? The drink. The pull of the drink was too strong. Imagine. Staying alive so he could keep drinking.

"Yes, what I said about the vaccine is true," she said. "The vaccine protects babies in utero from Medusa. It's how Will survived."

"How many doses do you have?"

"About a thousand."

"Would the girls be able to give birth down the road?"

"Yes," Rachel said. "The vaccine self-replicates."

A thousand doses. So many, and yet so few. He grabbed a notepad and did some rudimentary calculations. A year from now, there could be a thousand new babies within a hundred-mile radius—a new garden of humanity. Two decades from now, those kids would begin to have their own children. It would be tight, and they'd have to play their cards just right. But it could be enough to seed humanity's future. Salvation for them all.

"And how did you come to possess this vaccine?" he asked.

Rachel chuckled softly. Then she tapped a finger against her lips as though considering how to answer his question.

"OK, so this won't be easy to hear."

"Try me."

She clicked her tongue for a moment. Then she answered:

"I was vaccinated against Medusa."

"What?"

"Four years before the pandemic."

Dr. Samir Malik dropped the clipboard. It hit the floor with a terrific clatter before coming to rest. Then, a deep silence descended on the room. It was quiet but for Will's rhythmic breathing.

She told Samir everything, starting with the earliest days of the pandemic, the deaths of her mother and stepfather, discovering that her father had also been immune to Medusa, continuing through Adam's death, and wrapping up her tale with the destruction of Olympus and her recovery of these precious vials of vaccine. It came out in a rush, this tale of her life, the remarkable twists and turns, how her life had been so tightly braided to humanity's fate. He could tell it was cathartic for her, cleansing and healing her, not much different than the healing underway in Will's body.

Her voice was hoarse when she finished, and her eyes were wet with tears. Samir was in shock. His mind bubbled with so many thoughts, questions, and emotions that he could not keep them straight.

"Someone did this?" he asked in a small voice.

"Yes."

Samir gently covered his mouth with his hand, his eyes wide and far away.

The first thing he felt was rage. Rage that someone had done this to them. This terrible fate had been visited upon them not by nature or chance but by their fellow man. It was difficult to comprehend such savagery. How broken a mind must have been to sign up for this madness. To willingly participate in this mass extermination, this genocide of all genocides.

It was hard to wrap his head around it all, including the revelation that Rachel's life was so tightly bound to it all. It was almost impossible to believe her, and yet he did. It would take the deepest of delusions to fashion such a fictional story, and no one that mentally ill could be as put together as Rachel was.

"Do you mind if I ask you a few questions?"

"Be my guest," she said. "I certainly don't have any secrets left."

"Why did they do it?"

"The most cliched reason possible. To give humanity a fresh start."

He scoffed and shook his head.

"Well, this was definitely a way to go," he said.

"Yep."

"Do you know how the vaccine works?"

"It's a kind of nanotechnology," she said. "It targets and destroys the virus."

"Would it protect women who are currently pregnant?"

"Yes," she replied. "The vaccine transfers protection to the fetus in utero. It's how Will survived."

"My God."

"I know it's a lot."

"Are you sure it works?"

Rachel smiled wistfully.

"After I got to the compound in Colorado," she said, "they were taking me up to see Gruber. Escorting me down this long corridor when I suddenly heard this sound. One I hadn't heard in years."

"What was it?"

"The sound of children playing."

A chill ran up Samir's spine.

A chance. They finally had a chance. Finally, a weapon to push back the sadness and the malaise that had descended upon their community, upon the world at large. With each passing year, it had become increasingly difficult to shake the sense that everything they did was for nothing. They were rearranging the deck chairs on the *Titanic*. He allowed himself a moment to picture a world teeming with people again. It would take decades, perhaps centuries, for the population to recover. He wouldn't be around to see it, that was for sure.

"This changes everything," Samir said.

"Yes," Rachel said. "It does."

10

———

Riverview was much different than Dixon, the little town guarding the bridge across the Missouri. Ashby College sat on about a hundred acres along the western bank of the Mississippi. There was no bridge crossing here, but the river still played a massive role in the lives of the little village's nearly five hundred residents.

An eight-foot-high wrought iron fence ringed the campus, which was what had attracted its initial settlers after the pandemic. Its eastern border sat roughly a hundred yards from the riverbank. Fishing was Riverview's most important industry, as the river here was heavily stocked with catfish, crappie, perch, and bass. Overfishing was a thing of the past; within two years of the pandemic's end, the fish population recovered to levels not seen since the Industrial Revolution.

A brick building that had housed the college's administration office sat at the center of the town and served as the town hall. It had stood a hundred years before the plague and would stand a century more. The building served as the heart of the community. To the west lay the growing fields, barren now at the end of the growing season. From a distance, Rachel saw workers clearing the last autumn harvest and preparing the fields for their winter nap.

A small open-air market had built up in the center of campus; despite Riverview's relatively small size, the variety of wares on display was impressive. Farmers sold the week's produce haul; hunters put up their catch, wild turkeys, rabbit, among other game; vendors with goat milk, cheese, and salted meats; artisans who made clothing, tools, and utensils; and medicinal supplies derived from nature that had become like gold after the survivors had exhausted the supply of manufactured pharmaceuticals.

A chilly wind blew as Rachel arrived at the medical clinic, which was housed inside the administration building. Samir, June Richards and Alice Tirico were waiting for them. Alice was a wisp of a thing with slender arms, legs, and, currently, a swollen belly. Her hair was jet black, styled in a pixie cut that reminded Rachel of the frontwoman of a 1980s hair band. Alice's hands remained stationed atop her round stomach, a defensive posture as though she could somehow protect her unborn child from its dark fate.

Ironic, since the threat lay within her own body.

"I'm Rachel," she said, extending her hand toward Alice.

Alice pushed aside the hand and stepped in for an embrace. Despite her petite frame, she was deceptively strong, and her hug nearly took Rachel's breath away.

"Alice," she said. "So nice to meet you."

She stepped back and placed her small, warm hand against Rachel's cheek.

Will remained hospitalized as he recovered from the gunshot, but he was getting stronger by the day. He was awake and reading a comic book when she had left him to attend Alice's vaccination appointment.

Outside, a small crowd had formed. Word of the vaccine had spread quickly through the community, and for the last two days, it had been all anyone could talk about.

"Alice, are you ready?" Samir asked.

"You bet," replied Alice.

There was nothing to it, really.

Alice took a seat next to the vaccine station Samir had set up. Latex gloves, a syringe, and a vial of vaccine. It held nearly twenty doses' worth of the serum. Samir donned the gloves and set to work preparing the dose. He drew up the liquid and rapidly flicked the needle to clear any air bubbles. He laid the syringe on the table and cleaned Alice's left upper arm with a small wipe.

"Ready?"

"Very."

Her voice was firm and steady. There was no fear in this woman. Rachel admired her deeply, and she'd known her less than thirty minutes.

Samir, however, hesitated. He looked back at Rachel.

"Are there any side effects?"

"I don't know," she said. "It's been a long time since I was vaccinated. I don't remember anything unusual. But that was me. It could affect different people in different ways. I suppose there could be your basic side effects. Pain, swelling, maybe some fever and fatigue. Run-of-the-mill stuff. I'm not a doctor."

Samir nodded and then turned back toward Alice. He picked up the syringe and held the tip of the needle to her skin.

"You still okay with this?" he asked.

"Let's get on with it already," she said. A hint of annoyance had bled into her voice.

"Here goes nothing."

It was like riding a bike. He injected the needle into her outer bicep and depressed the plunger in one graceful maneuver. As he withdrew the syringe, a dot of blood bloomed at the injection site. He slapped on an adhesive bandage and squeezed Alice's shoulder.

Alice gently brushed her fingers against the bandage, her eyes wide and vacant. Besides her own vaccination, which she did not even remember, Rachel had never seen anyone inoculated against Medusa. It was a remarkable thing to behold. A sudden easing of the clench in Alice's face. A clench that likely had been there for years and most certainly since she'd learned that she was expecting. Then she looked down lovingly at her swollen stomach and patted it gently. As if to tell her baby that it was going to be okay.

"I want to keep an eye on you for a bit," Samir said. He was pulling off the gloves and disposing of the used syringe. "Let's cool our heels here."

June Richards watched the proceedings with a mixture of interest and apprehension. Alice stood up.

Then she collapsed.

～

11

———

Will couldn't sit still. It felt like bugs were crawling all over him. He wanted to get up and go. The nice doctor was checking his bandages, but it was taking forever.

Come on, come on.

This was no ordinary checkup; it was his final examination before discharge. Four weeks had passed since his injury, all of which had been spent inside this clinic, inside this room. But if everything were up to par, Dr. Samir would send him on his way. Will would continue recuperating in the home they had established for him and his mother.

"Everything is looking good," he said. "Healing nicely. No sign of infection."

"Good to hear," Rachel said.

As always, his mother was standing at his bedside. Will was glad she was there, but he was ready for a little time alone. She was always around. There when he woke up. There when he ate his meals. He had to stop her from being there when he went to the bathroom! She said it saddened her to think of him eating alone, but it didn't bother him.

The food in Riverview wasn't half bad, and he was content to eat quietly. Be alone with his thoughts.

The doctor began applying the new bandage, gently placing the gauze over the healing surgical incision. After a minute or two, Samir finished taping off the edge of the bandage and paused to review his work.

"How does that feel?"

"Good," Will replied, tapping the bandage gently.

The pain from the injury had largely dissipated. He felt discomfort only if he twisted funny or bumped too hard against something. Wearing the dressing had become second nature. In a way, it was reassuring—an extra layer of protection.

Because he'd been shot.

It still didn't seem real that he had taken a bullet. That he had almost died. It felt like he'd been watching it happen to someone else. He had not even heard the report of the gun firing. His first indication something was wrong was a sharp, sudden pinch in his side. Like a cramp when you drink a glass of cold water too quickly. And that was immediately followed by the sensation of wetness on his shirt. He pressed his hand against his abdomen, which came away tacky with bright red blood—seeing that much blood leaking out of him was the weirdest thing he'd ever experienced.

His mom hadn't even realized he'd been hit. It shattered him, having to tell her. For a moment, the notion of not telling her zoomed across his traumatized brain. At the time, it seemed like a good idea. But of course, a few seconds later, she would know and deem herself a failure. Unable to keep Will safe.

This was ridiculous, of course. Even he knew that. He might have been only fourteen, but he understood their world; something terrible could happen at any moment. He knew how much it broke her that she could not give him the same upbringing she'd had. His childhood had been very different than hers.

Not to say that he didn't envy her. He liked hearing the stories she told about the world before, even if they made him slightly sad. Sometimes, it was hard to believe how the world had been, how easy it had been, but the evidence was there. The echoes of what had been. The civilization that had once been. The massive grocery stores with shelving as far as the eye could see. He remembered the times they'd gone hungry, experiences that had cut him deeply, so it was almost impossible to believe you could walk into one of them and find three different kinds of coconut milk.

And then there was the technology. The small handheld devices with shatterproof screens. Darkened now but once upon a time, multipurpose devices to communicate, play games, and research, the sum of the world's knowledge accessible by anyone at any time. He'd collected a few smartphones over the years; sometimes, he would stare into the dead gray screens, looking at his faded reflection in the glass.

"Well, Mom," Samir said to Rachel, watching anxiously at Will's bedside. "He's good to go."

"Thank you again," she said.

"I showed him how to change his dressing," he continued. "Every day for a week. And keep an eye out for infection. Redness, fever, any discharge, you let me know right away."

"I'll take care of it," Rachel said.

Annoyance bubbled up inside Will.

"I know how to do it, Mom."

He did know how to do it. It was time for him to start

taking charge of his own destiny. He wasn't a baby anymore. Sometimes, it felt like his mother didn't understand that. Sure, she taught him a lot, reminding him she wouldn't always be around, but she still tried to do everything for him.

Like, which is it, lady?

"We'll do it together," she said.

Together. That was her idea of compromise. She would say that and then do it herself anyway. He let her comment go; he would change it when she wasn't looking, and then she would see.

"He's free to go," Samir said. "Ready to get moving, champ?"

Will nodded. He'd been walking a little in the last few days, mainly to the bathroom, but a few circuits around the clinic. His legs were still a little shaky but felt stronger with each passing day. He swung his legs over the side and eased down to the floor. His head swam a little from getting up so quickly, and he could sense his mom moving toward him. He grabbed the side of the bed and waited for the dizziness to pass.

"Very ready," he said.

"By the way, how's Alice?" asked Rachel.

"She's fine," Samir replied.

"And the baby?"

"Baby's fine."

Rachel released a sigh. He knew his mother had been anxious about the woman who'd gotten the vaccine. Rachel would blame herself if something happened to the baby or her mother. She had put all her faith in the vaccine she carried; she had transferred this faith to the people of this community.

"How are people taking it?" Rachel asked.

Samir clicked his tongue.

"Hard to say," he said. "They're a little freaked out by Alice fainting."

"She's pregnant," replied Rachel. "It happens. You get up too fast, your center of gravity is off."

"Once people get an idea in their heads, it's hard to change it. Vaccines were always a touchy subject, even before."

"Yeah," Rachel said quietly.

He wore thick pajama bottoms and a hooded Arizona State sweatshirt *(college was another oddity his mom had taught him about)*. He put on his shoes, a heavy pair of hiking boots that had come halfway across the country with him. The boots were like an old friend at this point, someone he'd been through the fires with. As they left the room, Will glanced back at his hospital bed, thankful to be leaving it behind.

The cold air was a welcome slap in the face. A largely overcast sky hung over them. But the air was fresh and clean, spiced by the tang of a woodstove burning some- where. Rachel kept close to him as they walked, constantly reaching for his elbow. He kept tucking it out of her reach, pretending he didn't know she was doing it. Hurting her feelings wasn't his idea of fun.

It was late afternoon; the market was slowing down for the day, and the vendors were packing up their wares. Will was amazed by the sights, by the sense of permanence and community. They'd had this back in Evergreen, but that was long ago. Evergreen had been more aggressive and desperate, its lifespan governed by the contents lining the warehouse's shelves. Already, he was forgetting some of the details of the only permanent home he had ever known.

"Mom, can we stop at that one?" he said, pointing to the last kiosk on the row.

"Sure," she said.

His eyebrows jumped with surprise. He assumed she would insist on getting him home and back into bed. But going back inside was the last thing he wanted right now. He'd been stuck inside for two long weeks. They eased off the midway and paused at the stall.

"Welcome," said the vendor. "You must be the new folks."

She looked to be in her forties or early fifties. Her deep chestnut-colored hair, streaked with white, was pulled back in a tight ponytail. Like most survivors, her face looked hard and weathered from the difficult years. She wore faded jeans and a dark blue denim shirt.

"Rachel," said his mom, extending her hand. "This is Will."

"Marla Jennings."

The women shook hands.

"Good to meet you."

"How are you feeling, big man?"

"Better," Will replied.

"Glad to hear it."

She grabbed a small, wrapped package from the table and handed it to Will.

"A slice of fresh bread? My treat."

He took it.

"Thank you."

"You've been through a lot. I'd say you've earned it."

His mom and the woman chatted as he nibbled on the delicious bread. He checked out her wares—a variety of breads. Some were hearty and thick, others thin and light. While he browsed, Will became aware of a presence behind him. When he turned, he was surprised to see a thin dog eyeing him slowly. His fur was primarily black except for a stripe of white running from his throat down to his belly. Will tensed, having had little experience with dogs.

"Oh, that's Moose," said Marla. "He's kind of the village dog."

Moose was eyeing the chunk of bread still in Will's hand. His head was tilted in that curious way dogs had.

"Can I give him a piece of this?" asked Will.

"Sure," she said. "Can't promise he'll take it, though."

"Is he mean?"

"Not at all," she said. "But he's not very trusting of people. We think he was abused before he showed up in town."

Will knelt, his heart pounding in his chest. He wasn't exactly afraid of dogs, but animals made him a little nervous. The memory of their friend Charlotte was never far from his mind. The memory of how she had died, mauled by a feral wildcat, was harrowing. And it had been because of him—his immature stupidity.

Moose's tail wagged frenetically as Will held out his open hand, but he kept his distance for the moment.

"Come on, boy," Will said.

Moose took a hesitant step forward before retreating two more.

Will sat on the ground with his legs cris-crossed. He set a small chunk of bread on the ground before him. Moose took a few steps closer; he was now only a few feet away from Will. Will sat still, maintaining eye contact with the dog but making no other movements. He felt calm and relaxed, more than he had felt in a long time.

The dog inched closer to Will, close enough to bump his snout against Will's nose before backing away again.

"Wow," Marla said. "He normally doesn't get that close to folks."

Then Moose dropped to the ground and rolled over onto his back. His tail thumped against the gravelly road. Will slowly extended his hand and scratched Moose's belly. He noticed a thick, winding scar on the dog's stomach. He ran a finger across the thick cord of tissue.

"Looks like you were in a fight, boy," he said.

"Yeah," Marla said. "He was pretty bloodied up when he showed up here. He wouldn't let anyone near him, so it had to heal on its own. We weren't sure he was going to make it. But he was here every morning for water and his breakfast."

Will scratched the dog's belly for a few minutes; they were the happiest few minutes he could recall in months, if not ever. Eventually, Moose hopped back onto his feet and nuzzled his snout against Will's neck. Then he lowered his mouth, snapped the bread chunk from the ground, and trotted off.

"Looks like you've got a new friend," Marla said.

Will nodded, watching the dog scamper off.

12

———

Each day, Will waited for Moose at Marla's stall. He did not show up every day, but he did most days. Almost always at the same time, when the sun was highest in the sky. Some internal clock was running inside his canine brain. It had been a month since Will's release from the hospital, almost six weeks since the shooting. His wound was healing nicely. Dr. Samir checked on him every day. Will liked the doctor quite a bit, although Will suspected that Dr. Samir had his eye on his mother.

He didn't know what to think about that.

If he was being honest with himself, he didn't love the thought of it. It made him think about his father, Eddie Callahan, and thinking about his dad made his head hurt. The final moments of his father's life often returned to him in dreams, but he had never told a soul about them. Certainly not his mother.

After all, she'd been the one who'd killed him.

True, his father had been trying to kill Rachel because he was going to surrender him to that awful woman, Priya. Priya had pursued them across time and space until she, too, had met her end at his mother's hands. Priya wasn't the first person his mother had killed. He doubted she would be the last. One important lesson from Will's life was that it was unwise to cross his mother.

It was easier to push it to the back of his mind. His father was dead, and his mother had killed him. That was a strange thing to have in your past. Even he understood that. As he lingered by the stall late that morning, an older girl named Jade approached him. She was a couple of years older than Will. He'd spotted her earlier in the week, but they had not yet interacted. Until Will's arrival, Jade had been the youngest person in town, one of the youngest naturally immune survivors. Very few babies and toddlers had survived the pandemic, even if they'd been immune to the virus. It was why the adults were so sad all the time. With babies always dying, it didn't take a scientist to figure out which way the wind was blowing.

Jade kept to herself most of the time. When she wasn't in school, she was assigned to the fields. School was also in Will's future; the powers that be insisted that everyone keep learning. The younger folks took lessons in the liberal arts, science, mathematics, reading, and writing. As they grew older, the teaching became more specialized, learning how to operate and maintain the systems that kept them all alive.

Jade's jet-black hair was spiked, reminding Will of the style he'd seen on old music posters from the eighties. She wore tight black jeans and a matching black leather jacket. Her eyelids were lined with black eyeshadow, giving her a fearsome visage. Will didn't know if he was in love with her or terrified of her.

They had not spoken yet, but it looked like that was about to change. His heart was racing as she drew near him. She was as casual as a grilled cheese sandwich.

"Your dog show up yet today?" she asked.

She was direct and confident, but her voice carried no malice.

He shook his head.

She sat down next to him.

"I'm Jade," she said, as though he didn't know that.

"Will."

"I know who you are. How did it feel?"

She knew who he was?

"How did what feel?"

"Getting shot."

She certainly was direct.

"I don't know. Like it wasn't really happening."

"Did it hurt?"

"Yes."

"I'm sorry that you got shot."

"Me too."

They sat silently for a bit longer, but there was no sign of Moose.

"Guess he's not coming today," Will said.

"Guess not," she agreed. "Were you really born after?"

"After?"

"After the pandemic, dummy."

He felt like a circus freak.

"Yes."

She picked up a stick and started drawing in the gravel road.

"I don't remember much of it," she said. "I was maybe three when it happened."

Will did some quick math in his head. That meant Jade was eighteen, maybe nineteen.

"Where are you from?"

Will was endlessly fascinated by the pre-Medusa world.

He could listen to stories about how things used to be all day.

"Near Springfield. In Illinois. At least that's what the people who found me tell me."

Jade's face had taken on a blank look. Will worried that he'd opened doors that she'd preferred remained closed. But she continued to speak.

"I just remember little flashes of it," she said. "We lived outside of town, kind of in the country. It was a little house. I remember a white pickup truck. I remember a swing set in the yard. I remember my dad smelled like gasoline all the time. I think he worked on trucks and cars.

"I don't remember it, really," she said. "Things get a bit hazy. Maybe my brain was trying to protect me from the really bad memories. Do you think the brain can do that?"

Will realized she was asking him a question.

Come on, Callahan, wake up! This stunning creature is talking to your dumb ass.

"Oh. I don't know."

He had never considered it before, but it made sense. Her intellect awed him.

"It was a miracle anyone found me. I remember being so scared. And I was so hungry."

Will knew about hunger.

"Marla and another woman found me in a field eating wild strawberries. I was sunburned to a crisp. But they took me in and took care of me. I still remember those straw-berries."

Will watched her from the corner of his eye, too intimi-dated to look at her directly.

"Even now, I can't eat strawberries. I stayed with them for a couple of years. But then the other woman died, and it was just me and Marla. Eventually, we ended up here."

She paused, still scratching away in the dirt with the stick.

"I wish I remembered more," she said. "I don't even remember my parents' names."

Will tried imagining what it must have been like for four-year-old Jade: the terror she would have felt, the loneliness, everything yanked away from her when she was too young to understand what was even happening.

"I'm sorry," Will said. He didn't know what he was sorry for, but it seemed like the right thing to say.

"Thanks," she said. "I'm sorry, too."

"For what?"

"For boring you with my sob story."

"That's okay."

"Let me make it up to you."

"How would you do that?"

"I'm gonna give you the grand tour."

THE NEXT FEW weeks saw Jade and Will spending more time together and venturing farther and farther from Riverview. Initially, these outings were not popular with his mother and triggered a doozy of an argument.

On the morning of their latest tiff, Jade had been sitting on the porch of the small guesthouse where they were staying, waiting for them to go.

"The doctor said it was fine for me to go!"

"I don't know, Spoon," she said. "It's only been a couple of months since you got hurt."

Unbeknownst to Will, Samir had also told Rachel that without a compromise, he would just sneak out on her. Will assumed the doctor wanted to spend more time with his mother without him around; he was okay with that. They could do whatever they wanted if it got him out from under her thumb.

Spoon.

Her longtime nickname for him had started to annoy him. It was from a different part of their lives, when he was little and completely dependent on her. He wasn't a little kid anymore. He was fourteen. He was taller than his mom. Okay, maybe not taller, but he could look her square in the eye.

It was his trump card. There was no reason not to play it immediately.

"But I'm your mother. The final decision is mine."

"Mom, please," he said. "I'm so bored."

"Bored means you're safe."

"I'm not a little kid anymore!"

He was sick of it. Unless he stood up for himself, she would continue to see him as the little boy he'd once been. Rachel glanced out the window, tilting her head to check out Jade and her spiky hair on the porch. He knew his mother had done a background check on the girl; Jade's reputation in the community was sterling. Quiet, perhaps, but a hard worker, well-behaved, and respectful of her elders.

Will could see her working it all out in her head. How protective was *too* protective? Where was the line?

"I don't like it," she said.

Then she had said something that truly surprised him.

"But I guess I'm going to have to get used to that," she said.

Her eyes glistened with tears; Will kept his gaze toward the ground so he wouldn't have to watch her cry. She didn't cry often, but he hated it when she did. She leaned in and hugged him tightly, the force of it nearly taking his breath away. He returned the hug, letting himself sink into it a little. There hadn't been many mothers like Rachel Fisher. Her life had been difficult, complicated, a surreal nightmare, from struggles as mundane as growing up with a largely absent father to the almost incomprehensible achievement of navigating the apocalypse as a teenager.

"Love you," he said softly.

"Love you too," she had replied.

And that was how they'd reached a détente about this new phase in Will's life. He was growing up, as Rachel was fond of saying. And Will had grown up faster than most. He could hunt small game, find clean water, and he'd become an astute tracker, as he had proven on their approach to Dixon. The world had forced that on him.

His mother did not know this yet, but he had started keeping a daily journal. They were at the beginning of something new, something wondrous, and it seemed important to document the journey. The first decade-plus of his life had been a fight to survive, not just for him but for everyone. But because of the vaccine, the world was changing, even if it didn't know it yet. Future generations would want to know what they had done and how they had lived. The history of the world before the apocalypse fascinated him. The years immediately following the fall of civilization would undoubtedly interest others.

They had seventeen outings under their belts. Although he'd crossed much of the country in his short life, it was as if he was seeing the world for the first time. Until this exploration had begun, a bird's-eye view was the only one he'd had of the world. The trees rather than the forest. Something he was just passing through. But underneath it all was the world as it truly was.

Moose frequently joined them on their adventures. His energy was boundless, and his protective instincts served him and Jade well. He was constantly on alert, sniffing the trail ahead and guiding them away from pathways that left him growling and unsettled. At night, Will sat in bed with his journal by candlelight and noted everything he could from the day's events. His first volume was filling quickly.

After finishing the day's entry, he often flipped through the pages, reflecting on their adventures. The craziest thing they'd found had been the passenger jet that had crashed into a cornfield long ago. The pilot of the Liberty Airlines 777 had crash-landed the plane, splintering it into three distinct sections upon impact. The skeletal remains of dozens of victims were still buckled into their shattered seats. Will tried picturing what had happened; perhaps some of the passengers had survived the crash, many infected, and made their way elsewhere after no help had arrived.

He tried to discern why the plane had gone down, but the cause of the crash would forever remain a mystery. Maybe the pilots had been ill with Medusa and could not control the aircraft. Perhaps sick passengers and crew members had rioted and overwhelmed the cockpit. Whatever the case, if the crash hadn't gotten them, Medusa certainly had. It was these discoveries that got him out of bed in the morning. He had chores and studies, of course, but those were boring. This was how he learned. This was his real education. Understanding the world as it was before.

He and Jade had set out a little after eight on that dank January morning. It was midday now, and they were about ten miles north of Riverview. The pair paused to take their afternoon meal. It was cold and cloudy, and Will was starting to wish they hadn't bothered today. It had been a tedious slog through the river valley, and everything was beginning to look the same.

"So where are we headed again?" he asked, chewing on a piece of cured beef.

"There was this guy in Riverview," she said. "A scientist. He said there was a pharmaceutical lab not far from here. I thought we could check it out. Maybe there are some medicines there we can grab."

Will believed this was unlikely. Medicine was one of the first commodities stockpiled after the pandemic. Survivors might have been immune to the ravages of Medusa; however, they still needed antibiotics, antivirals, beta-blockers, blood pressure medications, blood thinners, cancer drugs, insulin, antidepressants, and anything else they could get their hands on.

"He used to live in Riverview? Not anymore?"

"Yeah, one day he just took off," Jade replied. "He was a bit of a strange guy."

When they reached their destination, about twelve miles north of Riverview, an eastern suburb of Kansas City, the sun had just begun its backslide toward the horizon. Jade paused and opened a map on the hood of a rusted-out sedan. She murmured as she checked their progress, sliding a finger from one waypoint on the map to the next.

"We're here," she said.

They were at the top of a dead-end street, which ran west for a quarter mile before terminating under a train trestle. A row of low-slung buildings stood to their right, once home to long-defunct businesses. A self-storage facility. A fabric wholesaler. A moving truck rental office. On the far side of the overpass lay a large tract of cleared land, bordered on one side by twin mountains of gravel and coal.

Four buildings, green with mildew, their windows long since blown out, loomed just beyond them.

Jade sat down on a cluster of broken concrete and opened her pack. She tore off a section of a dried beef strip and handed it to Will. He chewed it slowly, savoring the saltiness of the meat. Even in the colder months, it was easy to get dehydrated.

A fifth building caught Will's eye as he nibbled on his snack. Something about it seemed out of place. At first, the basis of its oddness eluded him, but it was interesting enough to send him toward it for a closer look. Moose, who'd been lapping from a puddle of fresh rainwater, looked up curiously as Will approached the cluster of buildings.

"What do you see?" asked Jade.

He pressed a finger to his lips.

As he drew within fifty yards, then twenty, of the building, the anomaly finally dawned on him. The building appeared abandoned, like the others, but it had seen use very recently. The remains of a small camp sat in front of the building. A single chair sat before a round metallic firepit. Will drew a deep breath, his nostrils searching for the residue of smoke, but all he smelled was the cold dampness of the day.

If nothing else, it was a strange place for a camp. It was relatively exposed and fairly removed from wild game or water sources. Nevertheless, someone might be living here. Jade drew up behind him, placing her hand on his elbow.

"We should go," she said.

There was a nervous edge to her voice that was unfamiliar to him. Confidence was typically her default setting. She unhitched the rifle from her shoulder and tucked the stock under her arm. Rachel required them to carry weapons on these trips. Will's heart was racing, and for a moment, he understood his mother's anxiety and reluctance to let him grow up. It could be scary out here. But his curiosity outweighed his fear.

"There's something here," he said. "We should check it out. There could be supplies."

"Will, wait," she whispered.

But he ignored her.

It took less than a minute to cover the distance to the building's front entrance, protected by a concrete overhang. Something continued to nag at him, an itch the discovery of the campsite had not scratched. He scanned the ground, not sure what he was looking for. Threads of rainwater ran along the cracked asphalt and concrete, the residue of an overnight shower looking for the lowest point. The water sluiced away from the building and toward a section of concrete recessed into the ground. A heavy metal lid lay flush against the concrete. This immediately drew his interest.

The metal lid was covered in mud and grime, but a name was stamped into it. He knelt and brushed away the detritus until the name was clear to read.

The words stamped into the cover stopped him cold:

PENUMBRA LABORATORIES – RESEARCH & DEVELOPMENT

13

———

"Holy crap," he muttered.

"What is it?" Jade asked.

Even Moose was interested, the dog sidling next to Will and sniffing at the hatch covering.

"Penumbra," he said, pointing to the metal.

"What's Penumbra?"

He paused, taking time to consider his words. His mom had told Samir much of the story, so there was little harm in telling Jade the truth. He liked the idea of confiding in someone.

"They're the ones who made the virus."

Jade's eyes widened with shock.

"Someone made the virus?"

Of course, there was more to the story, namely his familial connection to this whole mess, but he wasn't ready to share that with her yet. And there was much he did not know. But what he knew was bad enough. His great-grandfather had been one of Medusa's architects. Everything about William Callahan flowed from that dark, terrible truth.

"Help me lift this," he said, wedging his fingers into the gap between the cover and the recessed ground.

"Will, someone might be down there."

This gave him pause. She had a good point. But he didn't want to give up on this spot, which felt worth exploring. He wanted his mother to see he wasn't a kid anymore. And what better way to do so than to find something really useful?

He glanced at Moose, who remained on guard but did not appear concerned. Will told himself the dog would have already lost his mind barking if someone were down there. Instead, his snout was on the ground, sniffing away quietly.

"Well, our little alarm system hasn't gone off yet," Will said, nodding toward the pup.

Jade chewed on the corner of her lip, as she often did when she was deep in thought.

"Fine," she said. "But I'm gonna have the final say. If I say we run, we run. Deal?"

Will considered her offer. He was supposed to defer to her.

"Or we can leave."

He grunted in frustration.

"OK, fine," he said. "Now help me."

Working on either side of the hatch cover, they tried swinging it open. But it was heavy, constructed of thick steel, and held fast. They were about to give up on it when a dull motor started to whir; as they pushed back from it, the cover slowly opened automatically. A metal staircase descended into the darkness below.

"You really want to do this?" Jade asked.

Will ignored her question. The terror ran deep. If he opened his mouth to reply to her query, he might throw up.

He couldn't have Jade thinking he was a little weenie. So, instead, he nodded as convincingly as he could.

"I can't believe I'm agreeing to this," she said.

Neither did Will. She was more cautious than he was. But the allure of whatever was hidden down below was proving irresistible. For a moment, neither made a move. Moose put his nose into the opening and sniffed. His tail wagged, but he did not bark.

Will took a few hesitant steps down the stairs, pausing to look back at Jade. Her eyebrows were furrowed with concern, but she did not attempt to stop him. He scampered down a few more steps, committing himself to the venture. Moose raced ahead of him.

"Moose, heel!"

The dog froze, waiting for Will to come alongside him. The passage darkened quickly as he descended into its depths. His heart raced, and his breath caught in his throat. But it was also exhilarating.

"Coming down," Jade called out above him.

He kept moving downward, pausing briefly to turn on the flashlight that he carried with him. He was judicious in its use. Batteries were getting harder and harder to find. You didn't waste them.

The cone of light shone downward, revealing the bottom of the steps only a few feet down. Will eased to the final step and hopped down to the floor. A cloud of dust kicked up and tickled his nose.

"I'm down!" he called up.

His voice echoed down the long passageway, and a ripple of regret radiated through him. There would be little chance of escape if anything went wrong. But as the echo faded away, he took some comfort in his belief that this was a dead place. There was no one here. He felt it in his bones.

As he processed this internal debate, Jade finished her journey and edged alongside him. Will shone the flashlight down the corridor. It was narrow, just wide enough for two people to walk abreast. Its smooth concrete walls were built to last. Will pressed his hand against the nearby wall and found it damp and cool.

Suddenly, he felt Jade's hand patting his shoulder. She was pointing at something. He followed her lead and spotted a small surveillance camera mounted in the upper corner of the corridor. At first, Will thought nothing of it, but the buzz of the camera shifting as they moved startled him. Above him, the sound of gears grinding caught his ear. He looked up, confused, as the daylight began to disappear. Then it hit him. The hatch cover was closing remotely, trapping them. Until now, electricity had been nothing more than a fairy tale for Will Callahan. He'd ridden in vehicles, marveled at their digital clocks, and listened enraptured at the hiss of static from the built-in radios, but an uninterrupted power supply was like magic.

And he'd been a fool.

They were not alone.

He felt Jade's hand on his elbow. She'd heard it, too.

They took another few steps, and the camera adjusted behind them. Then, a light in the passageway flickered to life. Will was scared beyond anything possible, but his feet carried him forward. Moose stayed by his side, his hackles up, his teeth bared. Just off his hip, he could hear Jade breathing raggedly.

Behind them, the lights illuminating that section of the corridor switched off, and a new panel activated above them. Their movements triggered the lights; when they were no longer within the range of those particular sensors, the lights they controlled switched off.

And still, there was no sign of life.

At the terminus of this section of the corridor, the passageway opened up on a large circular room. Again, the lights behind him went dark. But this time, a panel of lights running along the ceiling switched on, bathing the room in light. It was a large, perfectly round room with a radius of about forty feet.

Three curved video monitors were embedded in the wall to their right. Two were darkened, but images flickered on the one on the far end. A long table ran nearly the room's length, bisecting it into two semicircles. It was a mess, covered with files, books, and binders.

Across the room was another smaller passageway leading deeper into the bunker.

"It really is like magic," said Jade.

She had drifted toward the video screen, her eyes fixed on the playing video. William focused on it for the first time. A man wearing a dark blazer addressed the camera, but the volume was muted. But seeing this video replay was mesmerizing.

"Is there a way to hear it?" Will asked.

"Maybe," Jade replied.

She ran her fingers around the screen's bezel, but the sound remained muted. She mock-smacked the screen in frustration. A window suddenly appeared onscreen, causing her to take a sharp breath.

"The screen is sensitive to touch," said Jade.

They studied the various options on the window.

Will pointed at the icon of an up-and-down arrow.

"Try that one."

Jade tapped the up arrow once. A bar appeared on the lower half of the screen and grew horizontally.

"Do it again."

She tapped the arrow several more times, and a harsh sound burst forth from hidden speakers, piercing their ears. She tapped the down arrow and reduced the volume to a reasonable level. The voice of the man onscreen filled the room. He sounded desperate, raw, panicked. His eyes were wet, and tears were streaming down his cheeks.

"...everything we could. Please. I hope you understand that."

The image hitched once, and then the video began to play again, this time from the beginning.

"My name is Aaron Wilson," he said. "I'm a data scientist with the Penumbra Corporation. I'm assigned to Penumbra - Kansas City. Today is Friday, the fourteenth of August. As I record this, it's estimated that a billion people are dead worldwide, a hundred million in the United States alone. We were too late."

At that moment, Wilson paused and looked at something off-camera. He spoke to someone out of view before turning back toward the audience.

"It's out of control now," he said. "There is no stopping it. When it's over, there will be very few of us left."

His jaw set, he leaned forward in his chair. He turned the camera toward a bank of monitors to his left and zoomed in on one in the middle. According to the graphic striped across the bottom of the screen, it was an aerial view of New York City. There was no sound, but none was needed. A chaotic battle was underway. At one end of a street, a phalanx of soldiers fired upon a crowd of civilians attempting to break through the line. But that wasn't all. Nestled behind a barricade of smashed-up vehicles, a second group of soldiers was firing on the first. It was absolute mayhem. The date stamp onscreen read 14-Aug, about two weeks into the acute phase of the pandemic. Everything was good and well screwed by that point.

"To anyone watching this, please know that we tried to stop them. Not everyone in PenLabs was in support of this … this monstrosity. Our colleague, Dr. Adrian West, was supposed to meet with the FBI in late July to blow the whistle, but he disappeared. We think they killed him. We thought we could protect him. Not that it matters now."

There was another pause. He glanced down and rubbed the stubble on his chin. It hissed with a melancholy sound.

"Maybe we should've gone to the authorities sooner."

Then he laughed.

"Jesus, listen to me. Obviously, we should have."

The video froze for a moment and then picked up again. The man was midsentence when it picked up again, suggesting that a part of the recording had been lost.

"…leaving in the next couple of days. To anyone still out there. Please know that we did everything we could. Please. I hope you understand that."

The screen darkened briefly before Holloway's face appeared once more, and the short movie began to play again.

Jade's hand was pressed against her mouth, her eyes wide with shock. The video had rocked even Will on his heels. Despite his familiarity with the general outlines of the apocalypse, seeing this footage from the past was terrifying.

"Someone did this," she said softly, more to herself than to Will. "On purpose."

"Let's keep looking," said Will.

~

14

———

Jade muted the video and backed away gingerly as though it might come to life and attack them. The only sound remaining was the clocking of their heels on the cold concrete floor. Will turned his attention to the long island in the center of the room. Darkened video screens embedded into the counter. At the end of the table was a small charging station holding three satellite phones, each parked in its own slot.

Scattered across the table were a series of thick binders and composition notebooks. The binder on the top bore a cover that was stamped OPERATION: COBALT. It was about two inches thick, its contents divided into a dozen sections separated by numbered blue tabs. It appeared to be a manual governing the operation of this particular bunker. He flipped through it quickly, but much of it was undecipherable for his fourteen-year-old brain. Perched on the edge of the table was a Penumbra coffee mug. Its bottom was stained with the residue of its final cup of joe.

"What are we looking for?" Jade asked softly.

"I'm not sure," Will replied, his voice a whisper. "But there has to be something here worth taking."

Jade nodded. If she didn't necessarily agree, she didn't object, either.

Will continued into a small passageway from the bunker's control room. It split into three narrower corridors, each leading to a different room. Will followed the left branch to its end, coming across a door to a small barracks. A recessed light flickered in the corner, giving the room a haunted, washed-out look. The room was rectangular and featured four bunkbeds, enough for eight people. The beds were in various stages of disarray.

Will slowly crept through the room to a closet opposite the door. A dozen beige-colored jumpsuits hung from the clothes rack bolted to the wall. Patches bearing different names were sewn to the breast of each jumpsuit. Disappointed there was nothing worth taking, he retreated down the corridor to the spoke in the bunker's wheel-like layout. A wave of anxiety rippled through him as he realized he'd lost track of Jade.

"Jade?" he said hesitantly. There was a noticeable tremor in his voice, and he was embarrassed. Being scared was something he could no longer afford.

There was no reply but for the echo of his voice.

"Jade!" he called out again, louder and more confident this time.

That'll show'em.

But now his whole body was trembling. He turned back down the passageway toward the control room. As he padded carefully down the corridor, he drew on the lessons his mother had taught him (*his mother, holy moly, she would kill him dead if she knew what he was doing right now*) to keep his wits about him.

Stay calm, above all else.

Losing your cool was the quickest way into the ground, his mother would say. He took a deep breath and let it out slowly. A hand on the wall of the passageway helped steady his feet beneath him.

"Jade's in here!" called out an unfamiliar male voice. It was high-pitched and reedy, peppered with a bit of manic.

Will's throat closed up with fear.

That's it, they were dead, this man would kill them and then eat them.

He should've listened to his mother. If they got out of this, he would never disobey her again.

"Get out here now, or the girl gets a bullet!"

The voice had reached a terrifying new pitch. Will's bladder struggled to hold on. As he neared the control room, the passageway brightened. On the far wall, he could make out two shadows.

Jade.

And someone else.

He took a shaky breath and let it out slowly. He had to be brave for her. Will Callahan carried no weapon; he was five feet, six inches tall, and tipped the scales at a hundred and thirty pounds, but he would go in there and save his friend.

He stepped out of the corridor into the large room. Jade was on his right, her hands flat on the table. Across from her was a thin, wild-looking man dressed in jeans and a dirty lab coat. He wore silver horn-rimmed glasses, and his hair stuck out in a hundred different directions. The rifle in his hands was aimed directly at Jade's chest.

"Okay, okay!" Will said. "I'm here!"

"Who are you?" asked the man, pointing a gun at Will's chest. "What are you all doing here?"

Will held out his palms to relay that he was no threat. The man was short, just a little taller than Will was. The name Holloway was stitched above the breast pocket of his coat. It was yellowed, stained with blue ink. Holloway. His short dark hair had gone wild, now long, grey, and tied back in a messy ponytail. He wore silver half-moon glasses.

"We're just looking around," Will said as calmly as he could.

"How did you find this place?"

Jade answered this one.

"There's always been a rumor of a government science lab around here," she said. "We just wanted to check it out."

The gun dipped slightly, and the man seemed to relax a bit.

"What's your name?" Jade asked. "I'm Jade."

Smart, Will thought. *Connect with the guy. Calm him down.*

"I'm Dr. Elias Holloway."

"I'm Will."

He waved unassumingly. The man's shoulders sagged as the fight went out of him.

"I'm sorry," Holloway said. He set the gun down on the table. "I hate guns. But I haven't seen another person in a long time."

His eyes cut to the ground.

"A very long time."

"Look, we're sorry to have bothered you," Will said. "We'll be on our way."

He held his breath, hoping this man would unlock the hatch and let them leave.

Holloway looked at Will again, but he appeared to be studying him this time. He turned his head this way and that, scrunching up his face, closing one eye. It made Will uncomfortable. Maybe he was sizing Will up for a rotisserie in the back. There were cannibals out there. He'd seen them himself.

"You're very young," Elias said.

"I look young for my age."

Holloway took a few steps toward Will, who, in turn, backed away.

"No," Holloway said, eating up the distance between them.

Will found himself backed against the wall video screen. Next to him, Holloway's video continued to play on a loop, the images flashing.

Holloway's face looked manic again.

"No," he said. "You are young. You were born after."

Will's eyes cut toward Jade, who shrugged. Will didn't see any point in hiding it any longer.

"Yes," he said. "I was born after the pandemic."

Holloway took a step back, a hand clapped to his mouth.

"Can we go now?" Will asked.

"Yes," Holloway said, a gleam in his eye.

He made no move to show them the exit.

"I just need to press this here," he said, pointing to a green button on a control panel.

"Can you press it?" Jade asked, a hint of concern in her voice.

"You have to do one thing for me first."

WILL SAT in the chair in the lab. A rubber tourniquet was wound tightly around his left bicep. Holloway was poking around in a cabinet in the corner, muttering to himself while he gathered the requisite supplies. When finished, he plopped down on a stool and wheeled toward Will's chair.

The lab was spacious, almost as big as the bunker's main nerve center, but was square-shaped. Will had missed it entirely in their initial sweep of the bunker. It was on the far side of the bunker, beyond the three narrow corridors he'd begun to explore. A series of computer workstations sat on one side of the lab. In the middle of the room lay a collection of lab equipment that Will did not recognize. The various pieces might as well have been from another planet.

"Just one little blood draw," he had asked. "I have to see it. Then I will let you go."

Holloway unpacked the hypodermic needle, the adapter, and the vacuum-sealed tube that would catch Will's blood. He swabbed Will's arm with an alcohol wipe and carefully guided the needle into the vein protruding under the crook of the boy's elbow. It reminded Will of the times his late grandfather had drawn his blood. Adam Fisher had been obsessed with discovering the anomaly that had spared three generations of his family, and he had died never knowing the truth. Will missed his Pop-Pop desperately. The day Adam died had been the worst of Will's life.

But that was the nature of their world. People died—all the time.

It happened quickly; Holloway was talented with the needle, and the tube swiftly filled with Will's blood.

"All done," Holloway said excitedly as he sealed the tube.

He wrote Will's name on a sticker affixed to the vial.

"Why are you putting my name on it?" he said. "Are there others?"

Holloway glanced at Will and chuckled.

"Good point," he said. "Just an old habit."

For the next half hour, Holloway examined Will's blood. Using a pipette, he deposited a tiny dot of Will's blood on a prepared slide and topped it with a small amount of a bright blue liquid from a second vial. He carefully layered a second slide atop the first and placed it on the platform of the high-powered electron microscope. Then he pressed an eye to the eyepiece and fiddled with a knob for a moment. Then he just sat quietly, studying his sample.

"My God," he said after a few minutes. "It really worked."

"What worked?"

"The nanovaccine," he said. "I've never seen it before."

"Don't you have it?" Jade asked.

"Oh sure, sure, that's not what I meant," he said, pressing his eye to the microscope. "The vaccine in Will's blood was transferred in utero. From his mother. Remarkable."

Will didn't care. He was ready to go.

"You promised we could leave," Will said.

"Yes, of course," he said. "Give me one moment to load this sample into the database."

Holloway removed the slide from the microscope's platform and inserted it into a data drive attached to a computer monitor. The drive whirred to life while Holloway sat at the large monitor. The screen flickered to life and began displaying various metrics. Will had no idea what any of it meant.

"What the hell..." Holloway said quietly.

"What is it?" Will asked.

"I don't know," Holloway said. "This computer is reading information from your blood sample. I didn't expect this."

Anxiety bubbled up inside Will's chest. Holloway's demeanor had changed. Will centered his gaze on the green button that would open the doors. Jade had moved closer to a storage cabinet. On top was a metal test tube holder. She grabbed it and cut her eyes toward Will. He nodded. The computer monitor still occupied Holloway's attention, and he was oblivious to events unfolding around him.

"Are you going to let us go or not?" Will asked, distracting him from Jade as she closed in on him.

"I'm sorry," he said. "But not right now. I have to understand this."

Jade made her move.

"Screw you, weirdo!" she howled, lunging at him, rearing back with the heavy metal rack and swinging it hard toward the back of Holloway's head. Her swing was pure. Holloway glanced up a second too late; the rack collided with his face and rocked his entire head backward. His momentum carried his entire seat backward, and he tumbled to the floor.

"Will! Now!"

Will zipped toward the control panel and slammed his fist against the green button. An unseen machine hummed, cranking the door to the lab open. Jade raced toward Will, grabbing him by the elbow. This galvanized him; he sprinted toward the door, close on Jade's heels. Behind them, Holloway moaned in pain as he struggled to regain his footing.

"Wait, you little brats!" he called out, his voice thick and slow.

Will did not look back, focusing instead on the path ahead. Jade crossed the threshold into the corridor and back into the control room. The door to the far corridor was still open, but Will wasn't sure how much time they had.

"Run!" Will said.

His heart was pounding; his lungs burned like they were full of sand.

They were back in the first passageway, racing back toward the stairwell that would hopefully deliver them aboveground before it was too late. God, if they could get out of here, he would never do anything like this again. Jade made it to the stairs first; she stamped up the steps like she'd been shot from a cannon. Will kept pace as best he could, stealing glances over his shoulder for the mad scientist. *What the hell had they been thinking?* He crashed into the wall at the edge of the passageway and turned up the steps; Jade was already back up top.

"Hurry, Will!" she shrieked. "It's closing back up!"

The heavy hatch cover began its slow swing, eating up the daylight as it lowered into a closed position. Will scampered faster up the steps, scrambling skyward with all the speed he could muster. The hatch door was closing quickly. Claustrophobia squeezed Will's heart. The closer he got, the smaller the opening seemed to get.

Tears welled up in his eyes, but he ignored them. His legs ached, his lungs burned, and he was half-blinded by the tears. Then he was there. He wriggled through the opening, edging halfway out before the lid pinched against his side. Jade's hand gripped his, and she yanked as hard as she could. The extra hand thrust him through the opening and out of the hatch just as the cover closed shut with a terrifying finality. He climbed to his feet, but his legs buckled, and he fell to his knees. Then he vomited. A few more seconds and the hatch would have closed with him still inside.

Still inside with that maniac.

He felt Jade's hand on his back as he caught his breath. His face was clammy.

"You okay?"

He nodded, maintaining his downward dog pose.

"We need to get out of here," she said.

"We're never gonna tell anyone, right?" he asked desperately.

If Jade planned to rat them out, he might as well stay here and die. Death would be better than whatever his mom would do to him. The idea of his mother finding out about this near miss made his stomach water.

"Never."

He nodded again and pushed himself up to his feet.

"Okay," he said. "Let's go."

They fled.

15

———

Victor Hale and his men were the first to arrive.

It was just after midday. A bright sun shone down on this hard, cold afternoon. His two most trusted guards flanked him, the trio riding horseback. Hale enjoyed riding, and it was only a few hours' ride from his compound. They drew up in the parking lot that had once served this abandoned textile mill.

They set water down for the horses as Hale stretched his back. He watched the pair work. These were tough men, hardened by the years since the pandemic. Everyone had been hardened by these times. These two, Baez and Jepson, had been with him almost since the beginning.

The building was in a rundown industrial area on the outskirts of Cohen, Missouri. It was here Hale and the others held their quarterly summit. Roughly equidistant from the three communities represented here. Before the plague, the textile mill had been a busy place. Industrial sewing machines, looms, and related equipment sat silently in the cavernous space. Debris from long ago still covered the floor. Large spools that had once held thread sat empty, their contents long since deteriorated into dust. A conveyor belt ran from the main level to the mezzanine.

The three leaders met here quarterly to keep the peace, trade, and discuss current events. The groups traded frequently, each offering something the other two communities did not have. He liked his fellow leaders and respected them. They understood the heaviness that came with wearing the crown. But that didn't mean they could be trusted.

Each of the attendees was permitted two guardians at their meetings. There was a cautious trust among them, but they were still careful. It reminded him of an embroidered pillow in his late grandmother's home that read *In God We Trust, All Others Pay Cash*. Even when attending a regularly scheduled meeting with his main trading partners.

The Coalition made its home in a prison, nestled in a small town about thirty miles from St. Louis, sprawling across the outskirts of what was once Alton, Illinois. To say the town had been struggling before Medusa was an understatement. In fact, it might have been hard for a casual observer to correctly guess whether a particular iteration of Alton had existed before or after the plague.

On the far side of Alton was a railyard. Not far from the prison was a train depot where several locomotives were parked in the wheelhouse. Getting the trains rolling again was one of Hale's long-term goals. The shelter had helped preserve them somewhat, but they would need some work before chugging down the tracks again.

Hale was on edge but confident. What he was planning was risky, but the time had come. His vision was slowly becoming a reality, but the danger was also real. Assassination was always a threat, and today warranted extra caution. Because it was time to change the status quo. The vaccine would soon be in his hands. It would be a turning point not just for Victor Hale, not just for his group, the Coalition, but for the world beyond. Everything was about to change. At this very moment, Coalition forces were preparing to strike the communities of his two comrades. Brutal? Yes. Unfair? Almost certainly.

But the status quo didn't change itself. Someone had to give history a nudge. By nightfall, the Coalition would be thrice as large as it had been this morning. And this was only the beginning.

Hale stepped inside the chilly main room. Skylights capped the large room's vaulted ceiling, but those were long broken. A weak sun shone down on him, doing little to keep him warm. Hale stood at a long metal table, tamping a plug of tobacco into his pipe. After igniting the leaves with a small torch, he took a deep pull from it.

At nearly six-foot-six, Hale cut an imposing figure. Standard military fatigues stretched across his thick frame. The fatigues and a pair of heavy black boots constituted his daily wear. Wearing the same thing every day eliminated an unimportant decision from his life. Using any brain power on such trivial matters was anathema to how he lived and worked.

Cameron Wu was next to arrive. She wore her usual garb, blue jeans and a thick sweater. She was in her mid-fifties now. Her community was large but not well organized. But she was an agricultural wizard, able to produce large crop yields regularly. Hale's Coalition produced some food but not enough to feed its residents. Wu's group helped the Coalition complete the puzzle of survival. In exchange, Hale offered limited weaponry, ammunition, and military advisors. Never enough to launch an attack against the Coalition, of course. Only enough to repel an offensive.

He rose to shake her hand, as was his custom. Etiquette mattered. Manners mattered, especially on a day like today.

"Nice to see you again, Victor."

"Cameron," he said, nodding respectfully.

She stood barely five feet tall, petite but lean. There was power in her tiny body, Hale was sure of it. Hale eyed her figure admiringly, wondering what it might be like to bed her. But it was not to be. They'd become comfortable with one another, and it was this comfort that Hale sought to exploit.

As they traded pleasantries, the last of the trio arrived. Hale did not know the man's name; he was known only as the Professor. This amused Hale. They lived in a post-apocalyptic wasteland, so why not have a guy known as the Professor? It added a little spice to their lives. He was a big man, about six feet tall, and built like a house. He lumbered as he walked, reminding Hale of a triceratops. He wore dark glasses all the time, rain or shine.

"Greetings, my friends!"

Hale nodded at the Professor but kept the greeting to a minimum. The man's voice was grating. He was from the northeast, perhaps Massachusetts or New Hampshire, betrayed by how he pronounced water like *watah*.

Hale had a slightly different arrangement with the Professor. The Coalition offered engineering and construction expertise in exchange for medicine and medical supplies. His town was west of here, and its people were skilled in developing medicines from herbs and plants. The Coalition's prison was on the outskirts of Tomlin, Missouri, roughly halfway between the prison and the other two communities, separated by less than twenty miles.

"Let's get started," Hale said.

"You in a rush?" Cameron asked.

They typically set aside a full day for the summit, ensuring they covered as many issues as possible. Revealing his impatience was a mistake he couldn't afford to make.

"Just like to be efficient," he replied.

"How about a toast before we get started," said the Professor. "This is the second anniversary of our little alliance."

"Great idea," Hale said, hoping his enthusiasm would mask his earlier slipup. The Professor wasn't the brightest bulb in the drawer, but Cameron was extremely sharp. She might already be on alert.

The Professor reached into his bag and retrieved a bottle of bourbon and three small glasses. The bottle was nearly full, but it had been opened. A healthy pour in each followed before he handed the libations to the other two. The trio clinked glasses; Hale waited while the Professor put on the show that would make any liquor aficionado proud. He swirled the liquid in the glass, tucked its lip under his nose, and took a dramatic sniff. Then he took a tender sip of the amber elixir. Neither Hale nor Cameron followed suit.

The Professor wiped his mouth with his hand and laughed heartily.

"What?" he asked. "Too afraid to accept a drink from me? Think I'd poison you?"

He and Cameron exchanged a glance.

"Well, you just saw me put this one down," he said, a hint of annoyance spicing his voice. He took another sip.

Cameron set her glass on the table with a heavy clang.

"Maybe you've built up a resistance to whatever's in here," Cameron said.

The man looked at Cameron before shifting his gaze to Hale, who continued to hold his drink. Then he scoffed.

"Do you know what this is?" he asked, holding up the bottle.

No reply.

"This is Pappy Van Winkle," he said. "God Himself could not have made a better whiskey."

Neither Hale nor Cameron was moved.

"I would sooner eat broken glass than adulterate this whiskey."

An awkward silence followed.

"Well, that'll be the last time, then."

He pointed at Hale's drink. Hale handed it to him; the Professor poured the bourbon back into the bottle and threw the glass across the room. It shattered with a mournful tinkle. He repeated the display with Cameron's drink.

"Now we can start," the Professor said. His cheeks were rosy from the flush of the bourbon. He took a deep breath and let out a contented sigh.

They took their seats. Cameron handed the men copies of the agenda she had prepared. For each meeting, the duty of preparing the document rotated among them.

"Last week's food delivery was more than a day late," Hale told Cameron.

"Couldn't be helped," she said. "We had a fuel shortage."

"Not my problem," he said. "The next ammunition shipment will be reduced by fifty percent."

"That's crap," she said, raising an eyebrow.

"Too bad," replied Hale. "I'm within my rights."

He was referring to the Contract, the document they'd drafted two years earlier to govern their interactions. Wu gritted her teeth but said nothing more. She had no defense. The consequences for breaching the agreement were designed to be severe. Her reaction was of no interest to Hale. He was simply making time. The pieces were in place.

At this very moment, Coalition forces were preparing to strike the communities of his two trading partners. Their residents would surrender, or they would die. There was no turning back from this. The old world was dying; a new one was about to be born.

This type of thing had to happen from time to time. Before long, someone would make a move. It was a cliché, of course, that the only true constant was change. But far too many people failed to grasp that simple concept. And they died because of it. Sooner or later, they would view him as a threat. Sooner or later, they would make a move against him. Perhaps not today, perhaps not even this year, but eventually, they would realize how dangerous he'd become.

But it was a big thing he was attempting. A move beyond the scope of anything that had come before. And it was possible now only because of the astonishing intelligence that had found its way to him a few months ago.

The vaccine.

He'd been looking for it for nearly three years. Victor Hale was an original member of Cobalt, the project that had precipitated the ultimate slate cleaner—the development and release of what would eventually come to be known as the Medusa virus.

The tragedy of it all was still raw three years on. It had been a clear winter day, the mountains dusted with a recent snowfall. He and his team were returning home after a long-range reconnaissance mission that had kept them on the road for two months. The first hint of trouble was the snow still covering the pass climbing toward the Olympus compound. Snow removal was a priority at Olympus. It had taken a whole day to make it up the mountain; eventually, he and his team had reached the entrance and found nothing but rubble. Ruins. Some were still smoldering; he hadn't missed the conflagration by more than a couple of weeks.

Many of his comrades were dead, the rest missing. He'd found the body of Leon Gruber in an old sport utility vehicle in the circular driveway fronting the chalet. His body was gray and desiccated but recognizable from the gold cross that lay at the hollow of the corpse's throat.

At least a dozen bodies belonged to people he did not know. The cold had preserved many of the remains, but their faces were unrecognizable to him. The entire scene was a giant mystery. He hadn't been aware of any force this size operating in the area.

He and his team camped at the site for a week, trying to understand what had happened. Troubling signs quickly began to emerge. Nearly all the dead were adults—no sign of the children that had lived here. Whether they had been kidnapped or simply run off was not immediately apparent. If someone had discovered their existence, Olympus would be an attractive target. They had been fanatical about security, but that didn't mean they were infallible. Someone could have taken the kids and poked and prodded them until they figured out how they existed at all.

The next discovery, however, had rocked him to his core. The Medusa vaccines were missing. More alarmingly, *only* the Medusa vaccines were missing. But again, that did not tell him what had happened to them. Several possibilities came to mind. Someone from Olympus might have made it out with the vaccines before Olympus had fallen. The more worrying possibility, of course, was that someone *outside* Olympus had taken the vaccine. And if that was the case, someone outside Olympus knew the vaccine existed in the first place.

Either way, he had to find the vaccine. When he had left Olympus on his reconnaissance mission, their lab housed nearly a thousand vaccine doses. Preliminary work was underway to manufacture additional doses; however, the work was moving slowly.

But he'd had no idea where to begin his search. The continent was so incredibly vast, much of it empty now, getting emptier every day. But what choice did he have? Without the vaccine, there was no future. He would have no leverage. And thus began his quixotic, desperate search for a special valise that carried his redemption, his salvation. For the first year, the search had been fruitless. The vaccine was gone into the ether.

But then.

A hint.

A lead.

A story of a six-month-old baby in Colorado. It had survived Medusa's initial onslaught in the days after its birth. Without the vaccine, a virtual impossibility. A miracle birth. He'd heard it on the road from a caravan of traveling musicians who played for their food and never lay their heads in the same place twice.

He'd tracked the mother, Allie, to a refugee camp in western Nebraska but missed her by a week. However, other residents who knew her confirmed the story of the baby's successful battle against Medusa. The baby had *lived*. There had been a woman, they'd said; she'd shown up about a week before the baby's birth, claiming to have a vaccine. She had spent time with Allie. Then she was gone.

But he had the bit between his teeth now. Reports had the woman continuing east, and Hale had also gone east.

Reports trickled in of another baby in northeastern New Mexico, near the sliver of the border with Oklahoma. Again, another tale of a woman who'd come bearing a vaccine. This time, he'd gotten a physical description. About five-foot-six, lean, rugged, capable. But bearing a soft spot for pregnant women.

"Victor, are you even listening to me?"

He'd been daydreaming, his mind on a future yet to come. He had most certainly not been listening to the Professor. He leaned forward in his seat and rapped his knuckles on the table.

"Professor?" Hale asked.

"Yes?"

"What's your real name?" he asked loudly.

The man looked at Hale with a bemused, slightly annoyed look.

"What?"

"Your name. What is it?"

The Professor glanced at Wu, who shrugged indifferently.

"Why do you want to know my name?"

"Because this is silly," Hale said. "We're trying to build something here, right? How are we supposed to build something when we can't trust each other on something so simple."

His sincerity was genuine. The Professor's identity foolishness was part of it. Hale had big plans for the future, which depended on people he could trust. If he did not control it, he could not trust it.

A sheepish look crossed the Professor's face.

"I guess it is kind of silly," he said.

He wiped his mouth with his hand and took a deep

breath. A set jaw and tight lips replaced the sheepishness on his face.

"To a brighter tomorrow," Hale said.

It was the signal to his men.

Two gunshots rang out almost simultaneously, followed by two more in rapid succession. Baez and Jepson had eliminated the security details for Cameron and the Professor. As they turned their heads to the source of the sound outside, Hale reached for the pistol in his ankle holster.

He came up firing, one shot into each of his contemporaries, before they even realized what was happening. At such close range, there was no chance of failure. Wu's head rocked backward before she face-planted into the table. The Professor, who'd just been about to reveal his name was Kevin Dodd, was blown off his chair by the impact.

Hale got up from the table. The air was cold, the echo of the gunshots still reverberating in the cavernous room. Outside, his men were retrieving the horses. They had done well, and he would reward them for their service. Killing was no small thing, even in their world. To take a life, to close the book on everything and anything someone had been or would ever be, was an existential punch in the face.

Less than five minutes later, the three men were astride their horses, headed back to the prison, a new future awaiting them all.

16

———

Rachel could not sleep. Again. It was the dead of night, three or four in the morning, and she had been tossing and turning since setting her head to the pillow hours earlier. She'd always been a light sleeper, as far back as she could remember, but she could typically grab a few restful hours every night. It didn't look like sleep would come tonight, though.

Part of it was the newness of it all. They'd been on the road for so long she'd forgotten what it was like to have a home base, even temporarily. Being on the road was easy. Simplistic. You had a destination, a certain number of miles to cover, and that was the focus for the day. There were risks and obstacles, of course, and you had to be mindful of those. But the road was a kind of home in and of itself.

This was different. It required a recalibration. The long years in Evergreen had been filled with securing their food supply, with tension, fear, and the always-on-edge feeling of believing there were no post-pandemic children other than Will.

But so much had changed. There was a future now.

Now, distributing the vaccine would be her life's work. Ensuring that each dose found the right home, the right person. To maximize humanity's potential. And finally, she had a partner she could trust. Samir was a good and decent man. He was everything that Eddie Callahan had not been. Samir's eyes lit up when they discussed potential distribution plans. He'd lived in darkness for so long, watching humanity fade away a little bit at a time. A spark of hope inside him was catching fire. How exciting it must have been for him.

It made her miss her father. She wished he could have lived to see this future ripe with possibility. He'd told her once—in fact, on the day he had died—that life would find a way, that their generation would not be humanity's last. He had been so sure of it. At the time, she worried they'd been on a fool's errand. There would be others like Will, he had always told her. And he had been right.

But he was gone now, dead three years. Not only had he died without seeing the future regenerate with possibility, but he had also died not knowing the truth about their family's legacy, their connection to the plague. Perhaps it was better that way. There were times she wished *she* hadn't learned the truth.

Riverview had put Rachel and Will up in a guest house on the east side of the college's bucolic hundred-acre campus. It was a lovely setting, albeit a bit shaggier looking than it had been before the plague. The tree-lined quad at the center of the campus now served as Riverview's community square and marketplace. The community had established its gardens around the perimeter of the quad, near the freshwater lake in the north-central section of the campus.

She got out of bed and padded over to the window overlooking the small front yard. Like most yards, it had long returned to seed, back to its natural state. This house didn't see much use, so its care was an afterthought. Besides, it wasn't like anyone was doing any landscaping these days. After eighteen years of perfectly manicured San Diego lawns kept alive by water piped in from the Colorado, Rachel had come to prefer yards gone wild. Each one was different. There was a beauty to it all. No two yards alike.

This time of year, they saw goldenrod and coneflower, geranium and bellwort. A medium-sized silver maple tree grew in the corner of the yard. Come spring, it would cast a lovely shade in the afternoon. She wondered if they would still be here by then. It wasn't much, but for now, it was theirs. It was a small two-bedroom ranch, the right amount of space for her and Will. His bedroom was across the hall from hers. He had settled in nicely; the stability was welcome after more than two years on the road.

A flutter of movement caught her eye. She ducked out of view under the window sash. Then she raised her head an inch, coming level with the bottom of the window. Outside, moonlight shone down through broken clouds. At first, she saw nothing, thinking that she'd imagined it. Her body started to relax, but a moment later, another flicker. Someone was out there.

There!

A shadowy figure lurked behind the maple tree. He ducked low and skittered to the corner of the house, on the opposite side of the structure, disappearing from her line of sight. Quickly, she retrieved a handgun from her nightstand and edged her way out into the hall. It was silent except for the insistent susurrations of her heavy breathing.

The home's narrow kitchen bisected the bedrooms and the home's main living space. From there, the back door opened on the narrow strip of land in the back. If she moved quickly enough, she could intercept the intruder before he could reach Will's bedroom window. She didn't know his destination but wasn't taking any chances. As she hurried down the hallway, she checked her weapon. Something she had done so often that it was second nature. Muscle memory.

She turned at the short corridor leading to the kitchen. Here, she trod more carefully, taking her time, keeping her eyes fixed on the glass panes in the door's upper half. As she crossed the threshold into the kitchen, a shadow crossed the glass of the door. She skidded to her right, ducking just below the oval-shaped kitchen table.

Suddenly, the window shattered, the shards crashing and tinkling on the kitchen floor; a second terrific crash followed. Rachel felt a hollow thud against her flank, an impact against her ribcage that took her breath away. The sudden panic that she'd been struck threatened to overwhelm her. She fired once blindly.

"Shit," hissed the assailant, his voice cloaked in whisper.

Rachel lunged for the door, but her quarry was quick, reaching the back fence in seconds. She bolted toward it, lunging and grabbing a leg as he tried scurrying over. The intruder kicked hard, his foot catching Rachel on the cheek, a blow decisive enough to shake her loose. He slipped over the fence and melted into the night beyond. The top of the fence was just beyond Rachel's reach; after stepping back, she leaped toward the barrier and pushed off with her right foot to catapult her high enough to grab the top. But her first try came up short, and she slid back to the ground.

She barreled back through the door, finding a perplexed Will in the kitchen.

"You okay?" she asked as she zipped past him.

He nodded.

She continued through the living room, out the front door, and into the yard. But it was futile. She stood in the yard, her hands on her hips, her heart racing, her body glazed with sweat. The night was silent but for the sound of her labored breathing.

"Dammit," she whispered.

RACHEL WENT to see Samir early the next morning. She was exhausted, and her face was sore from its collision with the intruder's boot. The blow had left a waffle-cut bruise on her face. Her flank ached from where the object launched through the window had struck her. Fortunately, it had not been a bullet. The light of dawn revealed its true nature – a red brick bearing a hastily scribbled message in black paint: NO VACCINES. It seemed that her gift was not universally welcome in Riverview.

Unsurprisingly, she had not returned to sleep. She'd spent an hour patrolling the house, ensuring every window and door was locked. Afterward, she'd sat in the living room, the gun on her lap. Will slept on the sofa; she wanted to have her eyes on him. Her eyes drooped shut a few times before she jerked back to attention. It was going to be a while before she slept soundly again.

Samir was busy when she arrived at the medical clinic, seeing patients. Six or so folks sat waiting their turn. For such a small community, its residents needed extensive medical care, and the good doctor was always busy. Despite the radically reduced population, several pathogens were circulating, and survivors still had to deal with the garden-variety chronic conditions that had plagued them before the actual plague. Not one corner of the globe had escaped Medusa's wrath; that said, Rachel had no idea what the rest of the world had been up to these last sixteen years. That said, America had not been a bastion of good health before Medusa. Diabetes, cancer, and heart disease problems endured, and conditions that had been treatable once upon a time often became a death sentence.

She sat in the waiting room, leafing through an old news magazine, perhaps its final issue. The cover featured an image of the Medusa virus under a microscope and bore the headline: HOW BAD COULD IT GET?

Well, pretty damn bad.

Fifteen minutes later, the door to the sole exam room opened, and Samir emerged with a middle-aged man she did not recognize. He was tall and lean; a baseball cap was pulled low over his forehead, largely disguising his face. Her body tensed as she studied the man's movements, trying to draw up the vague silhouette of the man who'd been in her home the night before. Perhaps he was here getting his arm looked at.

"Come back if it doesn't get better," Samir said.

"Will do," said the man as he approached the exit.

Samir moved toward the reception desk and grabbed the clipboard. She came up behind him and touched him on his arm, startling him.

"Rachel," he said. His usual warm smile disappeared as his eyes zeroed in on the bruise on her face.

"What happened?"

"Can we talk?" she said. "Now."

His eyes cut toward the patients waiting for their turn. She could feel them watching her, this carpetbagger cutting into their precious time with the doctor. But this couldn't wait. She could only hope they would forgive her. She had faced this moment in every place they'd tried to make a home. An inflection point would arrive, and they would run. Every time. But not this time. Her gut told her to stay, not to run. It was time to put down roots for good this time.

Samir motioned for her toward the exam room. He followed her in and closed the door behind him.

"What's this all about?"

"The man you just saw, who was he?"

"His name is R.J.," he said. "Farmhand."

"What was he here for?"

Samir smiled thinly.

"You know I can't discuss my patients with you."

Rachel clicked her tongue against her teeth. It was hard to tell where caution crossed the line into paranoia.

"Someone came after us last night," she said. "While we were sleeping."

His face tightened with worry.

"My God," he said. "Is Will okay?"

"He's fine. Slept through most of it."

Samir pointed at her face.

"And that?"

"I chased him over the fence," she replied. I got an arm around his leg, but he booted me and got away. I didn't get a good look at him. It was dark."

Samir took a seat in the plastic chair in the corner. He leaned over and propped his elbows on his knees. He took a deep breath and let it out slowly.

"Crime is almost unheard of here," he said. "Any idea what he wanted?"

She tapped the backpack.

She removed the brick from her sweatshirt pocket and handed it to him. When he saw the message scrawled on its surface, his eyebrows jumped.

"But why?" he asked.

"Not everyone is going to be pro-vaccine."

Samir scoffed.

"I guess some things never change," he said. "Without vaccines, humanity would have never reached its potential. Not if half the population died of diphtheria before age twenty."

"You sound like my father," she said.

"Sounds like a smart man."

He paused and started to laugh.

"Then again, maybe all this never happens."

"You can't look at it that way," she said. "The plague happened because bad people caused it to happen."

"I guess," Samir said.

He held up the brick.

"What do you propose we do?"

"I am going to find out who did this."

17

Rachel arrived early on her first day, bright-eyed and ready to spread the gospel about Leon Gruber's beautiful, terrible vaccine. For the past week, she had been working to set up a vaccine outreach office, and with Samir's help, she had done just that. He had given her a small office in the Ashby medical clinic.

Sleep eluded her the night before the opening. As soon as the sun rose, she was out of bed, dressed, and taking a small breakfast of fruit and a small corn tortilla.

The little house had been quiet as she ate. The trauma of the attempted break-in had begun to fade, and she was sleeping a bit better than she had the first few nights after it happened. Her gun was never far from her side.

After finishing her breakfast, she woke Will up; he was scheduled for field work this morning before his studies. He didn't complain much, happy to be settled in a place again. There weren't many teenagers, but there were a few; he'd been spending much of his free time with the punk rock girl Jade. There didn't appear to be any teenage shenanigans between them, but Rachel kept a close eye on them anyway.

Will dressed and ate quickly, as was his norm. They left together, leaving Moose behind. He'd swiftly adjusted to life in their home. The dog loved the company of his masters, but he also was content to spend the day curled up on the sofa.

She had prepared a stack of handwritten pamphlets, designed a large posterboard displaying key facts about the vaccine, and readied a list of questions people might have. *No pressure, Rachel.* Only the future of the human race. There were a lot of questions about the serum in Riverview; she would be happy to answer them.

There were many more vaccine doses than there were women of childbearing age in Riverview, which itself created a new set of problems. But one thing at a time.

The office was small, not much bigger than a walk-in closet, and sparsely furnished with a table and a chair, but that was enough for her.

She got her first visit a little after ten. A younger woman, maybe twenty years old, was loitering at the door to the outreach office. Rachel recognized her but did not know her name; she'd been just a kid during the pandemic, old enough to carry some memories of the world gone by. She was petite, three or four inches shorter than Rachel, a hundred pounds soaking wet. She wore jeans and a baggy sweatshirt that all but swallowed her up. Her light blond hair was tied back in a messy ponytail.

"Hey there," Rachel said as welcomingly as she could.

The woman did not reply.

"What's your name?"

"Taylor."

"I'm Rachel."

Taylor nodded. After looking around, she wandered

toward the table, picked up a pamphlet, and leafed through it.

"Would you like to learn more about the vaccine?" Rachel asked.

She chuckled as the words spilled out of her mouth, feeling like a religious zealot knocking on an unsuspecting homeowner's door.

"I guess."

"What do you want to know?"

"Is it safe?"

"I've had it."

"That means it was safe for you."

Rachel smiled.

"That's true," she said. "But I met a lot of people who'd had it. And they were fine."

"Who else got the vaccine?"

"The people who made it."

"How does it work?"

Rachel steeled herself to deliver a more detailed explanation. The people of Riverview deserved to know the truth, even if it made them uncomfortable. The vaccine had flowed through Rachel's veins since she was a teenager. Without her mother's consent, not to put too fine a point on it. Yes, it had protected her from Medusa. It had made Will possible. But that didn't mean she knew everything there was to know about it. All she could do was be as transparent about it as possible.

"It's a very special vaccine."

"Special how?"

"It's a nanovaccine," Rachel said. "Tiny machines that are programmed to destroy the virus."

"Like robots?"

"Kind of," she said. "But they're microscopic. No bigger than the proteins in a regular vaccine."

"How does it protect the babies?"

"The nanoparticles are always looking for the virus. If it enters the body, the vaccine destroys it instantly. That's how it keeps the babies safe. That's how it kept me and Will safe."

"You're not immune to the virus?"

A chill ran through her. But for her family's hand in this entire sordid mess, Rachel would have almost certainly died in the pandemic. Choking on her blood, impossible fevers burning her alive. There was a recurring nightmare in her repertoire of nightly dreams, one where she found herself burning with fever and a bloody nose, and it always felt so real, even when she was telling herself that it was just a dream, until she shot up in bed, bathed in sweat, breathing hard. On those nights, sleep was hard to find again.

"Without the vaccine? Probably not."

"Oh."

She ventured deeper into the office, pausing and taking the empty chair across from Rachel.

"What powers the machines?"

Rachel's brow furrowed in confusion.

"Not sure I understand the question."

"The little robots," Taylor said. "Do they have batteries?"

Rachel opened her mouth and then closed it again. The question stumped her. The provenance of the nanoparticles' power supply had never crossed her mind. She didn't have the first damn clue. Perhaps they generated their own power. Or relied on the body's electrical system to keep the particles charged. As she scrambled for an answer, a look of concern darkened Taylor's face. Rachel was losing her.

"Well, I got the vaccine a long time ago, and it still seems to be working."

But Taylor was standing up even as Rachel tried to recover.

"Okay, thanks for your time."

Rachel stood as well.

"Would you like an appointment to get the shot?"

She was backing up toward the door, holding her hands up in surrender.

"I'm not sure," she said. "I'll have to think about it."

"Do you want to have kids?" Rachel asked.

This froze Taylor at the door.

"I don't know, to be honest with you."

"Want to talk about it?"

"I don't know."

Rachel gestured toward the chair previously occupied by Taylor.

"Let's talk."

Taylor eyed the seat momentarily and then glanced over her shoulder at the door to the waiting room beyond. She seemed torn; Rachel did not speak again, figuring that pushing too hard might push her right out the door. A moment later, Taylor eased into the chair. Rachel breathed a sigh of relief and took her seat.

"It's not that I don't want kids," she said.

She bit her lip, and tears welled in her eyes.

"I forgot what kids sound like."

Rachel knew the feeling. It was hard living in a world largely devoid of children. Even the time she'd spent with Will and the kids from Olympus had been fleeting. You needed kids around, a massive injection of them to stay sane. To remind the world that it was worth saving.

"Must have been nice, you and your son."

"It was wonderful," Rachel said. "And it can be that way for you."

"Even if I took it, what kind of person would I be bringing a child into a world like this?"

Her eyes cut to the floor, apparently embarrassed by her comment.

"No offense."

"None taken," Rachel replied. "But to your question. You won't be the only one bringing a child into this world. You'd just be one of the first. And others will follow."

"How many?"

"How many what?"

"How many vaccine doses do you have?"

"Almost a thousand."

"We don't have anywhere near that many women here," Taylor said.

"I know," Rachel said. "But there are other communities out there that we could share it with."

She and Samir were batting around that option regarding the excess vaccine supply. Trading it for goods and services made the most sense from a survivalist perspective. Once proof of concept was established, people would pay almost anything for it. It felt barbaric, however; selling doses to the highest bidders would immediately put the less fortunate at a disadvantage. Rachel did not begrudge those who embraced the mentality that *only the strong survive*, but this vaccine was beyond that. It transcended post-apocalyptic capitalism. The vaccine was their salvation. To barter with it felt borderline sacrilegious.

But Rachel's pipe dream was manufacturing the vaccine. If she could somehow find a way to reproduce it at scale, it would immediately lose its value while remaining priceless. There would be no reason to fight for it, to hunt her down, to kill her for it. But counting on such a capability was the most desperate of fantasies. Both the Citadel and Olympus were gone, in ruins, and to the best of her knowledge, those were the only sites on the planet that had created the vaccine.

"We can worry about that later," Rachel said.

The tide was starting to turn; Rachel could feel it in her bones. A few more minutes would convince the young woman to take the vaccine. That was how a shower became a storm, how a storm became a flood. She just needed a few people to believe.

A sharp knock at the door interrupted them. Rachel looked up to see June Richards looming ominously at the threshold of the small office.

"I've been looking for you, young lady," June thundered.

Rachel's brow furrowed in confusion. She had no earthly idea why June was looking for her. Rachel glanced at Taylor, whose face had tightened considerably.

"Well, you found me," Taylor said, acid virtually dripping from her voice.

"Let's go."

"I'm not done here," Taylor bit back.

"You're done when I say you're done."

Rachel decided it was time to cut in.

"Is there something I should know?"

Taylor laughed sharply.

"She thinks she's my mother."

"I assume she is not?"

June stepped deeper into the office, her eyes fuming with rage.

"I have raised this ungrateful woman since she was four years old," June said, never taking her eyes off Taylor.

Now, it made sense. June had rescued Taylor as a child.

And now she believed that Taylor should always be indebted to her. It was a hell of a guilt trip to play. Rachel wondered how many relationships just like this one were playing out worldwide. Survivors who believed they were owed something by the children they had helped raise after the pandemic.

"Remember how I found you? Alone in that playground? Starving? Half dead?"

It was Taylor's turn for her face to fill with rage.

"Yes, I remember," Taylor said. "And I guess you'll never let me forget it."

June's face softened just a little bit at that moment.

"Just a little appreciation is all I ask."

Time for a bit of diplomacy.

"June, what seems to be the problem?"

The woman turned her attention to Rachel.

"We haven't survived this long by being rash. I understand you want to help. But you need to understand the danger you've brought to our doorstep. Not everyone will roll up their sleeves and let you inject them with this so-called vaccine. For all I know, you're here to murder us all."

Rachel chuckled at that.

"That would be a pretty novel approach, wouldn't you think?"

June scoffed.

"I think it's pretty simple. You come in with this wild claim of having a vaccine. People go crazy and the next thing you know, everybody's dead. You could be an advance team for an invasion force. And just like that, you've got everything we own."

"But you've seen my son," Rachel said.

"I haven't seen a birth certificate," she said. "He could be small for his age. He doesn't even look like you."

June Richards was proving to be a much bigger problem than Rachel had anticipated. And given the influence she wielded in Riverview, Rachel needed to tread carefully. It wouldn't take much for June to turn the residents against her and the vaccine. After all, the idea that the savior of humanity had waltzed into town was a bit fanciful. That someone was out to get them all was far more believable. All Rachel needed, however, was for Alice to give birth and for the baby to survive more than a few days. Then, Rachel would have all the proof she needed.

"June, I want to be a mother someday," Taylor said. "I'm not saying I'm getting the shot today. But I don't want to wait forever. What if the supply runs out?"

June was chewing on her lower lip now. Her eyes were glassy.

"I've already lost two children," she said.

June looked directly at Rachel.

"You think I'm some kind of monster," she said. "Just some obstacle in your little quest here. But I had two beautiful daughters. Monica and Ellie. They were eleven and thirteen. Eleven and thirteen! And I had to watch them get sick, drown on their own blood, cry out for me, and then die. You know what that's like?"

Rachel shook her head.

"No."

Rachel had met many women who'd lost children to Medusa; she had heard their stories, she had sat with them and cried with them, but she would never truly understand their pain, their heartache. Every such story pierced her soul. She'd lost many nights of sleep simply worrying about something terrible happening to Will. And nothing had.

June was standing behind Taylor now, caressing the young woman's hair. Taylor's eyes were focused on her lap, where her fingers fumbled together. June's little monologue had had an impact on her. She was drifting out of Rachel's reach.

"Let's go, Taylor," June said.

Rachel chose to end the battle for the time being. Taylor looked at her, waiting for her to say something, but there was nothing to say. Rachel was a guest in Riverview, and she could not afford to ruin that. It was going to take a little more time than she'd thought. It wasn't ideal. Every day, the human race got smaller. Every day, they drew closer to the point of no return. The terrifying moment that the surviving population fell below a certain threshold that would prove impossible to recover from. It would no longer matter how many vaccines she administered. As it was, she could only hope they hadn't hit that mark already.

Taylor's shoulders sagged; a look of confusion was etched across her face. Fear of taking the vaccine, fear of not taking the vaccine, fear of alienating the woman who had saved her life. Taylor got up and made her way to the door. June gave Rachel a hard stare before following Taylor out.

The encounter left Rachel quite rattled. She sat quietly for the next fifteen minutes, replaying the scene in her mind. It had been the right call not to push any harder with Taylor; trying to win the argument with June may have cost her the war. She had no other takers that first morning. Traffic to Samir's clinic was steady; eventually, someone's curiosity would get the best of them. She tried not to worry.

Samir came to see her around midday.

"Any nibbles?" he asked hopefully.

"Just one."

"Who was it?"

"Taylor."

A look of understanding crossed Samir's face.

"Ah," he said. "I was wondering what June was doing here."

She shook her head.

"Don't sweat it," he said. "I'm telling everyone that comes through."

"I know."

"Samir?"

"Yeah?"

"Is June going to be a problem?"

He crossed his arms and sighed.

"I don't know."

18

Victor Hale sat on the roof of the prison administration building, his legs dangling over the edge. It was a cold and gloomy afternoon. A sharp wind blew in from the west, cutting through the heavy black duster he wore to ward off the chill. The grounds of the prison stretched out before him. People hurried to and fro, attending to their duties. Setting up shop here had been a wise decision. It had the infrastructure he needed to build his small community, but it also was easy to secure.

Before Medusa, this had been the Waterside Correctional Center, one of three large prisons in Missouri. It had housed fifteen hundred inmates, nearly all of whom had died of Medusa. Statistically speaking, a handful of the inmates would have been immune to the virus, but they died all the same, of thirst or starvation, trapped in their cells when everything had collapsed. It was a morbid thought.

The prison sat on about seventy-five acres of low-lying Missouri plains, ringed by chain-link perimeter fencing topped by barbed wire. The terrain was elevated, protecting against the river's floodwaters, which worsened with each passing year without man-made defenses. It was isolated from nearby communities, surrounded by forest and swampland. A combination of oak, hickory, and maple made up most of the woodlands surrounding the prison. When Hale had set up shop here, the fencing was buckled and broken in several places; its repair had been one of the Coalition's priorities upon moving here.

A single road serviced the prison, running right up to its main gate. At its opposite end, the road connected with Missouri State Route 58, branching off toward New Madrid north and Talleysville south. Most of the prison staff had lived in one of the two towns.

They had been here for two years, and it was starting to feel like home. More than that, it felt like a new beginning. A new beginning for the world. Some might have called him insane or delusional. But Hale liked to think of himself as ambitious. That was why he'd signed onto the most secret of Penumbra projects so many years ago. And yes, it had gone bad. Real bad. But that didn't mean you threw out the baby with the bathwater.

The vaccine was out there. Somewhere. Rarely did a month go by without a rumor of babies surviving beyond infancy. Tales of a young, determined woman carrying a vaccine. And it would be an absolute game changer. Hale's thoughts lay beyond the walls of the prison, to the desolate wastes beyond, out past their little patch of the Mississippi River watershed. Someday, new nations would rise from the ashes of the United States. New leaders who would forge their places in history. Why not him? Why shouldn't future generations learn about him, study his life and times, see how he had put it all back together? To be great, one had to do great things. And if he had to do terrible things to further the greater good, history would treat him kindly.

A rustling sound behind him broke him from his train of thought. It was Trevor Gresham; he could identify the man by his footsteps, heavy and lumbering, a bit off-kilter thanks to a permanent limp, a parting gift from a bullet he'd taken in an ambush some years earlier. Trevor cleared his throat. He was an average-looking fellow, average height and build. He wore forgettable clothes and kept his jet-black hair fastidiously trimmed.

"I'm sorry to bother you, sir."

"Mmm."

There were strict protocols. When he was on the roof, he was not to be bothered. His best thinking took place here.

"I wouldn't be here if it wasn't important."

Usually, he'd tear any interloper a new one, but he was in a reflective mood. They were approaching a paradigm shift, and silly, angry outbursts did him no good. They added stress and raised his cortisol levels.

"Well, out with it."

"Gamma team is overdue," Grisham said.

The Coalition frequently sent small teams on various missions, including supply, reconnaissance, survey, and secret missions like Gamma's. Burns and his team were pursuing a lead on the mystery woman carrying the vaccine. If Hale's math was correct, they'd been gone about six weeks.

Hale's head dropped as he let out an exasperated sigh. This wasn't what he was hoping to hear. Recovering the vaccine was critical—one of many items on a long to-do list. Finding it was never going to be easy. But any delay in its capture slowed the entire process down. It was on the *critical path*, as they might teach in project management school.

"Any clues as to what happened?"

"Not yet, sir," he replied. "We have a few leads to chase down. I've got a team ready to move with your approval."

Hale raised a hand to wave Gresham off, but then he stopped. He swung his legs up and around and stood to his full six-foot-six height, towering over Grisham. This was too important to leave to another team without further discussion. If he wasn't careful now, it could be lost forever.

"Gather the executive team," he said, marching past a surprised Gresham.

FIFTEEN MINUTES LATER, they were gathered in Hale's office, once the bailiwick of the prison warden. Three other men were in attendance, all members of Hale's high command. Each had come from a wildly different background, but the pandemic had brought to the surface a particular set of skills, a persona that had lay dormant when the world was spinning along as it had been. These were intensely loyal men, and he did not fear any attempt that they would try to overthrow him. That said, the idea was not impossible, so he watched them daily to make sure. He had a network of spies working the community, acting as his eyes. These spies even spied on each other. He was realistic.

Marcus Trenton hailed from Detroit. He'd owned a small auto repair shop before the plague and knew his way around every kind of engine. He was tall and lean, his skin darker than night. Eliot Graves had been with Hale at Olympus. Young, in his early thirties. Once a summer intern in Penumbra's security division, he had been with Hale on the recon mission. He was short, topping out at about five-foot-five, but built like a truck. He worked out fanatically, two hours a day in the prison gym without fail. Hale suspected it was to compensate for his more diminutive stature. Seated to his right was Cole Redfield, a mountain of a man, usually gentle but a man who could go nuclear at any time.

It had been a short meeting.

Hale decided to lead this search-and-rescue mission himself. As good as his people were, the job of finding Gamma team was too important to leave to someone else. Redfield would join him.

He and Redfield left that afternoon, pressing south with the tiny bit of intel that Gresham had gathered. They continued well past sunset, Hale believing that time was of the essence. But when the night clamped down on them, leaving behind a black sky with no moon, Hale relented, and they made camp about ten miles south of the prison.

"You think this woman actually exists?" asked Redfield, tending to the fire and roasting a rabbit he had snared earlier in the day.

"I do," said Hale. "It adds up."

Redfield offered him some rabbit, which Hale ate mindlessly. He did not care about food, consuming only what he needed to keep his body in shape.

"Too many rumors flying around now," Hale continued. "And if Gamma team ran into trouble, that just tells me she's desperate. They were close."

Hale barely slept, keeping the fire going while Redfield caught some shuteye. Hale watched him sleep, wondering if the man understood the paradigm shift in the offing. At dawn, Redfield rose and padded off into the woods to relieve himself while Hale broke down the camp. After a quick bite of the remaining rabbit, they set back off.

They reached the trading post a little bit before midday. A light snow had begun to fall. He and Redfield pulled up the horses, slowing down in the last mile to let their bodies cool. Stopping them too quickly increased the risk of injury. They dismounted and removed each animal's tack before securing them to the wooden fence. The horses lowered their heads to drink at a narrow stream babbling nearby.

The post was housed in an abandoned gas station. Half the canopy had collapsed onto the pump, and the glass windows of the attached convenience store had been blown out. It was operated by a peculiar black man named Sanford. Sanford was harmless and seasoned with just a dash of crazy. He spent most of his days sitting on an old beach chair under the awning covering the pumps. His sole hobby appeared to be reading. He lived inside the convenience store. He was an information broker, trading intel for supplies.

Sanford looked up as Hale and Redfield tended to the horses, but he made no move to interact with them. People came to Sanford. Sanford didn't go to anybody. They approached him cautiously because you never knew when the man might snap.

"Morning, Sanford," said Hale.

"It ain't morning no more," he said, pointing up at the sky. "Sun is on its way down."

"So it is," replied Hale. "How're you doing?

"Pretty good, pretty good," the man replied, never looking up from his book.

"I need some information from you, buddy."

"Is that right?" Sanford replied.

"You're the man regarding this kind of thing."

"Don't I know it," he said.

He lay the book face down in his lap, ready to hold court for his visitors.

"What kind of information are you looking for?" Sanford asked.

"Looking for a couple of folks."

"Friends of yours?"

"You can say that."

"Are they lost?"

"I just want to know where they are."

"They're big boys. I'm sure they'll find their way home."

"They should have been home a few while ago. You hear about anything going on?"

"I don't know, maybe?"

Victor Hale sighed. He glanced over at Redfield and nodded, which was the signal to offer up a day's worth of rations.

Redfield returned to their horses and removed some supplies from the saddle bags.

"Hey Sanford, how about you let us do the cooking tonight?"

Sanford glanced at Redfield as he returned from the horse carrying his offerings.

"What you got there?"

"Some beef jerky, some fruit, some oats."

"Got any New York strip in there?"

"From your lips to God's ears, Sanford. From your lips to God's ears."

A few moments of silence followed as Sanford decided how much to share and whether he could hold out for a little bit more. Hale was always willing to reward Sanford if the intel was valuable enough. Redfield had once suggested torturing the man for information, but Hale didn't see the point. As his mother had said, you could catch more flies with honey than vinegar. It was an old, dumb cliche, but it was usually correct.

"I might have heard something."

"I'm listening."

"Some kind of explosion a while back."

"How long ago?"

"I don't know. Couple weeks. Maybe three weeks."

"Where was it?"

"South."

"What else do you know?"

"What else you got?"

"So, you do have something."

"I didn't say that."

"You don't have anything else?"

"I didn't say that either."

The back of Hale's neck prickled with irritation.

"Look, Sanford, I don't have time for this today. Tell me what you know."

Sanford had turned his attention back to his book. Mild irritation had mutated into heat crawling up Hale's back, up his neck, and his jaw tightened with anger. He could deal with and take a lot, but one thing he would not brook was disrespect.

He clamped the book between his thumb and fingers and slowly extracted it from Sanford's grip.

"Sanford, I know we work together a lot, and you're used to us, and you think we might be friends, but we are not friends."

Sanford's eyes remained fixed on Hale.

"This will end badly for you if you don't tell us what you know right now."

Hale could feel the anger in his voice, and he worked hard to remain calm.

"You ain't going to do anything to me. You need me."

Hale stepped forward and knelt beside Sanford. He took

the man's chin between his thumb and forefinger and turned Sanford's face toward his own.

"Sanford, have you ever known me to bluff?"

Sanford reared back, trying to pull his chin away, but Hale's grip was firm and held fast.

"Have you ever known me to bluff?" Hale asked a second time.

He was deliberate in his word choice, repeating the question exactly.

Now Willie's eyes widened with a bit of fright. He had never seen this side of Hale because Hale had never felt the need to show it. It was, however, called for now.

"South," he said. "Not far from Riverview. Old cabin in the woods. That's all I know."

19

———

Samir found himself thinking about Rachel on a troublingly regular basis. When he woke up. When he went to sleep. And most of the time between those two daily markers. It wasn't just that she was attractive, which she was. There was also a deep inner strength to her, a powerful force that Samir found almost impossible to resist; it was like a planet's gravity pulling him toward her. Then he would shake her off and go five or ten minutes without thinking about her. There was no time for it. Even if she reciprocated his feelings, they had too much to do. Distributing the vaccine without alienating the rest of the community was proving to be a tall task. Other than Alice, only a handful of women had taken the vaccine. But seeing Rachel had quickly become the highlight of his day. The days that he did not see her left him feeling empty.

It was becoming a problem.

It was getting dark on this late afternoon. He'd been on call for the last twenty-four hours and was exhausted. After such a long shift, he allowed himself twelve hours away from the clinic to decompress, sleep, and exercise. His nurse, Megan, could cover pretty much any medical issue. By this point, she was a *de facto* physician. It wasn't like there was a med school she could enroll in. Obviously, he was always available to respond to an emergency.

Early evening was his favorite time of day, when the sun began to set, taking off the edges from the hardness of the day. As he cleaned the office, his mind swirled around thoughts of Rachel. He swept the floors and mopped the countertops, hoping to maintain a semblance of infection control in his facility. These protocols still mattered to him.

His stomach rumbled; he had not eaten in several hours, maybe not since yesterday. When the clinic met his specifications, he grabbed his jacket and headed out the door. To his surprise, Rachel was waiting for him outside. She was carrying a heavy bag with her.

"Hey there," she said.

"Evening," Samir replied. His mouth was dry.

She waited awkwardly, unsure of what to say, it seemed.

"To what do I owe the pleasure?" Samir asked.

She held up the bag.

"I thought you might be hungry."

Stay calm, man, stay calm.

"I am hungry now that you mention it."

"Great," she said.

"Let's eat in my office."

Samir led Rachel to the clinic. His office was small, but it was enough for his purposes. There was room for a desk, a file cabinet, and a small loveseat on which he'd spent more nights than he cared to count. He offered her the loveseat and took a seat on his office chair. It wasn't the most comfortable spot to sit, but he would sit on a bed of nails for a few minutes alone with Rachel.

She set the bag on the desk and removed the pot. Once

free of its bag, the stew's hearty aroma made his empty stomach flip. The cozy smell of warm garlic quickly filled the room. It reminded him of his mother's kitchen. His family used garlic by the truckload, and its scent was a keystone of his childhood. Rachel ladled a serving into a bowl and handed it to him. She also brought a bit of flatbread, but not much, as it was not easy to make. He took a bite; it was delicious. Full of vegetables and a steaming hot tomato-based broth. A sigh of contentment emanated from him. He had been hungry.

"Not sure I ever properly thanked you for saving Will's life," Rachel said.

"Don't mention it," Samir replied. "That's my job."

"Yeah, but it's different now. It's not like I can take him to an ER."

"True, but I'm not going to let a kid bleed out if I'm able to do something about it."

"Well, thanks anyway."

They ate in silence for a few more minutes. Samir's bowl emptied quickly. Rachel poured him a second serving without asking him. He was still hungry but felt weird about asking for more, and he was deeply grateful for the additional portion. After setting him up with his second bowl, she sat back on the loveseat.

"You saved my kid's life, and I don't know the first thing about you," she said.

"Well, there's not much to know," he said. "Got lucky enough to be immune to the dread plague, and fifteen years later, here I am."

"Where are you from?" she asked.

"Well, my folks came here on the Mayflower," he said.

Rachel looked at him, her face frozen, unsure how to respond.

Then he started laughing.

The punchline dawned on her, and she started to smile.

He tapped his hands against his face, which had the dark brown skin tone of his ancestral people, immediately regretting his attempt at humor.

"Very funny," she said warmly.

She chuckled.

"Sorry, it's just been a while since I've heard anything in the edgy humor department."

"But that was funny?" he asked.

He hated how he sounded, as though he was groveling for her approval.

She looked at him with a broad smile.

"Yes, it was funny."

The ice broke, and he moved on.

"My parents immigrated here from Syria many years ago. My father ran a little grocery store in Lawrence, Kansas. My mother raised me and my three brothers. We all became engineers and doctors, the way children of immigrants are supposed to, you know."

They sat awkwardly for a few moments before they both spoke simultaneously.

"You go ahead," he said, extending his hand to her.

"Four boys," she said softly. "Your parents must've had their hands full."

He chuckled, thinking back to those formative years. Only six years separated the four Malik boys; he could only imagine the trauma his poor mother endured. They were clever boys, hardworking boys, but they were boys, and from time to time, they let off steam like Reactor No. 4 at Chernobyl.

"Yeah, it was chaotic," he said. "But my mother, well, she was something else."

"What was she like?"

"Getting deep here, aren't we?"

Rachel held her hands up apologetically.

"Don't mean to pry."

"Not at all," he said. "I'm glad we're doing this."

"Me too."

"She was remarkable."

It was an odd word choice, but it was apropos. While handling the business side of the family's grocery store, she found time to wrangle four boys, put dinner on the table every night, and God knew what else. His father pitched in at home when he could, but the business was all-consuming.

"My parents got along pretty well. That was pretty rare in an Arab marriage. Often, they were arranged out of convenience or to unite families. But my parents seemed to love each other."

And he paused, thinking about how they had died. Medusa had killed his mother on the seventeenth of August, his father the next day. By mid-August, it was clear that there would be no traditional funeral; civilization was in full-throated collapse. Samir had buried them in their back-yard, side by side. The fate of his brothers, who had been scattered across the country when the pandemic hit, remained unknown to him. His brothers, their wives, their thirteen children. All gone. His family was large; perhaps a relative somewhere had survived and was still eking out an existence somewhere. Maybe here. Maybe in Syria.

"Where did you grow up?" she asked.

"Kansas."

"What about work?"

"I worked at the University of Texas Hospital," he said. "In the emergency room."

"You were on the front lines."

"Yeah. Yeah," he said. "I was. I still remember the first case of Medusa. It was, as you can imagine, horrifying."

"I told you that my father was a doctor," she said.

He nodded, taking a hearty sip of the broth.

"He was an OB/GYN," she said. "He worked a few days straight during the worst of it. He only talked about it once. I think it hit him pretty hard."

"I'm not surprised," he said. "It was as close to hell on earth as you can imagine."

His sudden openness with her took him a bit by surprise. He had no doubt that he'd been suffering from post-traumatic stress disorder since those terrible days so many years ago. It was not the sort of thing you just sloughed off. Watching a person die in the most horrible way imaginable and then repeating the experience over and over and over again until you were near the brink of madness tended to do that to you. Especially when it was certain that you would soon be joining them. The virus struck down co-worker after co-worker, even those lucky enough to find protective personal gear. It was late August, nearly four weeks into the apocalypse before Samir began to truly believe that he was immune to Medusa.

Even now, he sometimes woke up at night drenched in sweat, reliving those days in that hospital. One recurring dream had him trying to escape from the hospital but never finding the exit. He would run down hallways he knew like the back of his hand, racing for exits he could never find. He told no one of these things, of these feelings, until this meal with Rachel. Part of him believed that they all just needed to suck it up. He knew how unhealthy that was, how terrible it was to hold it in, but he didn't want anyone to view him as weak.

"How was it for you?"

"Not as bad as for you, I'm guessing."

He was shaking his head even before she finished her sentence.

"It was bad for everyone," he said. "Don't minimize what you went through. Remember, I worked in an emergency department, so I had leveled up a bit. I had seen plenty of suffering before the virus."

Rachel opened her mouth to reply but closed it again. Her gaze drifted to the corner of the office. He noticed her lips, *oh my God, I'm staring at her lips, look at something else, anything else.* He turned his eyes down toward the remnants of his meal.

"I was getting ready to head back to CalTech for my sophomore year—"

Samir's eyes widened, and she must have noticed.

"Don't I look like a CalTech girl?"

He laughed and cut his eyes to the ground, embarrassed.

"No, it's not that," he said, looking for the right words. "I know what an accomplishment that would have been, getting admitted there."

"Well, thank you," she said. She chuckled softly to herself, and she smiled wistfully.

"You know, I did love it there."

"What were you studying?"

"Computer science," she said. "With a minor in machine learning/AI. Extremely useful these days."

Samir laughed out loud.

"You must have been an amazing student," he said.

"Well, I wasn't very popular in high school," she said. "Sort of made it easy."

He was reminded of his own high school experience.

Like Rachel, he'd been about as far from the center of the social universe as was humanly possible. His parents were wildly overprotective, but as it turned out, that was wasted energy. There wasn't anything to protect him from. His weekends were spent in the basement of his friend Jason Wu, where they whiled away their Friday and Saturday nights playing video games and watching movies. They tried weed a few times when Jason's parents had been out of town, but he didn't care for it. Or maybe he hadn't done it right.

"Yeah, I know the feeling," he replied.

"Anyway," she said, continuing her tale. "My stepdad locked us down. It was just him, my mom, and me. Somehow, she got it. I don't even know how. We were so careful."

"I think I can answer that," he said, holding up a finger. "I studied some virus after it was all over. It was encased in this extremely unusual shell that let it travel on air currents and remain viable for hours. There was simply no escaping it, even outdoors. If you breathed air anywhere on Earth that month, you almost certainly inhaled the Medusa virus. I guess we have your friend Chadwick to thank for that marvel of biomedical engineering."

Her lips tightened, and her eyes took on a glassy, faraway look.

"I wish I could see him die again," she said softly.

She turned to face Samir.

"Is that a terrible thing to say?"

He leaned back in his chair.

"No, I don't think so," he said.

"I think it a lot, and then I feel bad when I do."

"You shouldn't," he said. "You went through a lot. You know what?"

"Hmm?"

"I'm glad he's dead too."

They were quiet again, and Samir did not know what to say next. It was a heavy moment they had landed on, and he wasn't sure if he should pry any further. She remained quiet, making him think she didn't want to pursue this line of discussion either. But there was no tension, no awkwardness. Just two people gripped by the memories of a horrifying moment.

Rachel spoke first.

"Well, I hope I haven't intruded on your evening too much."

"Not at all," he replied. "I very much enjoyed this."

She nodded her head and brushed a finger against her lips.

"Yeah, I did too. Well, I'm sure you've got plenty to do without me bothering you."

"Trust me, it's no bother."

She was standing up, brushing off her jeans as she did so. He stood up as well, and for a moment, he had the courage to try and kiss her. But the moment passed, and he was glad it did because it wasn't right. He didn't want to come on too strongly. Then she leaned in and brushed her lips against his. Barely enough to count as a kiss, it startled him into paralysis.

"Thank you again for saving Will."

He nodded.

"I'm going to be heading out," she said.

He nodded dumbly.

"I've got some charting I need to do. But I hope we can do this again."

"So do I," she said.

Their eyes met for a moment in the dim office. As she moved past him, she reached out and squeezed his hip twice rapidly. It felt marvelous. And it would have to do. She left him alone in the office, and that was how he knew he was falling in love with her.

20

Hale sat on a stump next to a roaring fire, poking at the chunks of wood fueling the blaze. A weakened log split under the force of his thick stick, sending a plume of embers skyward. A few reached the ground and hissed in the fresh snowpack. He was on the final watch of the night; dawn was winding toward them. He had not slept much during his break, which had ended hours earlier. His body was physically tired, but his mind was racing, and he could not fall asleep. He always took the final watch because it was the most challenging shift. Most folks could not handle the strain of those final hours before dawn when the body screamed for sleep. Hale didn't trust anyone entirely on general principle, not even Redfield, and certainly not in a situation like this.

Three difficult days on the road had brought them here. He'd pushed his men hard and rewarded them by making camp an hour after sunset the night before. There was little chitchat, just the minimum necessary to clear the campsite and build the night's fire. It was good to be on the road again. Sometimes, you needed to get your hands dirty. Great things were built with dirty hands.

And now he was closer to his goal than ever.

The new day would bring an important piece of the puzzle—the identity of those responsible for the loss of Gamma team. And Hale believed the team was dead; every bit of intel they'd gleaned pointed toward the tragic outcome. The thought of it brought bile up his throat.

The darkness started to give way to the coming dawn. The black night softened, and the purple and indigo of imminent sunrise leaked into the sky. Victor stoked the fire as the stars receded. The men began to stir as the sky brightened with the first hints of dawn. They broke camp quickly and were on the move before full daylight.

Their destination was less than ten miles away—a small cabin in the rural wilds north of Antonia, Missouri. A community not far from the cabin made its home on a college campus, but Hale knew little about it. It was on his list of possible acquisitions.

For now, though, the cabin was his focus. Tracking down his team's last known location had cost them another day's rations, but it had been worth it. The intel sent them up Highway 726, three miles north of Seredni, then west along unmarked singletrack for half a mile.

They reached the cabin a little after midday, keeping to the far side of the river. They set up surveillance on the north side of the path, cloaked by a thick line of trees. The cabin was visible through a gap between two snow-dusted pines.

A series of defensive fortifications likely protected the cabin. Waiting out its resident was the right call. Their break came in the middle of the afternoon, just as the day's light started to fade.

The cabin's resident emerged from the front door, a rifle slung over her shoulder and a duffel bag dangling from her right hand. She made her way to the small Jeep parked in the semicircular driveway fronting the residence. Her departure from the property would bring her about fifty yards to their west, where her narrow drive broke through the treeline.

He gestured quickly to the men, and they hurried in that direction, setting up shop just as her engine roared to life. The little truck bounced up the dirt road, spraying a cloud of snow behind it. Hale's team remained hidden behind the trees, waiting for the right moment. Two large trees stood at the intersection of her dirt road with the main highway. It was the perfect spot for an ambush. As she drew near it, Hale and his comrades popped clear of the trees, their guns up. She brought the Jeep to a sudden stop, kicking up dirt and gravel as the tires bit into the earth. The men surrounded the vehicle, Hale standing before the hood, his men at each window. She kept her hands on the wheel. This unnerved Hale, and he took two giant steps back. He eased around toward the driver's side door. He stepped forward and rapped the window gently with his fist. She glanced at him before returning her eye to the road ahead. He knew what she was thinking – whether she could hit the gas and escape before her visitors' guns silenced her. But the road was treacherous, and making a quick getaway would prove difficult.

When she didn't comply, he fired a single warning shot into the air. She looked at him with a death stare; this was not a woman to underestimate. He fired another shot directly into the passenger side front windshield. The glass was reinforced and cracked into a spider-web pattern. He followed up with a third bullet into the right front tire. As the air hissed clear of the tire, the vehicle dipped toward its port side.

Finally, she surrendered, holding up her hands in clear view.

Hale made his way over to the door, Redfield covering him.

He opened the door and gestured for the woman to step out. She did so gingerly, never taking her eyes off of Hale.

"My name is Victor Hale," he said. "Do you mind if we have a little chat?"

"What can I do for you?" she asked. "There's really no need for this violence."

"This your place?"

She nodded.

"You alone here?"

She nodded.

"I'm not going to be pleased if you're lying."

"Yeah, I figured as much," she said. "Let's just get this over with."

"There's nothing I would like more."

"Why don't we talk inside?" Hale suggested.

She sighed mightily, a hint of defeat in her breath.

"Hands on your head, please."

She laced her fingers together and wrapped them around her head. She may have been many things, but dumb was not one of them. There was no need for this woman to die or even to suffer. All they needed was information.

The journey back down the gravel road laid bare the devastation wrought by her explosives. The incendiaries had blown down a line of trees, carving a half-moon of splintered and fractured trees. The trees were still accessorized with bits of clothing and bloodstains, all that remained of his team.

They reached her porch.

"The key's around my neck. You mind if I reach for it?"

"Do it slow."

She pulled the cord over her head and inserted the key into the lock.

"You try anything funny, and that'll be it."

"Yes, that seems to be the situation."

They stepped inside the house. The place was old and rustic. Wood paneling, the air rich with the spice of scented candles and firewood. She took a seat. Redfield grabbed a chair near the dining table. Hale remained standing.

"Care to tell me what this is all about?" she asked.

"You killed three of my men," Hale said.

"I didn't know they were your men."

"But you did kill them?"

"They were shooting up my house. What was I supposed to do?"

"Why were they shooting up your house?"

"Why does anyone do anything these days? I'm not particularly interested in the motivations of strange men trying to kill me."

"Nevertheless, it's an unacceptable loss."

"They shouldn't have tried to break in."

"I'm afraid we've gotten off on the wrong foot," Hale said. "How about we start over."

Meredith nodded. She was defiant but respectful.

"First of all, let's start with your name," Hale said.

"It's Meredith," she replied.

"It's very nice to meet you, Meredith."

"Can we do away with the chit-chat? I've got some errands I need to take care of."

Hale chuckled.

"First, I'll have my associate do a quick tour of your house. Make sure that we're all alone."

He nodded to Redfield, who began scouting the small cabin.

There appeared to be only four rooms: a large sitting area, two small bedrooms off the back, and a small galley kitchen. He returned and flashed his boss a thumbs up.

"How long have you lived here?"

"Five years? Maybe six?"

"And do you know why my men were here?

"Probably trying to rob me."

"They were not trying to rob you."

"How am I supposed to know that? I'm a lady living alone in the woods. Maybe they wanted to rape me," Meredith said.

Hale laughed at that.

"My people don't engage in that sort of activity."

"Such gentlemen."

She was starting to irritate him, but he let it go.

He paced around the room, studying its nooks and crannies.

"How do you stay in cocktail onions?" he asked.

"Excuse me?"

"It's an old saying," he said. "How do you eke out a living these days?"

"I do a lot of trading," she said. "Kind of a scavenger."

He retrieved the extra chair from the breakfast table and set it next to the couch where Meredith was seated. Her face was stone, her hands flat against her knees. He didn't like how this was going. She would be tough to break.

A large, irregularly shaped dark brown circle on the

couch caught his eye. Similar streaks ran down the front of the sofa, and a smaller one stained the rug.

"It looks like you took care of some impromptu surgery here," Hale said.

"I don't know what you're talking about."

"That's a lot of blood."

"Oh, I just cut my hand while I was doing some sewing."

"That's quite a bit of blood for a cut on the hand."

"I'm a bleeder. What can I say?"

Hale sighed and blew it out slowly, a bit of a theatrical way of showing his displeasure with his hostage. He did not want to hurt this woman, but she was leaving him little choice. They had to find out what had happened here.

"I don't think you're telling me the truth," he said.

"I don't know what to tell you."

He stood up and towered over her. Hale was a big man, and he was aware that his physical presence could be intimidating to many people. And he was going to take advantage of that now.

"Ma'am, we can do this the easy way, or we can do this the hard way."

A picture took shape in Hale's mind: his men had tracked the woman with the vaccine to this house. She had taken refuge here. Perhaps she was wounded. Possibly, one of her fellow travelers was injured.

But Meredith refused to comply.

"Don't make this harder than it needs to be," Hale said after an hour had gone by.

Meredith's face was bloodied, and her left eye was swollen shut.

Hale nodded to Redfield, who removed a small kit from his backpack. He opened it and set it on the table. Inside lay a series of sharp instruments: a scalpel, a dental scraper, and a large hypodermic needle featured prominently.

"Tell us where they went, or you will suffer like no one has ever suffered."

Meredith scoffed as she gazed at the tools of her imminent torture.

Then she started working her mouth strangely. It looked like her tongue was probing for something.

In a flash, a flash too late, Hale realized what she was doing. Panic flooded his chest. There was some kind of tablet secured in her cheek.

He reached for her chin and struggled to open her clenched jaw, but it was too late. She bit down hard on something and smiled.

Foam bubbled from her lips, and she let out a long, noisy breath. Then her eyes rolled back into her head, and she was still.

Meredith was dead by her own hand.

21

———

June Richards was reviewing the weekly harvest report when Billy Elliot came crashing into her office, virtually out of breath. Usually, she loathed any interruption during the mind-numbing but crucial work of ensuring they would have enough food to carry them through the winter. As usual, he was dressed in jeans and a thick flannel shirt. June wasn't sure he owned any other clothes. He wasn't a very bright man, but he was protective of Riverview. He paused on the carpet, bent over, panting, trying to catch his breath. His face was flush, and a glaze of sweat oiled his ample forehead.

"What's wrong?" June asked.

"It's bad," he said between gasps. "Real bad."

"What is it?" June asked.

"It's Meredith. She's dead."

"What are you talking about?"

"I hadn't heard from her in a few days. She was supposed to bring a load of meds up here but never showed. I went up to her cabin. She's dead, June. Dead."

"Any idea what happened?" June asked, dread squeezing her chest.

Any violent death near Riverview could mean trouble down the road for all of them.

"She was murdered."

He opened his mouth to say something but closed it again.

"Is there something else?"

He nodded.

"What is it?"

"It looks like…"

He paused again and cut his eyes to the floor.

"Spit it out," she snapped.

"Like she was tortured."

"Jesus," June said.

"It was real bad, June," he said.

"Wait a minute. She brought the Fisher woman here, right?"

"Yeah, I think so."

"Huh," June said. "Okay, thanks for letting me know. Get some water and rest for a bit."

He was still panting hard, and for a moment, June thought he might stroke out right there. He was a big man, and that kind of exertion probably wasn't good for him. After a few moments, his breathing stabilized, and he left her alone in her office.

She pushed back from her desk and stood up. She turned to the window overlooking the midway. It was a bright afternoon. The community was busy prepping for winter: canning the fall root vegetables and chopping firewood now that the fall foliage had dropped, leaving behind dry timber. Although the fields grew more fruitful with each passing growing season, the winters were harsh. She took no chances, ensuring they had enough fuel and food for the cold, lean months ahead.

Meredith's death had raced to the top of June's list of concerns. First things first, it was hard to believe the woman was dead. She had always struck June as the consummate survivor, made of a tough bark. Despite multiple invitations to live in Riverview, Meredith had always demurred, preferring the isolation, doing things her way, and never having to answer to anyone. June had respected the hell out of her. If someone had gotten to her, that was very concerning news indeed.

Her unnatural death had come barely six weeks after she'd brought that woman and her kid here. And their vaccine. June was careful not to jump to any conclusions. For now, she had no evidence that the two events were related. Perhaps someone was exacting revenge for her killing of the three scouts, ignorant of the fact that Meredith had brought the pair here. But June's job, if she were to be any good at it, meant considering all possible scenarios, no matter how remote. It was the unlikely scenarios, the black swan events, that bit you in the ass if you hadn't prepared for them.

Because if Meredith's killers wanted the vaccine, then everyone in Riverview was in terrible danger. If she had been tortured, she might well have told them about bringing Rachel here. And the only justification for torturing Meredith would be knowing that their target had the vaccine.

They might be on their way to Riverview already.

What to do, what to do....

These bandits, whoever they were, wanted the vaccine. If Riverview no longer had the vaccine, they would be safe. As it was, June already had grave suspicions about the vaccine's safety. For all its promise, that's all it was. Promise. Poor Alice had nearly cracked her head open after receiving her dose. If you removed the vaccine from the equation, however, there would be no reason for Riverview to suffer.

A plan began to take shape. The vaccine had not been universally welcomed in Riverview. Plenty of folks had been suspicious of vaccines before the plague; the pandemic had done little to change that sentiment. If anything, people had grown more suspicious of anything associated with the old world. After all, look where that had gotten them—life in a planet-sized graveyard. That said, if the vaccine flowing through Alice's veins actually worked, that sentiment could change quickly. She was due in a matter of weeks. The vaccine would have to be gone by then. And even before the baby came, she couldn't just give it away. It had to look real.

And it had to be done so that people wouldn't be heart-broken by its loss. Even better would be pinning the blame for its loss on Rachel herself. Alice's fainting episode might fuel conspiracy theories, convincing some that Rachel had brought death and ruin with her. And until the baby came, she could turn more people against it. That could serve as an effective insurance policy for her. If no one wanted the vaccine in the first place, they weren't likely to hold her accountable for its loss.

She dined alone that evening, thinking of possible options to reach out to these adversaries. It just required a little reverse engineering. News of the attack on Meredith's cabin would spread quickly up and down the river. Gossip still spread like wildfire, even faster than the virus itself sometimes. Human nature never changed. Information was still gold. Information was power. How you used that infor-mation and wielded that power often meant the difference between survival and disaster. The dead men's patrons would have found the site of their demise. And from there, Riverview would appear quickly in their crosshairs.

June believed very strongly that the Medusa pandemic had been God's judgment. Their world had been a wicked one. And God had seen enough. The vaccine, however, was anathema to His word. If humanity had been meant to survive, Medusa would not have continued to aim at their youngest and most vulnerable. God was speaking, and they needed to listen. God was reminding them of his plan. The lesson that God was above all else. It was a lesson they had forgotten. A lesson she had forgotten. But when she had survived the pandemic, when the world was quiet and empty, she had seen God's wondrous beauty as it was meant to be seen.

June had put it off too long, but they had to know what Rachel Fisher carried with her. It was unacceptable. It would not be allowed. Better to put the vaccine in the hands of the godless.

June waited patiently in the lobby of the prison administration building, sitting in an uncomfortable armchair. An old wooden table sat in front of her, covered with old magazines. She leafed through an old lifestyle periodical, intently reading an article about decorating your home for Halloween. Her heart ached. These reminders from the past were always difficult to see.

Getting here had been difficult, but she hoped the journey would be worth it. Her trek had started with discreet inquiries about the identities of the men who had perished at Meredith's cabin. She was met with more brushoffs than information, even when she had offered to pay for the tiniest morsel of intel. That had been instructive in and of itself, warning her that these were people not to be trifled with. Eventually, she had secured a name.

Victor Hale.

But she'd had no idea how to find him.

She had never heard of Hale before her recent work tracking down Meredith's killers. After making contact with an intermediary, she had shown subservience, making it clear that she wanted to make a deal. It had taken quite a bit of time to get to this point. Her travels took her to a trading post ten miles from Riverview; there, she had heard stories of three strange men who had arrived not long before Meredith's death. They were gone now.

It was there she met with Bishop, a man she did know, and it had cost her dearly to convince him to give up what he knew. He drove a bit of a harder bargain with June than with Hale, but that was because he didn't worry about June Richards ripping out his heart and showing it to him.

Further investigation turned up repeated mentions of a prison. Eventually, June narrowed it down to Waterside and another facility farther downriver called Sinner Correctional. Sinner turned out to be home to an all-female order of self-appointed nuns. Not the place she'd been looking for.

She continued north and arrived at Waterside at sunset two evenings ago, where she'd immediately been taken into custody. She was greeted with suspicion and held for fifty hours before she was granted an audience with Victor Hale. It was the farthest she had traveled from Riverview in some time, and she was surprised to see how quickly nature was continuing to take over their world. There just weren't enough of them to push back nature's unrelenting quest to retake everything that man had claimed and erase humanity's very existence. Part of this pleased her. This was

God's work, and God was taking back what was rightfully His.

Boredom had started to set in when a man emerged from a back hallway and gestured for her to follow. He did not say anything. She stood up, smoothed her pants and jacket, and accompanied the man down the corridor.

Her heart thrummed, and her legs felt a little shaky beneath her. The dim hallway pierced through the heart of the building for another fifty feet or so, ending at the door at the passageway's terminus. The young man knocked on the door twice and opened it without waiting for a response.

"He's expecting you," the man said as he gestured for her to enter.

She stepped inside, and he closed the door behind her, leaving her alone in this spacious office. Directly across from her was a large, ornate wooden desk. Behind it, two floor-to-ceiling windows looked toward a rolling hillside and some trees.

A sound to her right caught her ear. She turned to see a man standing against a dark wood-paneled bar, holding a tumbler of dark liquid. He swirled the liquid around and then took a sip.

"I understand you have some information for me."

She nodded.

"Yes. I believe I do."

"Then let's have a chat."

22

Rachel awoke with a start, the echo of a sonic boom rattling in her bones. She sat upright and blinked heavily, twisting the end of the bedsheet in her fingers, unsure of whether she had dreamed the sound or if it had pulled her from her slumber. It was the dead of night; even without a clock, you could tell you were as far from the end of the previous day as you were from the start of the next one.

She sat for another moment, ready to conclude that it had been a dream, when a second, much larger explosion boomed across the Ashby campus. It hit her deeply, down in her soul and bones, as though the detonation had occurred inside her. The world felt like it had shifted off its axis before snapping back into place. She scrambled out of bed, anxious and confused, instantly focused on the safety of Will and the vaccine.

Rachel had been around long enough to know that the wise move was to assume the worst: that Riverview was under attack. She shimmied the backpack onto her shoulder and hustled to her window facing south toward the campus' main entrance. The arched wrought-iron gate was closed, and the moonlight glinted off its black railings.

A desperate scream emerged from the depths of the night. She pulled herself from the window, crossed the room into the hallway, and pounded on Will's door.

"Will, wake up! Wake up now, buddy."

He was also a light sleeper and darted up to a sitting position.

"What's wrong?" he asked sleepily.

"We're under attack."

She left him to get ready; he had seen enough of the world that she could trust him not to dilly-dally. She had a partner in Will now. No longer her ward. It made her sad, but that was the reality. He was never going to have the childhood she had. Truth be told, he was never going to have a childhood at all.

Back in her room, she pulled on her jeans, thickest jacket, and heavy boots. She retrieved her AR-15 rifle from under her bed and slung it over her shoulder. In the drawer of her nightstand was a Glock pistol that found a place in the broad pocket of her jacket.

Like interlocking gears, Rachel and Will were quickly in sync. They reached the hallway together and were on the move. A third explosion shattered the once-quiet night as they reached the family room. It was clear now that Riverview was under attack.

"Stay behind me," she said.

He nodded.

She opened the front door a crack and peered toward the center of campus. Shadowy figures, silhouetted by the moonlight behind them, scampered to and fro in the darkness.

"Follow me," she said. "Administration building."

She handed the Glock to Will; he'd become an expert marksman, and she trusted him implicitly. A long way from his first lesson firing a gun, not long after they'd fled the ruins of Evergreen in Nebraska. He'd missed badly on his first shot, triggering a meltdown of epic proportions. Now, he could hit a knot in a piece of wood from fifty yards and field strip just about any weapon in his sleep.

She unslung the AR-15 as they ran alongside the edge of the house. As they neared the midway, the intensity and volume of gunfire increased.

"Mom," Will whispered harshly, tugging at her elbow. "Look."

She glanced back and followed his pointer finger. A pair of black-clad figures wearing masks and balaclavas had reached her door. They all wore masks and balaclavas. She let out a sigh between clenched teeth. Better than even odds that these attackers were here for the vaccine. Which meant someone knew it was here.

It would never end. The hunt for her would never end. The attacks would never end unless she ended them. If they could get through this night, she would vaccinate any woman who offered up her shoulder. There would never be a perfect time. There would always be skeptics, those who would simply not believe that the precious vials she carried with her offered them salvation.

She had been such a fool. All this time had been wasted. Her entire line of thinking had been flawed. Yes, the vaccine was precious. But unless it was in people's arms, it was also worthless. A Schrodinger's cat of a vaccine—worthless and priceless at the same time.

She and Will paused behind a large oak tree on the perimeter of the quad. Its trunk was wide enough to cover them while she ensured the last bit of runway to the administration building was clear. She recognized a handful of the people standing guard at the building's perimeter.

"It's Rachel and Will!" she hissed.

"Rachel!" said a familiar voice. It's Samir!"

Samir was flanked by three other men, all bearing heavy weapons. Riverview's arsenal was solid but small. Rachel did not know how big an assault the small community could repel. Now that they were inside the fence, the assailants could do significant damage. She hustled Will across the quad and into the relative cover of the stairwell.

"Any idea who they are?"

Samir shook his head.

She gritted her teeth before giving voice to her next thought.

"They might be after the vaccine," she said. "There was a group headed toward my house. Not sure if they knew I have it."

Samir nodded. He exchanged glances with the other men. In the gloom of the night, small arms fire continued.

"I had the same thought."

"I'm sorry-"

He paused.

"Why would they know to come to your place?"

In the commotion, the thought had not crossed Rachel's mind. But it was a good question with no good answers and several bad ones. He gestured for her to come close.

"There's a safe in my office," he whispered. "It's open. You can store the vaccine in there."

Rachel tensed at that. The thought of being separated from the vaccine filled her with anxiety. She could not afford to lose it. There was no more to be had. This was it. Either she started distributing it, or the curtain would begin to fall on humanity.

Could she trust this man?

Maybe he'd been the one to reveal its existence to outsiders. Who knows what he could have gotten in return? But she didn't think it was him. She'd learned to read people over the years. To understand what made them tick. Understand what drove them. Deep down, in her gut, she knew it wasn't him. His priority would be to protect the vaccine.

One of the men on the stoop stepped forward and fired a burst into the darkness.

"We've got incoming," the man said gruffly.

A burst from an unseen weapon illuminated the darkness. The slug flew so close to Rachel's face that she felt a prickle of heat as it screamed past her and into the chest of one of the other men. The round slammed him against the side of the staircase; he slid down to his bottom, dead.

"Inside!" Samir called out. "Everyone inside!"

About a dozen people emerged from the cover of the stairwell and scampered up the steps. Rachel kept a hand on Will's shoulder as the group made it to the porch and filed inside, one at a time. Samir and Rachel took positions inside the door as the others scattered for cover deeper into the building.

Rachel peered around the corner, picking up at least two, perhaps as many as three attackers in the tree line. She sighted her weapon; one of the assailants had left himself a bit too exposed. She steadied her hand, took a deep breath, and let off a shot. It caught the man's forehead, snapping it back before he dropped to the ground. The other two pulled back fifteen to twenty feet, taking further cover.

Samir grabbed Rachel's arm.

"The vaccine," he said. "Get it into the safe."

Again, she hesitated.

"Listen," he said, sensing her equivocation. "Enter the

combination. Seven to the left. Two to the right. Six to the left. There's a reset button on the back of the dial. Once it's open, hold the button down and pick a new combination. You'll be the only one who knows it."

A sigh of relief. She wanted to trust Samir, but until now, she hadn't gotten there yet. Now she had. He understood her need to keep it safe. He understood that trust was a rare commodity. You only had so much you could scoop out, that you were willing to spoon out. She reached out and placed her hand on the side of his face. It was warm and damp with sweat.

"We can hold them off."

She eased back into the darkness. The building was becoming a second home; she was able to navigate in the absence of light. The office was behind the second door on the left. She moved quickly but carefully into Samir's office, around his exam table, beyond the locked cabinet where he stored Riverview's meager supply of medications.

The safe was in the back of the supply closet, which smelled sharply of ammonia and rubbing alcohol. She dropped to her hands and knees and felt for the dial. She lit a match, using the small cone of light to illuminate the face of the safe. She entered the combination, working quickly. On the final number, the tumbler released, and the door drifted open. Inside, there were a few vials of medication and a box of ammunition. She unzipped the backpack, removed the valise and carefully set it in the back of the compartment. When it was secure, she reached behind the dial, finding the reset button.

Various replacement combinations swirled through her mind, and she had difficulty settling on a new one. This was taking too long. She had to get back to help hold the building. Her finger sat on the button. Enough, she decided.

Enough. Samir's code would work just fine. All her doubts about him dissolved at that moment. She closed the safe's door and spun the dial. Then she tugged on the handle. The door was secure. The vaccine was safe.

After checking her weapon, she hustled back into the office, picking her way back toward the corridor. Sporadic gunfire peppered the night. She edged her way back toward the main foyer. She spotted Samir near the doorway, recognizing his silhouette. He was leaning toward the opening, firing a burst from his weapon.

When his gun fell silent, she reached out and squeezed his left shoulder. He turned his head quickly.

"You're back," he said. "I think we held them off."

"Good."

They waited in silence for another fifteen or twenty minutes. Time lost much of its meaning in the darkness. Occasionally, a murmur in the gloom. The attack had died down, the gunfire easing like a bag of microwave popcorn nearing the end of its cooking cycle. But uneasiness scraped at her insides. Something wasn't right.

"Samir?"

"Yeah?"

"Is there another way into this building?"

"Actually, there is. Why do you ask?"

She ignored his question for a moment.

"Where is it?"

"There's a storm drain under the building."

"How many people know about it?"

"It's pretty common knowledge."

"But would it be easy to find if you were an outsider?"

He cocked an eyebrow.

"No, I suppose not."

"Where's the access point?"

"In my office," Samir replied.

Rachel tensed with worry. She reached for her gun, ensuring that the safety was off.

"Follow me," she said, gesturing toward him with two fingers.

Will got up, but she pointed back at him.

"You stay here. Look after everybody else. Understand? If anything goes bad, you get these people out of here."

"OK, Mom," he replied.

"Let's go."

They tiptoed down the hallway, her heart pounding in her chest.

"What's wrong?" Samir asked.

"Just double-checking something," she said.

The sound of footsteps in the corridor caught her ear. She pinned herself against the wall, trying to blend with it and make herself invisible. They slid along the hallway wall, stopping just outside Samir's office. She crouched low, controlling her breathing. Samir sidled up next to her, staying low and breathing hard. She turned to him and held an index finger to her lips.

He nodded, his eyes wide with fright.

She turned her attention back to the office door. She heard muted whispers of people speaking. There was no doubt now that their attackers had come for the vaccine, and they knew exactly where it was. It was the worst-case scenario. She should never have come to Riverview. This was why she had stayed on the road and lived her nomadic life. The vaccine would be safe nowhere but with her.

Hopefully, she could take the men by surprise before they got to it. She hoped the safe was strong enough to withstand a frontal assault. And if it wasn't, she could only hope the vaccine wouldn't be destroyed. As she listened, the murmurs of their conversation came into sharper focus.

"Set the charge," he said.

A controlled explosion followed a few seconds later.

"Got it!" a voice said in a loud but joyous whisper.

Oh no.

They had the vaccine.

23

They were running out of time.

A half-cocked idea formed in her head, and she acted on it before she could second-guess herself. She rushed into the room and opened fire, taking out the man standing closest to the safe. He dropped with a grunt, removing him from the equation. She turned her weapon to the second man standing to the far left, but her round flew wide. Samir came in behind her and fired, but his rounds missed their marks. The man returned fire, pushing them both back into the hallway.

"To the tunnel, to the tunnel!" the man yelled, obviously surprised by the sudden attack.

They hustled toward the back of Samir's office. The access panel lay flush with the floor near the rear wall. Rachel followed them inside, Samir staying close behind on her left hip. The rattle of the metal grate echoed in the dim office, followed by the heavy footsteps of the men running down the stairs to the tunnel. As the second man dropped in, he fired off another burst from his weapon, forcing Rachel and Samir back to the ground.

Once the coast was clear, Rachel raced for the tunnel, but before starting down the stairs, she felt Samir's hand firmly grip her forearm. "Rachel, wait," he said. "If you go down there, you'll be a sitting duck."

"But they're going to get away," she replied, desperate now and no longer thinking very clearly.

"We'll try to catch them on the backside as they come out."

"How far is it?" she asked.

"About a quarter mile," he replied. "If we hustle, we can get there."

"That vaccine is everything," she said. "Everything. If we lose it, we'll have nothing."

"I know," he said. "I know. Let's go."

They sprinted into the corridor and back out to the main foyer of the building. It was still quiet here. The guns had fallen silent. The attack on the administration building had been nothing more than a diversion. Rachel pushed those thoughts to the side. There would be plenty of time to second-guess her decisions. For now, they still had to get the vaccine. They still had a chance.

"Bobby," Rachel called out as they raced towards the front door. "Give us some cover fire."

Bobby leaned around the doorjamb, letting loose a long volley from his automatic weapon. There was no return of fire. Samir and Rachel stayed low as they approached the door. After another burst from Bobby's weapon, she and Samir booked it down the steps toward the center of campus.

As they ran, the scope of the devastating attack on Riverview came into focus. Bodies lay strewn about the Riverview campus. Rachel felt her heart cave in. She had brought this devastation to these people, and in the end, they would have gotten nothing for it.

Unless she could recover the vaccine

She stayed close to Samir as they sprinted down the midway, headed east toward the perimeter fencing. Her lungs burned in the cold air as they ran, and her quads felt like jelly. She'd once read that a human could maintain an all-out sprint for only thirty to forty-five seconds. Even if she wasn't running for her life, she was running for the lives of all those who would follow her, who would follow Will. She had to get there in time.

Samir's pace was starting to flag. He slowed down, paused, bent over, his hands on his knees, taking huge gulps of air.

"How much farther is it?" Rachel asked in between her own desperate gasps.

"It's just around that bend right there, maybe another hundred yards," he replied.

"Let's go," she said.

They picked up the pace once more. A few moments later, the storm drain came into view. It opened up into a narrow drainage ditch running toward the fence. They were fifty or sixty yards away when the first flutter of movement appeared in Rachel's line of sight. The first man shimmied out, his gun at the ready. Immediately, as he came out, he opened fire, sending Rachel and Samir to the ground to cover themselves. He wore the backpack holding the vaccine, forcing Rachel to hold her fire. The man slid down into the ditch, giving himself more cover. As the man lay down cover fire, the other men eased their way out of the tunnel. Rachel did open fire on them, drawing additional return fire.

The gunfire was heavy and kept Rachel and Samir

pinned down behind the chassis of an old vehicle. She huddled behind the wheel well of the car. The gunfire continued for another ten or fifteen seconds before ceasing abruptly. She gave it a count of ten, ensuring they would have some clearance before she poked her head out above the car.

In the moonlight, she could see the men running for the fence.

"Oh, shit," said Samir.

"What?" Rachel asked.

"There's a hole in that section of the fence. I'm guessing that's where they got in."

"What?" she asked in disbelief.

"Yeah. It's big enough for them to fit through."

"How would they know about it?"

"I don't know."

Someone inside Riverview had given these men extensive intel on how to get inside, get the vaccine, and get back out. They had a traitor in their midst.

Rachel broke clear of the vehicle's cover, sprinting after the men, caring little for her well-being. The game was just about up, if not already lost. As she closed the distance, an engine roaring to life shattered the still of the night. Sounds of men shouting mixed in with the revving of the engine. As they reached the gap, the thump of car doors slamming shut nearly brought tears to her eyes. The truck's engine revved again, and the wheels squealed as the driver hit the gas.

Samir dove to the ground and army-crawled through the opening, exclaiming in pain as an exposed piece of metal fencing dug at his leg. Rachel followed quickly behind him, barely noticing the sharp metal tearing at her skin. They stood up as the truck disappeared into the distance. Samir howled in frustration, emptying his weapon futilely into the darkness as the vehicle disappeared into the darkness.

THE DAY BROKE SHARPLY clear and cold, the sunrise revealing the extent of the horror and the damage the three bandits had inflicted upon Riverview the previous night. Rachel helped carry the dead and the wounded to the clinic, where Samir did what he could for those he could help. The initial count was sixteen dead—sixteen innocent people who had died because of Rachel.

It was the worst loss of life the community had ever experienced. Rachel did what she could with Samir in the clinic, calling back on the medical training her father had passed down to her. Her nursing days were long behind her; it felt good to help these people where she could. Dozens of survivors gathered at the clinic, waiting for word on this person or that one. Rachel could tell they were pushing on Samir's last nerve as he and Megan worked to triage the wounded.

"Let me talk to them," she said. "Maybe I can calm them down."

"That would be great," Samir said. "I need to focus on these patients."

She headed back outside, where a large crowd had formed in front of the administration building.

"Where's the doctor?" one man asked.

"He's trying to help the injured. A lot of people are hurt pretty bad."

"Yeah, thanks to you," one woman called out.

The woman's words were like a knife to her gut, mainly because Rachel agreed with her. She scanned the crowd for a friendly face, but all she saw were tight lips, set jaws, and burning anger in the eyes of these poor people.

"This is all your fault," someone yelled out.

A murmur of agreement followed.

Rachel began to get nervous. These people were mad, and her presence in front of the clinic was making things worse. She needed to slow things down. "Let me go inside and ask the doctor how things are going. I'll be back with an update."

"We've heard just about enough from you," another woman said.

Rachel turned to return to the clinic, but then she froze. Her eyes cut toward the ground.

"I'm really sorry this happened. I am so sorry."

Rachel hustled back inside, intent on escaping a crowd growing angrier by the minute. She wasn't sure they were wrong in blaming her for this nightmare. As soon as the acute phase of this disaster had passed, she would need to decide whether she and Will could stay here. And she already knew the answer to that question. The thought of leaving this place saddened her deeply. She had grown to like Riverview. The stability, the people, the sense of community. Samir in particular. But it looked like that time was coming to an end.

24

———

Rachel drank the last of her tea with a bit of flatbread they had baked. Another long day of work stretched out before them. She had been awake since before dawn, her slumber falling victim to the flash burn of a nightmare rousing her from sleep. Only its barest details remained, the rest of it dissolving like smoke. Something about a shopping mall, but that was all she could recall. The dream had left her uneasy; it was strange that something that had never existed could leave a scar on your mind.

Strange.

She and Will had been here about two weeks now. Two weeks since the disaster at Riverview. Two weeks since the promise of a new home had perished in a symphony of blood. Two weeks since she'd lost the vaccine. All that time, she had looked over it, protected it, kept it safe, and in one moment, it was all gone. And in a morbid twist, she and Will found refuge where this nightmare started. In Meredith's cabin, now vacant because Rachel had brought death to her doorstep.

It was cold outside. They were deep into fall now, closing in on the last page of the calendar. Calendars reminded Rachel of her CalTech roommate, Angelique. She was an astrophysics major from Brooklyn, as brilliant a person as Rachel had ever met. Her parents had died when she was thirteen, and she had raised her twin brothers almost by herself.

They got along well enough. Neither had been big into CalTech's social scene, to the extent that it had one, and they spent many weekend nights watching movies or shows on their laptops. Sometimes, they would order food and watch a movie together, but each woman mostly kept to herself, sitting on her bed, noise-canceling headphones keeping each in her own little world. Angelique was as close to a best friend as Rachel had ever had.

But the calendar.

Angelique had kept a monthly calendar on her desk, and she had a habit of X'ing out each day with a red marker before turning in for the night. Rachel had found the practice morbid, even though there were many more days ahead of them than behind them. Or so they had thought.

"It reminds me not to look back," Angelique had said. "The day is done; all I can do is look forward."

Rachel remained unconvinced.

"It's creepy," she said.

"Agree to disagree," replied Angelique.

Angelique had spent that final summer in Brooklyn, the outbreak's epicenter. As the outbreak grew in severity, they texted frequently. Their discussions had grown increasingly grim, from early thoughts that classes might move online to the unimaginable prospect of the school year being canceled to the brutal reality of the pandemic.

Then Angelique got sick. Rachel last heard from her

during the second week of the pandemic, and her final text message to Rachel remained burned on her brain.

August 13.

1:35 a.m.

Trust in Jesus. Jesus is Lord.

It was three hours earlier in San Diego, so Rachel was still up when the text arrived. Most of Rachel's time was spent glued to her phone, monitoring the rapidly deteriorating situation.

Are you okay, Ang?

No reply.

Over the next hour, Rachel sent her twelve more texts, but she left Rachel on *Read*. Rachel tried a voice call and a video call, but the line would not connect. Rachel never heard from her again.

Trust in Jesus.

Angelique had been deeply religious. It was a topic they steered clear of, as Rachel had little use for organized religion. The church had been important to Rachel's mom and her stepfather Jerry, and she hoped Angelique's faith had brought her comfort in those last days. As the months and years had unspooled, as they had lost track of the calendar, Rachel would think about those sharp red lines intersecting in the squares representing each day of her much-too-short life.

After breakfast, they spent the morning splitting wood. They were about fifty yards behind the cabin. A clear brook cut through this edge of the property. Beyond, the forest stretched toward the horizon. They would have enough wood until Rapture. The work was hard and left her spent before mid-day. Her body was glazed with sweat, and her hands hurt. It was cold; the skies were gray and lacquered with a low cloud ceiling. Rachel had spent no time in the

Midwest before and was still getting used to its wildly variable weather patterns.

"I need to take a break," she said to Will. "You keep going."

He paused his work long enough to nod. She took a seat on a stump and took a swig of water. Even in the cold morning, her body had grown warm. Will's energy seemed limitless. He did not complain, and he did not get tired. A pungent, sour aroma exuded from his body. Puberty was hitting him hard. She made a note to score a stick of deodorant.

After a short break, she got back to work.

"Mom?" he asked.

"Yeah?"

He knelt and adjusted a stack of firewood close to toppling over.

"What happens now?"

There was an emptiness inside her, a void that came from the sudden and violent loss of her life's true purpose. The past years had been difficult, but they were always gilded with a twinge of hope.

"I don't know."

WILL FELL ASLEEP EARLY, leaving Rachel alone with her thoughts. She wandered the house, studying Meredith's life. At the back of the house was a small workroom in which Rachel had spent little time, but it drew her attention that evening.

The square room, which looked like her workshop, featured a window looking north over Meredith's property. The wide strip of land ran downhill toward a thick line of trees. A fast-moving brook wound through the trees before curling off to the east, just out of view.

Several projects were underway, including sewing, various repairs, and meat drying. The faint aroma of sirloin and perhaps Worcestershire sauce hung in the air. Multiple pieces of art adorned the walls, some quite spectacular.

In the corner was a large drafting desk with a wooden chair underneath it. Rachel sat down at the desk and opened each drawer one at a time. In one, she found a stack of letters. She carefully removed them and flipped through the pages. Letters written by Meredith and addressed to someone named Ethan. There were dozens of them, each dating back to the days immediately following the pandemic. They formed a kind of diary, but one done in epistolary form.

Ethan.

She was initially hesitant to read them, but her curiosity got the best of her. There was an old saying that after dying, a person died two more times – once when their name was last spoken and once when someone thought of them for the last time. Their world was harsh, and soon, no one would remember that Meredith had ever existed. If Rachel read them, Meredith would live on a little longer. After all, Rachel was the reason the woman was dead.

She set the first letter on the center of the desk. The paper was wrinkled and the ink had started to fade. A dry brown spot in the upper right corner might have been blood. It was dated September 4 in the Year of the Plague. The pandemic would have been over by then. Rachel was on the road in early September, heading east toward Virginia. She had not yet made the acquaintance of the folks from the Citadel, which would change her life in ways that she could still scarcely believe so many years later.

Dear Ethan, she wrote in blocky lettering.

Another day has come and gone, and I am not sick. I am starting to think that I will not catch it, whatever it is. It has been about a month since we first heard about the virus. It is hard to believe how much has changed. If it had not happened to me, I am not sure I would have believed it. It has been a week since I last saw another human being. I was on a supply run, and we ran into each other at a grocery store. A heavyset man, maybe forty years old. He had a gun but he screamed and ran the moment he saw me. I suppose I should be pleased that he did not remember he was armed. I was, too, of course, but I am not sure I can ever pull the trigger. Time will tell.

Rachel set that one aside and leafed through a dozen before settling on another one to read.

January 6 (? not sure of the date anymore)

It's been five days since the snow started to fall, and it has piled up so high that I can't even open the door. Obviously, I don't need water, but my food supply is starting to run low. I just pop the window open and scoop out all the water I could want. It's really clean now, so there's that—the cleanest snow I have ever seen.

I am very hungry.

Rachel's heart started to race as she put that letter aside, reminded of her own dance with starvation a few years earlier. She would end it all before going hungry like that again. Never had she known such desperate madness, not even when the world had disintegrated around her.

She picked up another letter.

Summer, Year 3

I went to St. Louis, she wrote.

I saw the Gateway Arch! It's covered in vines now, really thick ones that have wrapped around it like a second skin. A completely green arch towering over the city. For all the land-

scaping and urban planning and sustainable growth, in the end, America had simply been waiting to return to nature.

Rachel stacked the letters back together and replaced them in the drawer.

The next drawer down contained a sealed bottle of bourbon. She pulled the bottle out and set it on the desk. It was not a brand she was familiar with, although she had enjoyed bourbon from time to time over the years. Something about the amber liquid made her mouth water.

Hell. Now's as good a time as any for a drink.

Before she knew it, Rachel's feet had carried her out to the kitchen. After finding a suitable tumbler, she carried the bottle and glass to the dining room. She sat at the window and looked out into the dark, its blackness softened by the light of the crescent moon.

The first bourbon went down smooth like it had been waiting for this moment. It washed down Rachel's throat and warmed her stomach almost instantly. She poured a little taller drink, two fingers, maybe three. She took her time with this one, swirling the whiskey in her mouth, trying to pick out the hints of oak and vanilla.

It was gone. The vaccine was gone. She was still having a hard time accepting that. Her entire *raison d'etre*, the most important mission of her life, and she had failed. She looked back down at the tumbler, which, to her surprise, was now empty.

Huh.

She didn't remember finishing the drink, but the proof was there. The bourbon was gone. She poured a third drink, this one about the same size, about two fingers. The alcohol was starting to work its magic now, burrowing its way into her extremities, making her warm. It did relax you, wasn't that the truth of it? Sitting here, the benefits were obvious.

She wasn't clenching her teeth as hard as she had been earlier. See, this was why people drank. It made them feel better. It did wash away your problems. Maybe she'd have a hangover tomorrow, maybe not. She was a big girl; she knew when to stop. Perhaps this was a blessing in disguise. Maybe losing the vaccine was the best thing that could have happened. It was too much for one person. Who was she to play God? Let someone else decide.

Yeah, that was it.

A light rain had started to fall. The patter of raindrops against the windowpanes was soothing. It didn't have to be her, did it? If the attackers wanted it so badly, they were welcome to it. They'd probably do a better job distributing it. Couldn't do a worse job than she had.

But what if they wanted to destroy it?

The thought bubbled up unexpectedly. A little voice from her soul, encouraged by the booze on board now. Shields down, self-censorship down. If they wanted to destroy it, then maybe that's what humanity deserved. If fate or the universe had wanted to give them a second chance with this vaccine, it shouldn't have put all its eggs in the Rachel Fisher basket.

Rachel sat up with the bottle of bourbon for a very long time.

25

Victor Hale sat in his office alone. The door was closed and locked; the blinds were drawn. Lanterns cast a shadowy, sickly yellow light into the room. On his desk lay the prize he'd been hunting for nearly two years: the small valise containing the Olympus vaccine. The case was open, the bottles nestled in the red felt compartments that had kept them safe all this time. It was truly remarkable that the vials remained intact after all this time. Perhaps it was fate. Maybe he was meant to have these in his hands.

The plan was back on schedule. He chuckled a bit at that thought because it reminded him of the villains from the Saturday morning cartoons he'd watched as a child, but it was true. There was a plan, and it was going well. Echo Ridge and Ironwood had recently fallen to the Coalition, although Hale's troops were still working to extinguish a few pockets of resistance in Ironwood.

A knock at the door startled him out of his trance.

"Come in," he called out.

Redfield and Graves, his top two lieutenants, filed into

the room. Their loyalty had remained strong over the years, especially as they entered this period of great change. He tried to lead these people, not rule them. Because if you led them, they would follow. Trying to hold them down or to oppress them cracked the foundation. He didn't want that. Especially not now, not with his final goal starting to come into focus.

He gestured for them to approach his desk.

"Come here; I want you to see this."

The two men approached the desk slowly as though Hale were holding a bomb. Their eyes were fixed on the vials, which shimmered in the light of the lanterns they carried.

"So this is it," asked Redfield.

"This is it," Victor replied.

"Hard to believe," Graves said.

"Believe it. We got it."

He closed the lid and secured the clasps.

"Alright," he said. "Let's get started."

The men retreated to the chairs opposite Hale.

"How many individual communities are there in a hundred-mile radius?" Victor asked. "Anything with, say, more than fifty people?"

"I'll take this one," Graves replied. "We think there may be sixty or seventy. Some with as few as fifty, a handful with a few hundred. Maybe one or two with upwards of a thousand."

Victor's heart raced with excitement. It was happening. A new world. He was going to be building a new world. And after all was said and done, there would be no doubt who the father of their new world was.

He stood up from his desk and poured drinks for the men.

"It's time for us to start expanding," Victor said, handing each man a tumbler of rare scotch.

"Yeah, I thought you might want to talk about that," Redfield said.

"How is this going to work?" Graves asked.

Hale carefully removed one of the vials and held it up. It contained fifty doses of vaccine.

"Because we can offer something no one else can—a future. People have given up. They think the sun is setting on the world. That humanity is about to blow away like dandelion seeds."

Hale paused to sip the scotch. He swirled the smoky liquid in his mouth, savoring its layered taste.

"How many women do you think are in an average community these days?"

"Honestly?" Graves offered. "Maybe thirty to forty percent. Truth is, it's been tough on women, this world of ours."

Hale nodded his understanding. Despondency among women had become common. Despondency about the babies. Despondency about their place in the world. Despondency that men often took what they wanted from them whether they agreed to it or not. It was a harsh reality. Hale did not approve of such treatment of women. But that didn't mean it wasn't happening. Everyone had a story. Women taken, exploited, or vanished.

HALE and his team had been on the road since first light. It had taken them almost three hours to get here, and now the sun was at its peak for the day, soft as that peak was. They were near the solstice, and the days had grown shorter. It was around noon, but it already felt like the day was on its way out. They stopped for a quick bite: some dried meat and stale flatbread. This would carry them over for the rest of the day.

Redstone was their destination today. It was about a hundred miles north of the prison, which would make it the Coalition's most remote colony. Home to about two hundred people, their intelligence put the number of women of childbearing age at about forty. More than most communities, for reasons unclear to Hale. But there were many mysteries in their world. Regardless, Redstone would become one of their crown jewels. These people would be beholden to the Coalition.

So far, their lightning-quick conquest of this part of the Mississippi River Valley had gone relatively smoothly. One town had put up more resistance than Hale was comfortable with, and he was not in a very good mood that day, so its twenty-eight residents had been liquidated on his orders. It was not the outcome he'd wanted. The loss of the three women of childbearing age was regrettable, but the benefit outweighed the loss. It was important for word to spread that resistance was not an option and would not be tolerated.

Within a month, twelve new communities had joined the Coalition. Each surrendered their armories to the fledgling nation, ensuring their decision was permanent. No takebacks. There was some pushback, as he had expected. Not everyone was willing. That didn't stop the Coalition from conquering those communities as well. But most women desperately wanted to have babies. Most men wanted the women to have babies. They wanted the human race to continue.

Hale didn't force a woman to carry his child. They were

not being coerced. They were free to walk away. He always made that very clear. And in the end, it was such a small thing he asked of them. A brief act. It was over in a short time. On the face of it, one might say it was an act not consummated with love. But Hale disagreed. It was love for a baby that would soon be joining them. Love for a baby that would be safe from the horrors of Medusa. Love for mankind.

He checked the gas gauge on the old Ford Bronco. The needle pointed at the halfway mark of the gauge, reassuring him there was enough for the trip home the next day. He eased into town, letting off the gas as he approached its border. The words *A Community of Peace* were etched onto the wooden sign bearing the name Redstone.

There was no fence, no wall to protect the people of Redstone. An old black man stood guard, carrying an ancient shotgun. He was in his mid-to-late fifties. His hair was cut close and was salted with gray. The guard was more for show rather than any display of strength. It was like putting a dog in your house to fend off intruders. Maybe the dog was gentle and harmless and wouldn't bite anyone. But criminals didn't like hassle any more than law-abiding citizens did. It didn't matter if the dog was vicious. You just moved onto the next house. The man held up his hand as Hale came to a stop. Hale's window was down, his elbow propped up on the sill—just a man out for a drive on a Sunday afternoon.

"Can I help you folks?" the man asked as Hale drew alongside him.

His manner was genial, which only made Hale's task harder. He retrieved the handgun tucked in his waistband and shot the man in the forehead—no need for the man to suffer. The shot echoed through the community. Hale replaced his handgun in its holster and grabbed the AR-15 tucked into the gap between his seat and the center console. Then Hale and his two comrades alighted from the vehicle, taking position in front of the hood.

There was movement ahead a little bit farther into the town, but they made no move. These people would come to him. A few minutes later, a young man, maybe seventeen years old, approached them, his hands up in surrender. His eyes shifted from the three strangers at his doorstep to the lifeless body of the guard.

"Please don't hurt anyone else," he said. His voice was high-pitched and reedy. "We have no quarrel with you."

"Who's in charge here?" asked Redfield.

"Governor Burton," replied the boy.

"Get him out here. Now."

"Her."

"What?"

"Governor Burton is a woman."

Hale nearly burst out laughing at the correction.

"Her, then," snapped Graves.

The boy turned and sprinted back toward town. Hale waited ten minutes before the de facto leader of this community appeared. She was a tall, thin woman wearing her silver hair in a long braid. She looked aghast, and she had been crying. That was okay with Hale. Violence was not his preference, but sometimes it was necessary. Besides, the crying told him all he needed to know. If she was crying, the battle was already won.

"What is it you want?" she asked. Her throat was thick with congestion.

Hale spoke for the first time.

"I'm Victor Hale. What's your name?

"Anastasia."

"Anastasia, I am sorry for what we had to do here, but we needed you to know how serious we are."

"All you had to do was ask," she said.

Hale doubted that. People needed to see how serious you were and that you were willing to do what they were not. That was how you got anywhere in this world.

"Be that as it may, we're here now, and now I believe you are ready to hear me with an open mind. And you'll be compensated for your loss."

Her eyes cut toward the body on the ground. The blood had spread into a thick puddle.

"Just please don't hurt anybody else."

Hale laughed at that.

"Hurt anybody else? I'm actually here to help you. I'm here to prevent any more loss of life. Is there somewhere we can talk privately? Trust me, you are in no danger of being harmed today."

"Today," she echoed.

"I don't think you'll have to worry about that. You have my word."

"Fine, we can retire to my office."

As a team arrived to recover the body of their fallen comrade, Anastasia escorted Hale's group to an endcap in a small office park that Redstone used as its headquarters. The quartet sat around a long table in a conference room. The cheap walls were unadorned. A window at the back of the room looked out over a parking lot. There were still cars parked there.

"After today," Hale said, "you won't need to worry about threats from the outside."

"Why is that?" Anastasia asked.

"Because we're going to protect you."

A wan smile appeared on her face.

"Look—Mr. Hale, is it? I won't beat around the bush or play coy with you. What is this going to cost us?"

"The cost?"

"I'm not stupid. There's always a cost."

"You're right. There is a cost, but it's very small. And in the end, you may not see it as a cost at all."

"That does not make me feel any better," replied Anastasia.

"How many babies have died here in the last five years?"

"What?"

"You heard me."

"All of them. You know that."

"But how many? Can you venture a guess?"

Anastasia set her teacup down. It clinked against the small saucer.

"Fourteen. Fourteen children lost."

"What if I told you that no more babies would have to die?"

Her eyes widened at that.

"I'd say that it sounds like you're a Nigerian prince who needs my bank account number."

His two men stiffened with tension. This woman was calling Hale a liar and a con man, but he understood. If he were in her shoes, he would think the same thing. The vaccine was almost too good to be true.

Almost.

He was going to have to lie to her a little bit—just a little white lie.

"Many years ago," he said, "I was in a counterterrorism unit. Bioterrorism, specifically."

Anastasia reared her head back.

"Well, you didn't do a very good job, did you?"

Hale chuckled at that.

"No, no, you're right. We did not. That said, we were working on a vaccine for the virus, but we just ran out of time."

"There was a vaccine," she said incredulously.

"There is," he replied. "But everybody that's left is immune for the most part. There may be pockets of people who were never exposed to the virus that are out there somewhere. But yes, almost anyone still walking around was immune to the virus."

"Except for the babies," she said.

"Yes. Except for the babies."

"But this vaccine would protect them?" Anastasia asked, a spice, a hint of hope in her voice.

"Yes. The protection of the vaccine is transferred in utero. So when the babies are born, and their natural immunity fades, they remain protected."

"My God."

THE FIRST REDSTONE ceremony was scheduled for the following week. Her name was Bethany, and she had been selected by lottery. She was about thirty years old. A high school senior when the pandemic hit. Hale would not have called her traditionally attractive. But that didn't matter. This wasn't about sex. This was about the future. And when history books looked back on this period, the history books that would exist solely because of him, future generations would understand that this had been an act of love—altruism at its very finest.

She entered the room wearing a robe. Hale was already in the bed. Outside the room stood a sentry, ready to pounce if a woman moved against Hale. One of Hale's most trusted men. She was a tall woman, all arms and legs. Her hair hung in a long braid down her back. It was brown but for a streak of silver near her forehead.

"Bethany, my name is Victor Hale," he said.

She nodded at him, but she did not speak.

"I want to tell you how much I appreciate what you're doing," he said.

She scoffed at that.

"Are you kidding me?" she said. "Just hand out the vaccine. That's all you've got to do. You don't have to do this."

She waved her arm at the ridiculousness of it all, this room, the bed. Perhaps he'd been tired. Maybe it had been a long week on the road. But a spark of anger flickered inside him.

"It's because of me that you have this opportunity at all," he snapped. "It's because of me that the human race will go on. No one is making you do this. If you don't want to have a baby that survives, you can turn around and head right back out that door. Fifty other women are ready to come in here and do their duty. To help save humanity."

She did not reply. She stood there, fidgeting, looking down at the floor. And he had her. The pushback perplexed him. He wasn't rough with the girls. He didn't force them. He usually let them lead the way. They understood the importance of this work.

"Couldn't you just jerk off into a little cup?" Bethany asked.

It was a legitimate question, and he had considered it. But he was worried about the sample's chain of custody. He needed to make sure that he was the one. It was a painstaking process. Intake, psychological testing, testing for sexually transmitted infections (difficult but not impossible as demand for such over-the-counter tests had been low), making sure that they were not already pregnant. There were many I's that had to be dotted and many T's that had to be crossed.

Moreover, Waterside couldn't store his samples properly. The natural way was best. It prevented the degradation of his sample and gave them the best opportunity for a viable pregnancy.

"No, my dear, it has to be this way."

She crossed her arms at her chest and looked at him. Hale remained quiet, knowing that each woman had to decide for herself. The choice was theirs alone to the last moment. There was nothing more for him to say.

Then she loosened the robe and let it fall from her shoulders. She went to him in the bed and surrendered to her destiny.

~

26

"**M**om!"

A grunt.

"Mom, wake up."

Another grunt.

"Mom, wake the fuck up!"

This did get Rachel's attention. Her head was pounding, her eyes were glued together, and her body ached, but the cracking pubescent sound of her son dropping the eff-bomb did get her attention. She yawned and smacked her dry lips together. Her mouth tasted like a sick dog had used it for a bathroom.

"Watch your tone with me," she said hoarsely.

Will ignored her.

"You need to wake up."

She was lying on the couch in the cabin's great room, her left hand tucked under her cheek. A light blue blanket covering lay askew. Will must have covered her the night before when she fell asleep.

Passed out.

Fine, she passed out.

It was nobody's business but hers.

Her eyes drooped. She could use a bit more sleep. That was not going to happen out here. Her bedroom, cloaked with dark curtains, beckoned and called. The front room was awash in sunlight streaming in through the bay window. Based on the angle of the sunbeams, it was at least midday and probably well past it. The many chores that needed doing weren't going to do themselves. But she found herself not caring. Her entire adult life had been nothing but one long chore. She was entitled to a bender now and again. After all, she must have been doing something right. Here was her son checking on his mother like a good boy. And good boys checked on their mothers.

Will grabbed her by the shoulders and tugged her into a sitting position. The room spun, and her mouth watered. She heaved once, but nothing came of it. No surprise, given how little she'd been eating these last few days. And whatever she had eaten the night before had likely come up during the night. It had been her SOP these last couple of weeks. A drink or two with dinner. Usually two. That got the evening going. A heavy buzz quickly gave way to blind drunkenness before a final stop at alcohol poisoning.

She leaned forward, placed her elbows on her knees, and waited for the vertigo to pass. Glancing down at the carpet, she saw a circle-shaped stain darkening the corner of the large area rug that stretched from one end of the room to the other.

"You spill something?" she asked Will, her voice cracked and hoarse.

It was an attempt at a joke, a bad one.

"No," he said coldly. "You puked. I cleaned it up."

There was a heft to his voice she had not heard before. The weight of disappointment that accompanied discovering that your parents were just as human as anyone else. Even the one who had walked through hell to keep you safe. For all she had done for Will, he would probably remember cleaning up his mother's puke more than anything else.

She chuckled.

"No fair," she said, her voice barely above a whisper.

"What?"

"Never mind."

The bottle of vodka was wedged in between the seat cushions. It was mostly empty, and hand to God, Rachel could not remember how much she had consumed the previous night—at least half the bottle. But there was plenty to go around. She had to hand it to the late Meredith; the woman had put together a hell of a bar in her time here. One basement wall was stocked floor to ceiling with every liquor imaginable.

As her headache faded, she looked around the room, which felt more lived-in with each passing day. Their lives had settled into a predictable routine. They worked all day, chopping wood, gathering eggs, setting traps, searching for supplies, and fortifying the cabin's defensive perimeter. The place was cluttered with various projects, including sewing and starter plants they would transplant outdoors in the spring.

This was home now. The days of searching for a permanent settlement were behind them. It had been a fool's errand, bringing nothing but misery to her, Will, and those she met. When the day's work was done, they made supper, followed by a board game or cards. After family time, Will retreated to his small bedroom, where he read or painted miniatures, a hobby he had picked up and cultivated when he could. His room was dotted with knights and dragons and wizards and warhorses. The exhaustion caught up with him some nights, and he was out well before midnight.

"What time is it?" she asked.

"Four hours until sunset," he replied.

Half the day was gone already.

"Today's a rest day," she said.

He laughed harshly, almost cruelly.

"We don't get rest days," he said, his eyes glittering with anger. "We have shit to do, and I need you to get up and help me with it."

He was talking to her like she was a child, like he was the parent and she was the out-of-control teenager.

"Don't you dare talk to me that way," she snapped. "I am your mother."

"I don't give a shit who you are."

"I'm taking the day off. I'm an adult. I can do whatever I want."

"Jesus Christ, listen to yourself."

Now he was yelling. She'd never seen him so mad.

"The vaccine is gone," she said mildly.

"So what? Who cares?"

She reached for the vodka bottle. She unscrewed the cap and took a long swig.

"Great. Keep drinking. That's all you're good for now."

The liquid burned down her throat and into her stomach. She wiped her mouth and re-screwed the cap onto the bottle.

"Don't you get it?" she said. "That's it. It's over."

"Why are you giving up so easily? Don't you want to fight? Don't you want to try and find it?"

"I don't know where the hell it is."

"Well, maybe if you got off your ass and stopped drinking, we could do something about it."

Her hand reared back to slap him, but her movements were slow and tired, and he saw it coming a mile away. He tensed up, but he made no move to avoid it. He was going to take it and let his mother slap him with her wildly telegraphed act of violence.

All the fight went out of her at that moment.

"God, I'm sorry," she said.

She began to cry.

Will stormed off.

She reached for the bottle again.

IT WAS LATE. Snow had fallen since mid-morning, blanketing the property with at least six inches. The air was crisp, and the world was silent as the snow absorbed the little ambient noise that their quiet world had created. Rachel sat on the covered porch outside, her trusty bottle of vodka at her side. She was cold but not uncomfortably so. Will was inside, tending to the crackling in the blaze in the fireplace. She could see him through the sliding glass door, poking at the logs. There was a certain peacefulness to his methodical movements. A poke and a bloom of flame. A poke and a bloom of flame. She curled her fingers around the neck of the bottle and took a long swig. Her eyes watered, and her throat burned as the liquor washed down her gullet.

They hadn't spoken since their argument. But that was okay because he always came back around to her. She had to do everything for him anyway. That was on her, okay, that was on her. She probably could've done a better job raising him.

A sound in the distance caught her ear. She got off the couch and moved to the screen, looking south toward the creek. She held her breath and primed her ears, listening for anything out of the ordinary, anything abnormal, anything that might pose a threat to her and her son. Initially, there was nothing but the familiar crack of the creek ice splintering. She started to relax, but then she heard it again. Again, another sound that didn't fit in the usual panoply of natural noises surrounding the cabin. She glanced back inside the cabin, seeing Will still at the fire, crouched low the way kids his age could, with nary a negative effect on their knees, beautifully oblivious to the dangers surrounding them.

Her mind worked to isolate the unnatural sounds from the familiar noises. Her brain worked, separating, cataloging, and finally zeroing in on the sound she knew was unnatural. Someone was out there. Someone was hunting them. Again. It didn't surprise her. It was always going to be this way. She could never rest. She could never relax. She would always be Will's caretaker.

Quietly, she slipped back inside the house, pulling the door closed behind her, careful to remain silent. When Will looked back at her, she held an index finger to her lips.

"Shh," she said. Will nodded.

She took a step towards the end table next to the couch where she kept the handgun. She stumbled a little as she did so, and the room spun slightly. She could not remember how much she had had to drink, but at least her senses were still sharp.

"Someone's out there," she whispered, nodding toward the door.

A strange look of confusion crossed his face. Then, he was the one resting his index finger against his lips.

"Why are you yelling?" he said softly.

"I'm not yelling. Stay quiet."

He sighed, his shoulders sagging, his face almost falling. As she turned back to the door, Will said:

"Mom, it's twenty degrees outside. What are you doing?"

"I'll be fine," she replied.

Once again, Will gestured at her to lower her voice.

"Jesus, how drunk are you, Mom? My hearing's better than yours, and I can't hear anything."

"Yeah, well, I was sitting outside. Something's out there."

She stumbled again, reaching out with a hand to steady herself against the door. She returned to the sun porch, looking attentively out towards the yard, searching for movement in the trees. She remained silent, dead silent. There was someone out there; she was sure of it.

Someone was coming to finish them off, but she wouldn't let that happen. She checked her weapon, her fingers fumbling over the trigger guard as she did so. She unhooked the clasp, secured the door, and gently pushed it open. It squealed ever so slightly, audible to no one but Rachel. She crept onto the porch and made her way toward the wooden stairs leading down to the yard.

Snowflakes stung her face and eyelashes. It was coming down at a steady clip, heavier than she had thought. But strangely, she was not cold. She took cover next to the railing, kneeling for a better look at the property, but still, she saw nothing. Her head was swimming a little bit now. Maybe she had had too much to drink.

Stupid, Rachel. Very stupid. Good way to get yourself killed.

The joke was on them, though.

There was nothing here worth taking. She had nothing left to offer. Their attackers had taken everything she had.

"I know you're out there," she yelled, her voice echoing off the blanket of snow.

Silence.

"Show yourself!" she howled. "Be a man!"

She staggered into the yard, kicking up little puffs of snow as she went down to the creek—still nothing. No shadows. No rustling of the leaves. The creek was a few yards ahead of her at the bottom of a gently sloping embankment. A wide clearing opened up on the far side of the creek, bordered by a thick cluster of woods. Rugged, inhospitable terrain, almost impossible to navigate. She would check the clearing and then turn back for home.

As she side-stepped her way down the embankment, her back foot slipped from under her, and she lost her balance. She struggled to stamp her right foot down, but that, too, lost its purchase. Her weight carried her over to the side, and she fell to the ground and slid toward the water. The grade here was sharper than she remembered, the ground slick with compacted snow. Her head struck a rock near the creek, and pain lit her body up. She did not lose consciousness, but the blow had stunned her into a sort of paralysis. Nausea swept up inside her, and she vomited, the evening's libations coming up in a rush.

"Mom!" a small voice called out.

And now she was hallucinating because what the hell was Will doing out here in the cold and the dark? He was just a little boy, and her job was to keep him safe. He was too young and weak and naïve and dumb to survive this world.

As she pushed herself upright, surely looking graceful on her bottom, her legs crossed under her, Will appeared at the top of the embankment. Standing there, his hand wrapped around a young sapling for support, he looked tall and strong. It was a trick of the eye, given that he was on higher ground, but he looked like a man to her for the first time.

"Are you trying to get yourself killed out here?" he asked, his voice dripping with disappointment.

And Rachel Fisher began to cry.

27

Two weeks had elapsed since the attack on Riverview. So much had been lost. The community was quieter now, more somber, nothing like the happy place Samir had come to love these past few years. A pall had fallen over the place since the night those men had come and destroyed so much, taken so much. It was a quiet he didn't like. A dismal, gray quiet. The type of silence that made you wonder if even worse things were in the offing, into which you packed your anxieties and dwelled on them. A reminder of what the world was really like now.

People got up, went to work, did their chores, and took care of their business with a bare minimum of discussion. Then they retreated to their homes, drew the blinds, and sat and waited for the next day. Not that Samir could blame them. This had been the worst tragedy many had experienced since the pandemic itself. The indiscriminate shedding of blood. Gone was the excitement and hope they had felt after Rachel had arrived at their doorstep. It was all gone, dissolved like morning mist.

The clinic was slow that morning, which surprised Samir as traffic was usually steady. There was always something to treat: injuries, chest pain, stomach upset, weird sores and lesions, malnutrition, and dehydration, and occasionally, subtle hints of something more ominous—cancer, heart disease, or one of the countless maladies that had stalked human beings before the pandemic and continued to do so long after it.

Cancer was the worst. He could do very little about it, assuming he even caught it. Which he rarely did. There was no imaging equipment, no advanced lab tests he could order. There hadn't been many, but there had been a few, and they had been awful. The fatigue, the loss of appetite, the constellation of strange symptoms. Then, months or weeks or sometimes even just a few days later, the patient would crash, and all he could do was offer palliative relief until they passed from this world to the next.

The lull in patient traffic gave him time to think. He retreated to his small office, hung his stained white lab coat on the hook on the door, and sat in the creaky old chair at the desk. It was an abomination of a chair, but he didn't bother replacing it. He rocked back and forth gently, playing the night over in his head. He doodled on a notepad, drawing a series of concentric circles.

The attackers were so quick and precise that the entire assault was over in less than fifteen minutes. They knew where to hit them, about the weaknesses in their perimeter security, and, most alarmingly, exactly where the vaccine was. Such detailed intelligence left only one conclusion.

Someone in Riverview had sold them out.

He had suspected as much even as the attack was underway. It had been inevitable; her cargo was too valuable, its existence too explosive to remain secret for long. But like

Rachel, like many of Riverview's denizens, he believed that the benefit outweighed the risk. How could it not?

"The future of humanity," he muttered softly.

The recognition that he was talking to himself made him chuckle. He leaned back in his chair and stretched, savoring the release of the tight muscles in his back. As he took a deep breath, it occurred to him that perhaps the vaccine was not lost. There was a traitor in their midst; there was no doubt about this. This person had to face justice.

But there was also opportunity.

Identifying the traitor could lead them back to the vaccine.

But the investigation was moving slowly to the extent it was moving at all. June Richards had spent more time consoling the victims than trying to figure out who'd been behind this heinous attack. Riverview's security chief, Jeff Rollo, had died in the attack, and no one seemed interested in stepping into his shoes. It reminded Samir of the adage that people waited for someone else to step up. Even if no one ultimately did. There was always that hope someone else would.

Well, he would step up. He would figure out who had precipitated this atrocity. A chill of anticipation ran up his spine as he committed to this critical task. For years, he'd felt helpless, simply going through the motions, doing what he could to ease the suffering, the pain, the hurt, to heal the sick and the infirm. It seemed like theater, a prologue to this.

No time like the present.

He made his way back to the clinic. The scene of the crime was as good a place to start as any. They had cleaned up the mess from the attack, which was probably a mistake. Evidence that might have shed light on the traitor's identity was now lost forever. The dead attacker had been buried at the back of their small cemetery with no fanfare. Samir and June had agreed on this quietly; it was the best option from a public health perspective. Cremation was beyond their capabilities, and dumping the body in the woods would create its own set of problems.

This was his first good look at the safe; in the chaos of the attack and its aftermath, he had not even considered how they had gotten inside. It was still open, its door still hanging askew. It was painfully, regrettably empty. He knelt and examined it closely. The unit was completely intact. The attackers hadn't forced their way in. This he found surprising. But he distinctly remembered them discussing setting a charge to blow the safe. In the chaos, it hadn't occurred to him that blowing the safe likely would have destroyed the vaccine. His fingers found no evidence of damage to the casing. The locking mechanism was still intact.

As a test, he closed the door and locked the safe again. The door was smooth and intact; it had not been damaged. Then he spun the dial to each notch corresponding to the combination: seven, nine, twenty-six. The safe opened easily. The attackers had known the combination to the safe; someone had given it to them.

Only three people in Riverview had known it.

Rachel.

Himself.

And June Richards.

THE REST of the day passed by in a haze. Samir saw a few patients that afternoon. One had heartburn, easily treated with an expired antacid. Will's friend Jade had an ear infection, and the third patient had developed a case of food poisoning. A short inquiry revealed that she'd eaten some beans left out overnight. All easily treatable maladies. It gave him the time to chew on the knowledge that June Richards had betrayed them. He could not believe it. The woman that they had entrusted their safety with had cost them a dozen lives.

Part of him wanted to march down to her office and confront her. But acting hastily was not in anyone's best interest. He needed to handle this correctly. June was crafty, a seasoned politician, and if he wasn't careful, he could find himself blamed for the betrayal. That he had no motivation to betray Riverview would matter little if that narrative took hold in the community. If June accused him first, the burden would fall to him to prove his innocence; even if he succeeded, the seed of doubt would thrive. It wouldn't take much. An accusation that their attackers had promised him a healthy reward. For something as valuable as the vaccine, the possibilities were endless.

As darkness fell, Samir decided to call it a day and locked up the clinic. He checked the supply of narcotics, making sure that the actual inventory of these addictive pills matched the count in the logbook. Megan would double-check in the morning, offering the necessary controls to ensure the pills remained accounted for. He rarely prescribed them, saving them for the most egregious injuries.

He returned to his small living quarters, reflecting on his time in Riverview. He'd been here now ten years. He'd spent ten winters here, shepherding these people, tending to them, trying to keep them as healthy as possible in a world that made it very difficult.

A light snow fell, dry and utterly silent as it dusted the

ground. The previous week had been bone-chillingly cold, so the snow accumulated almost instantly. He turned toward the cafeteria, hoping to catch the tail end of the dinner service. He had not eaten all day, and hunger came upon him in a rush.

As he neared the cafeteria, he noticed a figure rushing toward him in a sprint. He tensed, his mind immediately flashing back to the night of the attack. The person was waving a hand wildly, desperate to capture his attention.

"Dr. Samir!"

He recognized the voice instantly. It was Jade.

"Over here, Jade."

She broke back into a run, closing in on him with the easy speed of a teenager blessed with an athletic build.

"It's Alice!" she said breathlessly as she drew near him. She knelt over and put her hands on her knees. Her cheeks had reddened in the chilly air.

"She's going into labor."

Samir's stomach flipped.

It was time.

28

———

Rachel slowly came to. The first sensation she detected was pain. A throbbing, dull ache at the back of her head. She was on her back, cloaked in a blanket. The thought of moving was an unpleasant one, so she remained still. Just the idea of it made her feel nauseated. Her body felt tight and stiff, as she'd become accustomed to. She couldn't recall when she'd started feeling like an old lady getting out of bed. There was a time when not everything crackled or popped, and evidently, that time had passed.

Rachel's head was still smarting at the spot the rock had clipped her, but she had survived the experience not much worse for the wear. Thanks to Will, of course. If he hadn't been keeping an eye on his mother, she might have frozen to death by that creek. That was a fact. For the first time in their shared existence, she'd had to rely on Will for her survival. It marked a new phase in their relationship and the end of the old one.

She touched her hand to the laceration, wincing as her finger brushed against the tender spot. The bandage had come loose on one side. She went into the bathroom and carefully removed the other side, still bound to her skin. The gash was about an inch long and almost deep enough to have caused her real problems. It had crusted over several times, but finally, it was starting to heal. A nasty scar would form there, reminding her of her drunken brush with death for the rest of her days.

The snow had become heavy during her recovery, and ten fresh inches covered the ground when the snowstorm had pulled away. After a quick breakfast and a cup of hot lemon water, she began clearing the path in front of the house. By the time Will woke up and stumbled outside, she was halfway done with the sixty-foot walkway. She was finished by the time the sun had peaked for the day. Will offered to help, but she declined; he had done enough during her bender. She was starving, however, and she accepted his offer to make them lunch. She peeled off her heavy coat and sat at the wooden table with her son, and they ate quietly. She didn't say much, embarrassed by her recent behavior.

She opened her mouth to say something, but Will's eyes turned sharply toward the window. Something had caught his eye, and she tensed up, worried that someone was making another attempt on their lives.

"Hey, it's Dr. Samir," he said. "And Jade!"

Rachel turned to the window, and sure enough, the doctor and the young girl were approaching on cross-country skis. Behind him was the young woman who had bewitched her son, even if Jade had looked at Will as nothing more than a younger brother. She better have. Will was only fourteen. As for herself, she ignored the sensation of her heart racing in her chest. Rachel tucked the stray locks of her hair behind her ears, feeling a bit like a silly schoolgirl, but she couldn't help herself. She wanted to look good for him.

Samir paused at the edge of the snowpack and unsnapped his boots from the skis. He planted the skis in the deep snow and stomped onto the walkway, clearing snow from his shoes. He caught them watching him through the window, and he waved with a smile. He looked genuinely happy.

"I'm going to let them in," Will said.

Rachel nodded. She waited patiently at the door while Will welcomed their guests to the house. There were awkward greetings before they paired off. Samir and Rachel sat at the table while Will and Jade played outside in the snow. Rachel watched him through the window, loving how he was adjusting to life in the boonies. Maybe their lives would always be like this: nomadic, solitary, moving from place to place. She hoped Will was made of stern stuff, hard stuff that would carry him through the tough years ahead. The years were always tough; that's just how it was in their world.

"It's good to see you again," Samir said, drawing her attention away from the window.

"You too."

A moment of silence followed and threatened to widen into awkwardness.

"What brings you out here?" Rachel finally said.

"Well, Jade wanted to see Will, and honestly, I wanted to see you."

She wasn't sure what that meant. The kiss still hung between them as an event of great import that neither wanted to address.

"How are things back in Riverview?" she asked.

It was a good topic to keep the discussion moving and prevent things from sliding into weirdness.

"Well, to be honest, things got dark. It's probably best that you came out here."

"Yeah, that's what I figured," Rachel replied. "They blamed me, and they were right. It was my fault."

"No, you don't understand. Things have changed."

"What do you mean?" she said.

"Alice."

Rachel's heart stopped. Alice's pregnancy had been atop her mind since they had left Riverview.

"Did she have it?"

"She did."

"And?" Rachel asked hesitantly. Everything depended on Samir's reply. She found that she was holding her breath.

"It worked," Samir said, his voice bright, full, and happy.

"It worked," she repeated.

"Yeah," Samir chuckled to himself, thinking back to the week that had transpired since the birth of Alice's baby. "She's eight days old now."

"She?"

"Caitlin."

"Caitlin," repeated Rachel.

Repeating his message seemed to be all she could do. Then she heard the name as it rolled off her tongue. The baby was still alive; the vaccine had delivered.

Caitlin.

Not surprisingly, Caitlin's delivery had been unremarkable. Bringing babies into the world had never been the problem.

Virtually all the doomed babies were born healthy, coming out pink and screaming. Rarely was a newborn symptomatic at birth. In those first hours, the babies were still enjoying the protection of their mothers' immunity.

Regardless, the virus was insidious, and the babies were born doomed. Medusa almost always announced its presence in the first forty-eight hours, seventy-two hours at the maximum. The cough arrived first. It was a cute little hacking thing that ultimately deepened into the lung-stealing cough of Medusa. Fever quickly followed, and from there, it didn't take long—death, as certain as night following day.

That had been the longest stretch of Samir's life. The first three days had been a death watch, as it always was. He wouldn't dare get his hopes up, even knowing Caitlin had the vaccine on board. It was asking too much, a leap of faith he was unwilling to make just yet. He didn't know exactly when he'd let himself start to hope. Maybe around day four, when little Caitlin was still trucking along, nursing, doing all the things that little newborns should be doing, and none of the terrible things newborns should not have been doing.

He checked her temperature every hour on the hour and recorded the readings in the logbook. Every reading was normal. Megan insisted that he sleep, and finally, on the second day, he took a two-hour break to get some shuteye, demanding that he be woken up if there was any change whatsoever in Caitlin's condition. But she continued to thrive, looking pink, healthy, and wiggly. Sometime on the afternoon of the fourth day, he let a little hope through the blinds, starting to believe that Rachel Fisher had, in fact, brought them salvation and delivered them from damnation.

Samir was not a religious man—he never really had been. Religion had never clicked for him, as he was always hunting for rational answers. Proof, evidence, and certainty were the foundations of his intellectual curiosity, but those things were lacking in the world of faith.

Alice had been remarkable. Once the baby was out, he could see it in the woman's eyes, desperately wanting to know if the vaccine had worked. But holding back, simply keeping an eye on her infant daughter, not sure if it was a child or just a time bomb waiting to go off.

The ninety-six-hour mark came and went on a Thursday evening. It was bitterly cold under a clear sky, millions of stars shining down on them. He went to Alice's room, terrified that Caitlin would start running a fever, and he'd have to give her mother the bad news he always assumed he would be giving her. His heart was racing, and his palms were sweaty. And he wasn't sure he would get a correct temperature assessment just by using his hands.

He wrapped his fingers around her skinny little legs, but he was unable to tell if they were warm with fever. His internal thermometer wasn't functioning correctly. His mind was racing, unsure if he was feeling a normal temperature or just wishing he was.

"May I?" he asked Alice, holding his arms out for Caitlin.

Alice handed the child over to him, her eyes wide with fright and anticipation. He kissed Caitlin on the forehead with a gentle peck of his lips, finding nothing but cool skin. There was no fever. He listened to her chest. There was no rattling, rales, or signs or symptoms of respiratory problems. Her heartbeat was strong, her eyes bright, and she was feeding incredibly well.

"Mom," he said to Alice, "we might be in the clear."

And Alice had wept.

With each passing hour, Samir became increasingly confident that the baby would survive. No child he'd ever treated had made it three days without any symptoms. And now they were into the fourth day. Four days became five; five days became a week. And that was when he decided to visit Rachel. Because the birth of baby Caitlin wasn't the only news he was bearing.

He had to tell her about June Richards. He had to tell her what she had done.

"But that's not the only reason I'm here."

His voice was grim.

"I know who betrayed us," he said. "I know who gave up the vaccine."

"What?"

He held up a finger.

"I thought they had blown the safe open to get inside," he said. "I heard them talk about setting the charge before the explosion. But when I checked it the other day, there was no damage to the safe. No attempt to break into it. They had known the combination. And only three people knew it. You. Me. And…"

"June," Rachel said.

Rachel covered her mouth with her left hand. She couldn't say she was entirely surprised, but knowing that this woman had cashed in humanity's future for God knows what end still burned. Then Rachel stood up quickly.

"Wait a minute," Rachel said. "If she's the one that gave up the vaccine to them, she might know where it is. She might know where they've taken it."

"That was exactly my thought," Samir said.

"I've got an idea," Rachel said.

29

The plan was relatively simple, which was how Rachel liked it. The more complicated an endeavor, the more likely it was to fail. If just one little segment went awry, failure quickly followed. By the time Rachel and Samir had worked out the details of the gambit, the sun was setting. It was too late to make the risky trip home, so Rachel and Will welcomed their first overnight guests. Will and Jade worked all day and crashed hard after dinner. Jade slept on the floor in her room. Her assessment of Jade's feelings toward Will remained unchanged, but she didn't think it was wise to tempt fate with teenage hormones.

With the kids settled, Rachel and Samir returned to the great room, which glowed warmly with the light of candles. Samir sat on the couch while Rachel lingered by the bar.

"Can I fix you a drink?" Rachel asked, really thinking about her desire for one. She didn't like feeling this way. She wanted to drink, but she wanted someone to drink with. That had to be an improvement.

"No," he said. "Not much of a drinker."

"Oh," Rachel said.

"Don't hold out on my account, though."

She ran her thumb across the worn wood of the bar, wanting so much not to want a drink but finding herself wanting one anyway. Samir caught her eye, and a look of understanding crossed his face. He got up and crossed the room.

"You know, it's a wonder we're not all meth addicts," he said softly, placing a hand on her shoulder.

Rachel chewed on the corner of her lip, unsure of whether she was glad or embarrassed that Samir knew.

"The human mind is a remarkable thing," he continued. "But it has its limits."

Rachel's throat tightened the way it did before she cried, but she did not want to shed a tear right now. She did not want to cry in front of Samir.

"I did a psych rotation during my residency," he said. "And you know what I learned?"

She shrugged her shoulders, her gaze fixated on the half-empty bottle of vodka.

"That we're all a little mentally ill to some extent," he said. "No one is in perfect physical health, after all. Lactose intolerance, allergies, eczema, a million different physical ailments that plague the human race, most of them minor, but any one of which can interfere with your daily life."

He tapped the side of his head with two fingers.

"Why would we think the mind is any different?"

He went on.

"Mental health is as critical to survival as physical health. But mental health is different. It affects our perception of reality. And it's molded by internal and external factors. So, for example, you may be hardwired for anxiety, set like that at the factory, but your childhood experiences can help determine how much of an impact that will have. If your parent is calm and collected, you'd have a much different experience than someone whose mother was a nervous nelly."

"What are you getting at?" asked Rachel.

Because if he didn't get to the point soon, she would just as soon have another drink, her promises to eschew the bottle be damned.

"We were all a bit wacky before the pandemic," he said. "But then Medusa came along, and it blew everything we knew about mental health to hell. No one in human history has ever experienced what we went through, what we are still going through. And our minds simply couldn't process it. I can all but guarantee you that every person alive today has diagnoses of severe PTSD, major depression, anxiety, and probably a dozen other mental health conditions. All of which are basically untreated."

He nodded toward the bottle.

"So don't feel bad that you've looked for ways to self-medicate."

His eyes cut to the floor.

"I know I have," he said. "Virtually every single person has."

It was true. And it wasn't something he actively discouraged. Survival of his community was the primary consideration. If they were pickled, so be it, as long as they were alive. As for him, this was another day sober, and every day was a battle—a choice not to pour a drink. He had not had a drink since Rachel's arrival at Riverview.

"I can't afford to be like this," she said. "I have to think about Will."

Samir chuckled at that.

"Exactly. You have it even harder. It's one thing to mourn

all the babies that have been lost. It's another thing to actually raise a child in this godforsaken nightmare."

And it was a nightmare. Even if this vaccine proved their salvation, it was a promise for future generations. Their job would be to get them to it. So not only had they had to live through the horror of watching society collapse, of watching every single person they had ever known die, but they would not be around for humanity's rebirth, assuming it occurred at all. They were the dark, cursed, haunted bridge between the two worlds. It wasn't fair, not by a long shot, but that was what God, karma, or the universe had decided would be the fate of people like Rachel and Samir.

"How are we supposed to make it through this?" she asked.

"We have to rely on each other," Samir replied.

"I've never been good at that," she said.

Being mother to Will had been the great joy of her life. A mother's love was instant and eternal and, quite frankly, irrational. Some nights, she had lain awake, wondering if Will's existence had been worth its cost – the end of the world. And every time, God forgive her, she had landed on the same answer. An unequivocal yes. She would live through a dozen pandemics if it guaranteed her Will. Was that selfish? Absolutely. Did she care? She did not.

But so many other burdens chipped away at her, breaking off tiny pieces one at a time. She had never trusted anyone else. People meant well, but most did not share her demand for perfection in all things. The slightest slipup could mean the difference between life and death. Back in Evergreen, she had been fanatical about checking their stores of ammunition, supplies of propane, and the integrity of the canned goods that kept them alive. She did it to the point that it turned people against her. But she didn't care.

That had followed a near-disaster involving contaminated food. Rachel had been on trash duty during one dinner service. By chance, an empty can of baked beans had fallen out of the waste container; Rachel immediately noticed the odd bulge on the side of the can, its contents already mixed with the tray of beans on the buffet line. The bulge was a clear indicator of the presence of botulism spores, one of the deadliest toxins known to man. She screamed toward the service line, finding a woman carrying a small bowl of beans on her tray. She had slapped the tray out of Marilyn's hands, sending her lethal meal clattering harmlessly to the ground. Had she not noticed the can, a stroke of luck that defied logic, most of the population of Evergreen would have died that night.

They were standing close together now, with Samir at a slight angle, so their hips were nearly touching.

"You can rely on me," he said.

She looked up into his dark brown eyes, feeling weak-kneed with anticipation and anxiety. They were not at the point where a kiss was inevitable, but they were very close to it. Neither had looked at the other's lips, their eyes focused on one another. Their first kiss was never far from her mind.

"We have to get this vaccine back," she said softly. "We have to."

"We will," he said.

"How do you know?"

"Because I've been living in a fog. Once we knew about the babies, the world became unreal. I could manage to live through the apocalypse, but the knowledge that it had been for nothing, that we were just the final lights flickering out, was almost too much to bear. But now? Now you've given me life. You've given me hope. And I will die to get it back."

His eyes cut away from hers. The moment of romance had passed, and that was okay with her. If he had kissed her, she would have kissed him back. It would have been good, of that she was certain. And in the end, it probably would create more trouble than it was worth, as affairs of the heart often did.

"I've seen terrible things," he said. "I've done terrible things to survive."

"We all have," she said, recalling her own laundry list of things that haunted her dreams and fractured her sleep.

"With this vaccine, we can make sure future generations never have to see or do those things again."

30

They reached the outskirts of Riverview around noon the following day. Because the plan depended on secrecy, she and Will would camp a mile outside the town wall while Samir and Jade returned to town. It was cold, the chill like a tangible force reaching inside you, lacquering your insides with ice.

"If this works," Samir said, "I'll be back by the end of the day."

Rachel and Will got to work building a fire as Samir and Jade skied out of view. Their presence here would raise no alarm; travelers frequently camped along main thoroughfares. Jade and Samir said little, the short trip silent but for the susurrations of their skis knifing through the snowpack before it brought them to Riverview's main gate, which was still undergoing repairs in the wake of the attack.

The sentry, Tiffany Davenport, waved him and Jade through. They skied inside the perimeter, pausing to remove their skis now that they were inside the town, where they could negotiate its clear paths on foot. As they shed their gear, Jade spoke for the first time.

"You sure about this?" she asked.

"No," he replied. "But it's worth the risk."

"Need me to come along?"

The girl's bravery touched him, but he refused to put her in harm's way. He was pretty sure he knew how June would react, but there were no guarantees.

"No," he said. "You run along home."

She reached out with a clenched fist. He tapped it with his own.

"Be careful."

He nodded.

"Not a word to anyone."

"Believe me," she said, "I know."

He watched her go, thankful for her, confident she would be an important part of Riverview's future. As she melted into the ebb of the afternoon crowd, he turned toward Alice's dormitory, where she lived in a suite with three other women, wanting to pay her a quick visit. Notably, the baby's father had not been local. Alice had been with him only once, meeting him at a regional trading fair. His name was Travis, but that was all she knew of him. Incredible that this random drunken dalliance would bring them to this point.

Alice answered the door; her baby snuggled against her mother's chest. A hand towel was draped over Alice's shoulder, stained with the residue of infant spit-up—the sort of thing you expected to see in a newborn home. Alice was dressed in pajama pants and an oversized sweatshirt. She looked tired, her hair tied back in a messy ponytail, but an easy peace softened the edges of her face. It filled Samir's heart with joy.

"Hey, there," Alice said.

The baby was making adorable cooing noises.

"Hi, Alice. Is now a bad time?"

"Not at all," she replied.

The big smile on Alice's face told him all he needed to know. The baby was doing okay. Eight days old now and still healthy. It was hard to believe, even with the evidence before him. He wished he had the equipment to conduct a proper examination of baby Caitlin's blood. The notion that microscopic machines were now on patrol inside her body was straight out of science fiction.

Alice invited him in, and they sat in the common area. The suite was quiet.

"How's it going?" he asked.

"Really well. She's not much of a sleeper, but that's okay. Hungry little thing."

He chuckled.

"What?" she asked.

"All these years, I've done nothing but give new parents the worst possible news, and now, just sitting here talking about sleeping and feeding schedules, and it's about the best thing I've ever heard."

"Would you like to hold her?" she asked.

"Please."

She stood up and carried the baby to him. Samir cuddled Caitlin in his arms and gently rocked her back and forth. Her eyes were open, bright, and alert, seeking out the world around her. He looked down at her and then up at Alice, noticing a strong resemblance between mother and daughter. He was glad for that.

"I wonder if I should try to find her dad. He has a right to know. It was just one of those things. I didn't think I'd get pregnant."

"Do you want to find him?"

She nodded.

"He was nice," she said. "I think I owe it to him."

"Well, I can help you start looking for him. Have you had many visitors?"

"A few. People have been very respectful. When I go out for walks, though, she draws a bit of a crowd."

Baby Caitlin started to fuss, so he stood up and handed her back to Alice.

"Okay, I need to be pushing off," he said. "I just wanted to see how you all were doing."

"Thank you."

He was dreading leaving, dreading the imminent confrontation with June. He would much rather have stayed here and held baby Caitlin for the rest of the day. It filled him with life, with hope, with joy, but he had work to do. Important work for the future of Riverview.

"You come find me if you need anything," he said. "Day or night, it doesn't matter."

She nodded.

After tousling Caitlin's fine blonde hair, he stepped back outside. The door closed behind him with uneasy finality. He was on his own. Now, he was entering a world of deception and subterfuge, utterly alien to him.

The door to June's office was ajar when he arrived ten minutes later. She was working, her eyes down on one report or another. She didn't sense his approach, so he rapped gently at her door. She looked up and gestured for him to come in.

"Hey, Samir," she said.

His heart was pounding, and his mouth felt like a desert. He wasn't cut out for this kind of work. But he had no choice, and so he pressed on.

"June."

She held up a stack of papers.

"Riveting reading here," she said. "The latest food supply report."

Winter was tightening its grip on the area, and the food stores were running dry. People relied heavily on the potatoes, onions, and other root vegetables that emerged at the end of the growing season.

"How are we doing?" he asked.

His interest was genuine, June's treachery notwithstanding.

"Not bad," she replied. "About the same as last year. We should be good through the winter."

"Good."

"So, what can I do for you? I have a lot of paperwork to get through today."

He bristled at her dismissiveness. The woman had betrayed them all, and she was treating him like a nuisance.

"It's about Rachel."

June's face tightened.

"What about her?"

Her voice was coated with contempt.

"She wants to see you."

"She's here?"

"She came to the gate and asked to see us."

"Have you talked to her?"

"I have," he said. "I wanted to see if it would be worth your time."

Her face softened a bit at that. It seemed June liked the idea of someone running screens for her. It made her feel important, which made Samir like her even less, which was saying something given what she had done.

"What did she have to say?"

"That she has more vaccine."

June's eyes widened with shock.

"What?"

"She'd hidden it away."

"Why is she telling you now?"

"She wants back into Riverview. She wants her son to be safe."

"Where is this vaccine?"

"With her."

"You've seen it?"

"She said she would only show it to you."

June sat back in her chair, stroking her chin.

"Do you believe her?"

"I do."

June stood up and turned toward the window over-looking the midway. The market was bustling, and it looked as if most of the population was out there today.

"The vaccine put us in terrible danger," she said.

Thanks to you, he thought.

"But it worked," he said. "Think of all the good we can do with the ones she has."

"Was it worth the loss of so many of our people?"

"No one needs to know this time," he said.

Sweat glazed Samir's body. His throat was dry, and his lower jaw trembled. June turned back to face him.

"Where does she want to meet?"

"She's set up camp about a mile outside of town."

"Take me to her."

SAMIR AND JUNE strapped on their snowshoes and headed through the main gate. Tiffany bade them farewell, but June ignored the woman. Clouds had filled the sky, portending a snowfall later. Samir welcomed the chill; it kept his forehead clear of sweat that he was sure would give away his deception. A half mile out of Riverview, Samir's nose caught the smoky bite of Rachel's campfire.

His heart rate accelerated as they drew closer to the campsite. He trusted Rachel to deliver on her promise to get the information out of June. She was much more battle-worn than he was. She had seen things he had not seen. For all the terrible things he'd seen, it paled compared to what Rachel Fisher had gone through.

The sound of a branch cracking under the weight of the snow startled him. About twenty yards ahead, a pair of deer sliced through the woods. Beyond that lay a clearing. On its far side, he spotted Rachel's small temporary campsite. The fire was burning merrily. It was a good fire, kicking off very little smoke.

He reached out and gently grabbed June by the arm.

"Just a little bit ahead of us," he said, pointing towards Rachel's fire. "We're almost there."

"Good," June replied.

Samir's stomach flipped, and he choked down a dry heave.

When they reached the campsite, Rachel was crouched near the fire, warming her hands. When she noticed Samir and June, she rose to her full height and turned to face them.

"Rachel," June said.

Rachel nodded but said nothing in return. No love was lost between these women, but it was important to keep up appearances and not let June suspect they knew the truth about what she had done. Rachel gestured toward a stump near the fire. She had cleared it from the snow, making it the best seat in the house.

"Please, have a seat," she said.

"Thank you, I think I'll stand," June replied.

"Suit yourself," Rachel said.

"Samir tells me you have more vaccine."

"I do," Rachel said.

"Where is it?" June said.

"Somewhere safe," Rachel replied.

"I need to see it."

"I'll show it to you soon enough, but I need some assurances."

"What assurances are those?"

"I can't be in the wilderness for the rest of my life. My son needs a place to live. He needs a place to grow up."

"Understandable," June said. "And if you have this vaccine, I can make that happen."

"So where is it?" Rachel asked.

"Where is what?" June replied.

"The vaccine."

"I thought you would know. You're the one that has it."

"That's not the vaccine I'm talking about, and you know it. You gave the vaccine to that other group. Where is it?"

June turned to look at Samir.

"What's going on here?"

"Answer her questions," Samir said.

"I don't know what's going on, but I'm getting out of here," June said.

Rachel drew her weapon, moving as quickly as a cobra.

"You're not going anywhere. Have a seat."

Rachel circled June, pointing the weapon directly at her, taking a wide berth.

"Sit down on that stump, now."

"What are you going to do, shoot me?"

"I'll do what I have to do," Rachel said.

"I don't think you have it in you."

"You don't know what I'm capable of," Rachel replied.

Rachel's voice was so cold and so foreboding that it sent a chill down Samir's spine.

"Tell me where the vaccine is," Rachel said. "The game is up. We know you sold out Riverview."

"I didn't sell out Riverview," she said.

"Really?"

"I helped fulfill the prophecy."

"The what?"

"June, what the hell are you talking about?" Samir said, cutting in.

She turned her head toward him, a bright, terrible smile on her face. That was when he noticed her arm twitching. He didn't think much of it at first, but then he realized she had pulled her hand inside her sleeve, giving the illusion that she was missing her limb.

"The vaccine is where it is supposed to be."

June jerked her hand through her sleeve, and it came out bearing a small dagger about six inches long with an ornate handle. She launched herself from the stump, the knife held high, toward Rachel. They lunged toward June but were a fraction of a second too late. Rachel's hand clasped June's wrist just as the blade swept the air near Rachel's midsection.

The sudden attack took them both by surprise. When June wrenched her wrist free, Rachel took a step backward as she pulled the trigger of the Glock. Two shots rang out, both striking June in the abdomen. She did not make a sound, but her eyes widened momentarily, and she toppled backward off the stump onto the ground.

Rachel pulled herself to her feet and scampered around the stump up to June's head. The woman's mouth was moving, and blood was leaking from the corner of her lips, but she made no sound.

"Tell us where the vaccine is," Rachel said. "Please tell us."

June started to laugh, a strange high-pitched giggle that haunted Samir for the rest of his days. She bucked and seized for a moment, and then she was still. Her eyes remained open, but her chest stopped rising and falling.

June was dead, and the location of the vaccine had died with her.

31

Rachel was working in a basement pantry on a cold January morning, taking inventory of the remaining stocks of canned vegetables. It was tough, back-breaking work, but she never minded it. Her and Will's brush with starvation was never far from her mind. Anytime she started to feel tired, she would think about the dizziness, the hallucinations, the utter panic of not having something to put in that screaming belly. It was infinitely worse when she'd had nothing to give Will.

A week had passed since June died. Samir had taken the lead on reporting the news to the people of Riverview. He'd built up quite a reservoir of goodwill, and they had accepted his account of the vaccine's theft. The undamaged safe corroborated his story. And, of course, baby Caitlin was the best evidence any of them could hope for.

As such, the community's interest in June's passing quickly faded. She was one of many lost along the way. Still, her betrayal weighed heavily on Rachel. She had completely misread the woman. There was no indication that June would attempt something so drastic. But these were weird times that they were living in, and anyone was capable of just about anything at any time. The old ways of assessing motivations didn't apply anymore.

The scratching of Rachel's pencil on paper filled the quiet storeroom; she was careful and thorough in her count. Her focus was so intent that she did not hear April coming down the stairs until she was near the last step.

April was about fifty years old. Her hair was bright white, cut close like the soldier she had been once upon a time. Her parents had died when she was a child, and she had never married or had kids, so her landing after the apocalypse was a bit softer than for most people. There was a troubled look on her face.

"Hey, Rachel."

"Yeah," she replied, not looking back, keeping her eyes focused on her work, her mind blank.

"Someone's asking for Will."

Rachel's fingers froze atop a jar of cucumbers.

"What?"

"Some middle-aged man," April said. "At the gate. Wearing a dirty lab coat. A little weird."

"And he asked for Will? My Will?"

"Yeah."

"Who is he?"

"I have no idea. I've never seen him before."

"Jesus. Did he give you a name?"

April shook her head.

"He said he would only give it to you."

Rachel set her clipboard on a bare shelf and hustled toward the steps.

"He's not inside, is he?"

"We're not letting him inside the gate."

"Is he armed?"

"No."

"Who's with him now?"

"Charlie."

Rachel paused and thought for a moment. The last time someone had come looking for Will, it had ended with the deaths of a dozen people at Evergreen, including her father. Put another way, people looking for Will was rarely a good thing. She followed April up the steps. She didn't know where Will was, but that didn't matter. This visitor wouldn't come within sight of Will.

"You want me to join you?" April asked.

"No, I think I'll be okay."

The threat seemed low. Truth be told, anyone who meant them harm probably wouldn't have knocked. April accompanied her to the gate and then returned to the admin building. As promised, an odd-looking gentleman was waiting for Rachel outside the gate. He was dressed in khakis and a blue Oxford shirt. Over that, he wore a heavy winter coat. It was dirty and stained. His hair was nicely groomed, but he had a bit of an odd, loner look.

"Hello, Rachel."

"How do you know my name?" she said in surprise.

He smiled uncomfortably.

"My apologies. I'm not very good at social niceties. My name is Dr. Elias Holloway. Do you know who I am?"

She ignored the question for a moment and then repeated:

"How do you know who I am?"

"I will get to that in a moment. Do you know who I am?"

"No."

"Is Will here?"

"What the hell do you want with Will?"

Her voice was coated with anger.

"I promise that I mean you no harm."

"Will's dead. He died three years ago."

"I find that very hard to believe," Elias said.

"Why is that? It's a tough world. He didn't make it."

"I find it hard to believe because I met Will a month ago."

Punching her in the face would have had less of an impact on her. Rachel clenched her fists and opened them slowly, trying to tamp down her racing heart, her rapid breathing, and the urge to murder this man where he stood. She bit down on her lower lip, forcing herself to calm down and sort this out.

"Where exactly did you meet him?" Rachel asked, the fury nearly radiating from her body. Despite the cold air, a single bead of sweat traced a line down her back.

"He and his friend, the girl, stumbled across my bunker."

"What bunker? What are you talking about?"

"I used to work for Penumbra. I assume you know what that is."

Rachel stood there, frozen, certain that the shock on her face was evident.

Elias continued to speak.

"I do think I owe Will an apology. I'm afraid I frightened him. I really was looking for more information, and I came across a bit too strong, so he and the girl took off running. I don't blame them. I would have done the same thing."

"How did you find this place?"

"That's what I came here to tell Will. And you."

THE AFTERNOON'S events severely tested her newfound sobriety, but Rachel promised herself she would not drink on this day. Today, she had to sit and deal with the ramifications of Elias Holloway's visit. They were at a pivot point now; some great locomotive of fate was churning down the track, screaming toward them all.

Holloway was cooling his heels in Riverview's primitive lockup. After putting up the thinnest protest to his detention, he had since quieted down. Samir and Sean Jennings were watching him.

Rachel sat alone in her small living room, her knees drawn up to her chest, arms wrapped around her legs, almost in a fetal position. Her stomach rumbled, but she ignored the hunger pangs. It was nearly dark, and she was at the end of yet another very dark day.

Will wasn't home yet, but he'd be along soon enough. He was highly predictable, always showing up at dark for dinner. His appetite grew by the day. Part of her felt guilty, knowing that he would need extra rations to support his growing mind and body.

Like clockwork, the doorknob rattled as the day's last light ebbed out of the sky. Will came in, followed closely by Jade. As he strode in the doorway, mostly arms and legs now, his thin torso lean like his late father's, she was reminded how much she loved that kid. Just seeing him, just knowing he was in the world, always made her feel better, even when he was in a mood.

"Hey, Mom."

"Have a seat," she said, dispensing with pleasantries. "We need to talk."

She usually welcomed Will with a warm salutation, so the lack of one tonight would tell him something was amiss.

Neither of the teens replied. Immediately, strain appeared on their long faces, eyes cut to the ground. They came over and sat on the loveseat opposite her. Will's arms were folded at his chest. Jade sat with her hands in her lap. Her hands and fingers fumbled together like two large spiders.

As it often did, her heart swelled with love and frustration at her place as a mother in this world. Will had seen so many terrible things that she could not protect him from. If she stopped to worry about the impact of every single trauma, she wouldn't be able to function. It was a hard truth, but it was a necessary truth. They had to keep on keeping on.

"Is everything okay?" Will asked.

"Is there something you'd like to tell me?"

Both kids remained silent. They knew better than to roll over at the start of the interrogation. But they were kids, young, dumb, naïve, and they wouldn't hold out long.

Will shrugged.

"I don't think so."

He looked at Jade theatrically.

"Is there something I'm forgetting?"

Jade was a bit wiser, a bit warier. Her response was a bit more muted.

"Not that I can think of."

Rachel wasn't in the mood to waste time. She leaned forward in her seat and clasped her hands at her lips.

"Think hard," she said. "This is really important."

And she gave him the kind of look unique to each mother and her son, the type that told him she knew and there was no point in covering up the truth. There were no further denials, no attempts to explain away whatever series of events had brought them into Holloway's orbit. Jade studied her index finger, peeling away at a rogue piece of skin. Will's hands were balled up into fists, and he was lightly tapping them together.

Eventually, Will spoke.

"A few weeks ago, we were out on one of our adventures," he said. "You know how we do those."

She nodded easily, not wanting to spook him.

"Sure."

The casual reply was designed to keep him open and transparent. He was smart enough to know that this was an important moment for all of them. Extra patience would help tease out the whole truth.

"Actually, can I cut in here?" Jade asked. Will turned to her and nodded.

She looked back at Rachel.

"For as long as I can remember, there's been a rumor of a secret lab not far from here."

A dozen questions bloomed in Rachel's mind, but she said nothing, wanting them to tell the story free of her influence. She would have her moment.

Jade continued.

"Some people thought it was the old government disease research center ... what was it called?"

"The CDC. Centers for Disease Control."

"CDC. That was it. I also heard it might be a private lab. No one seemed to know for sure."

Jade looked over at Will, silently handing the story off to him.

He nodded to Jade and then looked back at his mother.

"Mom, it was a Penumbra bunker."

Penumbra.

She would never be free of that cursed organization. Its fate and hers seemed inexorably tied together, braided like two strands of DNA. As Leon Gruber had told her, Penumbra had been her destiny, whether she wanted it or not. Because of Penumbra, the world was dead. Because of Penumbra, she had Will.

"Did you go in?" she asked. Her voice was small and quiet.

Will's eyes cut to the ground. He looked back up.

"I know we shouldn't have. I know we should have told you about it first."

"You went inside," she said softly, in utter disbelief.

He nodded.

"Please don't be mad."

Rachel was furious. Her head felt like it might rocket off her shoulders and launch into outer space, but she said nothing. She wanted the whole story, for Jade and Will to tell her everything they had found. Reacting with anger might cause them to shut down. She sat on her hands, literally tucking her hands under her bottom, vibrating with rage, and kept calm.

"It's okay. I'm just glad you all are okay."

They looked at each other, and Will continued.

"What did you see in the bunker?"

His shoulders sagged, and he sighed as though he was unloading a great burden. He had been distant these last few weeks, but she had written it off to teenaged angst. Now, it seemed there was an explanation. Her son had been hiding something from her. Something big. Something important.

"It had electricity," he said. "Computers and screens and files. It was like a medical lab. We weren't there very long."

"Why not?"

"Mom, there was somebody inside. Someone who lived there."

"I know."

"You know?"

"He's here," Rachel said. "He found you guys."

32

———

They shoved off at dawn, just as the sun cracked the horizon and spilled its yolk-yellow light across the sky. It was a bright, clear morning encased in an icy layer of frost. Samir was at the wheel of the ancient Ford Explorer, the group deciding that this mission warranted using Riverview's scarce fuel reserves. The old SUV rumbled loudly in the morning silence as they put Riverview in the rearview mirror, then quieted down as the engine warmed, and they chewed up the miles.

Humanity's post-apocalyptic resourcefulness continued to amaze Rachel. The oceans of gasoline lying underneath the nation's countless fuel stations when civilization had screeched to a halt had gone stale over the next two years. Eventually, an enterprising petroleum engineer discovered a way to reactivate the inert fuel, and word spread rapidly from community to community. It wasn't easy, requiring a difficult-to-find substance that interacted with the fuel, but it was possible.

That wasn't all – from manufacturing medicines to making ammunition to growing weather-resistant crops, they'd all been busy keeping themselves alive. Humanity's ingenuity had always left a tiny pilot light of hope flickering inside Rachel's soul. And the vaccine, if they ever got their hands back on it, could be the spark that ignited a new future.

Rachel and Will sat in the back with Elias wedged in between them. Jade sat shotgun next to Samir.

"Start talking," Rachel said, nudging Elias's shoulder.

"It'll be easier to explain everything at the bunker," he replied.

Rachel leaned her head against the window, still frosted with a morning coating of ice. The cabin was silent as they rumbled down the highway. Samir moved slowly, about fifteen to twenty miles an hour, slaloming around abandoned or burned-out vehicles.

"He took a sample of my blood," Will offered.

"He what?"

She glanced at Will as he spoke. His lips tightened, and his face steeled with a grimace.

Jade jumped in.

"He wouldn't let us leave until Will gave a sample," Jade said. "He knew Will had been born after the pandemic."

"Then he let you leave?"

"Not exactly."

"What do you mean not exactly?" Rachel said, a little fire edging into her voice.

"We had to escape."

Rachel bit her lower lip so hard she tasted blood.

"Something in Will's blood got him all hot and bothered."

"Did he say what it was?"

"No," Will said. "Jade knocked him out, and we ran."

Rachel laughed in disbelief.

"When were you planning to tell me this?"

Neither teen responded.

The last remnants of civilized behavior still drifting through Rachel's soul kept her from strangling Elias there in the car. Just wrapping her hands around his throat until he stopped struggling. But they needed him, much as she hated to admit it.

She stared directly at Elias; he continued to look straight ahead, either unwilling to make eye contact with Rachel or simply afraid to. She wanted to smash him open like a pinata, knocking his secrets out of his head and down to the ground for all to see. But she had to remain calm. She knew that. For everyone's sake.

"How did you find us?" Rachel asked.

"It's complicated," replied Elias.

"Explain it to me."

"I promise I'll explain everything."

They reached the town limits a little bit before dark. The sun was setting, blanketing the town in a gloom. Unease crawled across her skin; even small population centers could be dangerous after dark. You never knew who was hiding, who was ready to do violence to weary travelers. Perhaps the day would come when cities would rise and thrive. Not now. Not for a long while.

Samir navigated through the outskirts of the little city, following Elias's directions. Mother Nature had had a field day here. Green vines carpeted every structure; nearly all the buildings' windows were long gone. The road was blanketed with weeds and small bushes that had grown through the cracks of the crumbling asphalt. A decade from now, this place would be completely swallowed up. Elias leaned forward and pointed toward the windshield.

"Next intersection, that building on the corner," he said.

Samir edged around the remains of a three-car crash blocking the intersection. In the rusted remains of an overturned pickup truck, the skeletal remains of the driver hung upside down from the still-fastened seatbelt. Samir eased onto the sidewalk, navigating a bus stop gazebo, then dropped off the curb. The squeaking of the suspension was loud in the eerie stillness.

"So, there's a Penumbra lab inside that building?" Rachel asked.

"Not exactly," Elias replied.

"Mom, it's underground," Will said.

"Oh," she replied.

These Penumbra bastards sure liked their secrecy.

That's how terrible things happened, she reminded herself.

Hidden away, in the dark, in the corners, places where nobody else looked. No one had been paying attention to Penumbra.

Samir brought the Explorer to a stop, and the quintet exited the vehicle. He clicked the lock button on the key fob, and the sound of the horn confirming the locking of the doors was huge in the massive silence of the town. Now and again, some ritual from the old world, like locking your car, would hit Rachel just right, like a well-strummed note on a guitar, and for the briefest of moments, the terrible memories of the plague just faded away.

Then she caught a glimpse of another skeleton lying in a small alleyway between this building and the next, and the moment passed. She was back in the present, in this terrible present that seemed to have no beginning and no end. Sometimes, she tried to recall the last moment of her old life, immediately before she first heard about Medusa, perhaps in a news story or on one of her social media feeds.

Even then, there was no way to fathom the horror that awaited them all.

"Lead the way, sir," Rachel said to Elias.

She couldn't believe Will had already been down here, but there was no point in getting bent out of shape about it. And perhaps this was the lucky break they would need. Hell, maybe there was a stash of vaccines down there!

"Here," Elias said, gesturing toward a heavy cover flush with the ground. It was simple, unassuming, unadorned, but for the stamping of the Penumbra name in the metal. She knelt and brushed her fingers against the cold lid.

Before he opened the hatch, Rachel searched Elias one more time, very thoroughly, running her hands up each of his pant legs, around his waist, under his shirt, in his coat. Satisfied, she let him open the hatch. A keypad was embedded into the cover; it was all but invisible, camouflaged by the lid's black paint. Elias punched in a long code; Rachel watched him and tried to commit it to memory, but the code was too long, and Elias typed too quickly for her to keep up. A thought occurred to her.

"How did the kids get in if it was locked?" she asked.

"I spotted them on the security cameras and unlocked it," he said.

"Why?"

"Honestly," he said, glancing away. "I was lonely. I wanted the company."

He certainly was a peculiar man.

As he spoke, the lid cranked open slowly. They descended one at a time, Elias first, followed by Rachel and the kids, with Samir bringing up the rear. It was pleasantly warm. Forced air hissed through an unseen vent. She had experienced electricity and temperature controls during her short stay at both Olympus and the Citadel, but for the others, this was their first time. As far as she knew, Will had never felt indoor heat.

Samir started to laugh.

"Been a long time since I've felt this toasty," he said.

Their movement through the corridor triggered the automatic lights. Once they reached the control room, Rachel stood in awe at the edge of the large oval-shaped room.

"This is the control center," Elias said, gesturing to the workstations and the large monitors mounted on the wall.

"Can we save the tour for later?" Rachel asked, cutting him off. "How did you find Will?"

He looked almost hurt by her interruption, his eyes downcast and his lower lip quivering, but she did not care. If she was too much for this man, that was his problem, not hers. He took a minute to gather himself and then sat at one of the workstations.

"The truth is, I didn't really find Will."

"I don't understand."

"I found you."

"You're losing me here," Rachel said.

"Okay," he said. "Let me start again. I did take a sample of Will's blood. And that was unethical."

"Yes, it was," Rachel said harshly. "He's a child."

"Mom, come on," Will exclaimed, obviously disappointed with her assessment of his maturity level.

He turned to Jade and said, "I'm not a child."

"Shh," his mother snapped.

Elias continued.

"You're right. I'm sorry. I shouldn't have done it without asking you. I knew the vaccine had been designed to transfer in utero. I had never seen a real-world example of it, and I got ahead of myself."

"What made you think about checking Will?"

"He was obviously born after the pandemic. He's, what, fourteen?"

There was no longer any point in hiding the truth. The cat was out of the bag. Perhaps the cat had never been in the bag, and she had been living a lie.

"Fourteen."

"Anyway," Elias said. "When I got the slide under the microscope, I found something I didn't expect."

"What?" asked Rachel, her heart pounding against her chest.

"The vaccine is best described as a group of microscopic machines," he said. "Microscopic at an atomic level. I've never seen anything like it. They self-replicate."

"What does that mean?"

"They're programmed to make copies of themselves. It's almost like we created life that, in turn, creates life at the quantum level. Truly remarkable. It keeps a steady supply of the nanoparticles that target and destroy the Medusa virus. Medusa didn't go anywhere. It's still out there, constantly looking for a host."

This was a distressing thought. Medusa, the invisible killer that was always and forever hunting them. She supposed she should be thankful for this abomination inside her. Inside Will. Without this vaccine, she would be dead. Will would never have existed. She would have long since been dust and bones, her life short and devoid of any meaning.

"Some people are naturally immune, though, right?"

"Yes," he said. "But as we know, their babies are not. Babies are on their own when it comes to immunity."

"Antibody interference," Samir said, breaking his silence for the first time.

Elias glanced at him.

"I'm a doctor," Samir said. "That's why the babies die."

"Ah. I wasn't familiar with that phenomenon."

Rachel remained silent, deep in thought. Her arms crossed her chest, and she absently scraped a thumbnail across her lower lip.

"You were telling us what you didn't expect," Samir said.

Elias lightly smacked himself on the side of the head.

"Of course," he said. "Apologies for getting so off track."

Rachel was beginning to like the man. He was a bit eccentric but earnest and well-meaning. And this little roundtable discussion was likely the most human interaction he'd had in a long time. Perhaps it had been a blessing that the kids had found this place. It was a bit of a longshot that their visit had amounted to anything.

The bunker could just as easily have been home to a child-eating psychopath. It made her think about fate and destiny. Holloway was about to share with her a heretofore-unknown revelation about the vaccine, and it was only because of the lark and frolic of a couple of bored kids.

"I detected an unusual signature in Will's blood sample," he said. "I didn't know what it was, but I had to assume it was related to the vaccine nanoparticles. I used a centrifuge to isolate the vaccine particles and ran a spectrometry test."

"And what did you find out?" Samir asked.

"That it's giving off a low-level frequency. I ran it through some databases I can still access and found that it matched..."

"Oh my God," Rachel said.

"What does that mean?" Will asked.

Rachel turned to face Samir; the look on his face suggested he'd come to the same conclusion as Rachel.

"He's saying the vaccine is trackable."

"Exactly," Elias said.

33

———

The revelation hung in the air, an almost tangible thing they could reach out and touch. No one spoke.

"All this time, it's been trackable," Rachel said aloud.

A chill ran through her. The Medusa vaccine had been coursing through her veins for almost twenty years. Since she was fourteen, her place in the world had never truly been hers. It had belonged to Penumbra. Even if this signature had only revealed her location on a map, it was a staggering invasion of her privacy and sense of self.

"I guess the bigwigs wanted to track those they deemed worthy of this gift," said Elias.

"I guess."

Another thought bloomed in her mind, this one blinding, bright, and urgent, like a mushroom cloud sweeping away all the others. If the nanoparticles that made up the Medusa vaccine were trackable, they could potentially find the vaccine that had been stolen from them.

"How would you track the vaccine?" she asked.

"What do you mean?" asked Elias.

"Like, is there a program? How did you figure out where we were? You must have seen the information somewhere."

"Yes," Elias said. "It wasn't easy, though. That's why it took me so long to find you. I started trying to figure out how to triangulate the signal. I had some receivers here to work with. Eventually, I calibrated one to pick up the signal from Will's nanoparticles. Once the nanoparticles transferred to his body, they created a new signature that's unique to him."

"Is there a way to find other vaccines out there?" Rachel asked. "Find other people who are vaccinated?"

"I suppose," said Elias. "But I don't know their unique signature. I'd be starting blind."

"Is there anything in the bunker that could point you in the right direction?"

"Why do you need this?" Elias asked, suddenly suspicious.

Samir and Rachel exchanged a glance. He nodded and then tipped his head toward Elias. Samir wanted her to come clean with the man. But a tug of hesitation stilled her tongue. Trusting others was still something she struggled with. Nothing sprung to mind, but she was certain there was some way that Elias could exploit this information. Hell, he might still be in league with any remnants of Penumbra.

"I'll make you a deal," Rachel said. "You tell me everything; I'll tell you everything."

"Fair enough. I have nothing to hide."

"Why didn't you know about the vaccine's tracking feature?" she asked.

He chuckled.

"I wasn't that important," he said.

"Did you know?" she asked.

"Did I know what?"

She tilted her head and gave him a look a disappointed schoolteacher might toss a misbehaving student.

"Ah," he said, understanding.

"No, I didn't know what they were planning until it was too late."

"How did you find out?"

He pinched his lower lip and cut his eyes toward the ground, Rachel's question pushing him deep into the past.

"I'm a data scientist. I was hired right out of grad school. Georgia Tech. They hired me to run the data on its biomedical research. I worked with genomic data, clinical trials, that kind of thing."

A wave of nostalgia tugged at Rachel. Nostalgia for a life that she had never lived. A life that had been stolen from her in a cataclysm of disease. If not for Medusa, her career path may have mirrored Elias's. Hell, she might have ended up working for Penumbra.

"Did you always work in this bunker?"

"I was transferred here about a year before the pandemic."

"Any idea why?"

"They didn't say," he said. "But they doubled my pay. And told me I'd be here for two years."

"Were you here alone?" Samir asked.

"Not at first," he said. "I had a partner. Hadley. But he freaked out during the outbreak and took off. Never saw him again."

"I assume you're vaccinated."

He nodded.

"One morning—about four months before the outbreak —we got a company-wide message that we were missing a vaccine in our required inoculation series. I didn't think anything of it. Later that week, a Penumbra nurse showed up to give us the shot. That was that. I didn't think about it again."

"What happened when the outbreak started?"

Elias got out of his chair and disappeared down a corridor. He returned a few moments later with a bottle of liquor and three small tumblers clenched between his fingers.

"Sorry, kids," he said to Will and Jade. "Maybe when you're a little older."

"None for me," Samir said.

"I appreciate it, but I'll also pass," Rachel said.

"Suit yourselves."

He set the glasses on the table and filled one with a healthy pour. Rachel was unfamiliar with the name on the bottle, Jefferson Forest, but she knew little about alcohol brands. All she had cared about was drinking it

"Jefferson Forest," Samir said softly. "Almost worth living through the end of the world for this."

"I usually can't bring myself to drink it," said Elias, swirling the amber liquid in the glass. "Because this is my last bottle. And I don't know if I'll ever find another one."

Samir glanced at Rachel.

"It's very rare," he said. "A bottle of that might go for two grand. Used to, at least."

He took down the rest and poured a second healthy dram.

"A few days before the first news reports, at least any reports I heard, we got this strange message from Penumbra HQ. Told us to go into lockdown at our site. We tried to contact our supervisor, but there was no response. Somewhere around the middle of that first week, we got orders to analyze the virus's spread. This was before it was clear how bad it was going to be. Statistical modeling, machine learning to track the infection and mortality rates, anything and everything."

Rachel and Samir exchanged glances but said nothing.

"The next day, we got another company-wide message," he said. "It said, 'The future will be glorious.' That struck me as weird, almost like they'd been waiting for it. Then, one night at dinner that first week, my partner said something strange. Just offhand, more like a joke than anything."

"What did he say?"

"He said, 'What if that nurse brought us the vaccine for this?'"

This elicited no reaction from Rachel because that's precisely what this nurse had done, even if Elias and his partner hadn't realized it, even if the nurse herself did not know it.

"To this day, I don't know what made him think of it. Then again, he was a smart guy. Making connections no one else could see. I opened my mouth to argue with him but closed it just as quickly. Looking back, the whole mobile vaccine clinic thing *was* weird.

"Anyway, I hacked into the human resources database that night to access my personnel file. I checked my vaccination record. Guess what I found?"

"No missing shots," Rachel said.

"No missing shots," he said. "They were all there. Some given my first day, some after a month. Boosters. Multiple-shot series. All of them. That was when I really got scared. We kept running our models and watching the world die."

"Did you hear back from Penumbra again?"

"Every week, we got an automated message to continue our work and to keep our site active. After Hadley took off, it was a lot of work."

"What about supplies?"

"I had everything I needed for a year."

"Elias, did you have a family?"

His hands shook as he poured another plug of the bourbon.

"A son. He was in the Army. Stationed in Germany when it hit. He texted me once during that first week. It had gotten bad there quickly. He was sick…"

Elias's voice trailed off then.

"There was nothing you could have done," she said. "Absolutely nothing."

He broke down, weeping.

"A parent should never outlive their child."

She reached out and placed her hand over his.

"I'm sorry," she said.

He chuckled.

"Look at me, crying like a baby."

He wiped the streams of tears away from his cheeks. He took down the remaining finger of bourbon in one fell swoop. A sigh of, if not contentment, then peace followed.

"Now. What was it you wanted to tell me?"

"I had a thousand doses of the vaccine," she replied. "And they were stolen from me."

She glanced at Samir.

"From us."

Now, it was Elias's turn to be shocked. He sat there, his eyes wide. He opened his mouth as though he were about to speak, but then he closed it again. A moment later, he did speak, uttering a single word.

"Wow."

∾

AFTER RACHEL PROMISED to tell all, Elias started working on triangulating the signal. Rachel, Samir, and the kids enjoyed a small meal from Elias's stores as he worked.

"If he finds the vaccines, what's our next play?" Samir asked.

"We're going to have to go get them," Rachel said.

"That could be dangerous," Samir said.

"It's going to be incredibly dangerous," Rachel replied, "but we have no choice. We have to get that vaccine back."

"Maybe we should just let him do whatever he's going to do with it," Samir replied. "If he wanted to destroy it, he could have. He's just going to distribute it to women who need it. After all, the vaccine has no other purpose."

They sat silently while Rachel pretended to consider Samir's suggestion, even though she had no intention of going along. It was tempting. The burden would no longer be on her. Its new custodian could decide who got the vaccine. Did it really matter what he did in exchange for it? Humanity's continued viability was the only priority. What difference did it make if it went to someone in Riverview or Kansas City or Tupelo or Chicago?

But in the end, such a decision would mean abandoning her principles and turning her back on who she was. She had to do something. Until today, it seemed the chance to do anything was lost forever. The vaccine was gone, like smoke in the wind. Before today, doing nothing was the only choice she had.

The world was just too big, too vast, too empty. It was one of the more depressing aspects of a post-Medusa world. When someone was gone, they were gone. She thought about all the people they'd lost over the years. Not just the people who had died, and there had been plenty of those, but also those who had gone their separate ways. Like Jess,

Carla, and the kids. She hoped they'd made it across the bridge safely. But there was no way to know for sure. But here, technology had come out of the past to give them a chance, to give them a chance at redemption.

"But then they decide how and when and to whom it's distributed," Rachel said. "God knows the price they'll exact in exchange for a shot in the arm."

The hours passed in stasis, Rachel and the others caught between the past and the future. Jade and Will watched old clips of news coverage from the pandemic. They sat with eyes wide open, their jaws hanging partially open, stunned at the media coverage that used to exist, especially during a disaster like the Medusa outbreak. It didn't seem to faze them one way or another. After all, it was just a history lesson for them, not something they had endured. Samir watched a few minutes of the video coverage with them, but then he had to step away.

"It's still too raw," he said. "Can you believe that? Even after all this time, I still can't watch it, even though I lived through it."

The kids were jarred by the number of people in the news clips. Their lives had been spent in the wide open of a largely empty continent. At most, one might see a couple hundred people at a community market, and that seemed like a huge crowd.

Elias stayed tucked away at his workstation, muttering to himself, tapping away, looking at the signature in Will's blood, trying to reverse engineer it. Rachel dug through the files. Elias gave her free rein. After all, what was the point of keeping anything secret? The hours crawled by, second by second, a brutal war between their patience and Rachel's desire to know if they would have a bead on the location of the vaccines.

Around three in the morning, Elias pushed his chair back from his workstation. He stood up, stretched, and let out a loud sigh. Initially, Rachel didn't think anything of it. He'd been hard at work for hours without a break. He wandered over to them, his hands on his hips and eyes sunken. Huge bags sagged underneath the eyelids, hinting at the exhaustion the man must have been feeling.

"I found it," he said.

34

———

They gathered around Elias's computer monitor.

"Like I said earlier," he began, "I knew the signature that Will's nanoparticles were giving off. I constructed a receiver to detect his particular signature. The problem with the stolen vaccine is that I don't know the specific signature they're giving off; I only know that they're giving one off."

He turned to Rachel.

"How many doses in each vial?"

"Twenty."

"Okay, so that tells me the entire vaccine supply, before it's injected into someone, has a very general identifier specific to each vial. Once it's inside you, it creates its own unique signature. Now, I have no idea how the hell they did that. It must interact with your body at a cellular level."

He drifted into silence.

"It's just incredible," he finally said.

Rachel shook her head in disbelief. Pondering what Penumbra had done before the pandemic and what it had done since frightened her a little. The thought that the vaccine itself had interacted with her humanity, her essence, left her uneasy, but she pushed that out of her mind for the moment. After all, there was nothing they could do about it. Whether she liked it or not, whether she wanted it or not, the vaccine was part of her—part of Elias, part of Will.

"An algorithm creates the unique identifier once injected into the human recipient," Elias continued. "I realized if I just changed the receiver to detect the general identifier rather than Will's specific signature, I might be able to find it that way. I was a little worried that proximity would be a problem, that if it weren't very close by, I would never find it. But we got lucky. We might be right on the edge of the transmission zone, but we're still in it. About eighty miles from here."

"Holy crap," Rachel said, "you found it."

Relief shot through Rachel like electricity. She felt alive. There was much to do, of course, and the outcome was not guaranteed. But it was a turning point of sorts. Back from the dead, rising up when all had seemed lost.

Elias wrote out the vaccine's location coordinates and then plugged them into a separate terminal's mapping software. As the computer processed those coordinates, an aerial view of the Earth zoomed in toward the American Midwest, drawing in closer over a large compound about thirty-five miles north of Riverview in Tomlin.

"What is that place?" Will asked.

Rachel studied the three-dimensional image carefully, tilting her head this way and that until it clicked in her head.

"It's a prison," she said.

"How can you tell?" Elias said, still examining the image.

"Look," she said, touching her index finger to the screen.

"This is the perimeter fence. It runs around the entire

complex. You can see the barbed wire running along the top."

She touched three other points on the image.

"And these are cell blocks. A-Block, B-Block, and C-Block. It's painted on the rooftops."

"She's right," Samir said.

"So what now?" Elias asked.

"We go to this prison," she said, "and we steal that vaccine back."

Samir chewed on his lower lip and shifted his weight from one foot to the other.

"You up for this?"

He didn't reply at first.

"It's going to be very dangerous, very, very dangerous. I'm used to this sort of thing. I've been through this sort of thing before, but I can't ask you to do it."

"You could die," he said.

"Yes, I could die, but I have no choice."

Samir wiped his hand across his mouth and placed his hands on his hips. His brow furrowed in deep thought. He was a handsome fellow, lean and athletic but radiating intelligence. Losing him would be a terrible blow to Riverview, but his importance to the community would not matter much longer without the vaccine.

"Everyone wants the chance to save the world, right?" he said. "Well, this is my chance. I am definitely up for this."

"We'll need a vehicle and a full tank of gas."

"We can get it."

"Okay, I'm in," he said.

"I am as well," said Elias.

Rachel blinked in surprise. She hadn't thought this mousy scientist would want to join them on this mission.

"Are you sure?" she asked. "I can't guarantee your safety."

"Somehow, I feel partially responsible for all of this," said Elias.

He gestured at the bunker around them; on the video screen, an obviously ill man was bravely delivering news on the rapidly growing disaster.

"These last few years, humanity has been fading away. Erased like a pencil mark. I don't want that to happen. If I could do something to stop that, I'm going to. I lost my only son to this. I have no other legacy. This is something I can do. I may disappear into history, but that'll be okay. If I know that humanity will continue, that'll be enough for me."

Rachel looked at the man with a new measure of respect. If nothing else, a third body on this mission would be a plus. It opened up the playbook. She could teach him as much as she could during the trip to the prison. She had no idea if he would survive. She had no idea if any of them would survive.

"We're doing this?" Samir asked.

"We're doing this."

THE PENUMBRA BUNKER was a motherlode of supplies. The group got to work, stocking up for the trip to and infiltration of the prison. Rachel curated the weapons for their arsenal, Samir took responsibility for the medical kit, and Elias focused on calibrating a batch of communication devices for the group. They worked late into the night and were ready to go by dawn. The first leg of the trip would take them back to Riverview to drop off the kids and pick up a can of reserve fuel.

The drive home passed quietly.

"Mom, can I come?" Will asked as the gates of Ashby College appeared in the morning gloom

"No," she said, and her single-word reply popped with such finality that he did not even bother arguing.

There was no need to explain how dangerous it was, that she needed to keep him safe, or that his future was in Riverview. He understood all that. Her decision was just another waypoint in their relationship as mother and son. Eventually, he would continue without her, and she had to ensure he was ready.

Light snow fell as they reached the gates. The sky was an ominous gray, the clouds low, thick, and locked in. It was a good indicator of a big storm moving in. It was mid-morning, but it was already gloomy and dim with the twilight of the short day. The air percolated with dancing snowflakes and heavier snow in the offing. Samir eased off the brake as the dayshift guard opened the gate wide enough for the truck to navigate. He followed the main road toward Riverview's motor pool. After parking, Samir exited the vehicle and grabbed two gas cans, which he placed inside the truck's cargo area. As he took care of that, Rachel took Will and Jade to the side.

"Jade, I need you to look after him while we're gone."

"Mom, I don't need anyone—"

She turned to face Will.

"And you look after her."

She handled him now like the adult he was becoming, albeit with training wheels. Eventually, those would come off, or he would rip them off.

"Y'all listen to me," she said. "It's because of you we even have a chance. Because of a little insane bravery. And sometimes, that's what it takes in this world. You understand me?"

Will nodded stoically. There were no tears, which broke her heart because it meant he was hardening. But that was good because their world did not tolerate softness for long. Their world called for the sharp end of the knife.

"Jade?" she said.

"Don't worry," she said. "We'll take care of each other."

Rachel hugged the young woman fiercely, eliciting a gasp from her. Jade hugged her back.

"If we don't make it back, don't you give up," Rachel said. "This here is our best chance right now, but that doesn't mean it's our only chance. There could be other bunkers out there. Maybe more vaccine supply. You keep searching. You do everything you can to keep going."

Rachel did not know if she believed that, but Will needed to believe she did. Letting him think this was their only hope, their last chance, could deflate them. Collateral damage if the mission to the prison failed. Behind her, Samir was finishing up with the truck.

"Ready?" asked Rachel.

"Let's go."

35

S amir drove. They motored west for twenty minutes before turning south on Route 67, parallel to the river. The road doglegged west again toward the empty cities of Columbia and Kansas City and onward toward the Rockies before turning south again. The snow had already dusted the interstate here as the storm moved in from the north. For now, the big SUV's tires managed to traverse the highway without issue. They encountered the same traffic jams that had snarled American highways in the desperate last days of the pandemic, as though one could have escaped the virus by sitting in traffic.

As Samir navigated the quilt of abandoned vehicles and the ruins of smashups, Elias and Rachel studied the blueprint of the Waterside Correctional Facility. They had found it in the Ashby College library. Before Medusa, Waterside had been home to approximately two thousand inmates, many of them dangerous and violent. This meant it had many security features that a minimum-security prison did not, making its infiltration all the more difficult.

Outside, the weather continued to deteriorate. Light

snow showers were yielding to heavier precipitation. It reminded her of a night many years ago, when her father had come to rescue her from the Citadel, where the Medusa virus had been midwifed into the world. It had been an equally tragic and triumphant moment, putting an end to the madness but also costing them so many lives, including the love of her father's life, Sarah Wells. Even now, fifteen years later, she thought of Sarah often, a woman she had only met once but felt a special kinship to. Not only had she been willing to make the ultimate sacrifice for her loved ones, she had made it.

Rachel thought of this sacrifice when she'd had to make terrible decisions that put lives at risk. Nobody liked to lay their lives down, but someday, she might need to cross that bridge. Such a thought caused panic to bubble up, and when that happened, she would think of Sarah and calm down again.

"Rachel?" Elias asked.

She blinked twice, shook off the daydream, and thought about Sarah, her father, and everything that had brought them to this point.

"Yeah, sorry. Just checked out for a moment."

"No worries," he said. "I've been checked out most of my life, especially since Medusa."

The plan had come together the first hour out of Riverview.

"Got it. I found something on the blueprint."

Rachel raised her eyebrows.

"Tell me."

He pointed to a spot on the right side of the scroll.

"Right here. This appears to be a storm drain or sewer running from here to here."

He pointed out two spots on the map. It was about

fifteen hundred yards from one end of the storm drain back to the prison infirmary.

"We can access the prison through here. That'll get us inside the walls without going through the fence. After that, we're gonna need some luck."

"How big is the population?"

"I'd estimate at least a thousand," Elias said. "Maybe as many as two thousand."

"What do we know about this place?"

"Hard to say. If I had to guess, there's a hierarchy. Militaristic, almost certainly meaning a strongman. Not unlike a beehive. From the queen on down. A community of that size needs a lot of worker bees to keep the trains running on time. Maintenance, food prep, waste removal, that sort of thing."

"How can you be sure?" Samir asked.

"Way of the world. It's the way it's always been. The way it will always be."

"The bigger the better. At some point in the growth of a community, you stop recognizing everyone. We're gonna use that to our advantage."

"They probably keep records of their population. A census."

"True, but it's still maintained by people. And people are fallible."

"Look at you with the standardized test words!" Samir joked.

"Standardized tests," Elias said with a hint of nostalgia. "Sneaking in won't work when we don't know where they keep the vaccine. It's unlikely we will last long enough to locate our prize."

Rachel started to argue with him, but he was right. And she had already considered and dismissed the option of walking up to the prison's front gates and asking for refuge. That could easily land them in one of Waterside's many cells.

As though reading her mind, Samir asked: "What about just asking if they'll take us in? Hide in plain sight. Won't need to worry about hiding."

"Too much of a risk," she said, explaining her reasoning.

But as she spoke, another idea came into mind. A hybrid between a stealth infiltration and simply walking up to their front door. It would require a sacrifice on their part, but one that would be worth it if it worked. And if it didn't work, that was part of doing business. Without risk, there could be no rewards.

The best way to manage that risk was to offer Waterside something they didn't have. She tapped a fist against her lips as she wracked her brain. An idea continued to brush against the periphery. Then, finally, it burst into existence, fully formed. Ultimately, it was so obvious that she was annoyed it had taken her so long to think of it. The risk to Elias and Samir was not insignificant, which they would need to understand.

"I've got a plan," she said.

"What?" Samir asked.

She told them. She explained the risks involved.

And in the end, Elias and Samir were all in.

WHEN THEY REACHED TOMLIN, the town closest to the prison, it was closing in on dark. The skies were clear as night fell, and brilliant starlight shone on them. Tomlin was a small town that had relied on the prison for most of its employment prospects. At its peak, it had been home to about three thousand people, mostly small families who lived in cute little ranch houses with square front yards where everybody knew each other.

Samir killed the headlights well before the town limits and eased off the accelerator. Their adversaries would have night patrols, requiring extra caution. Samir parked the vehicle on the outskirts of the gas station's pump island. The group alighted silently from the car. The land here was flat and wide open. They were about a mile from the prison's entrance.

The trio split a small meal of flatbread and some salted meat. It wasn't much, leaving Rachel wanting more, but it would be enough. All they needed right now was the energy to get through their mission and complete it. The conversation was kept to a minimum. All of them understood how voices carried on the silent air of their world.

"We ready?" she asked as they wrapped up their supper. Both men nodded.

"This is it," she said. "No turning back."

They nodded again.

Their first task was to stash the bulk of the weapons in the convenience store's small office. The arsenal was too valuable. This would prevent them from falling into this group's hands. Back outside, the snow had intensified. Rachel tore a long strip of fabric from the old upholstery of the car's interior. After unscrewing the gas cap, she ran its length into the gas tank, exposing just a swatch. Then she swiped a match from Samir's supply and lit it. The tiny corona flickered in the immense darkness. A flare in a void of nothingness. She cupped the tiny flame to protect it from the elements, letting it light their way. The men's faces, awash in an orange glow, were tight but determined.

Samir nodded.

She nodded back and touched the match to the gas-soaked cloth. The flame bloomed immediately. Like a demon spotting its prey, a cord of fire dove into the tank, rippling down to the gasoline sloshing below.

"Back up," Rachel warned the men.

They hustled away from the truck, putting a couple hundred yards between themselves and the growing fire. It wouldn't be long. Deep in the truck's bowels, a correction was coming, entropy in its purest form.

Then it happened: a massive whoosh as the truck exploded, quickly turning the night into day. Rachel shielded her eyes with a hand. A sonic boom fractured the night silence and radiated across the land. The conflagration would not go unnoticed.

"I hope you know what you're doing," Samir said.

The SUV burned like hell, a gigantic, raging inferno blinding them with its deep orange rage.

"Me too," Rachel said.

They didn't have to wait long. Fifteen minutes later, the shine of headlights appeared in the distance. Behind that set came another – they had sent two vehicles. Of course, Rachel and the others would be quickly taken into custody, and that was the plan.

The pair of SUVs decelerated as they approached the scene. Like sharks, the pair slowly circled Rachel's burning truck, assessing the situation. Then they idled momentarily, their occupants scanning the area, determining the risk that might have been present.

One of the windows lowered, and a man's face appeared in the darkness like a specter.

"Hands on your head," he said.

36

Rachel's group complied and awaited their fate. The die was cast now, and there was no turning back. A door in the lead vehicle opened; a man carrying a military-style assault rifle emerged from the back. He was dressed in a heavy winter coat and a black winter cap. A gaiter was pulled up across the lower half of his face. He was of average height, on the shorter side, and average build. But a swagger to his movements made Rachel immediately wary of him. Two more men emerged from the second SUV, each drawing close to Elias and Samir.

"What's happening here?" asked the first man out of the truck.

She marked him as the leader. The others were clearly deferential to him.

"Oh my God!" Rachel exclaimed, cautiously but enthusiastically jogging toward the man. "Thank you so much for stopping! This was crazy. I thought we were gonna die."

She talked rapidly and loudly, hoping her theatrics would sell her story of the damsel in distress. The man held up his hand in a *stop* gesture, clearly startled by Rachel's sudden movement toward him.

"Hey, hold up, hold up," he said. "I can hear you fine from there."

Rachel pantomimed a big show of surrender, holding up her hands to show that she posed the men no danger. Behind her, the other men had already begun searching Samir and Elias, who were both armed, but that was also part of the act. A search was inevitable. It would be more suspicious if they weren't armed. No one traveled unarmed these days.

"Our car caught fire," Rachel said, ramping up her breathing a bit to simulate unhealthy exposure to a fog of smoke. "It just caught fire."

She used her most desperate, most vulnerable voice. Behind her, their SUV continued to burn. The flames hissed and popped as they interacted with falling snow showers.

"How did the fire start?"

Elias jumped in.

"We were moseying along, and then I started to smell smoke, and the next thing I knew, flames were shooting out from the gas tank."

"Where you headed in this weather?"

"Texas," Elias said. "Weather took us by surprise."

"That can happen," the man said.

The leader pointed at two of his comrades.

"Get them in the trucks, and we'll take them back to base. Keep the men together; the woman will ride with me."

"Where are you taking us?" Rachel asked, this time spicing her question with a bit of panic.

Her concern was genuine. Being held captive by strange men was not her idea of a good time. A cord of worry wrapped around Rachel like a python, but all she could do was go with the flow. They had jumped into the river of their plan, and the water would carry them where it would. Their captors loaded them into the trucks. Rachel climbed into the lead vehicle, her friends in the trail car, and they set off through the snow.

The cars moved slowly, the drivers cautious in the poor conditions. Even with snow chains, the tires' grip on the roadway was tenuous. The darkened landscape eased past them; snowflakes danced in the beams of the vehicles' headlights. The man asked Rachel no questions. She wondered if any discussion was happening in the other cars, although she had cautioned her friends to stay quiet.

As they neared the prison entrance, a large sign reading *Waterside State Prison* mounted over two tall black posts greeted them. It was simple and unadorned. A hidden sensor activated, and the two black gates cranked open long enough for the two vehicles to enter. As they cleared the gate, the gates closed back up again.

Rachel's entire world shrank to the confines of this prison. She would either leave this facility with the vaccines or not leave it at all. She hoped that Elias and Samir understood the risk that lay ahead. The vehicles pulled around behind a building at the center of the prison grounds. The marquee on the façade of the building read *Administration*. The driver braked underneath a sally port—an open but covered area used to transport inmates inside the prison upon arrival.

Rachel's vehicle pulled in first, and the second trailed just behind. The trio was escorted into a large lobby area inside the administration building. The dim light of oil lanterns cast the room in an eerie yellow glow. There was very little chit-chat among their captors. The leader of the group escorted Rachel over to a holding cell. He gestured for her to enter it and closed it behind her.

It made sense to separate each of the prisoners. That way, they could be interrogated and see if their stories matched up. Even the slightest discrepancy would cast doubt on their credibility, so they'd worked so hard on it until it felt like the truth.

Her cell was about six-by-six feet square. A small window was embedded into the concrete wall, but it was too high for Rachel to look through even after pushing herself up on her tiptoes; the view remained maddeningly elusive. A commode sat in the corner; next to that was an old but clean bucket flipped upside down. Atop the bucket was a half roll of toilet paper.

The administration building was quiet. The activity their arrival had stirred up was dying down. At least two guards were on duty, their whispered chit-chat betraying their presence. Samir and Elias must have been nearby, but their cells were out of Rachel's line of sight. The adrenaline in her body faded as the first phase of their operation reached its end. There was a long way to go, but at least they had made it this far. The vaccine was somewhere close by, just beyond her reach. As her heart rate eased and her breathing calmed, a wave of fatigue washed over her.

The bedroll was calling to her. It was time for rest, an overlooked tool in a survivor's arsenal. Fatigue made you sloppy. You made mistakes, and mistakes could be deadly. Pacing the cell while waiting for someone to visit her would do her no good. They were on this group's time now. As if to drive the point home, she yawned. She lay down on the bedroll, keeping her jacket on. It wasn't bone-chillingly cold, but it certainly wasn't toasty. And there was no blanket.

She tucked a hand under her head and stared at the ceiling, unable to relax, anxious to meet with their hosts. Even after it was clear no one would be coming that night, she remained on edge. Sleep was hard to come by; her brain ran through one scenario after another.

Finally, she slept and dreamed. She dreamed about a large soccer field overrun with children. The hot sun beat down on them, and they were dressed in summer clothes. Their faces were slicked with sweat; their bangs matted down on their damp foreheads. The children ran aimlessly to and fro but were very earnest in their aimlessness, their faces sharp with furrowed brows and tight lips.

She reached out to tousle one kid's hair, but just before making contact, the entire field of children dissolved into nothingness. Then she blinked, and they were back. She reached for another, and again, the herd of kids vanished. No matter what she did, the children remained just beyond her touch. They were there and not there all at the same time. A Schrodinger's child. She woke up feeling uneasy, coated in a light glaze of sweat.

Then she slept again, and she dreamed again. This time, she dreamed not about children but instead about a dog—a little dog named Ajax she had met at the height of the pandemic so many years ago. With her mother already dead, Rachel had walked up to Brigid's Market, looking for medicine for her stepdad Jerry as Medusa overwhelmed him. While browsing the barren aisles, Rachel found a sick little girl alone in the store. When the dog growled at Rachel, the little girl—whose name Rachel had never learned—had said, "Ajax, shhhh," and being the good boy he was, he quieted down.

Rachel sat near the girl as the life drained out of her, and she had died in that little gourmet shop. Rachel tried encouraging the dog to follow her, but Ajax refused to leave.

Instead, he curled up into a little ball in his small, beautiful master's lap and would not budge. After gathering the few supplies still on hand, Rachel opened a few packages of food and left them near Ajax. She also filled several containers with water and set those out as well. Before exiting the store, Rachel propped the door open with a heavy cinderblock so Ajax could get out if he ended his vigil. Then, to doubly ensure he wasn't entombed inside the store, she shattered the front door and swept the broken glass clear off the stoop. That way, he could leave when he was ready.

She dreamed of Ajax often.

The stirrings of life in the booking area woke her from a thin, troubled sleep. Through the window, she saw a gray, low sky. The snow had lightened considerably and looked to stop soon. A new voice had entered the chat, this one firmer and more authoritative—undoubtedly someone superior to the two underlings who had kept the night watch.

The conversation ended and was replaced by footsteps clocking down the hallway. She rose quickly, straightening her bedroll, wanting to be on her feet when this new person arrived at her cell. She stood in the middle of the space, her hands folded at her waist. Two men appeared at her cell, one holding a tray of food. He wore blue pants and a blue work shirt. There was a blank look on his face. A pass-through slot was built into the door; he opened it on his end and handed the tray through. On it was a sandwich, a piece of fruit, and a small cup of water with a lid secured to the top. Rachel accepted the tray and set it down on the bedroll.

"Stand and face the corner," said the man.

Rachel complied. The cell door clattered open, sending her hackles into overdrive. She detested this sensation of vulnerability.

"Please have a seat facing me," the man said.

She turned slowly, lowering herself to her bottom and sitting with her legs crossed in front of her. A second man, dressed in military fatigues, hung back, remaining outside the cell.

"Thank you, Martin," said the man in fatigues.

Martin nodded and departed, leaving Rachel alone with her visitor.

"Hungry?" he asked.

Rachel nodded.

"By all means," he said, gesturing to the food. "I've had breakfast."

Rachel ate slowly, never taking her eyes off the man. The bread was hard, and between the two slices was a pasty nut butter. It was virtually tasteless, but it was hearty and heavy with calories. More importantly, it extinguished the worry of hunger for the time being. Fear of starvation remained braided to Rachel's DNA, bolted onto her like a permanent renovation. Even now, even the slightest hunger pang fired up a cauldron of panic. Not all software upgrades were good ones.

The man was patient and said nothing while Rachel ate her meal. When she was done, she set the tray to the side and took in the measure of her host.

"Greetings," he said.

There was a perkiness to his voice that Rachel found off-putting.

"My name is Victor Hale."

∼

37

It was mid-January.

Rachel, Samir, and Elias were nearing the end of their third week as probationary members of the Waterside community. She didn't see much of the others, only in passing during the day and occasionally at mealtime. She'd been assigned to a four-person custodial crew responsible for cleaning the prison's extensive common areas. Hale demanded perfection in the facility's care, so she worked twelve hours a day, seven days a week.

Elias was assigned to work on a technology detail. Samir's medical training earned him a spot in the medical clinic; unfortunately, Rachel's experience as a nurse had not earned her a spot alongside him. That likely had been deliberate. Divide the new arrivals and conquer them.

Rachel kept to herself initially. The other three in her crew, two men and a woman, were friendly enough but a bit cliquish. The woman was named Darlene. She was older than Rachel, probably in her late thirties, and very sharp. Her work was efficient but thorough. The men, Jalen and Timothy, frequently deferred to her leadership. She'd probably been new to adulthood when the outbreak hit. The cliquishness didn't surprise or much bother Rachel, to be honest. Such bonds were common. Outsiders were generally viewed with suspicion. Rare was the community that didn't have a horror story of a pleasant outsider burrowing in and then unleashing holy hell. And that, after all, was what Rachel planned to do herself.

As she scrubbed the tables after that morning's breakfast service, her initial meeting with Hale played back in her mind. It had gone reasonably well. He was a tall man in his mid-to-late fifties. His fatigues fit him well and accentuated the trim figure underneath. The sleeves on each arm were folded up, revealing lean forearms belted with firm muscle. A long scar ran from the crook of his left elbow to his wrist. He struck Rachel as careful, cautious, and thorough. She would need to tread carefully.

When he asked her for her name, she had given the false name she and the others had developed for themselves.

"I'm Lillian," she said, offering up her alias.

"And your car caught fire," he said.

"Yes," she said. "And again, thank you for helping us. Not everyone does that these days."

"Well, it wasn't entirely altruistic, as I'm sure you understand. You see an explosion near your border, you're going to investigate."

"Of course."

"I sent a team out there at first light to investigate the fire."

She tensed slightly. A skilled investigator might be able to deduce that the fire had been intentionally set. If they reached that conclusion, it would be a short mission.

"I'm afraid the truck is a total loss."

She closed her eyes and let her shoulders sag—a true display of disappointment.

"It had almost a full tank of fuel," she said with dismay.

That was true. Her disappointment was genuine. Although vehicles were a dime a dozen, getting them to start was another matter. A tank full of their precious fuel was indeed a sacrifice.

He stabbed a finger toward her.

"I assume you're the leader of this ragtag group," said Hale.

"What makes you say that?"

"It's obvious," he said. "The men defer to you. Just in the way they talk. Typically, in this thing of ours, one woman with two men doesn't usually end too well for the woman. I'm sorry to be so blunt."

"Not at all. I appreciate your honesty."

"How is it the three of you came to be together?"

"Evan is actually my cousin."

Evan was Elias's alias. Their tenuous family connection was another part of the fiction they had constructed. A wrinkle that was just odd enough to add a layer of authenticity to the entire production.

Hale's eyebrows jumped up at the revelation.

"Distant cousin, if I'm being honest," she said. "We're from neighboring towns in Oklahoma. We share a great-great-grandfather. I'd only met him at a family reunion a couple of years before the plague."

"And you found each other."

"Bit of a lucky break there," she said.

"Were you married?"

"No," she said. "I was just out of high school. Working as a med tech in a nursing home when the virus hit."

"That must not have been very pleasant."

She faked a full-body shiver.

"It was very bad," she confirmed. "Once it got in the building..."

She trailed off, not needing to finish.

"Did anyone in the building survive?"

She lowered her head in pseudo-shame.

"I don't know," she said. "My last day there..."

She trailed off. Her eyes remained fixed on a spot on the ground.

"I was the only one who didn't get sick. I kept working as long as I could because no one else was willing or able to. After the second week, I'm guessing most of the staff was dead. But I kept going in. My last day, I was trying to do rounds—fifteen rooms in a row. Every single person was dead. I lost it. I couldn't take it anymore. I ran out of there and kept running. Five miles."

Hale sat with his legs crossed as she spoke, tapping his fingertips together. When she was done, he said nothing. He removed a pipe and some tobacco from the breast pocket of his camouflage shirt and lit the bowl. For a minute, maybe two, he simply stared at Rachel, saying nothing as he smoked his pipe.

"I think you and your friends will be a good fit here."

"Hey, new girl," said Darlene, rocking Rachel out of her daydream. "Run and get me some towels off the cart."

The "new girl" moniker served as an insult, a reminder to Rachel that it didn't matter where she had come from, that she was at the bottom of the Waterside food chain. It didn't faze Rachel either way. She complied with Darlene's order, retrieving the towels and handing them to the woman.

"Thank you," Darlene said.

Rachel nodded.

"You know, we're rough on the new folks," Darlene said. "We need to make sure that you're committing yourself here."

"No, I get it," Rachel said. "It's not a problem. Trust me, you're not going to hurt my feelings."

Darlene chuckled at that.

"You might do all right here. What's your story?"

"Nothing special," Rachel said. "I had just gotten out of high school when the big virus came through. I was working at a nursing home. Then boom, everybody was dead, and here I am. Just me and my cousin Evan for the first few years, and then we met the doctor. So how did you end up here?"

Darlene scrunched up her face and looked up at the ceiling as though deep in thought.

"I've been here about two years," she said. "It had been up and running for about a year when I got here."

"What's it like?"

"Not bad," she said. "General Hale runs a tight ship. Better get used to that. This ain't a democracy. But we're safe, we're healthy, and we have what we need. No crime. No nonsense."

It reminded her of the Citadel, of the men who had created the virus in the first place. What they'd been willing to sacrifice for this peace and quiet of which Darlene spoke so lovingly. But maybe that was what mattered now. These people hadn't been responsible for the end of the world, so who was Rachel to judge how they lived now?

"Hey, Lillian."

"Hmmm."

"Lillian!"

The voice snapped Rachel out of a deep sleep. It was early in the morning, and it was still dark outside. She shook her head again and pushed herself up to a sitting position.

"What is it?"

It was Darlene.

"Get up, girl. We got work to do."

"Our shift just ended."

"Hey, when the boss calls, we got to get up and go."

"What do we need to do?" she asked.

"We have to clean his house. Now. It's for the ceremony," Darlene said.

"What the hell is the ceremony?"

"I don't have time to explain that right now. Just come with me."

Rachel yawned, rubbed the sleep out of her eyes, and swung her legs over the side of the bed. She dressed quickly as Darlene waited in the room with her.

Rachel was no closer to divining the location of the vaccines than she'd been since their arrival at the prison. Their days here had become rote, and they were spinning their wheels more than anything else. She was ready to give it up and head back home to devise a new plan. That was assuming they could get out of this place unmolested. But this was something new, a pre-dawn wake-up call to attend to the ceremony. If nothing else, it was something new.

"Let's go, Lillian," Darlene said. "Big man doesn't like to wait."

Rachel tucked her hands in her sweatshirt and followed Darlene to the gallery outside her cell. It was well before dawn, and the cell block was still quiet. The place had been unusually quiet the last few days, like something malignant was spreading silently. Something fundamental about Waterside had changed, and this ceremony had to be connected to it.

Rachel put Waterside's population at about a thousand people, give or take ten percent. Of those, about a third, maybe forty percent, were women, and of those, about two hundred were of childbearing age. If Hale vaccinated every woman in Waterside, roughly eight hundred doses would remain. Eight hundred doses to exert total dominance over the region.

Rachel followed Darlene through the guard station just outside their cell block. The night was chilly, and the skies were clear. An infinite sea of stars shone down on them. Snow from the last big storm remained on the ground. The bone-chilling temperatures had glazed the top of the snowpack, which crunched underneath Rachel's shoes as they walked.

Hale lived in the warden's house, about a quarter mile outside the facility's gates. It was an old stone structure with two stories, and the windows were framed with black wooden trim. It looked cold and uninviting.

"Hey, Darlene," Rachel said, grabbing the woman by the elbow as they neared the pebbled sidewalk bisecting the home's front yard. Darlene yanked her arm away from Rachel.

"Tell me what the ceremony is."

Darlene stopped suddenly and looked back at Rachel.

"It's something new. Just within the last couple of months."

"Go on," Rachel said.

Darlene sighed and blew out a long breath.

"I guess you've been here long enough. I can tell you

about it. When they tell you about it, just act surprised, okay?"

Rachel nodded, a picture of where this story was going forming in her mind.

"You know about the babies, right?"

Rachel nodded.

"Of course. The babies die."

"Right. The babies all die. Well, General Hale found a way to protect the babies. To keep them from dying!"

In the moonlight, Rachel saw that Darlene's cheeks were wet with tears.

"Are you serious?" Rachel said, feigning surprise.

"Yeah," she said. "We got a baby here that's ten days old already. No one has seen a baby survive that long since it happened."

"How is that even possible?"

"Hale used to work for some big pharmaceutical company."

A chill ran up Rachel's spine.

"Penumbra," Rachel said, a bit louder than she intended.

"Yeah," said Darlene, eyeing Rachel quizzically. "How'd you know that?"

"Lucky guess," Rachel said, covering her mistake as best as she could. "One of the big ones from before."

"I guess," Darlene said. "Anyway, he was able to get a big supply of vaccine. A vaccine that protects the babies inside their mamas."

Darlene took a step toward Rachel, curling her fingers around Rachel's elbow.

"Here's the thing, though. It ain't free."

"I don't understand," Rachel said.

Darlene tilted her head and raised a knowing eyebrow.

And then, all at once, Rachel did understand. She understood it all too well.

38

———

The import of Darlene's words froze Rachel into a moment of paralysis. Victor Hale's plan came into sharp relief. If Victor Hale had his way, his legacy would be secured. As many as a thousand babies could be fathered by him—future generations would trace back their lineage, their heritage, back to this man, this dark, evil man. She tried to do the math in her head, but as she considered it, the permutations, the future generations, all of which would trace themselves back to Victor Hale, her head began to spin. She realized Darlene was talking.

"Sorry, I zoned out for a second," said Rachel.

"I was just saying, do you know the worst part of this?" Darlene asked.

Rachel shook her head, chilled to the bone by the ramifications of her realization.

"He's not even forcing us to do it. You volunteer to do it, to let him be the father."

"Darlene, how many women live here?

"I think it's about a hundred, maybe a hundred twenty can have babies."

"How many have agreed to do this?"

"I would say almost all of them.

"But not everybody?"

"No."

"What about you, Darlene? Are you going to do this?"

The woman's jaw tightened and her face turned to stone.

"No, I will not do it. I refuse to give that man the satisfaction. If my bloodline ends here, so be it. At least it will end with dignity. It will end because I chose it to end."

Rachel's mind was racing. Darlene's opposition to Hale's new vaccine protocol made her a potential ally. She might help Rachel find the vaccine. The discontent in the woman's voice was evident. This might have been the break Rachel had been looking for. Time was running short. The pace of vaccinations would likely increase and begin eating into the remaining supply. And the fewer the doses, the harder it would be to restart civilization in a way that didn't carry the imprimatur of Victor Hale.

Bringing Darlene into her confidence was risky, so she kept turning it over in her head as she worked. Rachel cleaned silently, scrubbing every nook and cranny of Hale's private chambers. She wanted the place to absolutely shine. Her gaze drifted to the king-sized bed in the middle of the room. She wondered how many times each woman had to subject herself to Hale's advances before becoming pregnant and thus worthy of the vaccine.

Just thinking about it made her want to vomit. Even now, the patriarchy still burned brightly. It was who they were, as a people, as a species. And perhaps that's how things would unfold if she managed to get her hands back on the vaccine. Women would give birth to little boys, who might become men like Victor Hale. And she would have to fight them, too. Or Will would have to. Or Will's children would have to. But at least they would be charting their own future, their own way.

Another revelation slammed into her like a drunk driver running a red light. Nothing was more valuable than the vaccine, and once word of its effectiveness spilled out into the world, communities would be lining up at Hale's door. They would gladly trade dominion over their communities in exchange for a nursery full of healthy screaming babies.

This would be the first move to build a major new society since the pandemic. Until now, humanity had been splintered, pieces of a puzzle scattered across the globe. Soon, however, Hale would control manpower, arsenals, medicine stores, food supplies, and trade routes. It would snowball from there, Waterside growing larger and larger until no one was left to challenge it. Hale was only one man, but he was sure to find loyalists who would do his bidding and lord over these subservient communities.

There was nothing to stop him. A thousand doses of vaccine could seed dozens of smaller communities. And a virtual army of Hale's children would quickly follow. Even after his vaccine supply ran dry, his legacy would be secure. Future generations would look back to him as the father of their new world.

This new world would have been built on the backs of innocent women desperate to experience motherhood, not just for themselves but for humanity itself. It was wrong in so many ways, repugnant to the human experience. At the very least, he didn't deserve this legacy. He would have to take it from Rachel. Their old world had perished in a flood of disease. She would not let the new one be born in a maelstrom of rape.

"Darlene?"

The woman was chewing on a thumbnail, her face blank, her mind elsewhere.

"Hmm?"

Her nail-biting intensified.

"We can stop him."

FOR THE NEXT WEEK, Darlene and Rachel kept their ears to the ground, stealing snippets of conversation among Waterside's top brass. Rachel worked to position herself near Hale whenever he was around. She was careful to appear subservient, to make herself almost invisible. But not entirely so. She wanted him to notice her. Rachel knew her figure often caught the wandering eye of men she did not know.

This was a phenomenon that never ceased to amaze her. She had never viewed herself as an object of desire, but that was what she had become. High school Rachel would be amazed. Her body was lean and hard from the years of deprivation and struggle. But her femininity was a weapon, one she never hesitated to use. It was a lesson she had learned from a woman named Vania years ago. Vania had run a brothel, and she did so without shame or remorse. As she had told Rachel, she gave a man thirty minutes with her body, thirty minutes of herself, and she ate for a week. It was a lesson that Rachel had taken to heart, ultimately saving her life after Evergreen had fallen.

The rhythms and patterns of life at Waterside began to reveal themselves. Everyone worked hard. No one slept in. Mealtime was quick and efficient. Chitchat was pleasant but kept to a minimum. One cold, clear morning, Rachel was finishing her meager breakfast, anxious for the diners to move along so she could get to work on cleaning the dining room. One by one, the Watersiders made their way for the exits, dropping off their trays on their way out.

Hale came in as she was stacking trays. He moved gracefully, smoothly, like a jungle cat circling its prey. Rachel continued to work, keeping her eye on him. Now was not the time to act subserviently. Now was the time to demonstrate strength and femininity, showing Hale she was worthy of the vaccine.

"Good morning," he said, approaching her as she finished stacking a dozen trays.

"Hello," she said pleasantly.

His eyes remained fixed on her, making her feel like she was putting on a show for him. It seemed important to do the work well, so she was careful about it. As she worked, she occasionally glanced at Hale, cutting her eyes toward him.

"How are things going?" he finally asked.

"It's been good," she said. "I'm settling in well."

"Glad to hear it."

She moved on, gathering stray dishes and cups from the tables. Hale did not offer to help, instead sitting at the table closest to the cafeteria exit. Darlene was working in the back, pretending not to pay attention but keeping an eye out.

"Take a load off," he said, gesturing toward the seat across from him.

Rachel wiped her hands on the towel draped over her shoulder and took the seat.

"I've had my eye on you," he said.

Good, Rachel thought. *That was the plan.*

"You're going to make a fine addition to Waterside."

"What makes you think that?"

"Sometimes you just have a feeling."

"I see."

She remained quiet, hoping to draw more out of him. Men like Hale loved to hear the sound of their own voices.

"You've arrived here at an opportune time."

"Is that right?" she asked a bit coquettishly.

He smiled at that. Men were so damn predictable. That didn't mean he wasn't smart or dangerous, but knowing his behavior could be anticipated was reassuring.

"Yes," he said. "And I want you to be part of our future here. Because Waterside is just the beginning."

"How so?"

"What would you say is the biggest problem facing Waterside? Facing any community."

"The babies."

"Exactly. But what if I told you that we can scoot around that little problem?"

"I think you would quickly become a very famous man."

This was not hyperbole. It wasn't just fame. It would become the stuff of legend. The human race, rising up again. Perhaps that was what had held her back all this time. Knowing the attention this would all draw. In the end, fear had controlled her. It was tough to admit to herself, but that was a fact. She had lost the vaccine because she had been afraid. Now, she needed to climb over that fear and fulfill her destiny. After all, was it not her family that had, in part, brought humanity to this pass? Did she not owe a debt to the world, what was left of it, at least?

He chuckled at that.

"Yes, that's true. But fame is fleeting. As soon as you have it, it disappears again. And what good is fame in a world like ours? I want something more. Something more tangible. A legacy. Something that will last beyond us. We won't be here forever."

Longer than you might think.

"And how do you propose to build that legacy?"

"Do you want to become a mother, Rachel?"

She nodded.

"Yes."

"Have you been pregnant since the pandemic ended?"

She cut her eyes down and set her hands on the table. Her fingers fumbled together, acting the part of a woman wracked by ancient grief.

"Yes," she said softly. "Twice."

"I don't have to ask what happened to those precious babies, do I?"

"No."

"It doesn't have to be that way," he said. "You can become a mother and not have to bury your child long before its time. No parent should ever have to say goodbye to their child."

Rachel took in his words, wondering how women were reacting to this offer, this deal with the devil. He could just give them the shot, of course, with no questions asked. The ultimate act of altruism. Everything they had ever wanted, right there. In a different world, where the fate of her family had not been braided with the fate of humanity, perhaps this offer would have been dangled in front of her. It would be difficult to resist. She had to admit that to herself. It would be very tough.

"Come to my house tonight," he said, rising from his seat. "And I'll show you how to make that a reality."

"What if I don't want to?"

A broad smile spread across his face.
"No one is forced into anything against their will."
"Okay."
"I'll see you tonight."

39

———

Rachel moved through the dinner service robotically, focusing on the task ahead. Dinner was uneventful. Boiled potatoes, turnips, and a spoonful of beans for protein. Around her, people delved into idle chatter. Whispers of new things as she cleaned tables and collected stray trays. If she could generate a word cloud based on the conversations, the largest would contain the words "baby," "vaccine," and "shot."

It was moving into the mainstream now. Whatever Hale had planned, it was starting. After the in-house administrations were done, he would move on the neighboring communities and not stop until his grip over the region was ironclad. He would have to be stopped here.

The cafeteria slowly emptied. The Watersiders exited in dribs and drabs until Rachel and Darlene were alone. They drifted into the kitchen, each mopping a counter, their backs to one another.

"You ready?" Darlene asked.

"I'm ready," she said. "You'll get the message to Elias and Samir?"

After parting ways with Rachel, Darlene would find the men and deliver the coded message they'd agreed on—the signal to meet Rachel at the prison entrance.

"Yeah, but you'll be on your own."

"Then that's how it'll have to be.

Rachel took a knife from a dish drainer and tucked it into the pocket of her apron. She turned to leave when Darlene grabbed her by the elbow. As Rachel turned back, Darlene threw her arms around her and held her tightly. The embrace took Rachel by surprise. Although their friendship had been brief, their closeness had hardened like masonry.

"Be careful, lady," said Darlene.

Rachel nodded.

She left Darlene alone in the kitchen and crossed through the dining room to the exit. Outside, the cold slapped hard. The skies were clear and dark. She cursed herself under her breath. Her fears and her hesitation had brought them to this point. More than three years had elapsed since the destruction of Olympus; if she hadn't dragged her feet, there could have been dozens, if not hundreds of babies, born immune since. Instead, she had let the perfect become the enemy of the good. Not again, she swore to herself. If she survived this night, she would not repeat that mistake.

Pride goeth before the fall.

A sliver of memory from her Sunday school teachings bubbled up in her mind. A memory from childhood, from San Diego, when her mom would drag her to church once a week. Before they met her mom's future husband, Jerry. Away from her father, Adam, alone and miserable. For all that, she had forgotten the lesson anyway. It was the most important lesson that this world could teach you. You had to remain humble; if you ever started to think you were better than this world, stronger than it, well, you were in for a very rude awakening.

The cell block was dim, the flickering light of the lanterns casting a strange orange glow on its drab gray walls. The prison's nightlife was well underway. Each night, Watersiders assembled to play cards and drink the moonshine they distilled. Stitches of laughter fractured the evening air. These weren't bad people; Rachel liked many of them. But it could not be this way; Hale could not have the last word on how humanity's hard drive would be reformatted.

After reaching her cell, she changed into jeans and a dark gray sweatshirt. She laced up her heaviest pair of boots. One way or another, her time at the prison was coming to an end.

No one paid her any mind as she made her way to the end of the block and through the unmanned security checkpoint. She descended two dark flights of stairs into the main lobby of this building. After zipping her jacket tightly, she stepped outside into the cold, dank night. The temperature had plunged into the twenties. Very few people were out and about. It was cold enough in the cell blocks; it was downright dangerous out here. A single guard, warmed by a fire in a rusty old oil drum, kept watch at the prison's main entrance.

The walk to Hale's home took less than ten minutes, but it reenergized her. She felt alive. The end of a long journey that had started nearly fifteen years ago was in sight. One way or another, something was ending tonight; the status quo was changing permanently. These people here at Waterside, back at Riverview, people worldwide didn't know it yet, but the next few hours would change their lives. Maybe it would go her way; maybe it would not.

She cleared her throat and coughed as she reached the portico at the front of Hale's house. Her light knock on the door was quickly answered by the man himself. He was still dressed in his fatigues, which surprised her a bit. She wasn't sure why. Did she expect him to answer the door in satin pajamas and holding a brandy?

"Good evening," he said. "Right on time. Come in, please."

She crossed the threshold, and he closed the door behind him. It clicked shut with a certain finality. He led her to a sitting room. An antique settee sat on one side of the room; across from it was a very old wingback chair. A fire roared in the gigantic fireplace in the middle of the west-facing wall.

"I'll be right back."

He left her alone in this bizarre room and disappeared for ten minutes. She heard him fumbling around somewhere deeper in the house. The thought of moving against him now crossed her mind, but she decided against it. There was a plan. She needed him at his most vulnerable. Hale was a tall man, a well-built man, and things could quickly go south if she didn't have the upper hand.

He returned to the room, a bottle of wine in one hand and two wine glasses in the other; their stems were clamped between his thick fingers. He made quite a show of it, pouring a small dram of the purple liquid into one of the glasses. He spent a few moments swirling the wine in his glass, tilting its lip to his nose and taking in heavy sniffs.

"I allow myself this one indulgence," he said. "The amount of wine sitting in cellars around the ruins of this once great country is staggering to me. A lot of it is probably gone, victim to the savages who probably didn't even know what they were drinking when all they wanted was a good buzz."

He shook his head wistfully.

"But now and again, I'll find a very good one to savor."

God bless America, did this man ever shut up?

He wanted Rachel to like him. Maybe not *like* him, but he wanted her to respect him, to think he was a man of culture, of art, of renaissance, even while he was an oppressive dictator. That he was worthy of siring her offspring.

Rachel had taken the wingback seat lest he try to sit next to her. He handed her a glass of wine and sat on the sofa. She set the glass on the small end table next to the chair as he settled into his spot.

"Not a wine drinker?"

"I'm not a drinker at all."

"I can respect that."

"I'm sure it's delicious."

He took another sip and then set his glass on a small end table. He swirled the glass around, swishing the liquid to release its flavors.

"I'm sure you have questions about why I asked you here tonight."

"Yes, I do. How can you be sure that the babies will survive?"

As she spoke, she wondered if Hale knew who she was. After all, he was a Penumbra product. If so, this could be an elaborate trap that would end with her brutal murder, but she was committed now, and she could not turn back.

"Well, we don't know why the babies die, even when they're born to mothers who are immune to the Medusa virus. But we know that invariably they die."

Rachel nodded her understanding.

"But in the end, as bad as it is, Medusa is still just a virus, and it can be defeated."

"But how?"

"I've come into possession of a rather large stockpile of Medusa vaccine."

Rachel clapped her hand to her mouth, but she remained quiet. Silence was the appropriate reaction to such a revelation.

He smiled.

"And rest assured, it is the real deal."

"That's amazing," she said softly.

"With this vaccine, we can start anew."

"I did work as a nurse some years ago," she said.

She almost said she worked with her father, but that would open a can of worms she most certainly wanted to keep a lid on. Disclosing that both she *and* her father had survived the Medusa virus would invite a lot of questions. Her father's immunity remained a bit of a mystery. To this day, she did not know if he'd been vaccinated like her or if he'd been naturally immune. The most likely scenario was that her grandfather had vaccinated Adam, but she would likely never know the whole truth.

"I can help you administer the vaccine," she offered. "That would be my pleasure."

He laughed softly before taking another sip of the wine and finishing his glass. He poured himself a little more, but not as much. Only about half of what he poured the first time.

"Thank you, but we're all set in that department. What we need are women who are willing to accept the vaccine."

"Sign me up. I'm all for it. I'm all in."

"Wonderful. There is just one small price to pay."

"And what price is that?"

He stood up and threw another piece of wood on the fire. The log sparked a shower of embers as it landed on the dancing blaze; the fireplace coughed out a shower of warmth that felt rather pleasant against Rachel's cheeks. Then Hale knelt and worked the fire with a black poker.

"This has been a dark time for us all," he said. "When that damned virus broke free, it took away everything we had worked so hard to build, all the progress we had made for centuries. We put a man on the moon, for God's sake!"

Rachel kept quiet as his monologue continued.

"You know what I think about sometimes?"

"What?"

"The Voyager spacecraft."

He turned his head to his shoulder, revealing his face in profile, illuminated by the blaze in front of him.

"You know about the Voyager mission?"

"Yes," Rachel said.

The Voyager mission was one of NASA's shining accomplishments. Launched two weeks apart in 1977, the two small spacecraft, Voyager I and II, exceeded the agency's wildest dreams. For decades, they collected data and sent it back to Earth. The world had ended, but their lonely mission into interstellar space continued unabated, headed to unknown points.

"I think about those little spaceships," Hale continued. "We weren't even born when they were launched. Sixty years later, they're still out there, still tumbling through the cosmos. I think about them sending data back to Mission Control, even though there's no one there to receive it. I think about that, and it makes me sad."

Then he turned to face her, putting his back to the fire. The flames seemed to surround him, giving him an almost demonic visage.

"It's our duty to rebuild this world," he said, continuing. "And the only way to do that is together. We have to stand together. Or we will fall, each of us, alone."

"And this vaccine is part of that?"

"Of course," he said. "But that's not enough. Not nearly enough."

"What would be enough?" asked Rachel.

"Hope," he said. "The world needs hope. People need something to look to, to make them feel like they're going somewhere. They need to feel connected.

"Connection is important, wouldn't you agree?"

"Very," Rachel said. "We've drifted apart from one another."

Even as she said those words, her blood was boiling, listening to this man talk about community and togetherness, this man who had murdered innocent people to take the very vaccine he wanted to use for this come-to-Jesus moment for humanity. Her teeth sunk into her lower lip, and she clenched her hands into fists, waiting for this wave of rage to pass.

He smiled boyishly, almost embarrassed by what he was about to say.

"It's going to be me," he said. "I'll be the father of this new world."

"Not sure I understand."

He stepped toward Rachel, towering over her now, and placed a finger under her chin.

"If you want the vaccine, I'll be the father," he said, his voice sharp and dark. "I'll be the father of each and every baby that's born. And I'm offering you this opportunity tonight."

❧

40

───────

A thin nightgown awaited Rachel on Hale's bed. It was light blue and made of cotton. She changed into it quickly, laying her regular clothes on a chair by the bedroom door. There would be little time to escape after she killed Hale. After she was dressed for the Ceremony, she climbed into his bed and pulled the comforter up to her chest.

He entered the room a few moments later, wearing a robe. It was dark green with blue pinstriping. Something about it was emasculating, like he was someone's grandfather, and it made her a little less afraid of what was about to transpire. Rarely had she ever felt this close to death, and every sliver, every strand, every thread of courage that she could find, she would take.

"I want to show you something," he said.

He knelt and removed the familiar valise from under the bed. Rachel's breath caught in her throat. He spun the combination lock and opened the lid. His hand emerged with a vial of the vaccine. Rachel's heart thrummed with anticipation.

"This is it," he said, holding the vial gently between his thumb and forefinger. "This is our salvation. Our redemption."

"Once you are with child," he said, "you'll be administered a single dose of this vaccine. It is foolproof. Your baby will be born healthy, and your baby will survive to see his first birthday and beyond. Your child will grow up and go out into the world, safe from the Medusa virus. He will have children of his own, and those children will be immune to Medusa. And a generation or two from now, Medusa will be nothing but a memory. A lesson. A warning. But no longer a threat."

"How many?" she asked. "Before me?"

"You'll be the twelfth."

"Eleven are pregnant?"

"Yes," he said, the proud papa-to-be.

It had really begun. Already, Hale had started executing his nightmarish vision for the future of their world. Her own hesitancy and self-doubt had condemned these poor women to an impossible choice. She wanted to find them, hug them, and apologize to them because it was her fault they were in this place.

Her eyes watered; Hale noticed.

"It's a remarkable thing," he said. "I'm glad you see that. It's not easy, what I'm asking you to do. But it's so important. The next generation must look back to a place they have in common, a place that we began anew."

She wanted to keep him talking as she readied her attack. With his focus on sex that was just moments away, she mentally reviewed her plan one last time. Her attack would come after he disrobed, when he was most vulnerable. But it had to be before he was in bed with her; he was simply too big to overpower. And if she waited until after he was finished, it might be too late. He didn't strike her as the type interested in a post-coital cuddle.

As he unlaced the cinch of his robe, Rachel got out of bed.

"Do you mind if I step into the ladies' room once before we start?"

He huffed softly at the inconvenience.

"Be my guest."

The half-bath was just off-suite. It was small, with just enough room for the toilet and the stand-up shower. She knelt at the base of the commode and reached behind it, gently probing the cool ceramic with her fingers.

There!

The gun was taped to the back of the toilet tank, just as Darlene had promised. The plan was rather ingenuous now that Rachel thought about it. Borrowed from a pivotal scene in *The Godfather*, the scene in which Michael Corleone assassinates two men as revenge for the attempted murder of his father. Who would've thought that decades after its release, it might serve as the linchpin for the redemption of the human race? She quickly peeled off the tape and crumpled it into a ball. Tucked behind the commode was a plastic bag containing a change of clothes and a pair of shoes. She changed quickly; if she dithered much longer, Hale would grow suspicious.

She stepped back into the room, her heart racing but her mind calm. Just moments away now. As she turned the corner, a shadow flickered against the far wall. Instinct sent her to the ground as Hale came crashing toward her. She fired a single shot desperately, more of a defensive maneuver than an execution of her now-botched plan. The gunshot was deafening in the enclosed space, but in its wake, she heard a primal grunt of pain. The shot had nicked Hale's shoulder. Not nearly enough to bring him down.

"You bitch!" he bellowed.

He kicked out hard, his foot catching the gun and knocking it to the floor. A quick glance for the weapon turned up nothing; she had to move now. If he got his hands on her, she would never get out of here. As he struggled to regain his footing, she bolted toward the nightstand on the far side of the bed. The vaccine lay where Hale had placed it. She grabbed the familiar case from the lockbox on the fly. An all-out sprint got her to the bedroom door just as a shot rang out behind her. A bullet smashed into the wall, splintering the drywall.

The hallway leading away from the bedroom opened to the small family room. Instead of bolting directly toward the exit, she ducked to the right and pressed against the wall just outside the door to Hale's bedroom. She looked around for a weapon. There was a sideboard to her right; atop it stood a squadron of liquor bottles, some fuller than others. She settled on a mostly full bottle of dark rum.

As Hale breached the living room, she reared back like a cleanup hitter and swung hard toward Hale's head. The bottle connected solidly with the side of his skull, staggering him and dropping him to his knees. He grunted like a wounded buffalo. The gun fell to the ground and ended up pinned between Hale's chest and the ground as he tipped forward into a prone position.

Rachel wedged a hand under his belly, trying to pull the gun free, but it was no use. He was just too heavy. He moaned in pain as he pushed himself to his knees. She reared back to hit him again, but he swung out his leg, catching her under the ankle. The sweep caught her off guard and nearly brought her down within arm's reach of

Hale. He swung his forearm wildly, catching the side of Rachel's head with a glancing blow. Her vision blurred, darkening just long enough that she feared she might pass out. She kicked hard, catching him in the cheek, which sent him back down again. But he was a tough son of a bitch, and he wouldn't be down long.

The gun was a lost cause. She had to move.

RACHEL HUSTLED toward the prison grounds, making her way toward the rendezvous point with Samir and Elias. The pack lay snug against her back, its heft reassuring. The night was silent but for the susurration of her rapid footsteps crunching down on the hard-packed snow. She made it back to the gate less than five minutes after escaping Hale's residence. There was no sign of her friends.

A guard shivered near the tower, standing near a blazing oil drum. He rubbed his hands together to keep warm. An insulated carafe sat on the lip of the tower's windowsill. After he was sufficiently toasty, he unscrewed the cap and took a sip. She gestured to the guard in the watchtower. He opened the gate for her, letting her back in.

"I'm not going to be here long," she said. "I just needed to grab something for my meeting with the boss."

"Sure, sure," said the guard.

A thin crescent moon lit the way, spilling just enough light to make navigation easy. After crossing the courtyard, she paused at the main entrance of her cell block and slowly opened the door. It screeched open with a loud squeal. She hustled inside, passing the front reception area to the stairwell beyond. Samir and Elias lived near one another, their cells on the second level of this block, a men's unit.

She took the steps two at a time, her boots twanging the metal stairs as she neared the top. The door to the cell block was ajar, as it usually was. Beyond that, the sound of conversation, the smell of burning tobacco so strong it made her eyes water.

Rachel hustled down the corridor. Samir's cell was halfway down the platform; Elias's cell was at the end. As she moved deeper into the prison, it suddenly felt very prison-like. This was a hell of a chance she was taking. But leaving the men behind was not an option.

Even if Hale regained his senses quickly, he'd assume she had taken off with the vaccine. Her return here would be the last thing he would expect. After all, she had the vaccine.

Or so she hoped.

Samir's cell was empty. Anxiety pricked the back of her neck. She continued along the platform toward Elias's cell, but it, too, was empty. This was the last thing she needed. The prison complex was big; there was no time to look for them.

"Dammit," she muttered under her breath.

As she turned to leave Elias's cell, something out of place caught her eye. As she crossed the threshold into the little bunk, she spotted it. The pillow had been shoved underneath the mattress. A last-resort emergency signal they'd agreed on—a coded message to meet in a backup location.

The rendezvous was between two dumpsters just behind the kitchen. The area was often deserted; the rich, thick smell of rot was overpowering on most days, even in cold weather. A cord of panic tightened around her throat. The news would not be good, that was for certain. After all, they'd be expecting her to have the vaccine. She scoured the cell for anything of value, gathering a few supplies. Then she left.

She eased her way back down the platform, retracing her steps towards the exit. A woman passed Rachel on the galley. They exchanged pleasantries, but Rachel did not stop to talk. The danger rose with every passing second. She burst through the door and into the courtyard, the panic rising in her throat like bile. The courtyard was deserted.

She cut northwest through the courtyard, around a grove of trees, reaching the path leading to the dining facility. Her heart was pounding. If they weren't there, she would have to leave without them. She had done all she could, but the vaccine had to take priority. The plan had been desperate and reckless from the start, but the whole thing depended on her getting access to the vaccine.

The smell of the trash receptacles hit her long before she reached them. In the dark and gloom, she kept close to the side of the building. The first receptacle sat just beyond the southwest corner of the building. She froze. Her ears detected movement between the two large metal containers.

"It's me," she whispered.

"We're here," came the muted reply.

Samir and Elias were huddled together in the shadows of the building. Both were incredibly excited, animated, worried.

"I got it," she said, gently tapping the backpack.

"Great, great," Samir said. "But we have a much bigger problem to deal with. Two problems, actually."

Samit had never been rattled in the short time she had known him. Not even on the night that Riverview had been attacked. But he was now.

"What?"

"Tell her," Samir said to Elias.

"First of all, they know who you are," Elias said.

She scoffed. That was why Hale had attacked her. It was a trap.

"And the second problem?"

"This one is much worse," Elias said.

"He has a kill switch," Samir said breathlessly. "Hale has a kill switch."

"What are you talking about?"

"He can deactivate the vaccines," Elias said. "All of them. The one in me. The one in you. The one in your son."

41

———————

The news buckled Rachel's knees, and it took all her strength not to crumple to the ground. After everything that she had seen, it was hard to shock Rachel Fisher anymore. But she wasn't sure she had ever heard something so truly macabre, so evil, so twisted. Instinctively, she stepped back from the men as if they were infected with Medusa, and she was naked, bare, devoid of any protection from the monstrous pathogen.

Will.

The virus was inside all of them. After exposure, Medusa took up permanent residence in the human host, like chicken pox or herpes. For most people, this fact mattered little because Medusa killed the overwhelming majority of its hosts. In a tiny portion of the population, perhaps no more than one in a hundred, the virus bounced around harmlessly, unable to latch onto a cell and begin its terrible work. These were the naturally immune survivors.

But then there were those like her.

Like Will.

Those who carried the artificial life support system that

was the vaccine, forever protecting them from the virus that would do them harm. The nanovaccine was everywhere inside them, standing guard at every corner. Without the protection of these microscopic machines, they would be doomed to a terrible fate.

"Are you sure?"

"Yes," Elias said. "That's what I've been working on. Hale's got a device that transmits the kill signal, but its range is very limited. They've been building a repeater, a transmission tower that can send the signal to a Penumbra satellite. From there, it can relay the signal all over the world."

"My God."

"The project has been on the books for years, but it's just now coming to fruition."

"Is he planning to use it?"

"Yes," he said. "And soon. There's something else."

"What?"

"Did you know about the vaccine's life-extending feature?"

"Yes," she said.

"What?" asked Samir incredulously.

She turned to look at him.

"I have not been sick since I received the vaccine," she said. "Not once."

"My God."

"It seems my lifespan will extend a bit longer than I once believed."

"Actually..." Elias interjected, holding up a finger.

Now Rachel turned to face him.

"Go on."

"That portion of the vaccine's programming has stopped working."

"Really? Any idea why?"

"No," he replied. "But it's fired Hale up something fierce. He knows that his time is limited, and this legacy is more important to him than ever."

Rachel did not know what to think about that. Part of her considered it an abomination to be absolved of the debt that every human being owed. You were born, you lived, you had your chance, and then you died, and the parts that made up the only you that would ever exist would go off and become something else. To live two or three centuries felt like an affront to nature.

But if Elias was correct, then it was out of her hands. And maybe that's how it was supposed to be.

"But we're still safe from Medusa."

"Yes."

Rachel tightened the straps of the backpack, as though it could protect the vaccine from Hale's deactivation device.

"I don't understand," she said. "If he uses it, then he deactivates this batch as well. The one in him and everyone here. It would be like a mass suicide."

"No. A geofence around the prison will protect this location from the deactivation signal."

A geofence was a digital border around a particular physical location. Anyone inside it would be safe from the effects of the kill switch. It was an old technology but had come into widespread use in the years before the pandemic.

"And if the vaccine is deactivated?" Rachel asked. "I mean, that's it, right? End of the road. We're dead."

Samir rubbed his chin thoughtfully.

"I don't know what will happen."

"But the virus is inside me. Inside Will. Inside Elias."

"Yes. Almost certainly."

"And without these nanoparticles, the virus can run wild."

Samir's face turned eerily blank.

"Yes," he said. "Unless you're naturally immune, I guess."

His voice trailed off, and he said nothing more. There was nothing more to say.

Sure, there was a chance she was naturally immune. A one percent chance. And Will bore that same chance. That meant there was a one-in-ten-thousand chance that both were naturally immune. But considering that both had been fortunate enough to be vaccinated, it felt like they'd used up their lucky shot regarding the virus. It was comical to hope that either would be naturally immune, much less both. There were no two ways around it. If Hale deactivated the vaccine, she and Will were doomed.

"Do you know where this transmission tower is?" Rachel asked.

Elias nodded.

"It's not far."

"How does the sequence work?"

"He needs to interface the deactivation device with the transmission tower," Elias said. "It's a bit of a fail-safe, so it's not initiated by accident. He can't do it remotely."

A chill ran through Rachel. That explained Hale's failure to return to the prison. He was on his way to initiate the deactivation sequence. He certainly wouldn't have thought that Rachel would return to the prison. And so, he'd decided to use the nuclear option.

"We have to destroy it," Rachel said. "Tonight. Now."

The men nodded their agreement.

"Can we get to a vehicle?" Rachel asked.

"Yes," Elias said. "I can get a truck from the motor pool."

"Can we go right now?"

"Yes, I don't think we have any choice."

"What about any explosives?" she asked. "Anything we can use to destroy the transmission tower?"

"I'm not sure about that," Samir said. "I can check the armory."

"You and I will do that while Elias gets the truck."

Adrenaline coursed through Rachel's veins. The point of no return was upon them. It was time to make their stand; they would either prevent Hale from activating the kill switch or they wouldn't. She couldn't believe that such a thing even existed. Recovering the vaccine hadn't been enough. It hadn't been the end. The finish line kept moving farther and farther back. Every time it felt like victory was at hand, a new obstacle rose to stand in their way.

It was as if the world preferred chaos. As if the world hadn't fallen apart enough already. Humanity did not deserve its dark fate. For all of its shortcomings, for all of its mistakes, for all of its flaws, humanity had deserved better than the Medusa virus.

"Everyone ready?" she asked.

"Yeah.

Rachel and Samir fist-bumped Elias, who then melted into the darkness as he headed to complete his part of the mission.

"You know that the armory is heavily guarded, right?" Samir said.

"That's why there's two of us."

"Yikes," he replied. "I don't like the sound of that."

"We don't have any other choice."

"I know, I know," Samir said. "I just wish one time the solution to a problem wasn't violence."

"Well, that's something we can aspire to, but for now, it's going to have to be violence," Rachel said, keenly aware of the flippant tone of her voice.

She didn't like it, but it was necessary. Sometimes, the world demanded violence. And when it was time to fight, fight like your life depended on it. When the rules had been stripped away, all that stood between them and chaos, total malice, was the willingness to do what the other side was already willing to do. You didn't have to like it. The willingness to do it was what mattered.

"Okay," Rachel said, "lead me to the armory."

"This way," Samir said, nodding to the north.

They remained close to the building until they emerged in an open plaza. The armory was housed in a separate building. The current iteration of Waterside had amassed a large armory far beyond what the prison would have needed. In the past month alone, Waterside had conquered a dozen communities as part of its expansion maneuver and confiscated all of those communities' arsenals.

The armory was about a hundred yards from the dining facility, near the west perimeter fence. There was a lot of open ground between the two buildings, which would leave Samir and Rachel extremely exposed. In the glint of the pale moonlight, Rachel spotted two guards patrolling the perimeter of the armory. These would be efficient, competent men he had there, men who were supremely loyal to Victor Hale. One survived an uprising by ensuring it never happened in the first place.

"How are we going to do this?" Samir asked.

"We need a diversion. We need to get at least one of the guards away from the armory."

"Hang on, I've got an idea," Samir said.

"Wait a second," Rachel pleaded.

"I can see the ring of keys on his hip," Samir replied.

Then he winked at her.

He broke clear of the cover of the building and strolled

toward the armory, just a man out on an evening walk. He drew the attention of the two guards, but they made no move. They just kept an eye on him as he approached them. He hadn't made any threatening moves yet.

Suddenly, Samir bent over, clutching his side and moaning in pain. He howled mightily, loud enough to draw the attention of the guards. They looked at each other. One nodded to the other and jogged over toward Samir. Rachel could hear much of their conversation in the cold silence of the winter night.

"What's wrong with you, man?" asked the guard.

"Not sure," Samir responded, gasping a little bit. "I've had a bit of a stomachache all day, and now it's really shooting up my side. Could be my appendix."

"Oh shit, that's bad," said the guard.

"Yeah, can you help me get over to the infirmary?"

"Not supposed to leave the post, man."

Samir responded to this man's reply with a blood-curdling shriek.

"Okay, okay, okay, I'll take you. Jesus. Just don't die on me here, man."

He looped Samir's arm around his neck and tried to guide him back towards the infirmary, but Samir made himself dead weight, making it hard for the guard to escort him.

"I can't walk," Samir said. "It hurts too bad, man."

He grunted and then tipped his head to the side and feigned vomiting.

"Don't puke on me, man. I'll puke if I see puke."

Samir gagged again.

"Hey, Oscar," called out the guard to his partner. "Help me get him over to the infirmary."

"We're not supposed to leave the armory, man. Some-one's got to be here at all times. Hale will throw a hissy fit."

"It's two minutes to the infirmary. I can't get the guy there alone. I don't want him to die right here in the courtyard."

The second guard scoffed with frustration.

"Christ. Alright, I'll be right there."

Oscar looked around for any surreptitious threats, decided the place was safe for a couple of minutes, and then jogged over to help the other man get Samir to the infirmary.

"Thanks, guys," Samir sputtered. "I really appreciate it."

Then he groaned again and leaned all his weight into the guard. As he did so, he released the carabiner securing the keys to the belt loop of the man's pants. The keys fell into the snow as the men escorted him toward the infirmary.

With the armory unguarded, Rachel made her move. She sprinted across the open ground, keeping her head down. Samir had bought them precious, valuable time, and she would be damned if she was going to waste it.

She ran.

42

———

The guard's keyring landed atop the snowpack, burrowing in enough to make her search a bit more exciting than she wanted. After a stomach-churning moment, a glint of moonlight on one of the keys caught her eye. A combination of adrenaline and excitement soared through her. She grabbed them and finished the final twenty-yard sprint to the armory.

The small, squat building sat inside its own perimeter fencing, but unlike the prison's exterior fencing, it was not topped with barbed wire. After reaching the fence, she hooked her toes into the chain links, scampered to the top, and shimmied down the other side. Despite the cold temperatures, she was sweating profusely. Perspiration glazed her shirt to her body.

She slid one of the three keys into the heavy door's lock and turned it, but the lock held. Her cold fingers shuffled to the next key, striking gold after sliding it home. The tumblers turned easily, and the door swung into the building's interior. An automatic light rippled to life, bathing the room in a soft white glow.

The armory was bigger than she expected, rectangular, about twenty feet long, and fifteen feet across. The ceiling was about twelve feet from the ground, the cinderblock walls colorless. Heavy metal shelves lined the four walls, loaded with weapons and boxes of ammunition. The scent of gun oil pierced the air. Hale's arsenal was staggering. Every imaginable size and caliber of firearm was on display. Other shelves sagged with the weight of tactical gear, gas masks, bulletproof vests, backpacks, riot helmets and shields, and night-vision goggles.

But there was no sign of the explosives she needed.

She scrutinized each shelf, her panic rising, before she spotted a panel in the floor secured by a heavy padlock. Holding her breath, she knelt and used the third key on the ring.

Bingo.

After she wriggled the padlock free, the panel cover opened easily, revealing a small compartment in the subflooring. There were more shelves here, each lined with grenades and bricks of plastic explosives. After retrieving her backpack, she carefully filled it with grenades and explosives. She had some experience with these incendiaries, lessons taught to her by Harry Maynard back at Evergreen so long ago. Just enough knowledge to be dangerous.

On her way out, she grabbed three weapons – a pair of nine-millimeter pistols, which she tucked into the waistband of her pants, and an AR-15 assault rifle. She secured the gun across her chest with the strap and then spent another minute gathering ammunition for each of the firearms.

Time to go.

She hustled back toward the armory's door, pausing momentarily to gather her bearings. She carefully pushed the door open, finding herself bathed in harsh white light. Her stomach flipped as she stood in the glow of the twin beams shining from a dark SUV pointed directly at her. Next to the truck, two guards stood on either side of Samir, a weapon poking his sides. He stood in a pool of light, his face bruised, looking miserable.

She was trapped.

A male voice boomed through a megaphone.

"Put down the bag," the man said.

Rachel's body went taut, scanning the scene, playing out the possibilities, the permutations, and combinations. But no escape route was immediately evident. She would have to wait.

"Do it now, or we kill your friend," the man said.

She'd seen the man before but had never interacted with him. His name was Murray. He was a top lieutenant to Hale. Bulky in stature, built like a brick wall. This was not a man to trifle with.

"Okay," she called out, holding up her hands in surrender.

She shrugged loose the weapon strap and eased the gun to the ground. Then she shimmied the backpack clear of her body and set it down next to the assault rifle.

"Hands on your head."

She complied. The motion lifted her shirt and jacket on her waist, revealing the two guns in her waistband. The security chief scoffed at her after spotting the weapons.

"I should kill you for that," he said, jutting his chin toward the guns. "But you've been cooperative. So I won't. Come toward me and keep those hands on your head. If your hands come one nanometer off your head, you both die. Understood?"

"Got it."

He gestured for her to start her perp walk. She stepped carefully, cautiously, not moving too quickly. This was no time for delusional heroics. They were caught; she would have to play this out until she could regroup.

"Put him in the truck," Murray said to his underlings, gesturing toward Samir.

The guards shoved Samir toward the rear passenger door of the Suburban. He moved like a man defeated, his shoulders slumped, his head down. As he neared the vehicle, Rachel reached her captor. He quickly removed the nine millimeters and tucked them into his waistband. As he did so, the air filled with the sound of a revving engine drawing near. The volume increased in intensity. She and her captor both turned their heads toward the sound. A pair of headlights approached rapidly, the beams of light widening as they drew closer.

"What the hell?" the man muttered.

Elias.

She delivered a high kick to Murray's abdomen, staggering him long enough to take cover behind the vehicle. The two guards abandoned Samir and moved to address the rapidly incoming threat. They raised their weapons simultaneously and opened fire. The night crackled with the staccato sound of small arms fire. But the vehicle kept coming, jagging left and right in a serpentine path, kicking up enough snow to almost conceal it from view.

The shooters' guns ran dry almost at the same moment, and they paused to reload. Before they could, the vehicle was virtually on top of them. One man dove clear of its path, but the second wasn't as lucky. The truck's front grill clipped the lower half of his body as he tried to jump to safety. The impact spun him around and catapulted him into the air. His broken body crashed against the armory fence and slid to the ground. The truck kept coming. She sprinted clear just as Elias slammed into the front of Murray's vehicle. The collision sent it spinning; Rachel heard the sound of the engine hissing.

The passenger side window of the attacking truck slid down.

"Get in, get in!" Elias shrieked.

The scene had descended into chaos. Samir, Murray, and the surviving guard were nowhere to be found. Reinforcements were streaming toward them from the north, the din of the battle audible throughout the prison complex.

"Samir!"

"Here," a weak voice called out.

His location was not immediately apparent. Her eyes bounced between scanning for her friend and the approaching vanguard.

"Samir!"

Another grunt.

Oh no.

The telltale sound of an injured man. Perhaps he'd gotten caught up in the collision. It wouldn't take much contact between a three-ton truck and the human body to do significant damage. As she searched, smoke or steam billowed from under the hood of the damaged vehicle. It would buy them a little time.

If she could find Samir.

Behind her, Murray struggled to his feet, still staggered by Rachel's attack. She glanced back; he hadn't seen her yet. As she turned her head back, she spotted a lone figure lying prone in the snow. Samir. She rushed toward him, waving back at Elias's vehicle to zero in on them.

"You okay, chief?"

"I'll live."

She knelt, and he swung his arm around her neck. Using her for leverage, he pushed himself off the ground. The air cracked with the sound of gunfire again. Murray had retrieved a weapon and was drawing a bead on them. Elias gunned the engine again, sliding between Murray's vantage point and Rachel and Samir. The pair hurried across the snow. Rachel flung the door open and slowed enough to give Samir a shove inside. She followed him into the backseat.

Elias sped through the snow and the night as Rachel closed the door with a slam.

43

———

Elias raced toward the prison's access road, struggling to keep the vehicle under control in the snowpack. The truck fishtailed as the tires fought to find purchase in the ground; each time it happened, Rachel feared the car would go tits up, ending their little adventure—the end of her, the end of Will, the end of the human race.

But the SUV kept its balance until they reached the main road. Elias took the turn wide, which let him maintain a decent speed as they shifted east toward the exit. The truck careened down the road, hopping and bouncing as it hit the tiny potholes just beneath the layer of snow.

A hundred yards up the road, the guard station came into view. A guard opened fire. A round caught one of the headlights, cutting their illumination in half. Even with visibility reduced, Elias did not let off the accelerator. Another burst from the guard's weapon missed. His gun ran dry; he looked at it in frustration and hurried back to the guard tower. Seconds later, Elias hit the wrought-iron gate, crashing through it like a knife through flesh.

"How far is it to this tower?" Rachel asked.

"In good weather?" replied Elias, his voice high and panicked. "Ten minutes. In this? We'll see."

"Just push as hard as you can without rolling us over."

She turned her attention to Samir, still struggling with his injuries.

"You get hit?"

"Just a glancing blow when the other truck spun around," he said through gritted teeth. "Caught my flank."

Rachel gently pressed a hand to his side, triggering a painful grimace as she did.

"Sorry," she whispered.

Her worry level for Samir was high. Internal injury was a possibility, but she could do nothing for him currently. The truck barreled through the snow, and Elias became more comfortable in the inclement conditions. The snow intensified, and tiny flakes showered the windshield, giving them a surreal view of the onrushing landscape. After another mile, Elias decelerated rapidly, so quickly that Rachel thought he'd lost control of the vehicle.

"There!" Samir called out, pointing toward a small sign marking a narrow access road.

He turned sharply and killed the headlights, which made for slow driving but provided some cover at night. The snowflakes reflected light shining from a structure in the distance.

The tower.

The outline of the building was barely visible, atop a hilly outcrop rising from the otherwise flat terrain. It rose about three hundred feet above sea level, but making the summit wouldn't be easy in these conditions. And driving up the hill would loudly announce their presence to Hale. The truck strained to climb the mountain; every few yards, it stalled out while its tires spun in the snow. Finally, the car came to a complete stop.

"We're walking from here," Rachel said to Elias.

He nodded.

She glanced at Samir.

"You wait here."

"Absolutely not," he said. "I'll be fine."

She chewed on her lower lip.

"Look," he said. "It doesn't matter what you say. Even if you leave me here, I'm getting out and chasing after you."

"Fine," she said. "You fall behind, I'm just leaving you."

She said it with as much conviction as possible, which wasn't much, and she didn't even know if he believed her. He was a good man, and she cared about him deeply; these were emotions she had not felt in a very long time. Probably not since the earliest days of her time with Eddie Callahan, before he'd revealed himself to be the heel he'd been all along.

"Fine with me," he bit back.

Elias guided the truck to a halt and killed the engine. The warm engine ticked loudly as it cooled in the chilled air. They eased out of the vehicle, gently latching the doors shut. Rachel handed the pistols to the men, keeping the AR-15 for herself.

"Elias, how quickly can he broadcast the kill signal?"

"Not exactly sure. It can take time to upload the signal to the transmission array."

"How long?"

"About ninety minutes. Not much more than that. To be on the safe side, call it an hour."

Rachel did the math in her head. Hale had gotten at least a thirty-minute head start on her. Assuming he'd started as soon as he arrived, they had maybe thirty minutes before the signal was broadcast.

"Let's get moving," she said. "We don't have much time."

Elias took the lead, and Rachel followed, keeping Samir between them. The hillside was steep, the path narrow, and flanked by heavy vegetation with an icy crust. While it was passable on foot, it would have been an absolute nightmare in the truck.

Elias kept to the inside track, closest to the heavier brush, to better conceal their approach. As they climbed, moving as quickly as they could, Rachel's lungs burned, and her legs grew heavy. A sharp wind blew across the hillside, buffeting them and ripping the fabric of their jackets.

The backpack, which she had retrieved from Hale's quarters, hung heavily on Rachel's shoulders. The heaviness stemmed from more than just its actual weight. The implications carried their own weight. The explosives inside made her nervous but also filled her with exhilaration. These weapons, these devices designed to destroy and kill, would prove their salvation. And if they survived the night, she would begin injecting women with vaccines the very next day. If it were up to her, she wouldn't ask for anything in return: not food, not medicine, not weapons, not protection. This was too important to turn into an item of commerce. It was a miracle that they had the vaccine at all, and they should treat it like one.

After another ten minutes of silent trudging up the hill, Elias raised a fist, signaling the team to stop. Rachel and Samir froze.

"We're near the summit," Elias said. "The hillside flattens out here quite a bit."

"How far to the tower?" Rachel asked.

Elias tilted his head to get a reading on the distance.

"About a hundred yards," he said. "Maybe one-fifty."

Rachel edged up next to him, where the path flattened into a plateau on which the tower stood. Ahead, she saw two guards patrolling its perimeter. The wind had picked up, and the snow had started to fall even harder. A ghostly howl filled her ears as the wind whipped across the plateau. A single red beacon on the side of the tower blinked disinterestedly. She wondered where it was drawing its power from.

The tower stood about a hundred feet high, a latticed steel frame situated atop a square block building. At its point was a large concave-shaped disk with an antenna poking out from its center.

"Remember," Elias said, "try to destroy the transmitter first. That's priority number one. But if you can't, bring down the whole satellite dish."

"Agreed," Rachel said. Samir also nodded his agreement.

The sound of an engine whining behind them caught Rachel's ear. She glanced back down the hill, spotting the shine of headlights approaching rapidly from the south. The sight chilled her to the bone. A second front in this war was about to open, and she wasn't sure they could handle even one. Whatever they were going to do, they would have to do it now.

"Need another diversion?" whispered Samir. "I'm probably the region's preeminent expert at that now."

Rachel smiled. The dark comic relief was most welcome as they teetered on the precipice of the zero moment, the point at which their success or failure would be revealed.

"Not up here," she replied. "They see anyone out here, they're just as likely to mow you down."

"Yeah," Samir said. "Good point."

The men circling the tower's perimeter looked fierce, strong, and attentive. They were too far away to risk a frontal assault. The trio would be gunned down long before they reached the tower. The terrain surrounding the plateau was lined with rocky outcroppings, which might provide them a bit of cover as they moved in and flanked the guards. If they opened fire simultaneously, they could eliminate both threats in short order, giving her time to place the explosives.

"Samir," she said, gesturing toward the trail, as it were, on the right. "Go around that way. Move until the entrance of that building is at your nine o'clock. Elias, you go the opposite way and circle until it's at your three. When you get my signal, you open fire on that guard."

Elias took a sharp breath.

"I've never shot anyone," he said, his voice shaky.

"First time for everything," Rachel said gently.

"I, uh…"

"Listen to me," she said. "We don't have a choice. You don't have to like it. But if we don't act now, we're all dead."

As if to prove her point, the sound of the approaching vehicles intensified, the growl of the engines, the crunch of the tires moving up the hill. Their truck would prove an obstacle, albeit one they would remove in short order.

"I don't know if I can do this," Elias said softly.

"I need you, Elias. I need you to remember what they did to you, what they did to all of us. And what will happen if we don't stop them now. Tonight."

His brow furrowed, he massaged his forehead with his thumb and fingers.

"OK," he said finally. "I'll do it."

"After you take out the guard, you get out of here, back down the hill to the main road. I'll set the explosives and we go. We all clear?"

The men nodded.

The air felt charged, as though a thunderstorm was moving in. Rachel could almost smell the humidity and the sulfur of electricity, the potential energy of a maelstrom about to explode—the maelstrom of battle. The window to act was closing.

"Samir, you sure you can do this?"

He nodded decisively.

"Let's go," he said.

The trio broke apart. Rachel took the path carving up to the summit of the hill, hustling as quickly as she could. The men were shifting into position like chess pieces. So far, it did not appear they'd been spotted. The sounds of the approaching convoy were almost a blessing in disguise, covering much of the noise they were generating.

She took cover behind a large rock, trapezoidal and featuring a narrow but flat top. She set the rifle barrel on it for stability and sighted her target. The guard was moving methodically but predictably. A few moments of surveillance confirmed his pattern. He made a single circuit and paused to shift the strap of his weapon from one shoulder to the other before continuing his patrol.

She pressed her eye to the sight. The man neared the end of his circuit, unaware that he was nearing the end of his life. Rachel curled her finger around the trigger.

She fired.

～

44

___

As promised, the men delivered. Seconds after the burst from Rachel's weapon, which cut down the first guard, Samir and Elias opened fire as well. Their first rounds missed; Rachel's stomach flipped. The guard turned and fired. The sickening sound of hypersonic metal hitting flesh reached her ears. Elias went down hard.

"No!" Samir called out.

Rachel had killed more than a few people in her life, but it never got easier. That was a good thing, she supposed. If it ever became easy, she might as well put the vaccine vials underfoot and stamp them out of existence.

Samir fired again; Rachel turned her weapon on the surviving guard, and together, their twin assault brought the man down. As he fell to the ground, Samir scampered over his hillside and out of view just as the first Waterside vehicle reached the plateau. Rachel shimmied down the slope toward the access road, letting loose a burst from the AR-15 toward the car. The rounds caught and shredded the right rear tire, causing the truck to fishtail to the left. A second round splintered the rear windshield, the sound of the fracturing glass cracking the night air. Rachel and Samir rendezvoused on the back of the hillside on a narrow plateau. He was quiet when she reached him, rattled by Elias's death.

"Elias," Samir said. "He didn't make it."

"I know."

Sudden death changed you. She understood that as well as anyone. She wanted to comfort him, console him, but there was no time for that. There were only seconds to spare. She shrugged off the straps of her pack, gently shimmied it off her back, and handed it gently to Samir.

"Get this back to Riverview," she said. "Start vaccinating anyone there who wants it. Wake them up if you have to. The vaccine won't save humanity. Vaccinated people will."

He held it gingerly against his chest, like a father holding a newborn for the first time, which wasn't far from the truth.

"What about you?"

"I'll try to finish this, but the vaccine has to make it back."

He nodded.

"You go."

As Samir retreated down the north side of the hill, Rachel turned and made a beeline for the building. The front door was locked, but a short burst from the weapon took care of that. She swung it open, revealing a short corridor ahead of her. Harsh white light shone from fluorescent panels. The place was silent but for the buzz of the lights. There was a door at the far end of the corridor.

This was looking more and more like a one-way trip.

She would set the explosives, ensuring the destruction of this station and everything in it. The problem was that she would be one of those things. The plastique was equipped with a time-release fuse; getting out before it blew would be difficult.

Before taking another step, she double-checked her weapon, ensuring it was ready to fire. Then she continued down the hallway, keeping the gun up and her head on a swivel. The door behind her rattled but held fast, announcing the arrival of the Waterside reinforcements. She picked up the pace to a quick walk, followed by a brisk jog. The door ahead remained a cipher, with no hint of what lay behind it.

She gently touched the doorknob and turned it, but it didn't give. She fired a round at the locking mechanism, blowing it apart. The sound of the report was huge in the corridor. Any semblance of cover and stealth would be gone now. The hinges of the door were not readily visible. Using the barrel of her rifle as a lever, she gently prodded the door open, revealing a control room inside.

Carefully, she risked a look around the corner, earning a round whizzing by her ear. She ducked hard against the wall. She knelt and peeked again, spotting Hale seated at a semicircular bank of computers, his eyes bouncing between a work terminal, his gun aimed at the door.

"Figured you'd be long gone," he called out. "Rachel Fisher."

Hearing her name aloud was jarring.

"Yeah, I figured out who you were," he said.

"Congratulations," she said. "It's the worst-kept secret of the apocalypse,"

"How's that son of yours?"

Rage swelled up inside her.

"Tough break for him, though," he went on. "Damn shame the vaccine won't be protecting him much longer."

"Go to hell."

No reply.

"Give me the kill switch, and I'll let you live," she said.

"Wow, that's quite the offer," replied Hale. "Allow me to counteroffer."

He was buying time, of course. The commotion at the main entrance had reached a fever pitch, and his foot soldiers would soon have a clear shot at her. Seconds later, the door clattered open. She fired off a burst, striking the first man in and pushing back the rest of the squad. She ducked low and barrel-rolled into the control room, staying low as Hale opened fire again.

She risked a peek over a long desk. Hale's workstation was about thirty feet away from her, but the chair was empty. Amid the commotion of the approaching assault team, Rachel picked up the sound of a door opening and then closing again deeper inside the control room. She poked her head up again, stealing a glance around before ducking back down. She sensed no movement, no human presence inside the control room with her. She raised her head warily a second time, this time taking a longer look, but again, she heard no sounds. She was alone in the control room, at least for now.

She lowered herself into a crouch and began navigating through the maze of the workstations here. Hale's workstation was just ahead, abandoned. The dark screen bore the residue of a green glow as though it had just been shut off. It was a basic setup: a monitor, a CPU tower, and a keyboard. A cursory check of the desk for the device, but, of course, it was clear.

She moved deeper into the control room toward a dark corridor at the rear. At its terminus was a door, which opened on her twist of the knob and put her into a darkened stairwell. She flattened against the wall, expecting a burst of fire from above, but none was forthcoming. Carefully, she scaled the steps one at a time, keeping her weapon up and her finger on the trigger. She reached one landing, keeping her back pressed against the wall. She risked a peek to the next floor, keeping an eye out for her adversary.

On a higher floor, another door opened and closed quickly. A burst of cold air rushed inside the stairwell as a gust of wind screamed across the hilltop, chilling her to her core. Rachel's heart raced as she navigated the dark steps to the next landing, all the way to the top of the stairwell. The door through which Hale had just passed lay ahead. She moved slowly toward it, gently pressing the release bar to open it a sliver. A rope of snow blew in through the crack.

She edged her way onto the roof, pushing up against the wall of the stairwell access hatch. Much of the rooftop was occupied by the base of the transmission antenna bolted to its surface. The antenna itself stretched high into the night, tapering to a point about a hundred feet off the ground. There appeared to be a panel or circuit board near the summit of the tower. A metal platform ringed the neck of the tower; Hale was already at the top of the ladder, spearing a narrow opening in the dish.

Rachel sighted her weapon, placing Hale in her crosshairs. The temptation to pull the trigger was strong, but taking a shot now was unwise; for all she knew, he had already loaded the kill switch into the tower's interface. She had to be sure that he was stopped. She draped the strap of the rifle over her head, securing it across her right shoulder and under her left arm, and began the steep climb up the ladder. Hale seemed oblivious to her presence, focusing on the control panel. She scaled up a dozen rungs before her lungs started burning. She paused, gasping for oxygen, and took another glance skyward.

Now, Hale had noticed her. He pointed a weapon downward and fired a round, which flew by harmlessly. The wind had picked up, causing the structure to sway and making it hard to zero in on a target. He fired again, missed, cursed, and returned to his work.

A quarter of the way from the top, she took another break. Panic was starting to set in. Activating the kill switch would only take so long, and he'd had a several-minute head start. But he was still working, and as long as that was the case, she still had a chance. This would have to be her final rest break. She took a deep breath, drawing in as much oxygen as she could, and began her final assault on the summit. Her legs pistoned up the last few rungs. Hale tore his attention from the control panel to squeeze off a shot, but he was too late. She'd made it to the cover of the cylindrical spear of the tower, opposite the side on which Hale was working. She gasped for breath, her lungs on fire, her legs like lead.

"It's over, Hale."

"Nothing is over," he called out over the wind. "A few more minutes and your precious vaccine will be rendered inoperable."

"You'll die too," she said.

"No," he said.

He said it with such confidence.

Then it hit her.

He'd drawn the geofence perimeter to include the transmission station, which would protect Rachel. But Will was vulnerable—as anyone with the vaccine would be.

"You can't stop what's coming."

As he spoke, she knelt and carefully withdrew a brick of C-4. She affixed it to her side of the tower; it clung firmly to the icy metal. Two more bricks quickly followed. With each passing second, it became more apparent that neither she nor Hale would survive this. The detonator operated on a sixty-second time delay. Once she triggered it, introducing a firing signal, she needed to vamoose and clear the blast zone in less than a minute.

With her hand on the timing trigger, she felt a knock to the back of the head, sending her body careening into the central cylinder. The world spun for a moment, and then it briefly went black.

"I don't think so," Hale said.

Hale moved in to strike her again, but she side-stepped him and tried to deliver a kick to his groin; the man was quick and lithe, ducking out of the way. They circled the cylinder toward the computer terminal. One thing was certain—the elevation was an equalizer. Neither of them could survive a fall from the tower.

The lit screen filled the platform with an eerie blue glow. A progress bar at the bottom of the screen was about a quarter of the way full. She was running out of time. They circled each other even as both circled the tower's central pillar. A strange Fibonacci sequence was at play here. The problem Rachel faced was that Hale didn't have to do anything. He just had to outlast her. She needed to take the fight to him and that very quickly. And her weapon was all but useless; it would take too long to get a steady shot, leaving her exposed for Hale to deliver a final strike.

It was like being trapped in a cage match, and that put her at a disadvantage. The larger Hale could reach her in ways that she could not reach him. She would have to come up with a better way to defeat him. She filed that bit of information away.

Then, an idea bloomed in her mind.

"Hey, it doesn't matter what happens to me," she said.

"I've already planted the C4. It's going to blow in three minutes."

His eyes widened at that, and he rushed at her.

The metal platform had become incredibly slippery in the last few minutes, which informed her decision-making. She carefully sidestepped out of his way. As he reached out to grab her, his forward momentum carried him toward the railing. He tried to hit the brakes when he realized the trap she had set. The platform had become something resembling a sheet of glass, and he had difficulty decelerating.

The lower half of his body hit the handrail. Rachel slid behind him, reached down, and lifted him by the lower half of his legs, trying to push clear of the platform. His body went over the side, but at the last moment, he hooked an elbow over the railing. He hung by the crook of his left elbow, leaving his right hand free.

With his teeth, he bit the finger of his glove and pulled it off. Moving quickly, he reached for that gun in his waistband. Rachel turned to move out of the way, but her foot slid out from underneath her, forcing her to grab the railing to avoid falling. She steadied herself as he lifted the weapon from his hip, pointing it skyward towards her. She reached and wrestled with his hand, trying to break his grip on the railing.

He fired once, the bullet catching her just on the tip of the ear, so close that she felt its heat even in these cold temperatures. Blood splashed down on him, splashing against his hand and causing him to lose grip of the gun. As he struggled to reclaim it, while it fell end over end, he loosened his grip on the railing. She gave him a mighty shove, breaking his grip on the railing. And the inevitability of gravity took over.

His throat emitted a single noise resembling that of

surprise, and then he was gone. His body plunged to the roof below, striking it with an unsettling thump; Victor Hale died there on the rooftop on that cold winter night. Rachel slid to the platform floor, taking a moment to breathe. When she had the strength, she pushed herself back up to her feet and then turned back to face the computer screen.

Her work wasn't done yet. The progress bar was well past the halfway mark now. She yanked the device from its port, but the progress bar continued marching along. As she considered her options, she dropped the device to the platform and crushed it under her boot. But she only had a couple more minutes before the satellite would transmit the signal to deactivate the vaccine. She quickly set to work, unpacking the rest of the explosives. She affixed bricks four inches apart around the base of the tower and put two more directly under the computer terminal processing the uplink.

She set the timers, giving her hopefully enough time to clear the blast zone. After securing the final brick, she gathered her pack and weapon and activated the countdown. She hoisted herself onto the ladder and scrambled down as fast as she could. After reaching the last rung, she hopped down to the squat building's concrete roof. The four men of the assault team, all on the ladder on the opposite side of the tower, noticed her descent and turned their weapons on her.

She ducked and rolled out of range of the first volley as the rounds pinged against the tower's steel latticework. Her luck wouldn't last, though; eventually, one would catch her if she didn't clear quickly. She scrambled to the edge of the roof and took a peek over. It was about a fifteen-foot drop. Survivable. But it certainly wasn't going to be fun. She looked around, hoping to find another escape route, but then she reminded herself that perfect was the enemy of good. If this were good enough, it would be good enough, and she could get out of here.

She slithered over to the side of the roof, grabbing onto the edge with her fingers, which were stiff and cold but maneuverable enough to get a grip. Then she jumped. The ground rushed up at her quickly, and she hit the ground hard, rolling down a shallow embankment. Fortunately, the vaccine was no longer in her possession and hopefully safely in Samir's. If she'd hit the ground carrying the vaccine, they all would have been lost. Another reminder that she needed to trust other people. But there was no time to dilly-dally. Up on the platform, the timer was winding toward zero, no more than a few seconds now.

She pushed herself to her feet, scrambled down the shallow hillside, and booked it back down the access road. Desperation fueled the muscles in her tired legs. Her body was battered, and it hurt to breathe, but she ran like she had never run before, like she didn't even know she was capable of.

Boom.

The detonation was instantaneous, all at once, everywhere. The breath of the explosion was warm at her back, shoving her forward and toppling her to the ground once more. She was almost close enough to suffer a burn. The ice and the rocks scratched up her legs and her face, but she had survived. She looked back and saw everything in flames. It was over.

The vaccine was safe.

~

EPILOGUE

THREE YEARS LATER

Spring had come to the Mississippi Valley. It came slowly at first and then all at once, the greens, pinks, and reds exploding into being just as it seemed that winter would never end. The air was redolent with lilac, crepe myrtles, and azaleas.

Every winter they put behind them felt like a miracle. At least, that was how Rachel saw it. Never did life seem less promised than during the last days of winter. When food stores and moods were at their lowest. Life could feel like a video game on the hardest setting. But life never felt fuller of potential than in those early days of spring, when the mornings dawned cold, but the afternoon sun warmed your skin just so.

That was why Rachel liked to get out when spring came. Travel was safer, the days were longer, and the trade routes started pulsing with activity. It was a reminder that life went on. Life would continue. For all of them. Even the human race. Even if sometimes she wasn't sure the human race deserved this second chance, this reprieve, it had gotten.

This week, she and Samir were on a diplomatic mission to Ashvale, home to about two hundred people. The town was about sixty miles northwest of Riverview, situated near a tributary of the Mississippi in a largely wooded area that had seen little development before Medusa. Some enterprising developers had gotten their hands on the property before the end had come, but ground had barely been broken on the project before the work had ceased forever.

A rusted-out bulldozer sat at one edge of the tract of clear-cut land. But even that was falling victim to nature once more, as thick bushes and small trees had begun to blanket the previously scarred land. A decade from now, the forest would be back.

Ashvale was populated by a group of people who lived with the land rather than trying to retrofit their lives with the ruins of the past. A scout met Rachel and Will shortly after mid-day, about two miles outside their camp. Her name was Agnes, and she had the bluest eyes Rachel had ever seen. She had been one of the first to volunteer for a vaccine and was now the mother of a two-year-old girl named Maize. Rachel wasn't too crazy about the name but kept her thoughts to herself.

"Hiya, Rachel," said the ever-cheerful Agnes, approaching on an old mountain bike. "Hiya Doc!"

Rachel did not know Agnes well, but the woman always brought a smile to her face when she visited Ashvale. They set off back toward the settlement's main encampment. They were quiet for a while, and as they drew closer, Agnes began to relax. It was good to get off the road, even for a short while.

"How're things?" asked Rachel.

"Great," she exclaimed. "Two new little ones since you were here last!"

Rachel's heart soared at the news. No matter how often she heard it, she would never tire of it. Everything had changed since Samir had returned to Riverview with nine hundred and seventy-eight vaccine doses. Within a week, every girl and every woman of childbearing age in Riverview had been inoculated. But that had used less than twenty percent of the supply.

By the time Rachel completed her eight-day journey home from the prison, Samir was already vaccinating residents in other communities, including Ashvale. The trip had been worth it, and the cold and the hunger and pain of the frostbitten fingers had melted away. Will had almost given up hope after a few days, and the memory of Rachel's reunion with him brought fresh tears to her eyes each time. He was virtually a man now, eighteen years old. He and Jade were a couple, had been really for several years. Although Jade had a couple of birthdays on him, such variances meant little these days. Rachel allowed herself to think about becoming a grandmother, a prospect that filled her with joy.

Within a month of Hale's defeat, a hundred pregnant women had signed up for the vaccine, and within six months, every last dose had been administered. He conducted physicals on each woman and provided prenatal care to anyone who would accept it. He was so busy there had been no time to discuss the sparks that had flown between them. Probably better that way. At least for now.

Word of the vaccine spread quickly up and down the river. Demand had quickly outstripped the supply, breaking Rachel's heart. She was reminded why she had resisted distributing the vaccine in the first place. But then she remembered the chaos that had caused. That said, unrest had erupted in a few communities not invited to participate in the vaccine program. There was never going to be a perfect solution. They had to do the best they could with the resources they had.

"Looking forward to meeting them," she said.

The trail curled east through a dense forest before opening on a wide-open meadow close to the riverbank. Even before reaching the village border, Rachel's ears filled with the sweet, screeching sound of small children playing. She would never get enough of that sound. Ahead was a large clearing dotted with small huts and heavy tents. This type of lifestyle wasn't her vibe, but she liked coming to visit all the same.

She drew her bike to a stop.

A pair of small children, a boy and a girl, sat in a sand-box, making a mess. Nearby, a woman carrying an infant kept a watchful eye on them, mostly observing but offering parental guidance when needed. This was what was supposed to happen. This was how life was supposed to be —even better than the clinical, antiseptic nature of Olympus.

"You're the first ones here," Agnes said.

Rachel smiled.

Today was a big day, an important day. Riverview, Ashvale, and five other communities were signing an agreement called the Mississippi River Charter. Once they had seen the toddlers and babies from Riverview, the other communities had quickly signed up for vaccination. And from there, it had been a short trip to unity for security, trade, and a future, a new nation. Signing the documents would constitute the first step to forming a new government uniting multiple communities. It was all because of the vaccine.

Ashvale's commissioner was a Brooklyn native named Maya. Her thick New York accent hadn't faded in the years since the pandemic. Agnes guided them to Maya's tent. Although she was entitled to live in larger quarters, she chose not to.

In the three years since Hale's defeat, Rachel had met so many people who just wanted the best for what little remained of the human race. That didn't mean there weren't power plays, double-dealing, the kind of behavior built into human DNA. And, of course, bandits, mercenaries, and warlords still roamed the largely lawless lands, individuals who would always seek to undo and destroy. That was one reason Rachel was excited about putting her name on the Charter.

"How have you been, Rachel?" asked Maya.

"Doing great. Excited to be here today. Glad everyone is coming."

"It won't be too much longer."

"How are the babies coming along?" Maya asked Samir.

"Very well," he said, "very, very well. Up to fifty-six babies at last count across our new little community here."

Over the next half hour, representatives from the five other communities arrived for the summit. Rachel exchanged pleasantries with everyone and engaged in deeper conversations with those she knew best. Each arrival brought food or drink representing the character of their community. Maya had suggested the idea, and it was a good one. The best way to establish bonds was to share the things that were most personal to them.

Once everyone had arrived, the group retreated to a large bonfire set up for them to palaver and share some fellowship.

"Why don't we get started," Maya said.

Maya was becoming an impressive leader—potentially the leader of their new nation. Rachel certainly did not want the job, and neither did Samir. He was too busy with his medical practice, and Rachel was looking forward to peace and rest, watching Will grow up—or at least watch what little he had left to do.

Maya held up the three pieces of parchment making up the Mississippi River Charter, drawing a round of applause from the group. She set the pages on an old picnic table and weighed down the corners with small stones. A fancy-looking quill pen sat next to the last page. Rachel was surprised they had found any pen that still worked, as most of the ink had dried up in the past decade. Each representative read the document, absorbing the language to which they were all becoming signatories.

A silence fell over the group. It was not a sadness but a somber understanding of their commitment to each other. Ashvale went first, Maya putting her signature to the paper and then punching the air with a joyous fist. Next came the representatives from Havenwood, Ironcliff, Greenhaven, Stone Gate, and Shadow Creek. Each representative reviewed the document, pausing at the last page before signing their name to the signature block. As each person stepped away from the signed document, there were big smiles on their faces and tears in their eyes.

Then, it was Rachel's turn. She wasn't sure if they had intentionally left her until the end as a tribute for bringing the vaccine into their lives, but she was glad to be the last. A woman named Logan handed the pen to Rachel, and she stepped forward to the table. Seeing the names etched on the paper was indeed a thing to behold. One chapter was ending; a new one was beginning.

No, that wasn't right, she thought. It was much more than that.

A book was closing, the old story was ending, and a new story was beginning. So much had been lost in the years since the virus had consumed an unsuspecting public. The whole gamut of emotions rippled through her, including grief, pride, relief, and joy. She remembered so many loved ones who were now gone, including her father, Charlotte, and Sarah. Her father would have liked what they were doing today, of that much she was sure.

She placed the tip of the pen on the parchment and then looked up at her new countrymen, taking in the full measure of their faces one at a time. The tears continued to flow, but these were tears of happiness, fueled by thoughts of a future that had been unthinkable just a few weeks ago. They had done it. They had won. They had prevailed. Humanity would continue. It would not be a future like she had ever imagined when she left for Caltech as a seventeen-year-old, but it would be a future all the same.

She set the pen to paper and signed her name. The place was silent but for the *skritch* of the pen's tip on the rough parchment. She looked at her name scrawled on the page next to the others and felt one final emotion seep in.

Hope.

She looked up at Maya, who warmly watched Rachel and nodded.

"Ready?" asked Maya.

Rachel nodded.

"Let's begin," Rachel said.

THANK you for reading THE IMMUNE series. Keep the fun going with SHADOWS, the first book in my American Midnight trilogy, and find out what happens when all the world's lights go out - permanently.

AFTERWORD

While I was home from college for winter break in December 1993, I read Stephen King's THE STAND for the first time. I was immediately swept up in the story of Stu Redman, Frannie Goldsmith, Larry Underwood, Randall Flagg, and the other memorable characters that populate King's famous novel.

At some point, the desire to write a sweeping and epic post-apocalyptic novel gripped me and refused to let go. But for years, I was stuck. I had vague notions of becoming a writer someday, but I had no idea what that would involve. I also had no idea how to write a complete novel, a goal that would take another decade to accomplish, when I finished my first, still-unpublished novel, THE HONOR MEN.

Even after I had finished a few full-length manuscripts, my post-apocalyptic dream remained just that—a dream. I knew I needed something more than just a post-apocalyptic landscape. I needed a story. I needed that landscape to have a narrative spine.

One day, I found myself thinking about what surviving a pandemic like THE STAND's Captain Trips would be like and trying to imagine how awful it would be to see everyone you had ever known perish.

And then it hit me that there might be something worse than seeing your loved ones die—not knowing what happened to them at all.

From there, Adam and Rachel were born.

I began writing THE IMMUNE in the summer of 2011 and drafted about 150 manuscript pages in a few months. However, I put the book to the side because I was worried that no publisher would want it.

But I loved the story and regretted not finishing it, so in November 2012, I returned to it and never looked back. I finished the first draft in April 2013. The book was published in 2015, but finding an audience took a long time.

At its core, THE IMMUNE is a simple story—a father looking for his missing daughter when all seems lost. But it's about more than that, too. Post-apocalyptic fiction can teach us many things—from the danger of runaway technology, to learning what an ordinary person can do in extraordinary circumstances, to the simple lesson that no matter what, we will always look to others for comfort.

The IMMUNE series become the North Star of my publishing career. I have enjoyed every minute spent with these characters in this dark, demented, quiet, and beautiful world.

It's taken me 1,500 pages and thirteen years to tell this story, but I feel it's finally complete.

I hope you have enjoyed it as well.

David Kazzie

December 2024

ALSO BY DAVID KAZZIE

The Immune Series

The Immune

The Living

American Midnight Series

Shadows

Nightfall

Daybreak

Standalone Novels

The Jackpot

Anomaly

The Nothing Men

Good as Gone

ABOUT THE AUTHOR

David lives in central Virginia, where he works as a novelist and attorney. His first novel, *The Jackpot*, was a No. 1 Legal Thriller on Amazon in 2012 and was later published in Bulgaria. His second book, *The Immune*, made it to the top of Amazon's bestseller list for post-apocalyptic novels.

He is the writer and creator of a series of popular animated films, including *So You Want to Go to Law School*, which were featured in the *Washington Post*, the *Wall Street Journal*, and on CNN. They have been viewed nearly 3 million times and are always available on YouTube.

Email him at dwkazzie@gmail.com